WALKERS

Horror
Standalones

BLACK ANGEL
DEATH MASK
DEATH TRANCE
EDGEWISE
HEIRLOOM
PREY
RITUAL
SPIRIT
TENGU
THE CHOSEN CHILD
THE SPHINX
UNSPEAKABLE
MANITOU BLOOD
REVENGE OF THE
MANITOU
FAMINE
IKON
SACRIFICE
THE HOUSE OF A
HUNDRED WHISPERS
PLAGUE

The Scarlet Widow Series

SCARLET WIDOW
THE COVEN

The Katie Maguire
Series

WHITE BONES
BROKEN ANGELS
RED LIGHT
TAKEN FOR DEAD
BLOOD SISTERS
BURIED
LIVING DEATH
DEAD GIRLS DANCING
DEAD MEN WHISTLING
THE LAST DROP OF
BLOOD

The Patel & Pardoe
Series

GHOST VIRUS
THE CHILDREN GOD
FORGOT
THE SHADOW PEOPLE

WALKERS

Graham Masterton

HEAD
ZEUS

First published in the UK in 1991 by Sphere Books
This paperback edition first published in 2021 by Head of Zeus Ltd

Copyright © Graham Masterton, 1991

The moral right of Graham Masterton to be identified as the author
of this work has been asserted in accordance with the Copyright,
Designs and Patents Act of 1988.

All rights reserved. No part of this publication may be
reproduced, stored in a retrieval system, or transmitted, in any form or
by any means, electronic, mechanical, photocopying, recording,
or otherwise, without the prior permission of both the copyright
owner and the above publisher of this book.

This is a work of fiction. All characters, organizations,
and events portrayed in this novel are either products of
the author's imagination or are used fictitiously.

9 7 5 3 1 2 4 6 8.

A CIP catalogue record for this book is available from
the British Library.

ISBN (PB): 9781801101196
ISBN (E): 9781786695574

Printed and bound in Great Britain by
CPI Group (UK) Ltd, Croydon cro 4yy

Head of Zeus Ltd
First Floor East
5–8 Hardwick Street
London EC1R 4RG.

www.headofzeus.com

'On the steps of the bright madhouse
I hear the bearded bell shaking down the woodlawn
the final knell of my world.'

Gregory Corso, 'In the Fleeting Hand
of Time'

'If I should die...
There shall be
In that rich earth a richer dust concealed.'

Rupert Brooke, 'The Soldier'

'Merrimack sounds like the Gaelic words *mor-riomach*, meaning "of great depth".'

Barry Fell, *America BC*

I

He took his eyes off the road for no more than an instant, reaching across to the glove compartment to find his Santana tape, when something blurred and grayish white like a huddled child in a raincoat scampered across the road right in front of him.

He shouted "Ah!" and slammed his foot on the brake— slipped—slammed again. The station wagon slewed sideways across the slippery blacktop, its tires shrieking. Then it bucked and bounced onto the leafy bank and banged loudly against the trunk of an oak tree.

Jack killed the engine and sat shaking in his seat. Jesus Christ! Jesus Christ almighty! The misty rain began to prickle the windshield. He had been driving fast, for sure, fifty or sixty miles an hour toward a blind uphill curve. But the visibility hadn't been that poor, and he hadn't done more than glance to one side for just a split second. He didn't know how the hell he could have failed to see a child running out from the side of the road.

"Jesus Christ," he repeated, out loud. His voice sounded flat and unconvincing. He was still shaking uncontrollably.

He took a deep breath, unfastened his seat belt, and climbed out of the car. It was now facing back the way he had come, the offside rear end impacted against the tree. The road and all the woods around it were oddly hushed after the noise of driving. Nothing but the dripping of the rain from the overhanging trees and the intermittent pee-oo, pee-oo of a distant pewee.

Woods, woods, and more woods. His mother's father had always hated Wisconsin, because of the trees. His mother's father had been a farmer, and to him trees meant stumps. "All these frigging trees," he used to complain, even in retirement.

Jack sniffed, shivered, and looked around. There was no child lying in the road, thank God, and no sign of anybody on the nearby verge. No gray-white raincoat smeared with blood. No twisted training shoe.

Tugging up the collar of his sport coat, he negotiated his way back across the churned-up mud, trying not to mess up his new saddle brown shoes. Because the rubbery tire marks repelled the softly falling rain, he could clearly see where he had slammed on his brakes, and where he had started to skid. Four crisscrossing figure eights, scissoring their way across the tarmac. He hunkered down to look at them more closely. There was nothing to suggest that he might have hit anybody.

He didn't think that he had hit anybody. He couldn't remember an impact, except for the final collision against the tree. He turned around, shielding his eyes against the rain, and stared at the front of his station wagon. The front bumper wasn't marked, no lights were broken. He just hoped he hadn't clipped somebody a glancing blow and sent them hurtling into the bracken and the underbrush. He had heard of hit-and-run victims lying in the bushes just yards away from a busy main highway, and dying at last of exposure.

He walked a little farther back along the roadway. He cupped his hands around his mouth and called, "Hallo? Is anybody there? Hallo?"

He stayed quite still, and listened. The pewee called pee-oo, pee-woo, then pee-widdi. The rain fell as soft as the veil of a dying bride. It was hard to believe that he was only twenty minutes away from Madison, the state capital, and fewer than two hours away from Milwaukee.

He called "Hallo?" three or four more times. There was still no answer. His heart stopped churning, his breathing gradually returned to normal. He began to feel calmer. He took out his handkerchief, wiped his face, and blew his nose. In spite of the chill, his shirt and his underwear were soaked in cold perspiration.

Must've been a deer, right? Or maybe a goat. Some kind of animal, anyway. You didn't get too good a look at it, did you? I mean, come on Jack, let's be serious here, what would a child be doing right out here in the woods, on a wet Thursday afternoon, miles from anywhere? You wouldn't be here yourself, would you, if you hadn't had to check up on Dad's old summer cottage at Devil's Lake, and the only reason you came down this road is because it happens to cut fifteen miles off your journey through to Route 51.

I mean, what the hell would a kid be doing way out here?

The disturbing thing was, though, that Jack was sure that he had seen running legs, swinging arms, and an upraised hood. Common sense told him that it must have been an animal. But he could still picture a huddled child in a gray-white raincoat, darting out in front of him in that wild miscalculated way that children do.

He waited a few moments longer. Then, slowly, turning around from time to time, he walked back to his station wagon. An '81 Electra, in metallic red, misted with rain now; his dad's last car. Jack had inherited it along with the summer cottage, and roomfuls of sour-smelling books, and more newspapers than anybody could have counted. He had been forced to sell the apartment at Jackson Park to pay off his dad's taxes and funeral expenses (not that he could have persuaded Maggie to live there, not for anything, not for diamonds, because Maggie had always believed that cancer was somehow catching). A whole life of dreaming and working had produced nothing more spectacular than something to drive around in and something to read.

The car's taillights had been smashed, scattering dark red plastic fragments across the leaf mold. The tailgate had been pushed in, so that it sneered on one side like Elvis Presley's lip, and no matter how hard Jack banged it down, it wouldn't shut properly. He guessed it could have been worse. He could have hit the oak tree head-on and been seriously injured, or killed. It was probably just as well that he didn't know how to control a front-wheel skid. A better driver might have died.

He climbed back into the car and started up the engine. The fan belt squealed, but apart from that it sounded as if it were off and running. So long as it took him back to Milwaukee, he didn't mind if it sounded like the Pfister Bier-keller Band.

Just before he switched on the windshield wipers, however, he thought he glimpsed something through the silvery mist of the rain that coated the glass. A whitish flicker, in the woods, off to his right. He cleared the windshield and peered at it again, but it had gone. He opened his car door and climbed half out so that he could see more clearly. Again, the faintest of movements, the faintest gray-white blur, he was sure of it.

He reached across to the backseat and pulled over his raincoat. There was somebody down in those woods, no question about it—somebody or something. And whatever it was, it had almost totaled them both. If it were an animal, there wasn't very much that he could do about it. except report it. But if it were a child, then he wanted to know what the blue blazes that child thought it was up to, running around the woods on its own.

He left the car, slammed the door, and began to climb diagonally downhill. Underfoot, the slope was thick with sodden leaf mold, and he slid sideways with every other step. By the time he had reached more level ground, his shoes were dark with wet, and the pants of his mohair suit had been snagged by brambles. He stopped for a while to get his breath back and to wipe his face yet again.

"Shit," he muttered to himself. He didn't know what on earth had possessed him to set off down this wet tangled slope in pursuit of a child who probably wasn't a child at all, but somebody's dumb runaway goat. He could have been driving back home right now, sitting in his dry, warm car with Santana's Abraxas playing at top volume to drown out the noise of his squeaky fan belt.

"And I hope you're feeling better... and I hope you're feeling good!"

He waited, and sniffed, and looked around. Behind him,

he could just make out the dull red fender of his station wagon, high up beside the highway. In front of him, the ground continued to slope downward, but into a dark and overgrown cleft, dense with brambles and dripping ferns. He could hear water running somewhere, the clackety sound of a small stream, but on this wet afternoon under a heavy gray sky, it somehow sounded flat and depressing instead of cheerful.

He could have gone back. *It is not logical to continue, Captain.* Even if the gray-white figure had been a child, he plainly hadn't killed it. And if it was a goat, it could easily outrun him, and climb hills and valleys for which Florsheim shoes were not just unsuitable but downright dangerous.

"Hallo!" he called, one last time. "Is there anybody there?"

He was beginning to shiver again, from cold this time. He needed to pee, too, urgently. He stood up against a clump of ferns and his urine steamed in the afternoon chill. It seemed to go on for ever. But he hadn't even halfway finished before he saw the grayish white figure again, only for a second, way down at the bottom of the cleft between the trees.

"Hey!" he called out. "Hey, you!" He zipped up and began to scramble after it. "Hey, kid, you just wait up there!"

The ground beneath his feet suddenly dropped more steeply. He slipped three or four times, and once he was forced to cling to some brambles to stop himself from falling, and he tore the heel of his hand, so that it bled. Sucking the blood, limping, swearing under his breath, he scrambled deeper and deeper into the narrow valley.

You stupid bastard, he told himself. *It's going to take you hours to climb back up to the car. And, damn it, it's raining even more heavily now.*

He slid down a gulley of loose stones, grabbed at the ferns to balance himself, and then fell heavily on to his back.

Shit! he raged. *Shit and double-shit!*

Slowly, painfully, he climbed to his feet. His pants were soaked at the back and gritty with mud. His new shoes were good for nothing but throwing in the trash. His right hand was still bleeding and he had bruised his left elbow.

This is it. Kid or no kid, this is where I turn around and head for home.

He stood up straight and took a deep breath, and then he shouted out, "Kid! Can you hear me? This is it! Forget it! If you're lost, that's just tough shit! You hear me!"

He listened, but all he could hear was the echo of his own voice, and the rain, and the clattering stream. "Stupid damn kid," he said under his breath. "Stupid damn—whatever-it-is, shit, goat. Who cares?"

He began to climb back up the valley. Right then, however, out of the corner of his eye, he saw the gray-white figure up on the bank to his left, only about twenty yards away—not moving, not running, but simply standing with its head bowed among the nodding ferns. He stopped and stared at it, his teeth chattering with cold. This time, for some reason, he didn't feel inclined to shout out.

"Right, now I've got you, you bastard," he said under his breath, and began to wade uphill through the ferns and the brambles. This time the figure stayed where it was, in its grayish white raincoat, its hood peaked up and its shoulders hunched. Jack thought it was odd that it hadn't turned around, that it hadn't moved at all. It must be able to hear him, after all. He was crashing up the slope with about as much subtlety as General Patton and the Third Armored Division.

He had almost reached the figure now, and still it didn't move. It was standing right next to a two-strand barbed-wire fence that ran diagonally down the side of the valley. It was definitely a child, rather than an animal. Yet it appeared to be a peculiarly hunched-up child, a distorted child; and for the first time Jack began to feel genuine unease.

"Hey kid!" he called harshly, but more out of bravado than anger. "Hey kid, you almost killed the two of us, back there on the road."

Still the child stayed where it was, against the fence. Jack stepped up to it at last, holding on to the top wire of the barbed-wire fence to prevent himself from slipping back down the hill.

It was only when he was almost able to touch the child that he understood that it wasn't a child at all. It wasn't even an animal. He grasped its "hood" and pulled it away from the fence, and all he had in his hand was a rain-sodden copy of last Sunday's Milwaukee Sentinel. Somehow it had become unfolded and blown against one of the fence posts in the shape of a hooded child.

He stood for a long time in the rain, frowning, with a bunch of wet sports section in each hand. He couldn't understand this at all; and in a peculiar way it was almost more unsettling than actually finding a child. He had seen this same-shaped figure running across the highway in front of him. He had seen it dart off down the hill and into the valley. From the gulley below, it had looked exactly like a child in a gray-white raincoat. How the hell could it turn out to be nothing but newspaper?

He unfolded the damp pages and saw the date. Last Friday's edition. Nothing special about it. Slowly he crumpled it up, and then he swung his arm back and tossed it away. He had one last look around the woods. There was no sign of anything else remotely like the child he thought he had been pursuing. No tantalizing flashes of gray-white raincoat among the ferns. He sniffed, and wiped his forehead with the back of his hand, and prepared himself for the long struggle back up to his car.

It was then, however, that he glimpsed the outline of what looked like rooftops among the trees. He climbed a few yards farther up the hill, and soon he could see it quite clearly. A huge building with yellow-brick towers, and shining blue-gray slates, and rows and rows of Gothic-style windows. Now, what the hell building was that?

Jack stretched apart the strands of the barbed-wire fence, ducked his head, and eased his way through. The building stood on the far side of the valley from the highway, its towers concealed among huge white oaks, so that even though it had been built with such a commanding view of the surrounding woods, it was almost impossible for anyone to see it from the highway.

It was fiercely protected from the outside world by the natural environment all around it, like Sleeping Beauty's castle. Jack could tell that the woods must have been cleared once, twenty or thirty years ago maybe; but now he had to struggle his way through thorns and wild rosebushes, and by the time he had reached a stand of oaks about two hundred yards below and southwest of the building, the tails of his raincoat had been ripped twice and his socks were in ribbons. Forget about the hundred-and-seventy-dollar shoes.

What intrigued him so much, though, was the way in which he felt he had been led here: as if he had been destined all his life to discover this building, on this particular afternoon, at this particular hour. As if it had been waiting for him.

When he was a boy, he had spent almost every summer vacation up here at Mirror Lake or Devil's Lake or Lake Wisconsin, and he and his friends had crisscrossed these woods on hundreds of hiking expeditions and "jungle explorations."

Yet he had never seen this building before now, in spite of its immense size. He had never even known of its existence. It was so grand and mysterious and atmospheric that Jack felt almost resentful that he hadn't found it when he was eleven years old. Think of the games that he and Dougie McLeish could have played around here! Prince Valiant! The man in the iron mask! Dracula! They could have had an incredible time! Why should he have had to wait to discover it now, today, when he was a forty-three-year-old married man living in Milwaukee, running a chain of quick-fit muffler shops?

The building looked like a castle, or a hotel, or a grandiose railroad station. It was built of that same pale yellow brick as the old Pabst Brewery on the west side of Milwaukee—that same brick that had once earned Milwaukee the nickname of the "Cream City." Its architectural style was

Austrian Gothic, with a square tower at each end of its two-hundred-foot frontage, each with a cluster of five spires, and decorative wrought-iron railings all the way round the gutters.

There were faces everywhere. Gray faces, cast out of lead, on each of the drainpipes. Yellow-ocher faces, carved out of stone, above the windows. Black iron faces, on the corners of the railings. Probably more than a hundred altogether. Unlike most gargoyles, however, none of the faces were ugly or grotesque. They were all calm and saintly and serene; although the strange thing was that every face had its eyes closed, as if it were blind, or asleep, or dead.

Jack made his way through the trees until he reached the white gravel driveway that surrounded the building. The gravel was overgrown with ivy and crabgrass. On the west tower the ivy had climbed its way up to the level of the third-story windows, clinging to the bricks like a dark and possessive mistress.

He had no doubt that the building had been empty for years, maybe even for decades. The gutters were badly corroded, and water had been trickling down the side of the main doorway, leaving a rusty stain all the way down the brickwork. Every window was dark and dusty and empty, and scores of the diamond-shaped leaded panes were broken. There were abandoned birds' nests in almost all of the chimney stacks, and wedged between the spires.

Over the entire building, as it stood in the softly falling rain, there was an air of quiet despair, of long-lost memories, and of elegant regret.

Jack walked up to the main door, climbed the stone steps, and tried tugging at the heavy bronze door handle. The doors were locked—probably barred, too. Not that there was much danger of the building being vandalized, out here in the woods where nobody could find it.

Beside the doors was an old-fashioned tug-down doorbell, with a cast-bronze face on it, the face of a saint with closed eyes. Jack tugged it once and did nothing but dislodge a shower of rust, but then he tugged it a second time, harder, and he heard a harsh clanging sound somewhere inside the building, a clanging that went on and on, like somebody madly ringing a handbell.

He stepped back in embarrassment. God almighty, supposing there were somebody here? He half expected the face on the doorbell to open its eyes and stare at him in disapproval.

But then the clanging died away, and the building was silent once again. The face on the doorbell remained beatific and blind. Jack shook his head and said, "Nerd," and grinned at himself for being alarmed.

He left the main door and walked farther along the front of the building until he reached the tower at the eastern end. He tried peering in at one of the windows, but the glass was so murky that it was impossible to see anything, except the shadowy outline of what looked like a sofa. Around the side of the building, the grass and the weeds had grown up almost to chest height, so he picked a branch, snapped off two or three extraneous twigs, and used it to thrash his way through the undergrowth. Indiana Jones. Stanley looking for Livingstone.

The silence and the dankness and the isolation of the woods somehow stirred up an excitement that Jack hadn't felt since he was a boy. He began to whistle softly between his teeth, a dramatic soundtrack to accompany his progress through the weeds. When he startled a squirrel, he whipped up his stick like a rifle, and pretended to take potshots at it as it fled up one of the nearby oaks. Kachow! Kachow! Kachow!

He passed the flaking blue-painted doors of what must have been the building's kitchens. Pressing his forehead against the windows, he could make out a huge old-fashioned range and two large sinks with upright faucets. There was a glass-fronted cupboard on the wall, which was still filled with stacks of white dinner plates and cups.

It was uncanny. It looked as if the building had been abandoned with everything in it—furniture, crockery, carpets. There was even a glass flower vase on the kitchen windowsill, with a spray of desiccated chrysanthemums in it.

Jack reached the back of the building. There was a long wrought-iron conservatory all the way along it, badly rusted now, with dozens of broken panes, and its glass roof thick with leaves and grime. From the conservatory, stone steps descended into a sunken garden, where gravel paths had been laid out in a formal cloverleaf pattern. All the flower beds were now tangled and overgrown, and a rose pergola that stood in the center of the garden had partially collapsed. Beyond the sunken garden, the grounds rose in terraces toward the woods. Off to the west, part of the grounds had been laid out as tennis courts, and next to the tennis courts was an outdoor swimming pool, with a tiled surround.

Jack walked the length of the conservatory until he reached the tennis courts. The rain was misting across the valley, miserable and cold, but Jack cupped his hands over his forehead to keep water out of his eyes and stood for almost five minutes staring into the distance. On a summer's day, the view across the woods would be breathtaking.

He slid down the wet grassy bank to the tennis courts themselves. The nets were sagging and rotten, with the dried-out corpses of birds tangled in them. But the red asphalt was still in good condition, and it wouldn't take much to have them back up to scratch.

He approached the swimming pool. It was tiled in white, with brown vine patterns around the edge: Edwardian and lavatorial, and quarter filled with greenish black water. Something was lying in the water, too, something shapeless and pale, just beneath the surface. He tried to reach it with his stick, but it was too far away. It nodded, bobbed, and rolled. It could have been anything.

You know—thought Jack, standing up and looking around the back of the building—*there's a whole lot of potential here. A fine building, basically sound. A tremendous location. Plenty of room for sports facilities. Cleverly redeveloped, this could become the finest resort hotel in the entire midwest.*

Slowly he walked across the tennis court and around to the front of the house once again. An idea was ballooning inside his mind. A business idea. A career idea. An idea that would take him away from the confines of the city, and away from the daily tedium of Reed Muffler & Tire. An idea that would bring him freedom and fulfillment and prestige and enjoyment, too—all in one stroke.

If the building had been left empty for so long, then obviously nobody wanted it, or nobody had realized its

potential. He should be able to pick it up for—what?—
half a million? Three hundred thousand? Maybe even less.
His friend Morris Tucker at Menomonee Savings would
be able to help with the financing. They had both attended
Wisconsin Business College, class of '67, and three or four
times every summer they still went out fishing together from
Whitefish Bay, with floppy sun hats and six-packs of Pabst
Blue Ribbon and Beatles tapes on the ghetto blaster.

No doubt about it, he would need millions to fix the
building up to international resort standards. But if Morris
could put together the right financial package—well, it was
a hell of a risk. A hell of a risk. Yet what did he stand to lose,
even if it all went wrong? A house in suburban Milwaukee,
a dented station wagon, and a crushingly predictable future
fitting mufflers onto other people's automobiles? That
wouldn't be a loss; that would be liberation; even if it all
fell through, and he had to go back to working in an office.

He reached the gravel drive and walked right up to the
building and pressed his hand against the wet brickwork.
*Once in every man's life, just once, a great opportunity
presents itself.* Jack was sure that finding this building was
his great opportunity. It *had* to be. *Just look at the weird
way in which I was led here. By a blown-away newspaper
that looked like a running child. If that isn't fate, my friend,
then I don't know what the hell is.*

He could see it now. The building restored, the grounds
all cleared, the sun shining, smartly dressed couples
strolling in and out of the conservatory. Helicopters landing
on the terraces, bringing guests directly from Chicago or
Milwaukee. A squash court, a glass roof for the swimming
pool, a golf course cleared out of the woods.

He would call it Merrimac Court Country Club. Owner and president, John T. Reed, Jr.

Slowly he backed away from the building, chafing his hands together and sniffing in the cold. As soon as he got home he was going to find out who owned the building and how much they would be prepared to sell it for. Then he would have it surveyed, just to make sure that the structure didn't have any defects that would cost more to put right than they were worth. Come on, you're going to be sensible and practical about this. You're not going to let yourself get carried away.

But he knew that there was no going back. His life had already been turned upside down. Even if this building was beyond restoration, he would find one that wasn't, and he would open his country club one way or another, even if it killed him.

Stand aside, Leona Helmsley. Jack Reed is coming through.

He gave the building one last long look, trying to fix it completely in his mind's eye, and it was then that he saw a face at one of the dormer windows, high up on roof. A small white face, like a child's.

He stood staring at the window, blinking the rain from his eyes. He felt intensely cold, and very tired. But he hadn't imagined it. He had seen it quite distinctly. Just for an instant, sure. But a child's face, way up high, looking down at him.

He didn't quite know what to do. It must be the same child that he had seen on the roadway, the same child that had led him here. The newspaper up against the fence must have been nothing more than coincidence. But even if there were a child inside the building, what the hell was he supposed to do about it? It wasn't his building; it wasn't his child. Maybe he ought to call the local police and tell them, in case the child was a runaway, or in some kind of moral or physical danger. But he couldn't see that his responsibility stretched any further than that.

Still—the child must have gotten into the building someway, and that meant there must be an open door, or a window that could be climbed through. Even if he couldn't find the child, he could at least take a look inside and see what condition the interior was in.

He walked around to the back of the building again. He tried the French windows at the side of the west tower; but they were firmly locked, and he could see that they were bolted, too.

He made his way to the conservatory doors and tried those. At first they wouldn't budge, but when he pulled the handles right down and tugged them again, one of them juddered open.

He hesitated. Technically he was already trespassing, just by walking uninvited around the grounds; but if he stepped inside he would be guilty of illegal entry, too. For all of its apparent dereliction, this might still be somebody's home; and if that somebody were here, he was going to have a whole lot of awkward explaining to do.

He knocked on the window with his knuckle. "Hallo? Anybody home?" he called out. Inside, the conservatory was thick with dust, silent, and dim. A cast-iron table lay tipped over on its side, and the pieces of the green ceramic pot that had broken when it fell were still scattered next to it. Against the opposite wall stood a collection of large earthenware urns, with dead yellowish plants trailing out of them. The air smelled of damp, and something else that was sourer, like vinegar.

"Anybody around?" Jack repeated. But the conservatory was silent, except for the persistent dribbling of rainwater through its corroded flashings.

Use your noodle, Reed, Jack told himself. *Nobody lives here. Only squatters maybe, or vagrants, or runaway kids. Nobody who has any more right to be here than you do. Nobody legitimate.*

He eased open the door a little further and stepped inside. The floor was gritty, and his shoes made a grinding, squeaking sound. He paused for a moment, then he crossed the conservatory and went up two steps to the doors that led directly into the building itself. They were stiff, too, but he was able to open them.

Here goes nothing, he thought, pushing the door just a little way and easing himself in.

The room in which he found himself appeared to be a large lounge or recreation room. There were cream-painted cane chairs all around, fifty or sixty of them, and cream-painted cane tables. On some of the tables, there were cups and saucers, marked mahogany brown inside with long-evaporated coffee. Magazines and newspapers were strewn across the green-carpeted floor. Jack bent down and picked up a copy of Collier's. It carried a cover story—"Walter Camp's All-America Team"—and it was dated 1926. He picked up a newspaper, with the banner headline hall-mills murder trial opens. The date was June 21, 1926.

He stood in the middle of the room for a moment and then carefully laid the magazine and the newspaper down on one of the tables. He felt strangely claustrophobic, as if the lounge were closing in on him. His immediate inclination was to get back out into the open air. Because, Jesus, this room must have been crowded with people back in June 1926, and for some reason they all upped and left, and the building was locked up, completely locked up, and nobody has touched anything here for sixty-two years.

He took a deep breath. The air inside the building was even colder than it was outside; and there was still that distinct sharpness of vinegar.

He listened, but the building remained silent. All he could hear was the rain, pattering on the conservatory roof. He looked around the lounge and thought to himself: This would make a terrific cocktail bar. A long antique mirror, running the length of the back wall, a marble-topped counter, gilded antique chairs. He crossed the lounge to the inner door, which was slightly ajar. This place could have such style.

He opened the door, and found himself in a huge cavernous hallway, with a galleried landing all the way around it. On each side a flight of marble stairs rose up to the second floor. What a reception lobby! A huge iron lantern was suspended from the ceiling high above. It trailed cobwebs below it like a slipping shroud. The floor of the hallway was tiled with red-and-white-checkered marble, but it was thick with dust and grit and fallen plaster and twigs from birds' nests.

At the foot of each staircase stood a life-size stone statue of a saintly figure in biblical robes, two identical statues, both with their eyes closed. Jack walked over to one of them and looked at it for a long time. He didn't know why he found all these faces with closed eyes so unsettling, but he did. I mean, who the hell makes statues with their eyes closed? Is it because they're supposed to be dead, or asleep, or is it simply that they don't want to look back at us while we're looking at them?

Whichever it was, he didn't like it. It gave him the unpleasant sensation that when he turned his back on them, they would open their eyes and stare at him.

He climbed up two or three stairs and called, "Hallo? Hallo! Is there anybody up there?"

There was no echo. But he heard a slight scuffling noise somewhere in the building. A squirrel, maybe. Or a bird. Or a small boy, who knew that he had done wrong by running across the road without looking and had hidden himself in one of the upstairs rooms.

"Hallo!" Jack shouted. "Can you hear me? Because I'm coming up to get you, ready or not!"

He mounted the stairs and climbed up to the second story, two or three stairs at a time. When he reached the landing, he looked back down at the two statues in the hallway. The light was beginning to fade, but they gleamed with an almost unnatural ivory radiance. Neither statue opened its eyes; neither statue moved. Jack, my friend, you should stop imagining things.

From the landing, two long corridors ran off in each direction, one toward the west tower and one toward the east. They were both dark, but Jack could just make out a glimmer of reflected light on their linoleum floors. He took a dime out of his raincoat pocket and flipped it. "Heads west, tails east," he told himself. The dime fell on the floor, tails up.

He walked along the eastward corridor. It was long and narrow and shut-in, but he supposed that he could always let in some extra windows. It was lined on both sides with rows of doors, cream-painted doors, all locked—but each door had a small spyhole in it, covered by a pivoting brass cover. He peered into three or four of the rooms. All he could see were beds and chairs, and in one of the rooms, nothing but a mattress.

Every sixth door, a short side corridor branched off toward the rear of the building, giving access to a window. Each window, however, was covered with a black steel diamond-patterned mesh, very fine gauge, which cut down the light by nearly half. What was more, the mesh hadn't just been bolted into place but welded. It struck Jack as pretty absurd that the building's owner had been security-conscious enough to protect all of the upstairs windows, yet hadn't thought to cover up any of the downstairs windows.

He went up the first side corridor, right up to the window, and squinted out. Through the dust-clogged mesh and the grimy glass, he could see part of the tennis courts and a corner of the swimming pool, and that tangled abandoned garden. He stayed by the window for two or three minutes, looking out. The rain was still falling, the sky was the color of Barre granite, the grass was poisonously green. He checked his watch and saw that it was already 4:30. He wouldn't get home until well after dark.

At the end of the corridor, Jack was faced with double stained-oak doors, not only locked but fastened with a steel hasp and a heavy-duty Ingersoll padlock. He rattled it, but it didn't budge. Whatever was kept in the east tower, its owners obviously wanted it to stay there. A valuable library maybe, or an art collection? Or maybe the floors had collapsed, and they simply wanted to keep people out for their own safety. But off to his left, another narrower staircase rose into the darkness, leading up to the next floor.

He found a light switch on the wall to his left, and he flicked it up and down; but of course it didn't work. The whole building would probably need rewiring, from top to bottom.

There was a window halfway up the staircase, but that, too, was covered with steel mesh. The mesh was dented in several places, as if something heavy had been hurled at it, again and again.

Jack set one foot on the staircase, then hesitated. It was growing late, and dark, and he didn't have a flashlight. Maybe he should call it a day and think about getting himself back home. He knew that Maggie would be worrying about him and that his turkey dinner would be all dried up. He was always so punctual; and he always called to let Maggie know if he thought that he was going to be delayed.

On the other hand, he had never come across anything like this building before, this chance of a lifetime. This was worth it. And what the hell was one dried-up Hungry Man dinner in the great scheme of human destiny?

He started to climb higher, his shoes scuffing on the marble. As he did so he thought he heard a noise, and so he stopped, and held his breath, and strained his ears.

It was a heavy, scratching, dragging sound, rather like the noise of concrete being mixed. But it was very indistinct, and he couldn't make out where it was coming from, and it stopped almost at once, so that he couldn't be sure if he had really heard it or not.

He stayed exactly where he was, listening until his neck began to creak with tension, but the noise wasn't repeated. It could have been rainwater, gurgling through the gutters. It could have been squirrels, pattering through the eaves.

He continued to climb the stairs, more softly this time. The next landing was even darker, and smelled even more strongly of vinegar. It was probably animal piss, of some kind. The whole building was probably a huge hotel for polecats and skunks and squirrels and birds. He remembered once seeing the roof stripped off a house on the outskirts of Madison. Squirrels had been nesting in it for five years, and the eaves had been packed with a huge wedge of torn-up fiberglass insulation, riddled with the half-decayed bodies of squirrel young. The stench of death had been overwhelming; and he had never again been able to look at a squirrel and think that it was cute.

Jack took a quick look along the third-floor corridor, but it was up in one of the dormer windows that he had seen the young child's face (if it had been a young child's face, and not an owl or a pigeon or some chance reflection off the window glass or something freakish like that). So he climbed the stairs yet again to the very top. Again, there was a window halfway up the stairs, and again, it was heavily protected by thick steel mesh.

Another odd thought occurred to him: steel mesh was usually fixed to the outside of windows, so that the glass couldn't be broken by stone throwing, and so that second-story men couldn't reach the windows in the first place. This mesh must have covered the windows so that they couldn't be broken from the inside.

But who would live in a grandiose building like this and have to protect the windows from themselves?

He reached the uppermost landing. Here the eaves curved inward to form a mansard roof, and even though he was right at the top of the house, Jack felt even more closed-in than he had before. If he wanted to escape from the house in a hurry, he would have to run down three flights of stairs, a long narrow corridor, another flight of stairs, across the hallway, through the lounge, and through the conservatory.

He waited for a moment, breathing deeply. He had never suffered from claustrophobia before, but there was something about this building that made him feel trapped. It was probably the windows, the way they were all covered over with mesh. It was the locked doors, too. He hadn't yet found a single room upstairs that wasn't locked.

He started to make his way along the corridor that ran the entire length of the building, through the roof. It was deeply gloomy now, and he could see only a dozen feet in front of him. He ran his hands along the top of the stained-oak dado, to guide himself. At each door he stopped and tried the handle. If the child had appeared at one of the dormer windows, it must have been able to enter one of the rooms. And just so long as it didn't have a key, and was able to lock the door after it, Jack would be able to find out where it was hiding.

"Hallo!" he called. "Anybody there?"

He rattled another door handle. It was locked. He went on and rattled the next one. That was locked, too.

He was halfway along the corridor when he thought he

heard that scraping noise again. He stopped and listened. It was behind him. A deep, low, dragging-a-bag-of-concrete noise. It was behind him and it seemed to be coming toward him.

He turned, his scalp prickling with alarm. There was nobody there. He could see for himself that the corridor was completely empty.

Yet the noise continued. Sssshhhhhhhhh-sssshhhhhh-ssssshhhhhh; thick and heavy and relentless.

Jack stood still for a moment, listening to it. Then he began to walk more quickly along the corridor, away from it, toward the west end of the house. He tried the first two or three door handles, but the noise kept after him, so he ignored the rest and began to jog. Sssssshhhhhhh-ssssshhhhhh-sssshhhhhh, along the walls, punctuated by a strange hollow knocking noise at every door.

It sounded as if something huge and invisible were chasing after him along the corridor, its body dragging against the walls and rattling against the doors. It began to sound louder and louder and faster and faster, sssshhhh-knokk! ssshhhhh-knokk! ssshhhh-knokk!

Jack broke into a run. The corridor jiggled darkly in front of his eyes. He hoped to God there was a staircase at the other end. It hadn't occurred to him when he started running that there might be only one.

The noise came pouring after him, sssshhhh-knokkk! sssshhhh-knokkkk! and he didn't know what it was or what the hell it might do to him, but he wanted out of that house as fast as his legs could take him.

He had almost reached the end of the corridor. There was another staircase, thank God! He plunged down it, leaping four or five stairs at a time, gasping for breath with every jump. But the noise came after him, shakka-takka-shakka-takka down the staircase.

He grasped the banisters and swung himself down the last half-dozen stairs, slipping and jarring his ankle. Then he sprint-hopped along the second-story corridor to the landing, down the last flight of stairs, across the hallway, through the lounge, through the conservatory, and burst out into the wet evening drizzle.

He turned around, panting. Whatever it was, he could face it now, out in the open. But just to be safe, he tugged an edging brick out from the side of the gravel path and hefted it in his hand.

He thought he heard the ssshhhhhhh noise coming through the lounge. He heard the lounge doors racket open. Then the conservatory rattled and shook as if it had been hit by a car, and several panes of glass pealed noisily on to the marble floor.

Jack took a step back, swinging the brick. But then there was silence. The noise had stopped. He waited and waited but the noise didn't return. He heard the rain in the gutters and the distant pewee singing peewoo, peewoo! But that was all.

He took two or three cautious steps back toward the conservatory and peered inside. He called "Hallo?" but nobody answered, because there was nobody there.

He listened to his heart beating for a while, then he stepped back inside. He wasn't going to be frightened off by this building; and he particularly wasn't going to be frightened off by his own imagination going ape-shit. He had been led here, right, by fate, and this building was going to be the Merrimac Court Country Club, owner and president John T. Reed, Jr., or bust.

Nerd, he told himself. *It was your own breathing, your own blood rushing through your eardrums. Same as hearing the sea, when you press a seashell over your ear. You just allowed yourself to get psyched.*

He picked up one of the broken panes of glass that had dropped from the conservatory roof. *No mystery about that, either. The doors banged shut behind me, and this ironwork is so darn corroded. I'm not surprised a couple of panes of glass fell out.*

He went back into the lounge. Empty. Unchanged. Not even a chair tipped over. If something had really been chasing him, he would have seen it, *ja?* He picked up one of the newspapers, went back into the conservatory, and closed the doors behind him.

All right, he still hadn't totally managed to convince himself that what he had heard was nothing but his own blood whooshing through his eardrums. But look at it rationally, Jack. There are no such things as ghosts; and something you can't see can't possibly hurt you, now can it? The very worst that it could have been was a squirrel running along inside the cavity walls. Yes, that was it. A squirrel, goddamn it, rushing after him to protect its young. They could be fierce, right? especially out here in the woods.

He was pleased with the squirrel theory. When he had the building surveyed, he would ask the surveyors to check out the wall cavities.

It was growing very dark now, even though the rain was beginning to ease off. He walked around the building one more time, trying to assess it as pessimistically as possible, looking at the very worst aspects of it, its collapsed gutters, its missing tiles, its rusted ironwork.

Come on. Jack, there's a hell of a lot of work here; and a hell of a lot of grief, too, before it's done. You could walk away and leave it, and that would be the end of it. Back to Milwaukee, back to Reed Muffler & Tires.

But he knew that he would never be the same again. He had been seduced by an elderly but alluring old lady, and he would never be able to get her out of his mind.

He slid-scrambled wearily away from the building, through the trees, and down through the ferns and the brambles to the barbed-wire fence. He had almost reached the fence when he saw a signboard lying flat among the weeds. He hobbled over and was about to lift it up when he saw that it was covered in black glistening slugs. He turned it over with his foot instead.

Through the greenish black lichen that obscured most of the board, Jack could just distinguish the words own risk. He let it drop back into the undergrowth. He took one last look at the rooftops of the Merrimac-Court-Country-Club-to-be, and then he ducked between the barbed wire and made his way back to his station wagon.

2

He had practiced his speech all the way home, but Maggie was still furious. She marched up and down the kitchen while he sat at the breakfast bench with a Pabst in front of him. The Hungry Man turkey dinner complete with fudge brownie had been consigned two hours before to whatever heaven awaits untouched TV meals.

"Tell me!" she demanded. "Tell me! Tell me just one thing that you know about running a country club! Just one thing, that's all, and then maybe at least I can begin to take you seriously!"

Jack shrugged. He was trying very hard to stay rational and coolheaded, and not to get crazy. For one thing, Randy was already asleep. For another, he always lost arguments with Maggie when he got crazy, because he had to say sorry for getting crazy, and as far as she was concerned that meant sorry for arguing as well, no matter how right he might have been.

"Point number one, I know how to run a profitable business," he told her. Profitable, her face said, in instant and silent scorn.

"Point number two, I also happen to have a pretty strong

29

idea of what I want out of a country club, as a paying customer."

"How can you conceivably have any kind of idea what you want from a country club?" she retorted. "You've never even been to a country club."

Jack looked down at his beer. "Well," he said, "I'm sorry, but that shows what you know. I went to the Kenosha Golf Club with Harry Whiteman; and I went to the Mud Lake Tennis and Racquet Club when we held that muffler dealers' convention at Madison."

"Oh, I forgot," said Maggie. "The Mud Lake Tennis and Racquet Club. Half a dozen potbellied men in Hawaiian shirts, trying to hit featherless shuttlecocks over a row of folding chairs."

"The net was being repaired," he snapped back; and then thought, Shit, she always traps me into details.

"But that's your pretty strong idea of what you want out of a country club? Mud Lake?"

He lifted his head and stared at her, giving her the evil eye. But he managed to hold back his temper. He had disappointed her, he knew that. He had disappointed her ever since they had been married. She had imagined him to be somebody else, some other kind of man, and for eleven years he had never been able to discover what other kind of man he was supposed to be.

He had tried asking her. "What the hell do you want from me?" he would roar at her, after too many beers. But she never told him. She just locked herself in the bedroom and put her hair in heated rollers. It was more than likely that she didn't know herself.

There was still love between them, although Jack found

it difficult to qualify just what kind of love it was. They still made "a smart couple" when they went out together. Jack was tall and long-limbed, with chestnut brown hair that always looked as if it were overdue for a cut, and one of those long handsome faces that people can never quite take seriously, like Dick Van Dyke's. He had a habit of overdressing—wearing a necktie when everybody else was wearing open collars—but even at the age of forty-three it was still difficult to shake the overwhelming formality that had been imposed on him by his father.

He had realized too late that his father's formality had been a symptom not of traditionalism and strength, but of shyness and chronic insecurity.

Maggie (or Margaret-Ann, as he called her when he was really crazy) was a second-generation Milwaukee German. Her hair was silver blond, her eyes were as green as grapes, and her chin was strong and Germanic and deeply cleft like her father's. When she was happy she was exuberantly feminine. She would dance with plump bare feet. But when she was angry she could look off-puttingly mannish. She was big-breasted, but her arms were big, too, and went freckled in the summer, and she always complained about her heavy thighs.

Her father was a retired printer, who had always harbored vague delusions that he was a European intellectual of some kind. His bookshelves were crammed with unread copies of books like Narziss und Goldmund and The Voyage of the Beagle, and he subscribed to Psychology Today. He smoked small cigars and talked of "worlds within worlds."

Maggie, who had once appeared to be quite contented with her part-time job teaching piano at Marquette University, had lately been showing signs of similar delusions. She had enrolled in an evening class in Expressionism, due to start in March. Jack didn't even know what Expressionism was.

He kept saying, "What the hell is Expressionism, anyway?" but she wouldn't tell him, or couldn't.

"We could live a life-style like you never imagined," he told her.

"Don't you think the real one is bad enough?" she replied. She marched up to one end of the kitchen, and then marched back again.

"You think it's bad?" he asked her. "You think the way we live is bad?"

"For God's sake, Jack, I didn't mean bad. Not bad bad. I meant, I don't know—stressful."

"What stress?" he demanded. "What stress? The only stress is that we have no stress. We have no challenges."

"And you think that running a country club is a challenge? Jesus! Some people's idea of a challenge."

She marched six paces one way, six the other. Five months and four days ago she had quit smoking, cold turkey. The Colonial oak cupboard fronts were disfigured with water stains, and the electric clock on the wall was never quite straight, and never right either.

Jack shook his head, trying to look as if he felt sorry for her because she didn't understand. "This building, honey... it's like something out of a fairy tale. You remember Sleeping Beauty? The castle all surrounded with thorns and stuff? You'll have to see it to believe it."

"I don't want to see it," Maggie told him. "I haven't even the slightest interest in seeing it. The whole thing, the whole idea—it's like you've gone mad. It's like you've come back home and told me you've contracted AIDS or something."

"AIDS?" he almost screamed at her. "AIDS? It's a building Maggie. It's a rambling old building right in the middle of the woods. It has potential like you wouldn't believe! It has everything you could ask for! Will you give me a break, for Christ's sake?"

He paused, shaking, and then he said, "AIDS, for Christ's sake."

Maggie stopped marching and pressed her hand against her forehead. "I never heard anything so dumb," she said, as if she were talking to somebody else on the telephone. "I can't believe that you came home two and a half hours late and told me you want to open a country club. Maybe I'll wake up tomorrow and you won't have said it."

Jack stood up. God, give me some strength here, please. He was close to the edge of going crazy. "Maggie," he said, as gently as he could manage. "Do you think I'd give up twenty-five years of Reed Muffler and Tire for something that wasn't going to work? Do you really think that? I'm not a cheesehead, Maggie. I'm a practical man. But what you have to understand is that I have an imagination, too. I have a vision. I may be forty-three but I still have ambition."

"Ambition," she repeated, nodding her head, as if she were still speaking on her imaginary telephone.

"Is that so wrong, to have ambition?"

Her green eyes swung to him sharply. "That's your ambition you're talking about, my friend. Your ambition. Not mine."

Jack walloped his fist down on the counter, splashing beer. "All right, Goddamn it! It's my ambition! But how the hell can I help you with your ambition if I don't even know what the hell your ambition is?"

The bedroom door slammed. Plaster sifted from the ceiling. Jack sat alone in the kitchen looking at his slopped-over beer. Blown it again, he told himself, with that familiar sick bitterness in the back of his mouth. Blown it again. Now the only options left to me are (a) give up the country club, or (b) divorce.

He was still sitting there when the door opened again. He thought for one irrational moment that it might be Maggie, come back to tell him that she was sorry. But it was Randy, tousle-haired, puffy-eyed, wearing his "A-Team" pajamas and carrying that hideous beige-colored sexless being that a feminist friend of Maggie's had knitted for him because it was totally nondiscriminatory.

Randy called it Waffle, because it had the skin texture of a waffle. Jack called it the Turd.

"How're you doing, ace?" Jack asked Randy, lifting him up onto the counter.

"You and Mommy woke me up," Randy said accusingly.

"Well, we were singing," said Jack.

Randy shook his head. "You were fighting."

"Nah. It wasn't a fight, it was what you might call a discussion."

"Mommy locked the door and when I looked through the keyhole she was putting on her rollers."

Jack sighed. "All right, Officer, I'll come quietly. It was a fight."

"What was it about this time?" Randy was very world-weary for a boy of nine.

"Oh, I don't know. This and that. The usual. The

impossibility of two grown people who have any opinions beyond the weather to live cozily and contentedly with each other. Is the universe shaped like a donut and if so where's the jelly. Your mom and I can argue about anything."

He paused for a moment and drank a mouthful of beer, and then he said, "Randy, would you like to move away from here?"

Randy held the Turd more tightly and frowned at him. "You mean move someplace else?"

"Sure. Like—I don't know—the woods, maybe."

"The *woods*?"

Jack nodded wildly. "That's right, the woods. You're beginning to sound like your mom. I say 'the woods' and she says 'the woods?' and I say 'the woods,' and so we go on, ad nauseam, ad infinitum, and for ever."

Randy stared back at him, mystified. At last Jack allowed himself to grin, and said, "Listen up, Randy. Let me give you the goods on the woods."

It was still raining the next morning when Jack drove out to Reed Muffler & Tire out on West Good Hope Road, next to Wisconsin Cuneo Press. He parked in the space marked reserved and hurried across the puddly concrete apron to the fitting shop. His mechanics looked as if they had their hands full. There were two cars up on lifts, having their exhaust systems replaced, while the tire bay echoed to the whirring screech of power drills and the deafening bang of inflated tires.

Jack's foreman Mike Karpasian gave him an oily-fisted salute and then came waddling beefily across the fitting shop in his outsize Oshkosh B'Gosh coveralls. Mike used to be a boxer, and spoke with a dumb-ox slur in his voice, but he was easily the most reliable and quick-witted man on the staff.

"What happened to your car?" he wanted to know, nodding out toward Jack's dented station wagon.

"Skidded, hit a tree," Jack told him. "You going to be busy like this all day?"

"Looks that way. We've got five more booked for this morning; two muffler replacements and three emissions tests. Tire bay ain't so tied up, but you never can tell. People start to worry about their tires when it gets slippery."

He sniffed, and then he said, "My cousin Waldo can fix that rear end up for you. He runs a body shop in Cudahy. Preferential rates."

"If he's anything like your cousin who fixed my trash compactor, I think I'll pass. I now have the only trash compactor in America that makes your garbage bigger."

Jack made his way through the fitting shop to the office. Karen was busy typing out invoices on the word processor, but she glanced up when he opened the door and smiled.

"Didn't expect you out here today," she told him. "I thought you were going to Wauwatosa."

"I came to see you," he said, closing the office door behind him.

Karen had worked for him for three years now. She was twenty-six years old, a bouffant brunette, very pretty in a pouting, baby-dollish, four-pairs-of-false-eyelashes kind of way. She always wore low-cut cardigans with no bra and tight short skirts and wiggled her butt when she walked.

She was a major attraction to the male customers of Reed Muffler & Tire, but she only had eyes for Jack.

Not that they were messing around together. Karen had just been granted a decree against her second husband, a 304-pound trucker named Cecil who had cracked her jaw in two places, and just at the moment she was taking what she called "an emotional vacation," nursing her heart and looking after her daughter by her first marriage, Sherry (short, improbably, for Sherrywine.)

Karen and Jack occasionally went to the Bierkeller across the street for a drink together after the fitting shop had closed for the day, and to talk sentimentally about things that were and things that weren't, and things that could never have been; but that was as far as it went.

"You and Maggie been scrappin' again?" she asked him.

"Well, not exactly." Jack sat down behind his desk and dry-washed his face with his hands. Behind his head hung a nude calendar, extolling the virtues of the HRS-71 low-profile tire.

"Want some coffee?" Karen asked him. "You look like forty miles of rough road."

Jack shook his head. "What I need is a Jack Daniel's; and a Blue Ribbon to chase it down with."

"Life can't be that bad," said Karen, tugging down her pink angora-wool cardigan so that she showed even more cleavage, and a gold-plated necklace with her name on it.

"I don't know," Jack replied. "Maybe it can. I mean—supposing you just happened to run across something which was what you always wanted, even though you didn't know it, but you couldn't have it, at least not without losing everything?"

"That a riddle, or what?" Karen demanded.

"Well, kind of," admitted Jack.

Karen looked at him for a very long time, chewing bubble gum, saying nothing. At last she said, "You want to tell me what's wrong?"

"I'm not too sure that I can," said Jack. It had suddenly occurred to him that if he told Karen he wanted to sell Reed Muffler & Tire and open a country club, he would be pulling her job security out from under her feet like a cheap nylon hearth rug. She had Sherry to care for, after all; and all the men at Reed had families to support. Where would Mike Karpasian find a job—fifty-seven years old, with slurred speech and a talent that stretched only as far as fitting new mufflers on cars?

Maybe he was acting more selfish than he knew. He had read about the male menopause in the Reader's Digest. After years of sobriety and responsibility, middle-aged men could unexpectedly break out like spoiled adolescents. Chasing women, driving too fast. Dreaming dreams of impossible grandeur, like running a country club.

But Karen said, "I've worked out the riddle. You've run across something you've always wanted. Maybe you didn't know that you wanted it—not before you ran across it— but when you ran across it, you thought, this is it, this is what I've always wanted."

Jack nodded, and then smiled.

"So what is it?" Karen wanted to know. "You're going to keep me on tenterhooks?"

Jack thought for a moment, and then he said, "I went up to Devil's Lake yesterday; just to check on my dad's summerhouse. On the way back I crashed the wagon. Not seriously. Sideswiped a tree, that's all. But when I got out to check the damage, I found this incredible building."

Karen said nothing, but shifted her gum to the other side of her mouth, which showed she was listening, and that she was interested in what he was telling her.

"It's hard to tell you what it was like," Jack told her. "It was huge, really huge, and old. But very grand, too. It hadn't been lived in for years and years."

"And you wanted it," Karen put in, in the softest voice.

"Yes," he said. "I wanted it."

"I could tell you wanted it," she said. "You had that same kind of hush in your voice that Cecil used to have when he talked about the sixty-eight Barracuda Notchback."

Jack gave her a wry grin. "Let me tell you something, Karen, if I had this building, it could change my whole life."

"But Maggie doesn't want you to buy it, am I right? But why doesn't she want you to buy it?"

"No reason. She just doesn't want me to buy it."

Karen said, "Uh-huh," and nodded her bouffant hairstyle up and down, and then said, "uh-huh." But then she said, "Pardon me for asking, but why exactly do you want to buy it?"

"I, uh—want to spread out, you know? Diversify, that's the word. I mean I got all my eggs in one basket, with RM and T. I'm thinking of going into hospitality, too."

"You want to open a hospital?"

"No, no, a hotel. A country club. Somewhere for people to hold conventions, you know, and play tennis, and swim, and have saunas. Somewhere elegant, do you understand what I'm saying, with fine food and fine wines."

"It sounds like heaven on earth," said Karen.

"Yes," said Jack. "It does, doesn't it? But Maggie is one hundred percent hostile. One hundred percent. She seems to think that running a country club is out of my league."

Karen watched him, and chewed. "So what are you going to do?" she said at last.

"I don't know," he confessed. He looked through the office window at a Riviera being lowered back to the oil-stained shop floor, at the silhouettes of his mechanics against the gray glare of a rainy day. That building had seduced him, all right. He could picture it now, standing abandoned in the drizzle.

Rescue me, it had begged him. *Make me grand again.*

And perhaps he recognized an echo from his own abandoned life, his own ambitions that had never come to be.

Karen said, "Let's get that drink, huh? You look like you could use it. Talk about the living dead."

They crossed West Good Hope Road together in the rain, Jack with his collar up, Karen click-clacking in her ridiculously high stiletto heels.

"Take me to see it!" Karen shouted as a truck drizzled past them.

"What?" he shouted back.

"The building! Take me to see it!"

He sat in the office most of the afternoon, calling realtors in Madison, before he discovered who was managing the building. None of them was helpful. As soon as he explained which building he was interested in, they said, "Oh, that building," as if he had mentioned some reprobate relative whose portrait had long been turned to the wall.

"Yes, that building," he told a brittle-sounding woman at Capitol Realtors. She asked him to hold; and after he had held for nearly three minutes, listening to a scratchy looped tape of the "Post Horn Gallop," she came back to say that ye-e-e-es, the building was managed by Capitol, in a manner of speaking, but that he would have to make an appointment to see Mr. Daniel Bufo.

"All right, that's terrific. I'll make an appointment to see Mr. Daniel Bufo."

He was home early that evening, with flowers. They looked too much like those hastily selected flowers that husbands buy for their wives to say sorry, too much spriggy stuff and too many hothouse roses. Maggie came in through the door and stood under that unflattering hall light and watched them for a moment as if she expected them to wilt in front of her eyes. Then she hung up her myrtle-colored beret and the knitted coat that Jack always called her mujahedin outfit, and walked briskly through to the kitchen, leaving the flowers where they were.

"Flowers," said Jack, nodding toward the hall.

She gave him a tight smile. "You didn't start supper?"

He glanced toward Randy, who was sitting on one of the kitchen stools, watching TV. "Randy had a bowl of Lucky Charms. I didn't know what time you were going to be back."

"The women's group finishes at six-thirty, you know that. You didn't even bring home a pizza?"

"I'm sorry. I thought maybe we could go out to eat. Maybe Schneider's, huh? Sausage, sauerkraut? Deutschland

über alles? Nothing like filling up the ethnic batteries."
The truth was that he hadn't thought about eating at all.
He had been too preoccupied with the Merrimac Court
Country Club, and his appointment to meet Mr. Daniel
Bufo tomorrow at eleven o'clock. He had already doodled
an elaborate letterhead for the country club—the letter M
for Merrimac, with the spires of the country club rising up
behind it.

"You booked a baby-sitter?" Maggie wanted to know.
Green eyes expressionless, waiting. Randy turned around
and saw that she was back, but didn't say anything. He
knew that there was a row to be gotten over first, before
he became a priority. He glanced at his father expectantly.

"Well... I didn't make any solid arrangements," Jack
admitted.

"You planned to take me out to Schneider's but you
didn't make any solid arrangements?"

"I thought maybe that Randy could come along."

Maggie's voice took on that terrible patronizing flatness
that always brought him to the brink of fury. "He's wearing
his pajamas, Jack. He has school tomorrow. You're going to
take him to Schneider's?"

"What the hell?" Jack retorted. "I mean, what the hell?
He's nine years old, he can come to Schneider's."

"Jack, he has school."

"He can skip school."

"Jack," she said, "you're crazy."

He nearly said Yes, I'm crazy, and swept his beer glass off
the counter, and slapped her face, but instead he lowered his
head and breathed deeply and didn't allow that alternative
scenario to happen.

Randy looked at his mother, then at his father. Expectant, but not afraid.

After a long while Maggie said, "All right," as if she hadn't cared about any of this argument anyway. "But if he skips school, you're going to have to take care of him. And you're going to have to write him a letter for his teacher."

"I'll do it, for Christ's sake," Jack assured her. "You want a note, I'll write you a note. For Christ's sake."

"You've been drinking," Maggie reprimanded him.

He covered his eyes with his hand, as if he were tired, and the light were too bright for him. *But let's face up to it, Jack, you're hoping that when you open your eyes again, everything's going to be different. Maggie will be smiling; and Randy will be happy; and none of this bitchiness will ever have happened.*

Maggie said, "Well... if we're really going to Schneider's, I'd better freshen up. Randy—go get yourself changed. And wear something respectable, for God's sake. Not your Alf T-shirt."

Randy switched off the television and ran to his bedroom to change. Jack looked at Maggie and Maggie looked at Jack.

"You know something?" said Jack. "We're not such a bad couple, you and me. We're not ill-suited. We go off at tangents, that's all. Kind of miss each other, if you know what I mean."

"That's your opinion, is it?" asked Maggie. He couldn't see anything in those clear green eyes that told him he might have won her over.

He nodded. He couldn't think of anything else to say. Maggie stood looking at him for a moment or two, and then went off to the bedroom to freshen up. He heard her turn the key in the door.

Jesus, he said to himself, *this marriage is over. Dead and buried. I should finish this beer and walk straight out of the door and never come back.*

But then Randy came in, wearing his new Levi's jeans and his bright red turtleneck sweater, and he was all smiles and ready to go to Schneider's. Jack held out his arms for him and clutched him tight, and smelled that hot biscuity smell of boy, and cursed God for making fathers love their sons.

It was raining hard when they reached the sloping turnoff a mile past Lodi. Sure enough, Mr. Daniel Bufo was waiting for them, in his saddle brown Sedan de Ville. Jack pulled up behind him and turned off the engine. He let down the station wagon's window a couple of inches, because the windshield was misting up. The rain was pattering noisily in the roadside laurels and drumming unevenly on the roof of the car. There was a moment's pause, and then the Sedan de Ville's door was thrust open wide, and a huge figure in a gray plastic raincoat and a gray plastic rain hat reared out of it and came lumbering toward them.

"Oh my God?" said Karen. "It's Moby Dick."

Daniel Bufo reached their car and thrust his dripping face close to Jack's open window.

"Mr. Reed? How's life treating you? And Mrs. Reed? Good to meet you, ma'am."

Karen crossed and recrossed her legs, and tugged down

the hem of her miniskirt, and uttered a peculiar high-pitched laugh.

"And who do we have in the back there?" asked Daniel Bufo. "Is that the smallest Reed?"

"That's Randy," said Jack.

Daniel Bufo wiped his face with the back of his hand. "Randy, hey? Once had a dog called Randy. No offense meant. Terrific dog. Swear he would've talked, that dog, if he would've stopped eating long enough." Jack saw pudgy fingers, thick gold rings.

"You folks follow me down the hill, off to the left. Easy turning to miss, so take it slow."

He returned to his car, and then they started up their engines and cautiously descended the winding road between the trees. It was so dark sometimes, under the trees, that Jack's station wagon automatically switched its own lights on. It was hard to believe that it was only eleven o'clock in the morning.

Protruding branches squeaked and scraped at the station wagon's sides. Then the road widened a little, and Jack could distinguish black iron gates, chained and padlocked. Daniel Bufo stopped his car, heaved himself out of it, and went across to the gates to unlock them. Before he heaved himself back into the driver's seat, he gave Jack an A-okay sign.

They drove up a long avenue of overhanging trees. Karen said, "It's kind of gloomy, isn't it?"

"Hasn't been cared for since God knows when," Jack replied, his mouth dry with anticipation. "If these trees were cut back, and the grass mowed."

The avenue seemed to go on and on, for at least a mile.

Then, without warning, the building appeared, even larger and more imposing than Jack had remembered it, and in some inexplicable way more surly, almost as if it somehow resented Jack bringing more people to disturb it. Karen said, "It's fan-*tas*-tic," but Randy sat back in his seat, his eyes wide, as if he didn't like the look of it at all.

They parked outside the main entrance, and Daniel Bufo climbed puffing up to the doors and searched noisily through a bunch of keys that would have done justice to Jacob Marley. "This is a fine historic building; truly fine; they just don't make 'em this way anymore. Can't find the craftsmen."

"So, how long has it been empty?" Jack asked him. He had asked him already, over the telephone, but Daniel Bufo's response had been inconclusive. "Awhile," he had answered. "Maybe somebody else knows for sure."

Daniel Bufo found the right key and held it up. It was unlike any key that Jack had ever seen before—more like one of those wavy Balinese daggers than a key. "Don't make keys like this, neither. Is that a key or is that a key?"

"What do you think, twenty years, thirty years?" Jack persisted.

Daniel Bufo shrugged. "Well, my partner says that it was built just before the turn of the century. Used to be a private house, first of all, built by Adolf Krüger who founded Krüger Beer. Seems like he sold it just after World War One, and after that it was converted into a nursing home."

He turned the key in the doors and eased them open. They didn't creak, or judder. Their hinges moved as noiselessly as if they were new.

As he walked in, Randy looked up at the blind bas-relief

faces and asked in a whisper, "Why do they all have their eyes closed?"

Daniel Bufo glanced up and then shook his head so that his jowls wobbled. "Your guess is as good as mine, my friend."

"They look like those kind of masks," put in Karen. "You know when somebody's dead and you make like a mold of their face."

"Death masks," said Jack.

"That's it, death masks. Creepy, isn't it? I mean, what if they *are*? A whole building covered with the faces of real live dead people."

They entered the huge echoing hallway where the ivory-colored statues stood. The building was utterly silent except for the scuffing of their shoes on the floor. Randy held his father's hand, and Karen gave a nervous little shiver.

"Well, cozy it ain't," she remarked.

"Mr. Reed, from what you told me on the telephone, you've been toying with the notion of converting these premises into some kind of a—what was it?—resort hotel?" said Daniel Bufo, looking around.

"That's right." Jack was standing still, listening. *Listening for what?* he asked himself. *Listening for whispers? Listening for rainwater running in? Or listening for that same sssshhhing noise that had pursued him down the stairs?*

"This property has all the potential, in that case," said Daniel Bufo. "Very generous reception rooms; very impressive indeed. You can see it all now, can't you? Lights, people."

"All I can see is dust and trash," Karen put in.

"We-e-ell." Daniel Bufo laughed. "Mr. Reed quite plainly understands that it's going to take a little vision to set the place to rights, not to mention a considerable amount of finance. It's been standing empty since the twenties, that's what my partner told me. So none of us are under any illusions here—are we, Mr. Reed? You're going to need to rewire, replumb, refit, strip the roof, bring the building up to local and state and federal requirements. Who knows what else needs remodeling. This is the first time I've ever been here myself."

Jack looked around and cleared his throat. "Donald Trump did it. No reason why I can't."

Daniel Bufo glanced at Karen and pulled a cautious face. By now he had realized that Karen wasn't Jack's wife, so he was making no direct sales pitch to her. In any case, it was obvious that Jack had dreams about the place, and that he wanted it, no matter what. A buyer like Jack had to be treated gently.

Jack walked up to the statue that stood at the foot of the east staircase. A tall draped figure, with her eyes closed. What have you witnessed? he thought to himself. What's been happening here, that you had to close your eyes for ever?

"You were talking about Donald Trump," put in Daniel Bufo. "It's possible that the state of Wisconsin might allow you to hold this building free of property taxes, on account of the fact that you're remodeling a historic structure and creating new jobs for the local work force. For a limited period, anyway. That's the deal that Trump managed to squeeze out of New York. I mean, don't tell anybody in Madison that I suggested it, but—"

Jack nodded. Karen's stiletto heels clattered and echoed on all sides, because she had worn down the heels to the metal tips. Randy turned around and around, staring up at the ceiling, and at the huge cobweb-draped lamp. He stopped because he began to feel giddy.

Daniel Bufo said, "What? You want to take a look around? Feel free. I'll just check out the cellar, see what kind of condition the utilities are in."

He shook out his huge yellowing blueprint of the basement and spread it on the hall table, while Randy began to climb the stairs and Jack and Karen circled the hall, hand in hand.

"Jack—are you really serious about buying this place?" Karen asked him, wrinkling up her nose. "It's so old. And so *cru*ddy."

Jack ran his hand down the robes of the ivory marble statue, almost as if he expected to find out that they were linen. "It's going to take a whole lot of money, Karen; but think about it. Try to imagine what it's going to look like when it's finished. People are going to fly in here from all over the world. The Merrimac Court Country Club, the place to be."

"You think so?" She looked around the hallway and it was plain that she couldn't imagine it at all. She had lived in a trailer for most of her life; what she saw was what there was.

Jack grinned and nodded. "It's a dream come true, Karen. Believe me."

"What about Reed Muffler and Tire?" she asked him. "I mean you going to keep that on, or what? You're not going to close it down? I mean for this?"

"I don't know yet," he lied. "It's kind of early to come to any decisions like that. But I want this place, Karen, believe me. There's something about it."

"Your funeral," Karen replied, blatantly chewing Bubblicious.

Randy climbed up to the galleried landing and looked down, waving to his father but not calling out, because the hallway echoed too much, and he thought that the echoes were frightening, like other people shouting your own words back at you.

Jack waved back, and so did Karen. They looked very small from up here. Randy liked Karen. She was fun and she smelled nice and she always gave him bubble gum, but he couldn't quite understand what place she occupied in his father's life. His father behaved even more affectionately to Karen sometimes than he did to his mother. Randy had seen him kissing her once or twice. Yet that was as far as it went. His father came home every night and kissed his mother, too, and told her he loved her. Sometimes he shouted at her that he loved her. Randy couldn't quite work this out, but said nothing, because his father seemed to expect him to say nothing.

He peered down the long linoleum-floored corridors that led away from the landing to the far ends of the building, east and west. The corridors were dark, yet Randy thought that they were strangely enticing. He had never been enticed by the dark before. He usually found it frightening. He insisted every night that his father leave on the corridor light (although, mysteriously, it was always switched off by the morning). He approached the eastward corridor and peered down it for a long time. Then he said, "Hallo?"

No answer. But no echo, either. He called "Hallo?" a second time, and he didn't know why he expected anybody to answer, but somehow he was disappointed because nobody did.

He was turning away to go back down to the hallway when out of the edge of his eye he glimpsed a small grayish white figure, rushing away from him down the very far end of the corridor. He turned back, shocked; his heart beating blompety, blompety, blompety. It had gone now. But it had been a child, it had to be. A little girl, in a hood, and a rustling rain cape. He hadn't so much heard the rustle as felt it—sssssshhhhhh, sssssshhhhh, sssssshhhhhh along the corridor.

"Dad," he called, but then he realized that he had whispered, rather than shouted out loud. "Dad," he repeated, but his voice was just as quiet.

He made his way cautiously along the corridor, his fingertips trailing along the walls and the doors on either side. The grayish white figure had disappeared from view, but he was quite confident that she was still there, waiting for him, somewhere in the darkness, and that there was nothing for him to be afraid of.

"Little girl?" he called. "Little girl?"

He passed one window after another. Each of the windows was barred by metal mesh. At last he reached the very end of the corridor and found himself on a landing. Another staircase rose to his left, dimly illuminated by a mesh-barred window. He could hear the rain whispering against the glass. He waited and listened. This time he didn't call hello. There were double doors in front of him. He tried to open them, but they were obviously locked. The little girl must have run up the staircase. He glanced quickly back along the corridor and then decided to follow her. She couldn't have gone far.

As he climbed he thought he could hear somebody singing, very far away.

"Lavender blue, dilly-dilly;

Lavender green.
Here I am king, dilly-dilly;
You shall be queen."

He had always liked that song, every since he was little. For some reason it had made him feel sad and happy at the same time. And somebody was singing it here! He reached the next landing. There was no sign of the little girl here, either, but he felt confident that she had climbed up higher, to the very top floor, and that he would find her there.

By the time he reached the attic floor, he was puffing. He stood with his arms by his sides, catching his breath. Then he looked around, blinking in the way that children blink when they mimic concerned adults.

"Now where are you?" he demanded.

He began to plod along the corridor, his red Keds squeaking on the linoleum floor. He tried to open one of the doors, then another, but they were both firmly locked. He could still hear somebody singing, "Lavender blue, dilly-dilly... lavender green..."

Halfway along the corridor he stopped. Ahead of him one of the doors was ajar. Only a little way, but enough to cast a shark's fin triangle of watery light onto the linoleum. He felt uncertain, but not afraid. He listened to the house and he felt that it was creaking and dripping all around him, like Noah's ark. He could hear himself breathing. He could hear his father's voice, echoing flatly along the corridors and up the stairs. And there, in front of him, was the half-open door, and the shark's fin triangle of light on the floor, and a feeling that I'm here, Randy, we're here!

Life happening at different speeds. Slowly pushing open the door. Slowly stepping inside. Blurry sound, unfocused vision. I'm here, Randy! We're here! A small room wallpapered with brown flowers; an iron-framed bed, painted cream, with a sagging mattress, stained by countless nights of helpless incontinence. A tilted picture on the wall, Susanna and the Elders, by Thomas Hart Benton, plucked eyebrows, curved breasts, cleft vagina, and men looking. Randy! I'm here, Randy!

He turned his eyes. He looked at the wall. Halfway up it, in the dim sloping morning light, he saw that the wallpaper was raised in the shape of a man's face—almost as if the decorators had papered over him, with brown flowers. The man's eyes were closed, but he was smiling. He looked friendly, in a way that you couldn't quite trust, like one of those practical jokers who whipped your chair away just when you were sitting down.

Randy stared at him, shivering. He didn't know if he was a real man or not. But how could he be real, if he was papered over? You couldn't breathe if you were smothered in wallpaper, could you? And he wasn't moving, he wasn't real, he was totally still, a bas-relief in brown wallpaper.

Randy approached him across the linoleum floor. The

linoleum was streaky green, with square black-and-white patterns that looked like squinting cat's eyes. The man smiled and didn't move, but every detail of his face had been captured in wallpaper: his eyelids, his lips, the cleft in his chin. Randy stared at him and didn't know what to do.

Are you afreet, Randy? You don't have to be afreet.

"Are you real?" he asked, his voice high-pitched with fear.

There was no reply. Randy stood and stared at the man's face and didn't know what to do next. He couldn't be real, could he? Yet he seemed to be breathing. You couldn't actually catch him breathing, yet he obviously was; you could hear it, sense it. In, out, in, out. Tight, suppressed respiration, like somebody hiding in a closet, in a threatening game of sardines.

"You're not real!" he cried, out loud. "You can't be!"

What do you call real, Randy? Do you think you're real, standing out there in the cold?

Randy bit his lip. He was right on the point of flying out of the room and running back downstairs. But although the man in the wallpaper was strange, he somehow wasn't threatening. There was something childlike about him, like that loopy boy George who worked for old man Hamner at the corner store.

"Can you talk?" Randy asked him. He took one cautious step closer. "Can you open your eyes?"

No need to open my eyes, Randy. None so blind as won't see.

"Who are you?" Randy asked him. "How come your face is in the wall?"

Name's Lester. Well, sometimes it's Lester. Other times it's Belphegor. That's a name, isn't it? Belphegor.

"How come your face is in the wall?"

How come you're here at all, Randy? It's Randy, isn't it? I heard your daddy calling you Randy.

"My father wants to buy this building and make it into a hotel."

He does? Well, there's a few people going to be pleased about that. Some that aren't; some that like things the way they are. But a few that will be.

"I don't know. I don't like this place. It's kind of old and smelly."

Well, maybe. But if you came to live here, you'd have dozens of new friends.

"This is way out in the country," said Randy. "Who lives out here?"

We do. All of us. And we could be your friends. And I could be your very special friend.

Randy hesitated. He could hear his father's footsteps, coming up the staircase, followed by the tappety-tapping of Karen's worn-down heels.

"I have to go now," he told the face.

Come here, come closer, the face asked him.

"I don't think so."

Come closer. You want to be friends?

"Sure, but—"

Come closer.

Randy stepped up close to the wall and lightly laid his hand on it, just below the face. The face said, You like mysteries, Randy? You like magic? You like naked women?

Randy didn't know what to say to that.

The face smiled a slow, secretive smile. *I can show you mysteries, Randy. I can show you magic like you never dreamed of. I can show you naked women, too.*

Randy shivered; he didn't know why.

Jack's voice came echoing along the corridor. "Randy? You there? Randy, where the hell are you?"

You want to see those things, you come back here Randy, you come back to this room, and you talk to me. But don't you tell nobody you saw me. Don't you tell nobody at all. Not your daddy, not your mommy, nobody. And especially nobody else that's in the wall.

"Randy!" Jack shouted, much more sharply this time.

"What do you mean, nobody else that's in the wall?" Randy asked hurriedly.

Word to the wise. Some of them aren't as friendly as me. Some of them are downright mean. Some of them are downright dangerous. Should have been kept under lock and key.

At that moment Jack pushed the door wide open and said loudly, "Randy? Are you in there?" The face that called itself Lester melted from sight as if it had been made out of jelly; and by the time Jack had stepped into the room and caught sight of Randy, the wallpaper was smooth again, utterly smooth.

"Can't you answer when I call you?" Jack demanded. "I've been looking for you all over."

There was a faint sssssshhhhhhhh—sssssshhhhhhh— along the skirting board. Jack laid his hand on Randy's shoulder and frowned and said, "Listen!"

Randy looked up expectantly.

"Did you hear that?" asked Jack. "Kind of a shushing sound."

Daniel Bufo had caught up with them, crepe soles squelching on the linoleum floor. "Rats, probably," he remarked, wiping the back of his neck with his handkerchief.

"Well, could be squirrels," said Jack.

Daniel Bufo glanced around the room and wrinkled up his nose. "Sure could use some cleaning-up around here."

They left the room. Randy turned when he reached the door and looked back at the brown-flowered wall. He didn't know whether he ought to tell his daddy about Lester or not. It sounded crazy when he thought about it. And his daddy would make such a fuss—feeling the walls, first, and when he couldn't find anything, feeling Randy's forehead, and asking him if he were feverish. And how could he explain about the naked women? His father wouldn't let him see any naked women, that was for sure.

He decided to keep quiet; for the time being anyway. Maybe they would never come back here. And Lester had asked him not to tell anybody. Word to the wise. Some of them are downright mean. Some of them are downright dangerous.

"I'm going to hear from you, then?" asked Daniel Bufo.

"Sure, you'll hear," Jack agreed. They were standing outside in the rain, while Karen and Randy waited in the car. Karen was fixing her lipstick in the rear view mirror; Randy was drawing patterns with his finger on the misted-up window.

"I talked to the present owners this morning," Daniel Bufo told him, wincing his eyes a little. "I have to tell you, they're what you might describe as reticent."

"You mean they're not keen on selling?"

"Hard to tell for sure. They're not given to straight replies, if you know what I mean. I said I had a party from Milwaukee who might be interested in coming to some kind of terms, and they didn't say nothing. Just 'hmmm,' and put down the phone."

"Just hmmm?" asked Jack.

Daniel Bufo leaned closer. There was a drip of rainwater swinging on the end of his nose, and his breath smelled of Hungarian salami and Binaca. "It might help if I could go back to them with some kind of a price."

"You mean, they don't have any particular price in mind?"

"I'm not too sure they have selling in mind, to tell you the truth."

"But they didn't tell you outright that they wouldn't sell?"

"No, sir. They said 'hmmm.'"

"Well," said Jack, "I was thinking in the region of five hundred, maybe five hundred and fifty."

Daniel Bufo made a face. "That's pitching it pretty low, Mr. Reed," he said, without much conviction. "There's seventeen acres of woodland here, as well as the building."

"Has anybody else made an offer?"

"No, sir."

"Well, that's my offer. Ask the owners, and see what they think about it. The worst they can say is 'hmmm.'"

"I guess so." Daniel Bufo took out his handkerchief and

blew his nose. "It would be really something to move this building off our books, believe me. It's an office joke, you know? Whenever anybody complains about a property sticking, they say that it's almost as bad as The Oaks."

"That's the name of this building? The Oaks?"

"That was the name they gave it when it was a nursing home."

"The Oaks," Jack repeated. He stepped back and looked up at the building one more time, its dark rain-glistening spires. He couldn't work out why it appealed to him so much. But he had fallen in love with it, with its deteriorating elegance, and with its mystery. He turned toward the car, and Karen gave him a little finger wave. Randy had his nose squashed dolefully against the rear window. He was probably wishing now that he had gone to school.

"All right," said Jack, and shook Daniel Bufo by the hand. "You put my offer to the owners; then we'll see what we can do. By the way, can you tell me who the owners are?"

Daniel Bufo shook his head. "I'm sorry, Mr. Reed. I'd like to, believe me. But client confidentiality, you know how it is."

"It's not the Wise Guys?"

Daniel Bufo made a noise like somebody playing the bagpipes and trying to laugh at the same time. "No, sir. It's not the Wise Guys."

Jack climbed into the car and banged the door. "How about a hamburger?" he suggested as he started up the engine.

"Whatever you like," said Karen, tugging at the hem of her skirt. "Will you look at my hair?"

They drove slowly down the avenue of dripping trees.

Randy twisted around in his seat to watch the building being gradually eaten up by the black shadowy leaves. They had almost reached the gate when he saw the grayish white figure of the little girl, standing in between the tree trunks, waving to him. One arm lifted, waving.

The strange thing was, though, that her face was hooded, as if her head were fixed on backward. Either that, or she had no face at all.

3

He came home three days later and Maggie was waiting for him in the sitting room, wearing her raincoat, her blue vinyl suitcase parked neatly beside her. He said, "What's this?" as if it weren't obvious.

Maggie said with well-rehearsed bravery, "I think they call it getting a breath of fresh air."

"Is that what they call it?" he retorted. "Aha, is that what they call it?" He had drunk one too many Blue Ribbons over at the Hunting Lodge. "That's funny. I call it running out on your husband."

"Jack—" she said, and when she looked up at him, he saw for the first time what all the arguments of their years of living together had done to her face. Or maybe it was just the unflattering ceiling light.

He said nothing. He looked around the room. It had no character at all, this room. Bland beige walls, sculptured shag-pile carpet in a color that was supposed to be honey but had turned out to be beige, too. Colorless paintings on the walls; a beige couch with brown-and-white flecks in it.

And sitting on the beige couch with brown-and-white

flecks in it, a wife he didn't really love, with her suitcase packed.

She gave him her prepared speech, picking at her fingernails as she did so. "I've been trying very hard to understand you, Jack. I've been trying to understand what it is that you want out of your life, and to give it to you. To help you find it, anyway. But you don't seem to know what it is. And if you don't know what it is, how can I help you find it? I feel as if I'm wasting all of my time and all of my precious energy, helping you to search for something that doesn't even exist."

He waited. Perhaps she expected an answer. He said, "Yes?"

"I'm not getting any younger," she said, with tears in her eyes. "I want to enjoy my life before I'm too old to enjoy it."

"Ohhhh..." said Jack. "I never realized! You want to enjoy your life! Why the hell didn't you tell me before? I wouldn't have made you wash my shirts, for Christ's sake, or cook my dinners, or clean my house! I wouldn't have given you Randy! I mean, you can't enjoy yourself with a kid around your neck, can you?"

"Randy's waiting in the car outside," said Maggie, standing up and picking up her suitcase.

"What do you mean? Whose car?"

"We're going to stay with my sister."

"Oh, God. The blessed Velma. Not to mention the blessed Herman."

"Jack, I have to get away from you. You're suffocating me. I don't want to leave you, not for good. I love you, but you're driving me mad. Ever since you found this building, you've been worse than ever. What do you ever talk about? How you're going to find the backing, how you're going to drain the swimming pool, how you're going to break the news to everybody down at the works that you're thinking of selling out, how you're going to clean the marble, how you're going to strip the roof. Jack, I can't take it anymore!"

Jack gripped her wrist. "Maggie—will you listen, for Christ's sake?"

"Velma's waiting."

"Listen to me, for Christ's sake!"

She snatched her arm away. "I've been listening to you for years, Jack. It wasn't good before and it's worse now. If you want to build this—this resort hotel, or whatever you call it—you go ahead and build it, but don't expect Randy and me to have to suffer for it. Live your life! Go ahead! But don't expect me to live it with you! You're too damned miserable and you're too damned obsessed and you're too damned everything! And you've been sleeping with Karen, haven't you?"

"What?" Jack roared at her. "What? You think I've been sleeping with Karen?"

"You're drunk," she said, tight-lipped. "I'm leaving. I can't discuss anything if you're drunk. Good-bye, Jack."

He seized her sleeve and twisted her arm around. He glared straight into her face and he felt that he could have killed her, right at that moment.

"Let me go," she said. He could hear the fear in her voice, and that made him angrier still.

"You think I've been sleeping with Karen?" he repeated, with such softness and reason in his voice that he frightened her even more.

"Randy said—" She turned her face away. The very thought of it made her flinch.

"Randy said what? Tell me, Randy said what?"

"Randy said you took Karen along with you to see the building. Randy said—you kissed her."

Without a word Jack released Maggie's sleeve and lifted both hands in a gesture of surrender, and backed away. He didn't feel angry anymore. He was almost relieved that Maggie had decided to leave. He hadn't slept with Karen, and the chances were that he never would. He couldn't be angry. It took guilt to stir up anger. Guilt, and frustration, and distress; and he felt none of those things.

Instead, all he could think was: *If Maggie and Randy stay with Velma for a while, I can concentrate all of my attention on The Oaks. I can make this deal happen for real. And when it's happened, and we actually open up, don't tell me that Maggie won't be happy then. Don't tell me that she won't promenade along that veranda. Queen of the Merrimac Court Country Club, with the sun shining and the pool glittering and the guests all nodding their hellos.*

Maggie said, "By the way, somebody called Bufo called you. He said they've accepted your offer, whoever they are."

"Daniel Bufo, he's the realtor," said Jack. "They've accepted it? That's what he said?"

Maggie opened the front door and stared at him for a moment. "God help you, Jack," she told him, and then she left, closing the door with commendable quietness. Jack stayed where he was. Then—when he heard Velma's Volkswagen pulling away from the curb outside—he went to the fridge and opened it and regarded its contents with the philosophical expression of a man who knows that he is probably going to have to eat out for quite a while.

After all, what can even the best chef create out of half a pack of Oscar Mayer bologna, five kumquats, an aerosol can of whipped cream, and some very old Roquefort? He was still gazing philosophically into the open refrigerator, however, when he heard the Volkswagen pulling up again. He closed the refrigerator but he didn't go to the door. He stood waiting in the kitchen while Maggie turned her key in the lock and came marching back in again. She was tugging Randy behind her with one hand and carrying his Rambo overnight bag in the other. Randy's eyelashes were glued together with tears. Maggie's face was taut and pale.

"He wants to stay with you," she announced, in a voice like somebody dropping an expensive wineglass onto a concrete patio.

Jack said nothing but turned to look at her.

"He says he likes the building and he's made a friend there; and he wants to stay."

Jack frowned at Randy. "Friend, what friend?"

Randy shrugged. "There was a sort of a man there, that's all."

Jack looked at Maggie. "What did Randy do, make a scene?"

"A scene? A cop came over and asked us to show our ID. He thought we might be—abducting him, for God's sake." Her nostrils flared.

Jack nodded. He didn't feel any sense of triumph. In fact, he would have preferred it if Maggie could have taken Randy with her. But he didn't want to fight, not now. He had begun to understand that part of his failure in life was his inability to cope with more than one thing at a time. He was capable of being a devoted husband, and an inspired lover, and a steadfast father. He was also capable of being a trustworthy employer and an imaginative real-estate developer. But he could only take on one of these tasks at a time. Trying to love his wife and bring up his son and console his workers and build for the future, all at once, that only confused him, and he ended up drinking too much with Karen and doing nothing at all.

This time Maggie slammed the door behind her so that the glass rattled. Randy stood awkwardly in the hallway with his hands by his sides. He was wearing a sweatshirt with the message "Experience Is What We Call Our Mistakes" printed on the front.

"How old are you?" Jack asked him. For the first time he saw Randy as another human being, as a person who was looking at him, the same way he was looking at Randy.

"Nine," said Randy. Unlike adults, children don't find it peculiar that you ask them questions to which you obviously know the answer. Teachers are always doing it.

"Nine," Jack repeated. "Jesus. If only I'd had your spunk when I was nine."

He picked up Randy's Rambo bag and unzipped it. Inside were pajamas, a clean pair of jeans, a red sweater and a T-shirt, and three pairs of carefully balled-up socks. "If you stay with me, you have to sort out your own socks, you got that?"

"Yes, sir."

"You want a chili dog?"

"I guess."

*

Under the fluorescent lights at Cap'n Dogg, their elbows ostentatiously propped on the Formica-topped table, with the jukebox playing bellbottomed-jeans-era music like "Salisbury Hill" and "Bummer in the Summer," they made a wonderful father-and-son mess of giant chili dogs and fries and pig's dinners to follow (nine flavors of ice cream swimming half-melted and khaki in a sundae dish).

"I feel sick," said Jack, swallowing the last of his beer.

"I don't," said Randy.

"You're nine, that's why you don't feel sick. Nobody of nine feels sick, not unless they eat adult food like squid, or escargots. Then they're sick."

"What's an escargot?"

"A snail. French for a snail. You bake them in their shells with garlic butter, right? And they're something special. Mm-hmm! You ought to try them!"

"Have you ever eaten them? Snails?"

"Not since I started subscribing to Greenpeace. I swore then that I'd never eat anything slower than myself."

Randy spooned up the last of his pig's dinner. Jack watched him, proud but uncertain. It wasn't easy, taking a son away from his mother. When you did that, you had to be gentler than usual; you had to be father and mother, and something else besides. Friend, spiritual counselor, and security blanket.

When Randy had finished, Jack leaned back in his seat and looked at him and smiled. "What friend?" he said at last.

Randy blushed.

"Come on," said Jack. "What friend? You know what I'm talking about. You told your mother you had a friend out at The Oaks. Now that was a whopper, if ever I heard one."

Randy said, "I'm not supposed to tell you."

"What do you mean you're not supposed to tell me?"

Randy said nothing for a very long time. The waitress came up and asked, "You folks through with all of this?" She had a very short skirt and very hitched-up breasts and black frizzy hair and a nose that you could have used to open a can of tomato juice. Jack wondered as she leaned in front of him to collect their dishes if anybody had ever made love to her, and if so what she had thought about it. There was such a gulf between picking up empty pig's dinner plates and reaching a sexual climax.

He suddenly realized that his frustration was showing. He sat up straight and tried hard to look disinterested and middle-aged.

"Are you really sick?" asked Randy. God curse children for their perception.

Jack shook his head. "I want to know what friend. And who says you're not supposed to tell me?"

"Lester," said Randy reluctantly.

"Lester? Who the hell is Lester?"

"Well sometimes his name's Lester and sometimes it's something like... Belfry."

Jack turned his ice-cream spoon over and over. "Randy—I want you to tell me the truth. This—what's-his-name—Lester, you made him up, right? You made him up so that your mom would allow you to stay with me?"

Randy shook his head. "I saw him."

"At The Oaks?"

Randy nodded. "He said I mustn't tell anybody. Not my mother or my father or anybody."

"Why not?"

"I don't know. Because. He said that I mustn't tell any other people, either, because they were mean, and dangerous. He said that some of them should have been kept under lock and key."

A parental alarm bell rang in Jack's brain. It occurred to him that Randy could well be telling him the truth, or a half-distorted story that was partly the truth. Children of Randy's age didn't naturally use phrases like "lock and key," not unless some adult had said it to them.

It was entirely possible that Randy had met somebody while they were visiting The Oaks. The building was big enough, and Randy had wandered off on his own. But who the hell was it? A squatter, maybe? Some kind of itinerant pervert? I mean, where do homosexuals and Hell's Angels and serial killers go, when it's raining?

That sssshhhhhhing noise—maybe that was him, maybe that was Lester, running along secret passages. A goddamned pervert called Lester, who had already wooed Randy with sweet-talking promises and peculiar threats.

And, Jesus H. Christ, who could tell what kind of black mischief somebody like that might have in mind?

"Randy," said Jack. "Are you sure about this? You saw a man there, back at The Oaks? This is serious, you wouldn't kid me?"

Randy nodded. "Cross my heart and hope to die."

"Well, you don't have to say that," Jack told him, laying

a comforting hand on his arm. "But I think that you and me, we should pay The Oaks another visit. What do you think? A surprise visit, so that Lester doesn't know that we're coming."

"When?" asked Randy.

Jack checked his Rolex. It used to belong to his father, and it had always run slow. His father had said that it made him immortal, this watch; because whenever the time came for him to die, he would always have two minutes of life left.

"It's eight-thirty. If we head out that way now, we could be there by ten. Do you think you can stay awake?"

Randy lowered his head. "You won't tell Lester?"

"What—that you grassed on him? I'm your father, for God's sake. And that building belongs to me now. Well, almost. Daniel Bufo has accepted my offer; all I have to do now is string him along for a week or two while I sort out the finance; and we're home and dry. And then there'd better not be any Lester or Belfry or whatever you call him, lurking around that building. Then I have legal rights to clear him out."

Randy begged, "Do we have to go?"

Jack stripped off two dollar bills, folded them, and tucked them under his saucer. "There's one thing you have to learn, Randy, and that's to face up to whatever it is that frightens you. It might be rats, it might be dogs, it might be spiders. Right now you have to face up to Lester, whoever he is, and tell him no. And I'll be there, right beside you, to back you up."

"But he's—" Randy began.

"He's nothing that you and I can't handle," Jack interrupted.

"He's in the wall," Randy finished miserably, and much too softly for Jack to hear.

Heading west, Jack suddenly changed his mind and swung north on Seventy-sixth Street, and up toward West Good Hope Road. The wipers dragged across the windshield with a rubbery juddering noise. It was raining too hard not to use them, but too sparsely to lubricate the glass. Ahead of them, the scarlet tail lights of other cars were reflected in the wet blacktop like exhaust flames from Buck Rogers's rockets.

"Thought we'd take Karen," Jack explained, driving one-handed.

Randy nodded. There was nothing else he could do, after all. If they took Karen, that would mean that he would be relegated to sitting on his own in the backseat. He stared out of the window at the stores and the gas stations and the brightly lit intersections, and he missed his mother more than he could have explained; not without crying, anyway, and he didn't want to cry.

Jack pushed a tape into the tape deck. The Eagles, singing "Hotel California."

They reached Karen's house. It was right on the corner of a side street, two blocks north of West Good Hope Road. It was small and scruffy, painted pea green, with a huge TV antenna, more like a shack than a house. A child's tricycle stood abandoned on the sidewalk. The only sign of life was the television, flickering against the drapes. Jack said, "Hold on, ace. I won't be a second." Randy sat and waited. The rain poured steadily and insistently onto the windshield, so that he couldn't see. He didn't think that he had ever felt so miserable in his whole life.

After ten minutes his father appeared on the porch arm in arm with Karen. They scuttled quickly toward the car so that they wouldn't get wet. Without being told, Randy unbuckled his seat belt and climbed over to the backseat. His father didn't even seem to have noticed. Karen jumped into the car with a little high-pitched squeal and said, "My hair!"

"You're hair's fine," Jack reassured her, starting up the car.

Karen buckled up and then turned around in her seat. "Hi, Randy! Late-night adventure, huh?"

Randy nodded without answering. Jack said, "He's tired. Not surprised, the way things have been." He steered the station wagon back south, toward 94. "If I'd known the way that his mother felt. If she'd only told me. You know, communicated."

"Well, some women just can't do that," said Karen, crossing her legs in her black fishnet tights. Her gold hoop earrings reflected the light from the street lamps, one orange curve after the other. "My sister was like that, she could never communicate."

Jack glanced in his rearview mirror. "Trouble is, running a country club, that needs communication, twenty-four hours a day. You know, response. People come to a place like that to be pampered, you know what I mean? It's just the same when they come for a muffler. They don't want to hear maybe, or wait, or come back Tuesday. They want the right muffler and they want it now."

Karen licked her lips so that they shone. "You don't think that you-know-who could hack it?"

Jack shrugged. "I'm not putting her down. Believe me, I'm not putting her down."

They turned onto 94 and headed west through the rain. Waukesha, Oconomonoc, Johnson Corner, the signposts swam by like signposts in an extended dream. Randy lay down on the backseat and closed his eyes, listening to the whishing of the tires on the surface of the highway, and the rubbery scraping of the windshield wipers, and the fluff-fluffing of the wind through the dented tailgate, where Jack had collided with the tree.

Jack was tired, too, but he felt determined, as if he were doing something positive for a change. If there was somebody squatting at The Oaks, some kind of sex pervert or whatever, he was going to roust him out and give him the hiding of his life. He was going to start taking control of his life, and everything around him. Maybe Maggie didn't care for him; but Karen did; and Randy did, too. We weren't talking mufflers and tires anymore; we were talking real-estate development, and stock-market quotations. Goddamn it, we were talking power.

Before he reached Madison, he turned north-eastwards; and twenty miles farther on he took a left to Lodi. The headlights jiggled through the rain; the tires blurted through roadside puddles.

At last they arrived outside the iron gates, and Jack parked close beside them. He opened the car door. The rain was nothing but a faint soft prickle now. He hefted the padlock in his hand. It was too big for him to force open; and in any case it was probably better if they approached the building on foot. That way, they could check if there was anybody squatting there without being detected.

Out here in the wet Wisconsin woods, miles from anywhere, the idea of flushing out a social misfit from a dark and abandoned building didn't seem like such an appealing idea. It hadn't occurred to him before, but maybe this Lester was armed. Jack had pictured him as a sniffling, creeping homo; but supposing he was six-one and built like Arnold Schwarzenegger, with a hand grenade dangling from each lapel, and one of those sawback knives that commandos used to cut their own gangrenous feet off?

Karen came around the car and stood beside him, shivering in her short scarlet raincoat. "Are you really going in?"

He cleared his throat. "Sure I'm really going in. Do you want to wait out here?"

"Are you kidding me? I'm not sitting out here all on my own."

"I'm just kind of debating whether it's really worth it."

He curved his arm around Karen's shoulders. She kissed his cheek. He turned his face and kissed her on the lips. She tasted of Peach Surprise lipstick and salt. He felt her heavy breast through her raincoat pressing against his arm and he realized how much he wanted her. Well, needed her, anyway.

"Hey, whoa," she said, and twisted away. Randy had woken up. He had switched on the station wagon's interior light and was sitting with his hair sticking up at the back like Alfalfa, watching them with pale-faced solemnity.

"Karen, uh—why don't you just wait here?" Jack suggested. "I'll take a flashlight, okay, and take a quick scout around."

"No way," Karen told him. "Wherever you go, I go."

Randy climbed out of the car, too. Jack said, "Hey, ace, close the door quietly. We don't want to let them know we're coming."

Randy said, "I'm thirsty."

"Well, listen, we'll just take a look around to see if there's anybody here, and then we'll find ourselves someplace to have a drink, okay?"

"Okay." Randy nodded.

Jack squeezed his shoulder. "Okay, then. Let's go. But any sign of anybody, and we back off, you understand that?"

Jack collected his flashlight from the glove compartment; and then they squeezed one by one through the gap in the hedge next to the gate. They walked Indian file up the shadowy avenue of trees. Their feet scrunched on the gravel. Karen was wearing high-heeled shoes, and twice she almost lost her balance, so Jack waited for her to catch up with him and then took hold of her arm. Randy plodded along behind them, with the collar of his windbreaker turned up. He kept glancing toward the trees where he had seen the little girl with no face. He very much didn't want to see her again.

Jack's flashlight darted this way and that, mainly illuminating the gravel in front of Karen's feet so that she could see where she was walking.

Gradually the silhouette of The Oaks came into view. Its spires and chimneys were outlined against the night sky like the complex pieces of some particularly difficult riddle. Jack had sobered up now, completely sobered up, and he was sharply regretting that he had brought them out here at all. They could be back home watching "The Cosby Show" and sharing a bowl of fresh homemade popcorn, instead of sneaking through the night ruining their shoes.

They walked around the back of the building, toward the conservatory. Karen looked up at the rain-slicked rooftops and the corroded railings and snuggled herself close to Jack's shoulder. "Is this place ever spooky. I mean, God. I've seen some spooky places."

They reached the conservatory door. It was closed; Daniel Bufo must have closed it. Maybe he had locked it, too. Jack found himself wishing that he had. It looked very dark inside, as black as an old-fashioned photographer's hood; and supposing Lester had already seen them coming, and was waiting for them?

The strange thing was, though, that even though the building was frightening, Jack found it alluring as well. It was decrepit, and it was claustrophobic, but for the past four days he hadn't been able to think about anything else; and now that he was back here, he felt just as excited as he had when he had first seen it. Approaching the conservatory door was like walking right up to the edge of a fifteen-story office building, and looking down at the street below, and being gripped by an irrational urge to jump. Or picking up a razor-sharp kitchen knife, and wondering what it would be like to slice it across his own tongue.

As he took hold of the door handle he realized that he hadn't come out here to look for a squatter called Lester; not really. He had come out here because he simply couldn't keep away.

He turned the handle. With a small off-key complaint, the door swung open.

Welcome back, Jack.

He took a deep breath, and he could smell that distinctive sour odor of vinegar, mingled with dust and damp. It was unpleasant, but strangely appetizing, like pickled herring. He probed the conservatory with his flashlight, but all he could see was broken glass and overturned pots.

Randy and Karen were holding back. Jack turned around to them and said, "So far so good. You coming in?"

He stepped inside, crossed the conservatory, and entered the lounge. Randy and Karen cautiously followed him. Karen said, "Would you turn the flashlight this way? I can't see a darned thing."

They reached the hallway where the two blind statues stood. Jack flicked the flashlight beam up toward the ceiling. It caught the lantern momentarily and whitened its shroud of cobwebs, and for a split second it looked as if some huge translucent spidery skeleton were crouched in the bottom of the dusty glass.

Jack listened. "Can't hear anything," he remarked.

Karen opened her pocketbook and took out a pack of lemon-flavored Bubblicious. She gave one piece to Randy and unwrapped a piece herself. They stood in the huge darkened hallway listening to the dripping of the rain and the endless mastication of Karen's gum.

"Where did you say you met Lester?" asked Jack, shining his flashlight toward the left-hand staircase.

"Upstairs," Randy whispered. "Right up at the top."

"All right, then," said Jack. "Let's go up and say hello."

He mounted the stairs, with Karen and Randy reluctantly following him. Karen's high heels echoed and reechoed throughout the building. "This is what I call a wild-goose chase," said Karen, hitching up her skirt so that she could climb the stairs more easily. "I must be crazy, coming out on a night like this, to a place like this. You know that? I must be losing my marbles."

Randy said nothing. Now that they had actually arrived at The Oaks, he was desperately worried that Lester might turn nasty because he had told his father about him. And what about those other people, the ones who were mean and dangerous, and who should have been kept under lock and key?

They reached the landing. For a moment Randy thought he heard somebody singing,

"Lavender blue, dilly-dilly
Lavender green.
Here I am king, dilly-dilly;
You shall be queen."

Jack stopped, his head inclined to one side, listening. "You hear that?" he asked Karen.

Karen said, "Jack, honey, you're imagining things."

But Randy said, "I heard something. Singing."

"Me too." Jack nodded. He began to walk slowly along the east corridor, trying all the door handles, even though he knew from before that all of them were locked. From time to time he leveled his flashlight through one of the spyholes and peered inside.

"There's somebody here," he said softly. "I'm sure of it."

"Well, who?" Karen wanted to know. "And where are they?" But all the same, she came trippety-tripping to catch up to Jack and take hold of his arm. "You know I truly hate this place. It's just like the hospital where my grandmother died."

But Jack kept on walking along the corridor, shaking the door handles, peering into the spyholes, faster and faster. He could sense that there was somebody here. The whole building seemed to be alive, like a building in an earthquake. There was a deep resonance within the building's walls, a dark rumbling excitement. A sensation of anticipation so strong that he could breathe it.

"Daddy!" screamed Randy; and Jack swung his flashlight down to the very end of the corridor. He was just in time to catch a glimpse of a grayish white coat, rushing toward the staircase.

Karen hadn't seen it. "What was that?" she cried, wide-eyed.

But Jack had already gripped hold of her hand and tugged her along the corridor at a breakneck run. Randy came behind them, panting with fear and effort.

They reached the foot of the staircase. Jack saw a flicker of grayish white, and then the child had fled upstairs. He was about to run up after it, but Karen pulled his sleeve and stopped him. "My shoes!" she complained, hopping on one leg and trying to take off her shoe. "I could never run in high heels."

"All right, all right." Jack held on to the banister rail and supported her while she took off her shoes. Randy stood beside them, trying to get his breath back.

"Have you seen that little child before?" he asked Randy.

Randy nodded. "I saw her upstairs, and I saw her in the garden outside when we were leaving. She waved to me, but she didn't have a face."

"Didn't have a face?" asked Karen, wrinkling up her nose. "What do you mean she didn't have a face?"

"I don't know. She was wearing a hood or something."

Jack said, "I saw exactly the same child. If it is a child. On the highway, first of all, that was the child I was telling you about, the one who made me crash."

"You mean the child who turned out to be a newspaper?" asked Karen.

Jack said, "That's right."

"And I suppose this isn't a newspaper, too? Or an owl? Or a rat, more likely?"

Jack looked at Randy and then shrugged. "Maybe you're right, maybe it's the same thing. Just a couple of sheets of newspaper."

"But it ran upstairs," Randy protested. "I saw it. It ran upstairs."

"Could have been a squirrel dragging a newspaper up to its nest," said Jack.

Randy stared at him in the light of the flashlight. Jack could see that Randy didn't believe him. A squirrel, dragging newspaper upstairs? But what the hell else could it be? Don't tell me some child lives here, rushing from floor to floor in a grayish white raincoat. Don't tell me it's a ghost, for Christ's sake.

Karen declared, "I want to go home. This place is giving me the creeps."

Jack took hold of her hand and squeezed it. Then he shone the flashlight up the stairs. "Come on, it can't be anything. Even if it is a child, are we afraid of a child?"

"Jack," said Karen, "if it's a child it won't be living here alone, will it? It'll be living here with its parents. Or one of its parents. Maybe this Lester creep."

Jack took the first step up the staircase. "Come on," he

coaxed her. "There's nothing to be scared of. This is only an old building, that's all."

"Jack, no," she said, trying to tug her hand free. "I'm frightened."

Jack tugged her hand again, but again she resisted. He turned to Randy. "How about you, Randy? You frightened?"

Randy swallowed. "No, sir," he said, in a thin, expressionless voice.

"There you are, then." Jack grinned. "Two to one we're not frightened. Motion carried. We're not frightened, so we press on."

"Jack—" Karen protested.

"What are you going to do?" he asked her. "Go back downstairs on your own, with no flashlight?"

She hesitated, and then she said, "Okay, okay. But I won't forget this. I never liked the dark. My daddy always used to shut me in the dark, and I used to scream and scream but he never came."

They climbed the next staircase; then the next; until they reached the attic floor. The vinegary smell was almost overwhelming, and there was an extraordinary trembling tension in the air. Jack directed the flashlight along the corridor. The beam reflected in crisscross patterns from doors to walls to ceiling.

"It was about halfway," said Randy. "It was the first door that was open."

Karen said, "If there's somebody there, Jack, I'm gone. I mean I'm out of here, flashlight or no flashlight."

He gripped her shoulder reassuringly. "Come on, Karen, everything's going to be fine." He felt breathless himself; but at the same time he felt compelled to carry on. If there was somebody there, he wanted to talk to him. He wanted to find out what he was doing here, and what he knew about the building. There were so many silent mysteries here. Why did all the sculptured faces have their eyes closed? Why were the windows barred? Why were all the doors locked?

And why had the whole building been abruptly vacated in June 1926, and left unsold and abandoned ever since?

The three of them walked along the corridor with Jack in the lead. At last they reached the half-open door where Randy had encountered Lester. They stopped. Jack said, "In here?" and shone the flashlight into the room. It looked as if it were empty.

"Hallo?" he called. "Anybody there?"

"Oh sure," said Karen. "The Ghost of Christmas Yet to Come."

Jack reached out with his left hand and eased the door open a little. It swung back smoothly except for a little grittiness in the hinges. He waited. The room was silent. The rain whispered softly against the windows, lavender blue, dilly-dilly, lavender green... He stepped into the room, turned, took two quick steps backward in case Lester had been hiding behind the door, lanced his flashlight left and right.

"It's empty," he said with a smile. "Nobody's here and nobody's been here."

"How do you know that?" asked Karen.

"Oh, come on, think about it. Have you ever seen a squat? Trash everywhere: blankets, empty bottles, dirty diapers, camping stoves. This room hasn't been used for sixty years."

Randy stood in the doorway serious and wide-eyed, saying nothing. Jack hunkered down in front of him and ruffled his hair.

"Maybe Lester wasn't quite so real as you thought he was, huh?"

"Are you mad?" asked Randy.

Jack shook his head. "Of course I'm not mad. It's been quite an adventure, hasn't it? And, believe me, ace, I would much rather find nobody here than somebody."

Randy said, "I guess so." He looked almost disappointed. Perhaps he had imagined Lester after all. And the little girl with no face, waving through the trees.

Jack said, "Let's walk right along to the end, just to make sure."

Randy frowned around the room. "Can I wait here?"

"On your own? In the dark?"

"There's enough light."

"Well, what are you going to do here, all on your own?"

"Rest, that's all. My feet are tired."

As a demonstration that he meant what he said, he slid with his back down the wall until he was sitting on the floor. Jack looked at Karen. Karen said, "He'll be okay, won't he? He must be bushed. We'll only be gone for a minute."

"Well, okay," said Jack. "But you stay right where you are. No wandering off. Parts of the flooring are not as safe as they should be, okay, especially along the far end."

"Okay," Randy agreed. He clasped his knees in his hands and lowered his head on his knees and he looked so small and weary that Jack felt like a selfish stupid bludgeoning ogre for driving him out so far so late at night, when he should have been tucked up in bed.

"Listen," Jack told him. He pulled the Turd out of Randy's jacket pocket and snuggled it up to his cheek. "We won't be a minute. Waffle will look after you, and you can shout out if you want anything. I just want to make absolutely double sure that there's nobody here."

"Okay," Randy repeated, and yawned.

Keeping close together, Jack and Karen walked farther along the corridor. They jiggled every door handle and looked into every spyhole.

When they had almost reached the end, Karen said, "You don't really think that there's anybody here, do you? You'd have to be out of your tree to live in a place like this."

Jack said, "It doesn't look like it, does it? I guess 'Lester' was just a figment of Randy's imagination. Poor kid. Maggie's walking out—well, he's taken it pretty damn hard. Maybe 'Lester' was like some imaginary friend, somebody he could talk to, apart from me."

"Sure," said Karen. She looked back down the corridor. "Breaking up is always toughest on the kids. I can remember how bad Sherrywine took it. She cried for a week, then she started stealing stuff from the Piggly-Wiggly."

She reached up unexpectedly and touched Jack's cheek. He flinched at first, not realizing what it was, but then she stroked it gently and touched his hair, and he turned his head sideways and kissed her wrist.

"How have you been taking it?" she asked him.

He kissed her wrist again. "I've been getting by."

"I don't know," she told him. Her eyes glistened in the darkness. "Sometimes getting by just isn't enough."

He gripped her wrist. Then he drew her awkwardly closer, hesitated for just a moment, and kissed her on the lips. It was a tentative kiss, to begin with, exploratory. But then she opened her lips wide and he pushed the tip of his tongue in between her teeth, and they kissed violently and hungrily.

"We shouldn't," Karen gasped. "Jack, we shouldn't." But she made no move to pull herself away from him; and she continued to kiss his lips and his face and his neck. "God, you don't know how long I've wanted you," she told him.

He fumbled at the buttons of her cardigan. The beam of the flashlight darted this way and that, picking out Karen's face, then the wall, then the ceiling, then the glossy black nylon of Karen's bra. Jack slipped his hand inside her cardigan and cupped her breast. She unbuttoned her cardigan even further and tugged it wide open. Then she pulled up her bra cup so that her breast was exposed. It felt warm and heavy in the palm of Jack's hand, the nipple crinkling in the cold of the night.

"Not here," she whispered. "We can't do it here."

Her short tight skirt had ridden up her thighs. Jack twisted it up even further, right up to her waist. Underneath she was wearing nothing but black fishnet tights. He ran his fingers tantalizingly around her thighs and she shivered, and nipped at his neck with her teeth. He caressed her between her legs. The swollen lips of her vulva bulged in diamond patterns through the fishnet. He slipped in his finger and she was slippery and hot and wet.

"Karen," he breathed. "Oh God, Karen."

It was then that they heard the noise drag past them. Sssssshhhhhhh—sssshhhhh—ssssshhhh. That slow, thick, cementlike sound.

They froze, both of them. Their breath fumed in the darkness.

"What was that?" said Karen.

"I don't know," Jack replied, still listening, still alert. His hard-on curled up; he drew his finger out of Karen's vagina.

"Randy?" he called. Then, louder, "Randy?"

There was no reply. He waited, listened. Then he shouted, "Randy!"

"Oh my God," said Karen. "What's happened to him?"

Jack hurried back along the darkened corridor. Karen tugged down her skirt and pushed her breast back into her bra and came running after him.

"Randy! Are you there?" called Jack.

They reached the open doorway where Randy had been sitting. The room was empty. Jack shone the flashlight from side to side, into the corners, up to the ceiling. Brown flowered wallpaper, a mildewed reproduction of Susanna and the Elders. A bed stained with brown tide marks of incontinence. No Randy, anywhere.

"Randy!" Jack shouted down the corridor. His voice was flattened by the deadness of the air.

"He was bored, probably," Karen suggested. "He couldn't have gotten far."

"I told him to wait here," said Jack. "I told him to wait here and not to move. Jesus! He should have come with us!"

"Jack, you're not to blame."

"I don't know what the hell I was thinking about, letting him stay here by himself."

Karen reached out and held his sleeve. "Come on, Jack, you know what you were thinking about. And so was I."

Jack shouted out, "Randy! Randy! Can you hear me! Randy!"

He listened. There was no reply. All he could hear was the rain gurgling in the gutters, and the soft creaking of a building that had been neglected for sixty years. Welcome back, Jack, the building whispered.

"We'll have to go look for him," said Jack. "God almighty! How long were we gone? Two minutes, three? Didn't I tell him to sit there and wait and not to move? Didn't you hear me say that? Randy!"

They walked back along the corridor as far as the stairs. Jack felt cold and prickly, and he couldn't stop swallowing. Supposing Randy had been right, and there was a pervert roaming the building? He could have murdered Randy by now, and dragged his body away, and how could they ever find him?

Even if they did find him, it might already be too late. Randy could have been tortured, abused, strangled; and all the time Jack had been sticking his finger up his secretary. What was he going to tell the police? What was he going to tell Maggie?

They hurried down the stairs. Their footsteps clattered in the claustrophobic silence. Karen said breathlessly, "He's here someplace, Jack. He's just wandered off."

"Randy!" Jack shouted, and shone his flashlight down the third-story corridor. He waited, but again there was no reply.

"Do you know how many damn rooms there are in this building?" he asked Karen.

Karen said, "I'm sorry, Jack. It's my fault, too."

"Of course it's not your fault. I'm his father. I shouldn't

have brought him out here. I shouldn't have come at all. I don't know what the hell—"

Far in the distance, like the muffled shout of a small child falling down a night-black well, he heard a voice cry "ammyyooowwww" and then die away again.

"Hear that?" he asked Karen.

"Something, I don't know. Maybe a cat."

"Cat? That was Randy. Randy!"

No answer. Jack ran along the third-story corridor until he reached the staircase at the other end. "Randy? Randy? Randy, it's Daddy!"

They spent two hours, searching every floor, rattling every door handle. The building had over a hundred rooms, and only the room in which they had left Randy was unlocked. There was no sign of Randy anywhere—not in the corridors, not in the kitchens, not on the second-floor landing.

At last they came down the stairs into the hallway. It was almost two o'clock in the morning, and Jack's flashlight was beginning to falter. Karen said, "I'm going to have to call Bessy, tell her I won't be back." Bessy was a waitress with thick ankles who had lodged with Karen ever since her divorce, and who baby-sat for Sherrywine whenever Karen wanted to go dancing or drinking.

"There's no phone," said Jack.

"There's a phone back at that gas station, at Lodi."

"So what do you think I'm going to do? You think I'm going to leave Randy here so that you can call your baby-sitter? Jesus, Karen, he might have been murdered!"

"He's not here, Jack! He's wandered off! We've been up

and down these corridors a dozen times! He's probably gone back to the car to get some sleep. We haven't checked the car yet."

"We haven't checked the cellars, either."

Karen rubbed her arm stiffly. It was a gesture of suppressed nervousness. "Jack, I'm frightened," she admitted. "I mean supposing this Lester is real."

"It won't take us long to check the cellars."

"Jack, I hate cellars. I really hate them."

"Well, do you want to wait here?"

Karen looked around at the blind and silent statues standing at the foot of each flight of stairs. "Here? In the dark?"

"Wait outside, then."

Karen bit her lip. "No, I'll come with you. Just so long as that flashlight doesn't give out."

The door to the cellar was on the west side of the hallway. It was wider than most of the doors in the house, and it was paneled in faded oak. Jack tried the door handle, expecting that it would be locked, hoping that it would be locked, but it swung open easily. A damp chilly draft rose from the darkness, and Karen shivered.

"You really think he's down there?"

Jack shone his flashlight into the doorway, and the waning amber bulb illuminated a flight of stone steps and a plain oak handrail.

"Randy?" he called. His voice didn't echo at all. He might just as well have been shouting into a pillow. "Randy?"

"He wouldn't have gone down there," said Karen, gripping Jack's arm.

"He's nowhere else," Jack told her, straining his eyes.

"He must have gone back to the car. He wouldn't have gone down there."

"Karen, I'm sorry. I have to look."

Karen took a deep breath. "All right. I know you do. I'm sorry."

Keeping close together, they went through the cellar door and down the steps. By the faltering beam of his flashlight, Jack could see that the cellars were vast. They ran the entire length of the house, with arched ceilings of lime-washed brick, supported by massive brick pillars. Underneath the floor of the hallway stood an immense dinosaur of a Kenwood boiler, its brass pipes encrusted with green corrosion and its dials blinded by grime. The rest of the cellars were crowded with packing cases, coils of rope, dried-up cans of paint, faded brown wrapping paper, empty carboys marked "Pickling Vinegar," boxes of nails, crates filled with murky-looking bottles of linseed oil, sagging sofas, dismantled iron beds, soiled mattresses, bicycle wheels, and a collection of fifty or sixty heavy glass accumulator batteries.

No sign of Randy.

Karen said, "Call him. Call him again."

"Randy!" Jack shouted. "Randy! You down here anywhere?"

The flashlight brightened momentarily and then faded. There must have been a window open somewhere in the cellars, because the draft was damp and cold and smelled of rain. "He's not here," said Karen. "We'd better go look outside."

As he turned to go, however, Jack glimpsed something beige and lumpy on the cellar wall, close to the back of the boiler. At first he thought it was fungus; but when the flashlight brightened again, he saw that it was something oddly familiar.

"Wait," he said, and went cautiously down the rest of the cellar stairs and picked his way across the floor. He went right up to the excrescence on the wall and shone the flashlight on it.

"What is it?" asked Karen, her voice unsteady with anxiety.

Jack reached up and touched it. It was beige, and woolen, and shapeless. It had the texture of a waffle. The Turd, halfway up the wall, inextricably stuck.

"It's Randy's toy," Jack called back.

Slowly Karen came across the cellar to join him. She stood beside him and stared up at the Turd in bewilderment.

"What's it doing there?"

Jack tugged at it. The Turd wasn't just stuck, it was buried in the brick, as if its atoms had become intermingled with those of the wall.

"You ever see anything like that?" Jack asked Karen. "I can't get it out."

He tugged again. This time he ripped the Turd apart, and he was left with a handful of torn wool and kapok stuffing.

God, he thought, *Randy's going to kill me.*

"How did he do that?" Karen asked. "And, you know, why?"

Jack said, "More to the point, where is he?"

"Maybe we'd better come back when it's light," said Karen. "I mean, he could be anywhere. I sure can't see him down here."

Jack tore away the last fragments of wool that still hung

from the brickwork. "I think we ought to call the police. The sooner they start looking, the better."

He shone the flashlight around the cellar. He lifted up some sheets of hardboard and shifted two or three crates. He prayed to God that he wouldn't find Randy lying dead. He moved a chaise with a collapsed seat, and he was just about to push aside some rolls of linoleum when he heard that noise again.

Ssssssshhhhhhhh—sssssshhhhhh—sssssssshhhhhhhhh dragging along the wall.

He stiffened, the skin at the back of his neck prickling. The noise went slowly along the entire length of the cellar, and then it started coming back again.

"Come on—I think maybe we're better off out of here," said Jack.

They retreated across the cellar floor, carefully at first. But the noise scraped nearer and nearer, faster and faster, like concrete being churned, like a body being dragged through gravel, thick and gritty but somehow soft. By the time they reached the stairs they were practically running.

"What is it?" Karen gasped, turning wildly around

"I'm not going to stop to find out," Jack panted back. "Come on, let's get out of here!"

They stumbled up the stairs. The noise was almost on top of them now, as deafening as an oncoming locomotive. Jack pushed Karen up ahead of him, gripping the wooden handrail and heaving himself up three and four steps at a time. They had almost reached the top of the stairs when his flashlight died; and at the same moment, without any warning, the cellar door swung shut.

They were immediately swallowed by blackness. Karen screamed, "No!" And the noise came rushing up the staircase after them sshhakkkk-attakkka-shhhaaakkkk-atttakkkka.

Jack tripped on the top step and fell heavily against the wall. As he did so he felt somebody gripping at his left ankle. He thought it was Karen at first, trying to stop herself from falling; but then his right ankle was gripped, too, and he found himself being pulled back down the stairs.

"Karen!" he yelled out. *"Karen, something's got me!"*

Big, powerful hands, wrenching him back. He snatched at the handrail, but he couldn't get a firm hold on it before he was pulled down four or five stairs, grazing his cheek and sharply knocking his chin.

"Karen!" he yelled. And at that moment Karen reached the cellar door and groped it open, so that the faintest of lights washed down the cellar stairs.

Jack twisted and turned around, kicking at the hands that gripped his ankles.

What he saw then made him shout out loud with terror. The hands that were holding him were gray and dusty, the color of concrete, and they rose directly out of the concrete floor.

A little farther away, a face had emerged from the floor, too. A man's face, with a heavy forehead and a strong jaw, and a fixed triumphant grin. It looked as if it had been smothered with dry cement. There were powdery wrinkles and cracks around its mouth. Its eye sockets were totally black—black, like night, no whites at all, as if the inside of its head were empty. But it was alive, there was no question about that. It had risen straight out of the concrete floor, in the way that a swimmer emerges from the dust-covered surface of a lake.

It was alive and it was grinning at him and it was gleefully trying to drag him under the surface of the concrete, too.

4

He believed for one long moment of panic that he was lost. The hands gripped him so tightly that his legs were almost numb. His left heel was pulled further and further down toward the floor, until at last it was pressed right up against the concrete. The pain was excruciatingly abrasive—like having his bare heel pressed against a spinning whetstone. He shouted and kicked and twisted, but the hands pulled him down yet again, until both heels were being dragged into the floor.

His fingers scrabbled for the wooden handrail. The first time he missed, but then he arched his back and managed to hook his fingertips around the lowest wall bracket that held the handrail in place. He stretched, and stretched again, and at last he managed to grip the handrail tightly.

Karen was screaming, "Jack! Jack!" but the pain in his feet was so raw that he could hardly hear her.

He kicked, and kicked, and kicked again. For an instant, the grip on his right ankle loosened. He twisted his right foot free and lashed out at the hand that was holding on to his left foot. The dusty gray face grinned even more wildly, as if it enjoyed the struggle, as if it were elated by sharing his pain. Then it opened its mouth wide and let out a sound that froze Jack to the backbone.

It was like the combined screams of three hundred people in a doomed airliner. It was like a subway train hurtling out of a tunnel. It was fear and rage and agony beyond all human understanding.

"Jack!" shrieked Karen, her voice scarcely audible over the deafening noise.

Lashing out with his right foot, Jack kicked himself free from the gripping hands. He rolled himself over and staggered back up the cellar stairs, sharply knocking his knee. Karen threw her arms around him and bustled him out of the cellar door. She was all ready to run straight out of the house, but Jack said, "Hold it, wait, hold it!" and slammed the cellar door shut, and turned the key.

"That ought to slow it down," he panted.

"But it came right out of the floor!" Karen squealed. "It came right out of the floor!"

Jack was trembling. He didn't know whether to stay where he was or to run. He wasn't sure that he could run, even if he wanted to. His whole body seemed to have lost its coordination. Karen stood a little way away from him, her arms clasped tightly over her breasts, staring at him in terror and uncertainty.

"Must have been what Randy was talking about," he said. He didn't even sound like himself. "You know, Lester."

"But how could it come out of the floor? How could it do that?"

Jack shook his head. "I don't know. I just don't know. But it pulled me in, too. At least it was trying to. I could feel it against my feet, I mean the pain of it. I never felt pain like that before. I mean it was actually trying to drag me down into the floor."

"That's impossible," Karen declared.

"Sure. It's impossible! Logically and scientifically impossible. People can't walk through solid walls and people can't come—rising up through solid floors."

"What are we going to do?" asked Karen. "Do you think it got hold of Randy?"

Jack leaned back against the cellar door and squeezed his eyes shut. All he could see was that greenish gray face, the color of cement. He didn't even want to think what it could have done to Randy.

Karen said, "Jack, if it got hold of Randy—"

Jack opened his eyes. "I'm just going to pray that it didn't. Do you know how strong that thing was? He wouldn't have stood a chance."

"So what are we going to do?"

"I don't know. Call the police, I guess." He wished he could stop trembling.

Randy, my poor Randy! Pray God that thing didn't get you; pray God you didn't suffer, if it did.

After a moment Jack managed to calm himself down. "Come on," he told Karen. He sniffed and cleared his throat. "Let's go find that telephone. There's nothing more that we can do on our own."

They crossed the hallway and went out through the lounge to the conservatory. As they were weaving their way between the reading tables in the lounge Jack thought that he could hear that dragging noise again. Sssssshhhhhh—sssssshhhhhh—sssssshhhhhh along the wall.

"Listen," he said, and laid his hand on Karen's arm.

Karen stared at him, wide-eyed. The noise stopped, as if somebody had been following them, and was waiting for them to continue. Waiting, watching, with bated breath.

"Let's just get out of here," Karen urged.

"No, wait. Listen. Can you hear something?"

"I can't hear anything and I don't want to hear anything. Oh God, Jack, I'm terrified."

But Jack stayed absolutely still. The rain dripped through the broken panes of the conservatory and rustled in the laurels in the darkened garden. But there was another sound, soft and powdery, like dead plaster sifting down behind age-stiffened wallpaper, like somebody hiding behind the curtains and not daring even to breathe.

Jack slowly, slowly turned around. The lounge was so shadowy that it was almost impossible to make out anything at all. Basketwork chairs, tipped-over tables. Magazine racks crammed with yellowed newspapers. But between the bookcase and the door, he thought he could distinguish a lumpiness on the cream-painted wall.

"Jack," pleaded Karen. She was so frightened now that she was practically in shock.

But without a word, Jack took three or four steps slowly back toward the door, staring all the time at the lumpy outlines on the wall. He would have done anything for a flashlight.

"Jack, please," Karen begged him.

"Do you have some matches?" Jack asked her. His mouth was so dry that he spoke in a whisper.

"Matches?"

"You know what I mean, matches. For lighting cigarettes with."

"I think I have some in my purse. But I left it in the car."

Jack took another step nearer the door. He didn't want to approach too close. His ankles were still sore from the hands that had seized him in the cellar.

Karen was fumbling in the pockets of her raincoat. "I have some book matches."

"That's fine, that's perfect." Jack reached behind him to take the matches without once glancing away from the wall. He opened the cover, bent the matches back, and struck all of them at once, with his thumb. They flared up brightly, and he lifted the matchbook and held it up as high as he could.

By the brief flickering light of the matches, he saw that the cream-painted wall bad raised itself in bas-relief, into the shape of a naked young woman. She was large-hipped, large-breasted, with narrow shoulders and a rather Negroid-looking face. Her hair radiated out from her head like the rays of the sun.

"Oh my God," whispered Karen. "Oh my God, she's right inside the wall."

In fact it looked as if the wall were nothing more than a thin sheet of glossy cream-painted rubber against which the girl was pushing herself from the other side. Her cream-painted eyes were open and she was staring at Jack without moving, without breathing.

"Who are you?" he whispered. He didn't think that he had ever been so frightened in his life.

The girl continued to stare at him, unblinking, saying nothing.

"Who are you?" Jack repeated.

She was alive, there was no question about that. She was

alive and she was staring at him. But how could she be, inside the wall?

Jack took two more hesitant steps forward. The flames from the matchbook were almost gone.

"*Who are you?*" he shouted at the girl. "*Where's my son?*"

The girl suddenly turned, with a faint sssssshhhhhh sound. Jack jumped back in fright. But she didn't attempt to grab him. She turned right around. He glimpsed her naked back, and then the wall smoothed itself out and the matchbook burned his fingers and she was gone.

He touched the wall with the flat of his hand. It was cold and solid. He could even feel the brush marks from the paint. A wall, that's all. He heard the sssssshhhhhhh sound dying away.

"You saw that?" he asked Karen, his voice shaky.

"I saw it," she replied. "A girl, just standing there. Then she disappeared."

Jack backed away from the wall and took hold of Karen's hand. "What do you think, you think we've eaten something and gone crazy? Or maybe there's some kind of gas leak around this building, something that gives people hallucinations."

"I saw it," Karen insisted. "It was real. A real girl, just standing there."

They left the lounge and walked out through the conservatory. Outside, on the gravel path, Jack checked his watch. It was almost three o'clock. They stood in the rain for two or three minutes, breathing in the chilly night air. Jack looked up at the building's dark spires, his eyes half-closed against the raindrops, and he didn't know what he thought about it now, whether he still wanted it, or whether he dreaded it. He knew that he had to have Randy back, whatever happened. He felt so desperately unhappy and frightened for Randy that he was close to tears.

"Do you think they were ghosts?" asked Karen.

Jack wiped the rain from his face with his hand. "I don't know. Maybe. I never saw a ghost before, and I never knew anybody who did. Who's to say that they can't come sticking out of the walls? I mean, everybody says that they walk through walls, maybe that's how they do it."

Karen said, "The cops aren't going to believe us, you know. They're going to think we're totally crazy."

"But it's true, it happened, we saw it with our own eyes."

"Forget it," said Karen. "I had enough of cops when Cecil started to beat up on me. Most of the time they tried to make out that it was all my fault, because I provoked him. You should of seen the size of that man, and I provoked him? One cop told me that in his opinion I deserved everything that Cecil did to me, and if I'd been his wife, he would have given me a beating I wouldn't have forgotten."

"We have to tell them, Karen. If somebody's taken Randy, or if he's hidden around the building someplace, we'll never find him without the cops."

"So what are you going to tell them? That there's a man in the floor who tries to grab your feet, and a nude woman in the wall?"

"I'm going to tell them the truth."

"Jack—" Karen interrupted. "Think about it. Randy's missing and how come we took him out to this weird old building in the middle of the night?"

"We were looking for some vagrant called Lester, remember?"

"Oh, sure. Some squatter. But you saw for yourself that nobody was squatting here, didn't you? So how come we left Randy alone?"

Jack glanced at her quickly. "We don't have to tell the police about that."

"Of course not. But how come we left him alone?"

"He was tired, that's all. Come on, Karen, for Christ's sake, he's my son. I'm just hoping and praying he didn't go down to the cellar. The police are going to be able to see for themselves how bad I feel about it."

"Sure you feel bad about it, but feeling bad about it isn't going to help us any. The first thing the cops are going to think is that we took Randy out here to get rid of him. You had a bust-up with Maggie, you wanted to hurt her, you found yourself burdened with a kid you didn't want. You can fill in the rest for yourself."

"Except you're forgetting one thing," Jack interrupted her. "It isn't true."

"That never worried any of the cops that I ever met."

Jack ran his hand wearily through his wet hair. "Let's think about the cops later, okay? Right now we ought to take a look down by the swimming pool. Maybe he wandered down there."

"Jack... I'm sorry," said Karen. "Please, honey, don't be angry with me. I want to find Randy just as much as you do. But I know what it's like when you call in the cops. Everything gets turned on its ass. After a while you don't know yourself what you did and what you didn't do."

"Jesus, he could be anywhere," said Jack, more to the night than to Karen. The wet shining on his cheeks wasn't rain. "Let's take a look by the swimming pool, then we'll go back to the car."

Holding hands, they walked across the tennis courts toward the swimming pool. It was so dark that Jack had to run his hand along the top of the tennis net as a guide. The canvas was cold and wet and unpleasant to touch. They said nothing until they reached the edge of the pool. They could just discern the surface of the water, circled and circled by the falling rain. The water was black and stagnant and stank of ammonia.

"You don't happen to have any more of those matches?" asked Jack.

"About half a book," said Karen, fishing in her raincoat pocket yet again. "I always pick them up, you know, out of habit. I used to have a collection. You know what, I even had one from William Holden's house. That was before he got drunk and cracked his head and killed himself."

She produced the matchbook. The first match was too damp, and the head simply mushed when Jack tried to strike it. The second match flared damply, and he held it up, peering through the smoke down to the water in the bottom of the swimming pool.

"There's something in there," said Karen. "Look, over there!"

Jack peered into the swiveling shadows, but the match died away. He struck another, which wouldn't light, then another. His last match burned just long enough for him to see a dark humped shape lying in the water.

"You don't think it's Randy?" asked Karen, in a petrified voice. "Maybe he saw that thing in the building and he was really scared and ran down here and didn't realize the pool was here."

Jack stood where he was, shaking with cold and indecision. "I saw something in the pool the very first time I was here. It was just a shape, I don't know what it was. Maybe that's the same thing. Maybe a tree stump or something that somebody pushed in the water just for the hell of it."

"But what if it's Randy?" asked Karen.

Jack hesitated one moment longer. Then he quickly unbuttoned his raincoat and stripped it off. He took off his sport coat, his necktie, his shirt. The rain spattered across his bare chest. He took off his shoes and socks, followed by his pants and his shorts.

"Oh, Jack honey," Karen begged him. "Please be careful."

"Careful? Are you kidding?" he shivered. He took off his Rolex and gave it to her. "Don't drop it, it used to belong to my father."

He hurried naked to the far side of the pool, where the steps were. Karen said, "It was just about there... maybe eight or ten feet from where you're standing."

His teeth chattering uncontrollably, he climbed down the metal ladder until his foot touched the water. It was deadly cold, and smelled so strongly that he retched out loud. He peered down into the darkness. God alone knew what was lurking beneath the surface. He climbed down two rungs further, the water clinging around his calves like garters of cold steel. His testicles shrank so tightly that they almost disappeared inside his groin.

Still holding on to the ladder with one hand, he leaned out across the pool, scooping his fingers across the surface of the water, trying to feel the mysterious shape in the darkness.

"I think I can see it," said Karen. "It's about three feet away from you. You're going to have to swim for it."

He swallowed. Then he said, "All right, I'll give it a try."

He took one more step down on the ladder, but unexpectedly there were no more rungs, and he suddenly plunged straight down into the water, right over his head. He shouted out underwater, in a gargled rush of bubbles. He could feel soft bulky things bumping against him in the darkness, and he surged to the surface in fear and disgust and desperation.

"Ah!" he shouted out, sucking in air.

"Jack, are you okay?" Karen called out. "Jack!"

"Ah!" he repeated. "Ah! Ah! Shit, I'm drowning! Shit, this is disgusting!"

Karen said, "It's over there, I can see it. Look, just there; you're only a couple of feet away."

"I can't see a goddamned thing."

"There! Look, there!"

Stiffly Jack swam across to the place where Karen was pointing. The water clung to his bare skin, more like chilled jelly than water, and something slippery trailed between his legs, making him thrash around with revulsion.

At last his fingers touched something floating in the slime. Something covered with heavy-duty cotton, like Randy's windbreaker. Something that bobbed on the surface soft and lifeless, like a drowned boy.

Jack grabbed hold of it. Then, slowly, his arms stiffening with cramp, he swam back toward the side of the pool, pulling the sodden object after him.

Karen came around to help him. Shuddering with cold and disgust, he climbed up the ladder, and then heaved the object onto the tiles. It made a deep, squelching sound, followed by a steady soft dribbling of water.

It was a mail sack, not a boy; but it was quite heavy enough to contain the body of a boy. There was something inside it that was repellently soft and shapeless, and it stank so strongly of decay that Jack regurgitated a mouthful of acid-tasting lunch.

"It's not Randy," Karen whispered, her face white in the rainy darkness. "It can't be Randy."

"I'm going to put some clothes on," Jack told her. "Then we'll just have to open the bastard up and see what it is."

Karen said nothing, but handed Jack his clothes from underneath her raincoat. He was bone-cold, so cold that he could scarcely think, and his shirt and pants stuck wetly to his skin. But once he had tugged on his shoes and socks and buttoned up his coat, he began to feel warmer and a little less shocked.

"Okay, then." He sniffed, hunkering down beside the mail sack. "Let's find out what the hell we've got here."

With stiff fingers he unlaced the top of the sack and pulled it wide open.

"Oh, Jesus," he said. The stench of decayed flesh filled up his mouth and his nose with nauseating sweetness.

"I can't see," he choked. "I can't even see what it is."

He pressed his hand over his face and peered intently into the darkness of the opened sack. He could make out something glistening, but that was all. Karen stayed well away.

"Oh my God, it's something awful, whatever it is," she whispered.

Jack stood up. "You don't have any more matches?"

She shook her head. But then she said, "My key ring! Why didn't I think of that before? Look, I have a little flashlight on my key ring!"

She jangled her keys until she found the miniature flashlight, and pressed it. "Cecil bought it for me. It's always so dark on my porch, I could never find the keyhole."

Jack took the key ring and knelt down beside the mail sack again. He directed the beadlike beam on to it and tried to make sense of what he saw.

A tangle of grayish pink flesh, mottled here and there with the bright greens and blues of decay. A swath of brindled fur, an upraised leg with the bone rotted right through the skin. A dog of some kind, probably a German shepherd. Certainly not a boy.

It was when he probed the beam further into the depths of the sack, however, that he prickled with shock. There was only one body, but two half-rotted heads were staring at him; two muzzles; two sets of snaggled teeth; two blackish tongues. Four yellow eyes, veiled with mucus.

He switched off the flashlight abruptly and stood up. "A dog," he told Karen. "Somebody drowned their dog."

"How could anybody do that?" Karen shivered.

Jack couldn't answer for a moment. His mouth was swimming with bile and saliva. "It was kind of a freak. Guess it was kinder, in a way."

Karen took hold of his arm. "At least it's not Randy."

"Let's get back to the car," said Jack.

Karen glanced back at the mail sack. "What are you going to do about that?"

"I don't know. Leave it for now. What else can I do?"

But it was right then that a very powerful flashlight shone in their eyes, and a dry-sounding voice said, "You could throw it, mister, and mind your own business."

The flashlight jiggled dazzlingly closer. Jack lifted his hand in front of his eyes; but all he could see was a dark silhouette of a man in a black fireman's waterproof coat and a huge floppy rain hat. Beside him, on a tight leash, he could see what looked like a Doberman, wheezing and whining for the man to let it loose.

"That was my dog," the dry-sounding voice remarked, momentarily flicking the flashlight beam across to the other side of the swimming pool. "You've heard of a dog with two tails being happy. But a dog with two heads, that's no fun at all. Lived for seven months, and I never saw one of God's creatures so miserable."

There was a pause, and then the man said, "You mind if I ask you people what you're doing here, trespassing around, at half past three in the morning?"

"Who are you?" Jack asked him.

"Sorry, friend. I asked first."

"My name's Jack Reed. I'm buying The Oaks."

There was another pause, much longer this time. Then, "You're buying The Oaks?"

"That's right. You can check with Mr. Bufo at Capitol Realtors."

"Mr. Bufo never told me nothing about that."

"Well, that's probably because the deal hasn't formally been concluded yet. But the owners have accepted my offer."

"Mm!" said the man. "They would."

"What's that supposed to mean?"

"It means what it means. They would, you'd expect them to. I'll bet they couldn't believe their luck."

Jack said testily, "Do you mind telling me who you are?"

"Sure," said the man. He suddenly shone the flashlight into his own face. He was quite an old man, midseventies, Jack would have guessed. He looked German, or vaguely Slavic. His eyes were very pale blue and his skin was the color of liver sausage and he had two rows of crimson scars running down each side of his nose.

"Name's Joseph Lovelittle," he said. "Parents changed it from Kleinlieb during the First World War. Little love, love little. Just about the only folks in Milwaukee who did. Most of them were proud to be German, still are."

He lowered the flashlight. "I saw your wagon, back on the road. I don't hardly never sleep, that's my trouble. Never could, that's why they gave me the job of watchman. Round about two in the morning, I usually take Boy here out for a walk. He likes to walk at night, same as I do. You see more, at night."

"Did you see a young boy back at my wagon?" asked Jack. "Nine years old, fairish hair, blue windbreaker?"

Joseph Lovelittle thought about that. "Can't say that I did," he replied at last. "Checked inside, too. You missing him?"

Jack nodded.

"Well," said Joseph Lovelittle, "The Oaks ain't the ideal place for wandering around at night. We get squatters, from time to time; or let's say would-be squatters. Hippies, dope addicts, bikers, you know the kind. But Boy and me, we do our best to discourage them from staying. Mind you, The Oaks ain't the kind of place you'd really want to stay, even if you was a biker."

"Do you think you might have any ideas where my son might be hiding himself?" asked Jack. "We searched the building."

He glanced at Karen, wondering if he ought to tell Joseph Lovelittle about the hands that had reared out of the cellar floor, and the staring impression of the woman in the wall, but Karen gave him a tiny shake of her head. They didn't really know who this "Joseph Lovelittle" was yet; and they didn't want to appear eccentric or unhinged. He could easily call the police and have them taken in for trespassing. Besides—Jack might have been right, and there might have been some gas leak or atmospheric peculiarity in the building that caused brief and frightening hallucinations.

Out here, on the rainy tennis court, it was difficult for Jack to believe that he had really been seized by a gray-faced man who had burst out of solid concrete.

Joseph Lovelittle picked up the sodden mail sack and slung it one-handed back into the pool. Then he began to walk back toward the building, dragging his half-asphyxiated Doberman along with him. Jack and Karen followed.

"No real use searching the building by night," Joseph Lovelittle remarked. "No use searching it without keys, neither."

"Randy couldn't have gotten into a room that was already locked," Jack pointed out.

Joseph Lovelittle's raincoat made a rubbery squeaking noise as he walked along. "I'm not so sure about that," he told Jack. "All those doors are self-locking, know what I mean? They lock automatically whenever you close them and you can only open them from the outside, and only with a key. So your boy could have found a door that was open, and gone inside, and closed it behind him, and then he wouldn't have been able to get out."

"I'm sure we would have heard him calling, or knocking, if he'd done that."

Joseph Lovelittle grunted in amusement. "Those rooms are pretty well soundproof, once they're shut. They were made that way, special."

As they reached the graveled path at the rear of the conservatory Jack looked at his watch. "Look—if we come back when it gets light, do you think you could help us to search the building?"

"Cost you," Joseph Lovelittle said promptly.

Jack reached into his back pants pocket and took out his money clip. He tugged out a twenty-dollar bill and handed it to Joseph Lovelittle without a word. Joseph Lovelittle scrutinized it in the beam of his flashlight.

"All right, come back by seven. It'll be good and light by then. That's supposing it ever stops raining." He sneezed, twice, into his hand. Then he said, "I'll meet you right here. Don't be late, will you? I've got enough to do without looking for kids who shouldn't have been here in the first place."

"I could always call the police," Jack challenged him, although he didn't really mean it.

Joseph Lovelittle laughed. "You'd have to pay the cops

five times what you just paid me just to come out here. Sheesh! They hate this place. They really hate it."

"We'll see you at seven," said Jack. "Meanwhile—you keep an eye out for my boy, you hear me?"

Joseph Lovelittle shone his flashlight directly into Jack's face. "You're pretty wet, ain't you? Better get yourself a hot shower before you catch pneumonia." He paused, and then he said, "You know who you remind me of? Dick Van Dyke, that's who you remind me of."

"I'm a little younger than Dick Van Dyke," Jack told him.

"I mean Dick Van Dyke when he's in 'The Dick Van Dyke Show.' You know with Morey Amsterdam and Rosemary What's-her-face and Mary Tyler Moore."

The Doberman called Boy wheezed at his leash, his tail thrashing against Joseph Lovelittle's raincoat.

"I'll see you later," said Jack. He felt defeated, very cold, and very tired. He would have done anything to have Randy back safe, and to be able to crawl into bed and sleep for the next two days.

"I'll be here," said Joseph Lovelittle. "You can count on it."

Obligingly he pointed his flashlight toward the avenue of oak trees that would lead them back to their car. Jack turned back once or twice to look at him, but all he could see was the dazzling lens of the flashlight.

"Was he creepy or was he creepy?" asked Karen as she balanced her way down the erratically lit driveway on six-inch heels.

But Jack countered, "What I want to know is, why should the owners be so goddamned delighted to have sold this place?"

"Come on, Jack," said Karen. "You saw what happened in the cellar. Don't tell me the owners don't know all about it."

"I'm not so sure... if anybody had ever seen that before... don't you think they would have gotten in touch with the press, or the television? This is a seriously haunted building we're talking about now."

"We were probably dreaming the whole thing. Did you ever see Nightmare on Elm Street?"

"For God's sake, Karen; that was a movie. This is real."

They squeezed through the gap in the fence, and Jack unlocked the car. As Joseph Lovelittle had told them, it was empty. They climbed in, out of the rain, and Jack switched the engine on and started the windshield wipers. It was 3:37 in the morning.

"There's a Howard Johnson's on Ninety-four, back toward Madison," said Jack. "You can call Bessy; and then we can both take a hot shower and get a little sleep."

Karen leaned across and kissed him. "I'm sorry, Jack. I'm sorry it all turned out this way. But we'll find Randy, believe me. If he's there to be found, we'll find him."

"And what about the ghosts?" asked Jack. He glimpsed himself in the rearview mirror. white-faced, exhausted. "What about things that come up out of the floor and grab you? What about women in the goddamned walls?"

"Jack, honey, we'll find a way to deal with it, okay? That geeky watchman was absolutely right. It's better to look in the morning."

Jack pulled the station wagon's gearshift into drive, backed up, and turned.

"Do you know something?" he said. "It's never going to stop raining. Never, ever, as long as we live. Never."

*

Jack took a yellow vinyl bar stool into the shower and sat under the hot water with his face upraised and his eyes closed tight. Karen opened a fresh piece of Bubblicious and sat on the end of the bed wearing nothing but her black nylon bra, and talked on the phone to Bessy with the thick ankles.

"Believe me, Bessy—if I'd've known what was going to happen! Bessy! You're an angel, Bessy, you know you are! You know that necklace you wanted? I'll buy you that necklace you wanted. I promise! I know it's a drag! Bessy, I'm sorry! But Sherrywine loves you so much!"

At last, just as Jack was coming out of the shower, she put down the phone. "Fuck her," she said, chewing noisily.

"What—she give you a hard time?" asked Jack, rubbing his hair dry.

"Oh, not exactly. Not in so many words. She keeps trying to make me feel like a bad mother, that's all."

"You're not a bad mother."

"You have bruises on your ankles. Have you seen them?"

Jack looked down. Both ankles were crisscrossed with reddish blue marks.

"That thing was real, wasn't it?"

Jack nodded. "Yes, it was real. It wasn't a ghost. It was real."

He sat on the cheap green nylon quilt cover, right next to her. She turned to look at him closely, her jaws working all the time. She was very pretty; even though one of her false eyelashes had become detached and was hanging over her eye. She had firm pointy breasts with brownish pink nipples as wide as coffee saucers; and even though her stomach sagged a little from having children, she was still very thin. He saw for the first time that she had carefully nail-scissored her pubic hair into the shape of a heart. She had copied it from Playboy.

"You can call the cops if you want to," she said. "I mean he's your son, you mustn't let me put you off. If the same thing happened to Sherrywine..."

"First, I want to search The Oaks properly," Jack told her. His voice sounded harsh and terrible, like Richard Burton about to die. "I don't know—I'm just convinced that he's still there. Those people in the walls. And the Turd, the way that was stuck in the bricks."

"That watchman—what was his name—" said Karen.

"Littlelove, Lovelittle?"

"That's it, Lovelittle. Do you hear what he said? Even the cops don't like visiting The Oaks. You'd have to pay them five times more. Now, why should that be, if there isn't something weird going down there? I mean something that scares them?"

Jack dropped his rough motel towel on the floor and lay on his back on the bed. He stared at the ceiling for a while, and then he closed his eyes. It was twenty to five in the morning. Outside the tangerine-colored loose-weave drapes it was already light; though grayly, because it was still raining.

Karen knelt beside him for a while, watching him. She shifted her gum from side to side. She liked him. She thought that she could probably love him, if destiny would let her. She read her horoscope every Sunday in the newspaper, but she didn't trust in destiny. After a few minutes she realized that he was sleeping. His fingers uncurled and he began to snore. She reached behind her back and unclasped her bra.

Jack murmured in his sleep. Nothing comprehensible. Karen stroked his face with her fingertips, touched his eyelids, ran her finger across his lips. He kissed thin air, dreaming. She ran her fingernails down his breastbone, lightly scratched his stomach. Then she took his penis in her hand, and squeezed it, and slowly massaged it up and down. It filled and stiffened, and Karen gripped it even tighter, but Jack still didn't wake up. He was far too exhausted by shock and anxiety and lack of sleep.

Karen circled her fingertip around and around the moistened opening of his penis; but then she took her hand away and lay by herself, watching the lights of passing trucks swivel across the ceiling.

She glanced across at Jack. He would never be hers. She wasn't sure that she could manage a man with a conscience. But she snuggled up close to him as the room gradually lightened, and she didn't sleep, and when he opened his eyes at twenty after six and stared at her, she smiled, and kissed him, and said, "Good morning, lover."

By daylight, Joseph Lovelittle looked even older and shabbier. He was waiting for them in the lee of the conservatory, the collar of his fireman's raincoat turned up, while his Doberman Boy sat beside him and shivered feverishly. The sky was quite bright, but gray, and the rain clattered straight out of it like water from an ornamental fountain. Their shoes crunched wetly on the gravel.

"Well," snorted Joseph Lovelittle. "Thought you wouldn't come."

"I'm looking for my son," Jack reminded him seriously.

"So you are, so you are." Joseph Lovelittle turned toward the conservatory door, a drip of transparent phlegm swinging from the end of his curved nose. "This the way you went in before? Sometimes it's locked and sometimes it ain't."

"You lock it?" asked Jack.

Joseph Lovelittle turned his head without turning his shoulders. It was quite unnerving to watch. "Sometimes I do. Sometimes I don't."

He swung the door open. Jack said, "Who locks it, when you don't? Daniel Bufo?"

"Sometimes."

"And who else?"

Joseph Lovelittle challenged him with pale blue eyes. "Who do you think?"

They stepped into the conservatory. Joseph Lovelittle took a deep, thumping breath. "You should've seen this conservatory, back in twenty-five. Tropical plants, cactus, you never saw nothing like it. Dr. Estergomy's pride and joy."

"Who was Dr. Estergomy?"

Joseph Lovelittle turned and stared at him yet again. "You're buying this place; you don't know Dr. Estergomy?"

"Is there any reason why I should?"

Joseph Lovelittle thought about that, and then shrugged. "I guess not, when you think about it."

"But who was he?" asked Karen.

"You know this place was a nursing home? That's what Mr. Bufo told you?"

"That's right. The Oaks Nursing Home, that's what he said."

"Well... Estergomy was doctor in charge. You know what I mean? Top banana."

"I see," said Jack. "And this conservatory here—"

Joseph Lovelittle smiled at him as if he were quite mad. "That's right, Mr. Reed; you got it. Dr. Estergomy's pride and joy."

"You remember it?" asked Jack, looking around at the shriveled leaves and the broken glass and the cracked flowerpots.

"Sure. I started work here in twenty-three, when I was twelve years old. Cleaning, washing dishes, helping out. Cabin boy you might say. Used to read stories to the patients, too, those that could understand."

He took off his hat and his eyes seemed paler than ever. "Dr. Estergomy's pride and joy. Used to grow grapes in here. Little green grapes. I can remember coming in here in the summer and stealing them."

He opened the door to the lounge and allowed Karen and Jack to go in ahead of him. Boy the Doberman thrust his muzzle up the back of Karen's skirt and she snapped, "Get off, wet-nose!" Joseph Lovelittle cackled, and winked at her.

They entered the hallway. Joseph Lovelittle unbuttoned his raincoat and hung it on the banister. Underneath he wore a sagging orange cardigan and baggy-assed jeans. "Best thing to do is to start from the attic, work our way down." He held up a key ring with a half-dozen odd-shaped keys on it. "Passkeys, one for each floor."

They climbed the stairs, right up to the attic. As they climbed, Joseph Lovelittle said, "When this was Mr. Krüger's house, it was called The Maze. Nobody ever knew why, because there wasn't no maze. That's why Dr. Estergomy changed it when he took it over. Dr. Estergomy was one of those practical-minded people, didn't like nothing you couldn't explain."

"When did the nursing home close down?" asked Jack. "I saw some newspapers in the lounge dating from 1926."

"Well, that's right, June fifteenth, 1926. Eleven-thirty in the evening."

Jack frowned at Karen. "That's a pretty odd time for a nursing home to close down, eleven-thirty in the evening."

They had reached the third-floor landing. Joseph Lovelittle let his Doberman off its leash, and it bounded up the stairs with its claws scratching against the linoleum. "If your son's around here anywhere, Mr. Reed, you can bet your bottom dollar that Boy will sniff him out."

"It won't hurt him?"

"Are you kidding me, Mr. Reed? That mutt?"

They heard Boy scuffling madly all the way up to the attic. When he reached the top, he barked twice to let them know that he was there. They plodded up after him. Joseph Lovelittle was badly out of breath and had to stop every now and then, his eyes bulging, the air scraping in and out of his lungs. "Smoked a hundred a day when I was younger, wish to God I never had."

Jack said, "Did you ever see a little girl playing around here? She would have been wearing a kind of whitish-colored raincoat, with a hood."

Joseph Lovelittle stopped a few steps short of the

top-floor landing, breathing hard and staring at him. "Little girl? You mean, all on her own?"

"That's right. No more than six or seven years old, I would have thought."

Joseph Lovelittle sniffed. "What would a kid that age be doing out here on her own?"

"I don't know. I was just asking if you'd seen her. Or him. I'm not entirely sure if it's a girl."

"Well, Mr. Reed, things ain't always what they seem."

"No, I guess they're not."

Joseph Lovelittle took out his keys and began opening doors, one after the other, and leaving them open. Jack and Karen followed him along the corridor, peering into every room. Most of them were completely empty, but a few still had beds and bedside tables. In one room there was even a cork bulletin board, with postcards pinned up on it, and a curled-up pinup of An Egyptian Houri, 1926.

Karen uncurled the pinup and smiled at it. "Sexy, huh?"

They walked along farther. Joseph Lovelittle said, "No scent yet. Boy always barks like crazy whenever he picks up a scent."

Jack looked into another empty room. "Was this a private facility? Or was it owned by the state?"

"It was private, but Dr. Estergomy was paid by the state of Wisconsin for some of the patients."

"Was it always full?"

"Oh, sure, always full. Full to busting. Night it closed down, we had one hundred thirty-seven patients."

"Estergomy must have been quite a doctor."

"Well, sure. He had all of these newfangled treatments.

They was new for 1926, anyhow. These days they're probably just about as antiquated as me."

They reached the end of the attic floor, but there was no sign of Randy. "Let's try the next floor down," said Joseph Lovelittle, selecting the appropriate passkey.

He went on ahead, shuffling down the stairs. Jack said to Karen, "If we can't find Randy in the building, I'm calling the cops, that's all there is to it. Even if I do have to bribe them to come out here."

Joseph Lovelittle turned around and said, "Do you have anything that belonged to your son, Mr. Reed? Maybe it would help Boy to pick up the scent."

Jack reached in his coat pocket and took out the shredded remains of the Turd. He held them under Boy's nose, and Boy sniffed at them and licked them and then tugged at them with his teeth.

"What was that?" Joseph Lovelittle asked, looking askance at the waffle-patterned shreds of wool.

"A nondenominational, nonracist, asexual, all-natural play item," said Jack.

Joseph Lovelittle stared at him. "I used to have a Jack Armstrong flying-saucer gun when I was nine."

"Well, you can't always have all the luck," said Jack. He was beginning to feel light-headed with tiredness, almost hysterical.

They walked the length of the next corridor, with Joseph Lovelittle opening up every door, and Boy trotting in and out and sniffing. Again, they found nothing. But Jack was surprised to see that the walls of every single room on this floor were thickly lined with grayish white fabric.

"Quiet rooms," Joseph Lovelittle remarked with a wry smile when he saw Jack touching the walls. "That's what Dr. Estergomy liked to call them."

They went down to the next floor. It was here that they came to the double doors that led to the tower, strongly padlocked.

"I guess he couldn't have gotten in there," Jack remarked.

"You want to look?" asked Joseph Lovelittle. He sniffed, and the swinging drip of phlegm vanished up his nostril as if by magic. "This was Dr. Estergomy's clinic. You know—where he did all of his treatment. He always kept it well locked up, on account of the drugs and all the other stuff."

Joseph Lovelittle fiddled with his keys, and then found the correct key for the padlock. He unlocked it and swung open the right-hand door. Jack hesitated. "Go ahead," said Joseph Lovelittle. "Nothing to be scared of."

Jack stepped inside and found himself in a dim, dusty room whose ceiling was two stories high. Heavily curtained windows looked out over the avenue that approached the house from the road; all Jack could see outside were wet oak leaves, kowtowing to the heavy rain.

In one corner of the room stood a large leather-topped partners' desk. It was still strewn with yellowed papers, as if somebody had been working at it only this morning. A fountain pen lay with its cap unscrewed on top of the ink-squiggled blotter. The only sign of how long it had been there was that its nib was rusty.

Not far from the desk was a high medical examination table, draped in a sheet whose hem had been gnawed at, probably by mice. In the center of the room, however, stood the most impressive piece of furniture: a huge squarish chair of sawed oak, with a metal cap attached to the back of it by a curved brass bracket, and leather restraints for the wrists and the ankles. The chair was connected by a thick brown fabric-covered cable to a huge bank of electric dials, like the flight deck of an old-fashioned flying boat. There were rows and rows of tarnished switches, and scores of little red light bulbs, and the whole bank was wired to a stack of glass accumulators, most of them dusty and cracked and encrusted with chlorine salts.

Jack glanced up. Over the chair hung a battery of black-painted spotlights, smothered in abandoned cobwebs. Even the spiders didn't live here anymore.

"It looks like something out of Frankenstein," said Jack.

"It looks like the electric chair to me," put in Karen.

Joseph Lovelittle leaned proprietorially against the open door with his arms folded, looking around the clinic. Boy stuck his head in the wicker wastepaper basket and worried some pieces of crumpled-up notepaper.

"You're both right, I guess," said Joseph Lovelittle. "This was one of Mr. Estergomy's big new treatments. Something about sorting out your brain cells so that they behaved themselves. He showed me once, with a magnet and some iron filings. He pulled the magnet past the iron filings and they all made a pattern. That was the way he tried to explain it to me, anyway. I guess I was too young to understand him; or too dumb; or both. I'm good with my hands, you know. Not too hot in the thinking department."

"So this was a nursing home for mental patients?" asked Jack.

"Mr. Bufo didn't tell you that? This was a famous nursing

home for mental patients. Over at the university they used to call it The Walnuts, instead of The Oaks."

"That explains the padded rooms and the doors that you can't open from the inside," said Jack. "What a dummy, I should have realized."

"They was all violent," said Joseph Lovelittle. "Every single one of them, totally ape-shit, excusing my French. The state penitentiary sent them here because the guards couldn't handle them. All kinds we had here. Ax murderers, mother smotherers, baby stranglers, fire-starters, you name it. Men, women, children too. One hundred thirty-seven the night we closed down."

"I had no idea," said Jack, shaking his head. "I never heard of this place before."

"Sure you didn't. They didn't advertise it when it was open, because the local residents wouldn't have relished a holiday home for dangerous criminal maniacs right in their backyard, now would they? And after what happened, they weren't about to advertise it after it closed."

"What did happen?" asked Jack.

Joseph Lovelittle whistled to Boy between his teeth. "You finished in here?" he asked Jack.

"Yes, I think we're all finished."

They left the treatment room and Joseph Lovelittle locked the door behind them. "You can look at the west tower if you like, but that's just books. Mr. Krüger left most of his library behind when he sold the house. Think he went off to Europe, someplace like that. He gave up the beer business, too."

"Is it possible that Randy could have gotten into the west tower? Or is it locked like this?"

"It's locked just the same."

"All right, then, let's leave it for now and check the downstairs rooms first, and then the cellar."

Karen said, "You're not going back down to the cellar?"

"I have to. The Turd was there."

Joseph Lovelittle threw Jack an odd sideways look. Jack still couldn't work out how he was able to rotate his head without moving his shoulders.

"My son's toy," Jack explained.

Coughing thickly, Joseph Lovelittle led them downstairs to the hallway, and then shuffled ahead of them around the kitchens, the rest rooms, the art studios, the closets which once stored coats and boots.

At last they ended up in the bathhouse, at the back of the building. It was echoing and cold and cavernous, with tiny windows that overlooked the tennis courts. There were five white-tiled bays, in each of which stood a massive white-enameled bathtub. Each bath had a wooden lid, with an oval hole cut in it—just large enough for a human head to fit through. On the sides of the lids, four brass clamps had been fitted so that the occupant could be screwed to the rim of the bath, restraining him from climbing out. Every lid was scratched and gouged and darkly stained.

"If any of the patients got really crazy, Mr. Estergomy used to leave them in here, up to their necks in cold water. Boy, they used to scream! Sometimes you could hear them way out by the swimming pool. They used to scream and they used to scratch, and the nurses would take them out of the baths afterward and the whole bath would be full of blood, and their fingers would be scraped right down to the bones."

Karen shivered. "Gives me the creeps."

Boy the Doberman prowled around the baths, his claws tapping on the tiles. "Doesn't look like your son's in here," Joseph Lovelittle remarked. "Last place to try is the cellar."

"You ever see anybody here?" Jack asked him as they left the bathhouse.

"I see dope addicts, bikers, but not too many of them."

"No, no. What I meant was, do you ever see anybody unusual?" He couldn't quite bring himself to say "anybody in the walls."

Joseph Lovelittle unlocked the cellar door. "Depends what you mean by unusual. I could say that you and your lady friend are pretty unusual, coming around here, looking for a son you can't even prove you ever had. How do I know what you're really here for?"

"Just wait up a minute," said Jack. "I paid you, didn't I, to help us look for my son? You took the money and so I wouldn't mind seeing a little cooperation, if you don't mind."

Joseph Lovelittle promptly stuck two fingers into his cardigan pocket and produced Jack's twenty-dollar bill. "You're not satisfied, here's your money back. I wouldn't take money from anybody who wasn't satisfied."

Jack pushed it away. "All right, I'm sorry. I just want to find my boy."

Karen said, "Jack... I think I'll stay here. I don't want to go down into that cellar again."

"Hey... there ain't nothing to be scared of." Joseph Lovelittle grinned, exposing teeth the color of old piano keys. "It's nothing but a cellar, that's all."

"All the same," said Karen, her voice off-key with agitation. "I'd just as soon stay right here."

"Suit yourself." Joseph Lovelittle sniffed. He reached up beside the cellar door and took down a green-enamel inspection lamp. God, thought Jack, if only we'd known about that lamp last night.

"You coming, Mr. Reed; or are you scared, too?"

The old watchman led the way down the cellar steps, swinging the wide beam of his lamp disconcertingly from one side of the cellar to the other, so that it looked as if the whole place was tilting. For one moment the lamp shone through his ears, so that they gleamed red and hairy and laced with dark red veins.

"I don't come down here too much anymore," he told Jack over his shoulder. "Was a time I used to maintain the boiler, but during the war there wasn't no spare fuel for it, and there didn't seem too much point, for a building that nobody was never going to live in no more."

At the foot of the cellar steps he suddenly turned and frowned at Jack as if he had never seen him before in his life. "What do you want to buy the place for?" he demanded in a querulous tone. "Fellow would have to be crazy to buy this place."

"You want me to keep you on the staff?" Jack asked him. "Caretaker, chief of security, something like that?" He was hoping that Joseph Lovelittle would be sufficiently impressed to behave a little more helpfully.

Somewhere in the depths of the cellar, Boy began to bark.

Joseph Lovelittle turned his back on Jack and said, "Chief of security? Don't give a shit, to tell you the truth. Just as soon retire."

Jack followed him across the rubbish-strewn cellar floor, past the domed and silent boiler. They crunched and splintered over sheets of plywood and climbed across three broken sofas. Joseph Lovelittle didn't seem to care what he trod on. He kicked two glass accumulators and one of them smashed, leaking battery acid all the way across the concrete floor. Jack climbed over the trash as carefully as he could, but said nothing.

Boy was standing by the lime-washed wall in one of the alcoves, barking loudly.

"You found something there, Boy?" Joseph Lovelittle asked him. He shone the inspection lamp on the bricks, but the wall was completely blank. "Dog's as stupid as shit, believe me. Every other Doberman—smart as paint. Not mine, though. This dog sees trespassers—what does he do? He brings them sticks so that they can play with him. I was never lucky with dogs. Never once had a dog that turned out right."

"Maybe there's something behind the wall," Jack suggested. He felt chilled but sweaty, and he wiped his hands on the sides of his pants.

"What's behind that wall, Mr. Reed, is solid rock, that's what's behind that wall."

Jack took out the shredded pieces of the Turd and offered them to Boy to refresh his memory. Boy sniffed and snapped at them eagerly, and then jumped up at the cellar wall, barking and barking and thrashing his tail.

"Will you shut up, you shit-stupid dog!" Joseph Lovelittle shouted at him, and lashed at him with his leash. "Never known a dog so goddamned stupid!"

"But he thinks there's something there," Jack pointed out.

"Oh yeah?" Joseph Lovelittle demanded. He seemed quite angry now. "What? What does he think is there? Come on, Mr. Reed, what the blue shit does he think is there?" He stepped noisily over a stack of hundreds of old wooden coat hangers and stood right next to the wall. "This is solid brick, solid brick! Hasn't been painted since 1924, hasn't been disturbed. There's nothing here, Mr. Reed, you take my word for it. Solid brick!"

He snatched at Boy's collar but Boy dodged him and circled and barked and backed away.

"You listen to me, you mutt! You quit that goddamned noise! You hear me! You just quit that goddamned noise!"

It was then that Jack was sure he heard that chillingly familiar dragging noise. That low, soft sssssshkhhhhh—sssssssshhhhhh—sssssshhhhhhh. He turned around quickly, trying to decide where it was coming from. But Boy's barking racketed and echoed from every wall, and it was impossible for Jack to hear the noise distinctly enough.

It was approaching, though. A soft, thick, gritty undertone.

"Mr. Lovelittle!" he called.

"What? What is it?" snapped Joseph Lovelittle.

"Mr. Lovelittle, I truly believe that we'd be doing ourselves a favor if we got the hell out of here."

"What? What the hell are you talking about? Boy—shut up that damned barking, I can't hear myself think!"

Sssssshhhhhh—sssssssshhhhhh—sssssshhhhhh. The dragging was louder still. Jack looked quickly and anxiously around the floor, expecting at any second that the trash would burst apart and a gray hand would reach out and snatch for his ankles.

"Mr. Lovelittle, come on!" he called, trying to sound coaxing. "I don't think it's really too safe down here, you know? Come on! Your dog will follow along when he's calmed himself down."

"Shit-stupid dog," Joseph Lovelittle repeated.

At that moment the sssssshhhhhh noise behind him was so loud that he turned in surprise and stared at the wall. "Did you hear that?" he asked Jack. "Maybe there is—"

Two powerful brick white hands came exploding out of the wall and seized Joseph Lovelittle's head.

"Jesus!" he screamed. But then the hands pulled his face smack into the brickwork. Jack heard the hollow turkey-bone snap as his nose broke.

With relentless force, the hands dragged Joseph Lovelittle up and down, up and down, chip-chop, chip-chop, so that his face was scraped against the brick like a cabbage against a metal grater. He screamed and screamed in helpless agony, one long high-pitched howl. His screams silenced even Boy, who stood stiffly among the rubbish with his ears pricked up and his eyes unblinking.

"Hold on! Hold on!" Jack shouted out, and rattled across the coat hangers and snatched hold of Lovelittle's shoulders and tried to pull him away. But Lovelittle was being wrenched up and down so violently that Jack was thrown back by his wildly flailing arms.

The skin from Joseph Lovelittle's face was stripped across the wall in thin bloody shreds, where it slowly uncurled. Then suddenly the gritty mortar tore through the last of his skin and into his flesh, and the brickwork was gaudily painted with circles of bright red shining blood.

The gray-white hands wrenched him right to left, right

to left, again and again. One of his eyes was dragged out of its socket, one of his pale colorless eyes. It stuck to the bricks for a moment on its stringy optic nerve, staring surrealistically toward the floor. Then it suddenly dropped and disappeared among the scattered coat hangers.

Jack backed away, slowly at first, then faster. Joseph Lovelittle was still screaming, still trying to cling to the wall to stop himself being scraped across the brickwork, but Jack could see that it was hopeless, there was nothing he could do.

"Jack!" shouted Karen from the hallway. She must have called before, but he hadn't heard her over Lovelittle's screaming, and the terrible cabbage-grating sound of his head being scraped against the wall.

Jack had almost made it to the steps when Joseph Lovelittle let out the most chilling scream of all. He didn't even sound like a human being anymore. The hands were dragging him all the way along the cellar wall, from one end to the other, ripping open his cardigan, scraping the fat white bulging flesh of his oelly, tearing away his corduroy pants, smearing the lime-washed bricks with a five-foot track of blood.

"*Jack!*" shouted Karen. "*Jack, what's happening? Jack, for God's sake!*"

Gasping with shock, Jack unsteadily climbed the cellar steps. By the time he had reached the top, Joseph Lovelittle had stopped screaming. Jack didn't look back. He blundered his way out through the cellar door and stood in the middle of the hallway between the two blind statues, swaying like a man on the edge of collapse.

Karen was standing right by the door to the lounge, ready to run if she had to. He turned around and stared at her.

"Jack?" she whispered. "Jack, what's happened?"

All Jack could do was shake his head and open and close his mouth.

5

Jack found a quarter bottle of Jack Daniel's in the station wagon's glove compartment. He swigged a mouthful, coughed, and then passed it over to Karen.

"No, thanks." Karen handed it back. "I'm just sick to my stomach already."

"We'll have to call the police," said Jack. He couldn't control his voice; and he felt as if his mind were leaping up and down on some kind of a trampoline. "We don't have any options anymore."

"Okay," said Karen, folding another stick of gum into her mouth. "If that's what you want to do."

"Well, what the hell else can we do? There's something down in that cellar that grabs people, and kills them."

"Sure," said Karen. Her tone was noticeably flat. "Something that comes jumping out of solid concrete."

"Karen—the police will be able to see what happened for themselves."

"Oh, sure."

"He was pulled up against that wall, sweetheart, and he was rubbed up against it, and he was torn to shreds, for Christ's sake."

Karen looked at him narrowly. The rain dribbled down

the station wagon's windshield and beaded the hood. There were dark smudges under Karen's eyes, and for the first time since he had known her, Jack thought that she looked old.

"What do you think the police are going to say about that?" she asked him. "About Lovelittle being scraped up against the wall?"

"It's there, Karen. The evidence is there. The body, everything. All they have to do is to look at the wall."

"And they're going to believe you when you tell them he was pulled up against it, from somebody inside?"

"What are you getting at?"

"They're not going to say that you pushed him up against it?"

Jack swallowed another mouthful of Jack Daniel's. There was only a drop left in the bottle now. He hesitated, and then swallowed that, too.

"Listen—" he said. "I'm assuming the police are going to be logical." He screwed the cap back on the empty bottle and returned it to the glove compartment. "They would only have to look at me to see that I wouldn't have the physical strength to scrape a man of Lovelittle's size all the way along a two-hundred-foot cellar wall. And if I wanted to kill him, why would I kill him like that? Why not stab him or shoot him or hit him with a baseball bat? I'm not a lunatic."

"Well, maybe I'm just prejudiced," said Karen.

They sat in the car a little while longer in silence. All they could see of The Oaks was a misty outline behind the oak trees.

At length, Jack said, "I'm pretty sure that Randy's down there somewhere."

"In the cellar?"

"The dog barked; that was the only time he barked. I let him sniff the Turd, and he went straight back to the wall."

"You think that Randy's in the wall, too?"

"I don't know," said Jack, rubbing his eyes. "I don't know what to think. I know what I've seen and I still don't believe it."

"But you expect the police to believe it?"

"Karen, the evidence—"

"Jack, honey, in my limited experience, the police don't give a fuck about the evidence."

Another silence. The rain dripped and rustled through the trees. Jack took out his car keys and picked out his ignition key. "He's my son, Karen," he said. "I can't find him on my own. I think he's in the wall, God knows how he got there. This Lester he kept talking about—"

"Look," breathed Karen.

Jack frowned and looked up. Between the dark trunks of the oaks, he could just distinguish a small grayish white figure, hooded, faceless, standing alone in the rain. It was no taller than a seven-year-old child. Yet what would a seven-year-old child be doing out here, watching them?

Jack opened the station-wagon door, but as he did so Karen gripped his arm. "Wait, it's waving."

The small figure had lifted both arms. Not waving, thought Jack. Beckoning.

"It wants us to follow it," he said.

"What, are you out of your mind?" Karen retorted. "Jack! You're not going back there? Not again?"

"You don't have to come," Jack told her. "But Karen—if there's any chance of finding Randy—"

Karen looked up at him tiredly. She knew that he would have to go. "I'll wait for you, Jack, listen to the radio. But if you're not back in twenty minutes..."

"If I'm not back in twenty minutes, call the cops. I mean it. You'll have to. Don't come after me."

He climbed out of the car. The small grayish white figure was still standing among the oaks, still beckoning. He squeezed through the gap next to the gate and began to trudge up the gravel driveway with his coat collar turned up. The figure lowered its arms and stood waiting for him. It was difficult to see through the trees and the rain, but it seemed as if Randy had been right. The figure had no face. Perhaps it was only newspaper, after all, sodden newspaper waving in the wind.

Before he could get too close, the figure ran off toward the back of The Oaks. It ran in a strange jerky way, just like a child in a new raincoat that was too big for it, but peculiarly disjointed, too. More like a speeded-up film than a real child.

Jack came around the back of the building. The small figure was waiting for him by the open conservatory door. It didn't beckon anymore. When Jack reached within twenty yards of it, it jumped in through the conservatory door and disappeared.

Jack knew with raw dread where this game of follow-the-leader was taking him. He hesitated at the conservatory door, breathing deeply to calm himself down. You don't have to go back. You could call the police.

There was no sign of the small grayish white figure, not unless it was hiding behind the door. There were no wet footprints across the conservatory floor.

But Randy was inside the building somewhere, he was convinced of it, he could feel it. He had no alternative but to go in to look for him.

He walked through the conservatory, through the reading lounge, into the hallway. The building seemed even more silent than usual. The cellar door was still partly open, as he had left it. He went across to it and pushed it open with his fingertips. He could hear his own heart pounding.

He was just about to step inside when a voice whispered, Welcome back, Jack.

He turned around. The blind statue on the opposite side of the hallway had opened its marble eyes and was staring at him.

Pleased you could come, Jack, said the statue.

Jack willed himself to cross the hallway. His feet dragged as if he were half-paralyzed. He stood in front of the statue and stared back at it. Its face was white and cold and mocking. It was alive, and it was formed in the image of a woman, and yet there was something utterly inhuman about it. A face of marble, a heart of stone.

You're looking for Randy, said the statue.

"He's here?" asked Jack hoarsely.

Of course he's here. We've hidden him.

"Who's 'we'?"

Well, my name's Lester... but there are many more of us. Don't you worry, Jack, your Randy's quite safe.

"Where is he? I want to see him."

All in good time.

"I want him back, damn it! I don't care who you are or what you are, you have no right to keep him here!"

Brave talk, Jack! But don't overdo it. We have Randy,

remember, and some of us are aching to do him a serious mischief! Some of the women... well, even Quintus has difficulty keeping some of the women in order.

"Quintus? Who's Quintus?"

Let's put it this way, Jack—the statue leered at him—*every social group has its leaders. Quintus just happens to be ours. As long as it suits us, of course.*

"What do you want?" Jack demanded. "Is it money? Just tell me what the hell you want!"

We want the priest, the statue hissed. Now it seemed to be talking about something it really hated. *You must bring us the priest. Otherwise Randy will be crushed; just as Joseph Lovelittle was shredded up; and just as something terrible will happen to you.*

"Priest?" Jack asked the statue. "What priest? What are you talking about?"

We want the priest! Bring us the priest! Unless you bring us the priest, your Randy will be crushed, and crushed, and crushed to nothing!

Jack raised both hands. "Please! Listen to me! If you want me to bring you a priest, I'll bring you a priest! But which priest? Any particular priest? Or will any priest suit you?"

The priest! screamed the statue, its marble mouth stretching wide to reveal a white marble tongue. *The priest! The priest! You must bring us the priest!*

Jack shouted, "I'm not bringing you anybody—not until you can show me that you've really got Randy—not until you can show me that he's safe! You hear me! Otherwise, forget it! I walk out of here and you never see me again!"

Fool! screamed the statue. And at that instant Jack heard Randy's voice, high-pitched and blurting, like a child trying to cry out underwater, and Randy's head rose up from out of the black-and-white marble floor, then his shoulders, then his arms, right up to his waist, like a boy standing in a shallow lake.

Daddy! he cried out, and lifted both hands in a desperate plea to be rescued. Daddy save me!

"Randy! Hold on!" shouted Jack, and ran across the hallway toward him. But before he could reach Randy's outstretched hands, Randy plunged back into the marble floor, as if somebody had pulled his legs from below.

Jack fell to his knees and pummeled the floor desperately with his bare fists. It was hard and smooth and cold, and completely unyielding.

"Let him go!" he roared at the floor. "You bastards! You bastards! Let him go!"

There was no reply. After a long while Jack wiped the tears from his eyes with his fingers, and stood up, and walked back toward the statue. The eyes were closed, and there was no sign of life.

"Which priest?" he asked it, in exhaustion and misery. "Which goddamned priest?"

But the statue said nothing. The building was silent. The people in the walls had told him what their ransom demand was; and somehow or other he was going to have to find the right priest for himself.

He turned, and was just about to walk out of the hallway when the cellar door opened. He stepped back, startled.

Out of the cellar trotted Boy, the Doberman. He came across the floor, his claws click-clacking. He was carrying something in his mouth.

"Boy... good Boy... what have you got there?"

The Doberman carefully laid down the object that he was carrying at Jack's feet, and then looked up appealingly, as if he wanted Jack to play throw-and-fetch.

Jack looked down at it. It was blue white and shiny, with a few tatters of red gristle at each end. It was one of Joseph Lovelittle's thighbones.

"So no police?" asked Karen, hitching up her skirt to make herself more comfortable.

"No police. Not yet. I want to find them a priest first."

"But they didn't tell you which priest."

"I don't know. Maybe any priest. Who knows. We'll just have to find out."

"Jack—I have to get back home. Bessy's going to be climbing the walls."

They reached the main road. Jack said, "Sure. I'm sorry. I shouldn't even have dragged you out here in the first place."

She leaned across and kissed his cheek. "I came because I wanted to."

He kissed her back and squeezed her thigh. "Do you know something? I should have met you years ago."

"That's what you think," said Karen, but she was obviously pleased that he had said it. Maybe, just maybe, when Randy was safe—

He drove her into Madison. Lake Mendota lay photographically gray under a photographic sky. Students cycled through the wet streets with tote bags over their heads to keep dry. He found her a cab downtown and gave the driver seventy-five dollars to take Karen back to Milwaukee. "Listen," he told Karen, "I'll call you later, okay? Tell Mike that I'll phone him this evening. Tell him I've had some family trouble."

"Well, you're not kidding, are you?" said Karen. She kissed him with cold lips through the partly open window of the cab. Neither of them dared to say "I love you"— not with Randy missing, and not with life so threatening and strange.

Jack watched the cab drive away, and then he crossed the street to the Jackdaw Bookstore for a cup of coffee and a donut. The bookstore was crowded with more students, smoking and talking and laughing. Jack sat on his own and forced himself to eat his donut, even though it stuck in his mouth like thick dusty glue. A pretty girl student with waist-length blond hair and wire-rim spectacles came past him and said, "Are you okay?"

He lifted his head. "Sure, I'm okay. Is something wrong?"

She smiled at him. She was almost young enough to be his daughter. "You're crying, that's all. Didn't you know?"

He raised his hand to his eyes. He was surprised to find that tears were running down his cheeks. He said nothing, but tugged out his handkerchief and wiped his face. The girl watched him for a little while longer and then walked out into the street.

Capitol Realtors wasn't difficult to find. It was only two blocks away from the bookstore, in a small smart new office development with tinted windows and air-conditioning and a mosaic-floored atrium filled with trees. Daniel Bufo was eating his breakfast on his desk when Jack was shown into his office: two huge lemon danishes and a mug of hot chocolate with "Green Bay Packers" printed on it. He scooped up the danishes on a property prospectus and carefully slid them into his top drawer.

"Don't let me interrupt you," Jack told him.

Daniel Bufo brushed the crumbs off his notepad with the side of his hand. Behind him, through the slatted blinds, there was a strangely clear view of another office building, where a man and his secretary appeared to be arguing with each other heatedly. On Daniel Bufo's desk was a laminated plaque awarded to Madison's Real Estate Man of the Year, 1975.

"Didn't expect you to come by," said Daniel Bufo with a fat unamused smile.

"I need some information," Jack told him. He could tell that Daniel Bufo was disturbed by his appearance: unshaved, his clothes crumpled, and obviously weary.

"How about some hot chocolate?" Daniel Bufo asked him. "It's Dutch; it's like a meal in itself."

Jack shook his head. "I want some background, that's all."

"On The Oaks? I told you, there isn't too much to tell. It's been empty since 1926."

"It used to be a lunatic asylum."

"Ah," said Daniel Bufo, rubbing the side of his face.

"Well, it's true, isn't it? It used to be a home for the criminally insane."

Daniel Bufo picked up a ballpoint pen and turned it around and around between his pudgy fingers. "It was a nursing home, for sure."

"A lunatic asylum. A nuthouse."

"All right, it used to be a lunatic asylum. But I don't see

what difference that makes. It hasn't been used for well over sixty years. And you're going to change the name, aren't you?"

Jack said, "I need to know how to get in touch with the owners."

"I don't think they're going to be too happy about that, Mr. Reed, with all due respect. They are—well, as I think I made it clear to you—reclusive."

Jack lowered his head for a moment. Daniel Bufo sucked at his hot chocolate, waiting for him to say something.

At last Jack said, "Either you put me in touch with the owners or the deal's off."

"I'm sorry?"

"You heard me. I want the owners' address and telephone number right now, or else the deal's off."

"Mr. Reed—you're putting me into a very difficult position here. I have to respect my clients' rights of privacy. They did specifically request that this transaction should be completed only through attorneys and not face-to-face."

Jack stood up. "All right, that's it. Forget it. As far as I'm concerned, there's no deal."

"Mr. Reed, please, believe me—the owners are very anxious to sell you the property. They like the price, they're pleased with your plans to keep the original building and turn it into a resort hotel. They're all in favor! But when a client asks me to guard her privacy—well, what else can I do? There's a code of ethics in realty, you know. It's almost like being a doctor."

"Proctologist, more like," Jack retorted, opening the door. Daniel Bufo reared up to come after him, but Jack lifted a hand to warn him off.

"If your clients change their minds, you can reach me at Howard Johnson's, on Route Ninety-four." He reached into his coat pocket and tossed Daniel Bufo a book of matches. "The number's on there."

"Mr. Reed—I really don't think—"

"Mr. Bufo, I need this information badly. Life or death. At least take the trouble to ask your reclusive clients whether they might consider talking to me face-to-face. Just consider it, okay?"

He closed the door, leaving Daniel Bufo frowning down at his cup of hot chocolate, like a big frustrated child.

His next stop was the offices of the Madison Times-Dispatch. They were located in an unprepossessing concrete building next to a run-down collection of auto-parts stores and Chinese restaurants. He spent most of the afternoon in a cramped back room, trying to dig out their files for 1926. They had microfiched their back issues only as far back as 1943.

A spinsterish woman in a black cardigan and a gray skirt was pasting cuttings. She clucked and huffed every time he pulled out another volume. The room smelled of sour old newspapers and ashes-of-roses perfume. The rain tinkled and tapped against the single window, and Jack began to feel bowed over with tiredness.

"Don't you ever eat?" the spinsterish woman asked him just after two o'clock.

He attempted a smile. "Some things are more important than eating."

At last, at the bottom of a stack of files with broken

spines, all marked "Awaiting Rebinding," he came across the Madison Times for June 1926. He laid it out on the table and read through it carefully, page by page, column by column.

After an hour he had found no mention whatsoever of The Oaks, nor of Mr. Estergomy.

He sat back and allowed the file to slap shut.

The spinsterish woman said, "Can't find what you're looking for?" It was almost four o'clock.

Jack shook his head. "They've got everything in here. Baby contests, marriages, who's dead and who isn't. I just would've thought—well, I don't know."

She inspected him through upswept spectacles. "What were you looking for in particular? What year is that?"

"Nineteen twenty-six."

"I was living here in Madison in 1926. My father was a professor in history at the university. Douglas Manfield, you might have heard of him. He wrote a very famous book about Etruscan inscriptions."

She stood up, and came across to where he was sitting. She held out her hand. "Helena Manfield," she introduced herself.

Jack stood up, too, and shook her hand. "Jack Reed."

"Not from round here?"

"Uh-uh, Milwaukee. Reed Muffler and Tire, five shops all around the city."

Helena Manfield perched herself on the edge of his desk. In spite of her age, she had a birdlike grace. Her gray hair was combed back into a black velvet bow, and although her skin was wrinkled now, she must have had a very strong face once. She reminded Jack of Katharine Hepburn, in a way.

She said, "What's a muffler-and-tire man doing searching through 1926 newspapers in Madison?"

"I was looking for any mention of The Oaks. It's a nursing home, out near Lake Wisconsin."

"I know The Oaks. I know of The Oaks, rather."

"You do? Seems like hardly anybody does; or if they do, they're not telling."

"Well, it was a mental hospital, more than a nursing home, that's why. Many of the local people objected to it when they discovered what it was. But in the end they closed it down anyway."

"Yes, I know that," said Jack. "I'm interested to find out why they closed it down, and under what circumstances."

Helena Manfield inclined her head to one side, interrogatively.

Jack said, "I've been thinking of buying it, as a matter of fact. Converting it into a resort hotel. I just wanted to know something about its history."

Helena Manfield thought about that for a while, looking down at the diamond ring on her left hand. Then she said, with great preciseness of speech, "You'll forgive me, Mr. Reed, for being inquisitive. But it seems to me that you've been searching for this history with more than what I would usually describe as a casual interest."

Jack gave her a wry smile. "Does it show that much?"

"Well... you've been here almost all afternoon, without any lunch. You look a little disheveled, I must say, for a man who's buying a resort hotel. And frantic, if you don't mind my saying so."

"Miss Manfield—" said Jack. "Do you happen to know who owns The Oaks?"

"Of course, I've known her for years, ever since she came here. Olive Estergomy, she was the middle one of the three Estergomy girls."

"And they were the daughters of Dr. Estergomy, The Oaks's previous owner?"

"That's right. Beautiful girls, all three of them. Alice, Olive, and Lucy. Beautiful! But then their mother was very good-looking."

"Do you happen to know why Dr. Estergomy closed The Oaks so suddenly?" Jack asked her.

Helena Manfield shook her head. "Nobody ever knew. We didn't find out that it had closed for months and months. Then one of our local storekeepers happened to mention that the Estergomys had canceled all of their orders for provisions."

She stood up and walked back to the table where she had been working. "The Estergomys left the area at the same time. The only one of them who ever came back was Olive. She never said much, whenever I asked her about The Oaks. She wouldn't talk about her family, either. In the end I could see that she didn't want to discuss it, so I left her alone. It was sad, though. Once upon a time the Estergomys were very good friends of ours. My father and Dr. Estergomy used to get along like a house on fire. But when they left, they didn't even stop by to say good-bye."

"So you never found out what had happened?"

"No," said Helena Manfield. "There were scores of rumors. But my guess is that the local residents managed to put enough pressure on the state penal commission to have them withdraw their funding."

Jack said nothing for a while. While Helena Manfield

had been talking, he had been unexpectedly visited by a vision of Randy. Those big serious eyes; that hesitant way of talking. He could almost feel him; he could almost smell him. His warm biscuity hair.

"You're crying," said Helena Manfield, in a matter-of-fact voice.

"I'm tired, that's all." This time he made no attempt to wipe away the tears.

"You must tell me what's wrong. Perhaps I can help."

"I don't know," said Jack. "I don't think anybody can."

"Well, you can always try me," Helena Manfield suggested. "I think I know something about emotional pain."

"What do you know about losing people?" Jack asked her.

Helena Manfield stood up straight. "I'm a spinster, you know. I shouldn't have been. My fiancé died in the war. He was in the air force, shot down at Ploiesti. Over three hundred young airmen died that night, in Romania; and all because Allied intelligence said there were scarcely any guns there."

She took a sharp breath. After forty-five years, her bitterness was still fresh. "After that—well, nobody else seemed to compare. I preferred being alone."

Jack said, "I'm sorry."

Helena Manfield smiled, her eyes out of focus. "Don't be sorry; it all happened a long time ago. I shouldn't whine. Have you lost someone, too?"

"My son, Randy, he's nine. I took him out to The Oaks."

"Yes?"

"Well, I know it sounds crazy. But he disappeared."

Helena Manfield said, "When?"

"Last night. Late last night. We searched the building from top to bottom, twice over, but we couldn't find him. He's hiding someplace. God knows where."

"Did you call the police?"

Jack shook his head. "He's still in the building, I'm sure of it. And, besides, I've been given the distinct impression that the police aren't going to be very amenable. Not when it comes to The Oaks, anyway."

"You've lost your nine-year-old son and you don't want to call the police?"

Jack shrugged. "Sounds irresponsible, doesn't it, when you put it like that. But I don't honestly think the police are going to be able to help."

Helena Manfield stayed silent, watching him.

"Let's put it this way," he said, "the first question the police are going to ask is what I was doing at The Oaks so late at night, with a nine-year-old boy; and the second question they're going to ask is why did I kill him?"

"You don't think he's dead?"

"No, he's not dead. Least, I don't think he's dead. I pray that he isn't. But things aren't as simple as they sound."

"Believe me," Helena Manfield replied, "they don't sound the least bit simple."

She thought for a moment, and then she said, "Why don't I introduce you to Olive? She's very shy, but she talks straight. Maybe she can give you some ideas where your boy might be hidden. Maybe The Oaks has a secret closet or a secret passage, something like that."

"Olive Estergomy still lives around here?"

"Certainly, she has a house out at Sun Prairie."

Jack said, "That's near enough. Fifteen, twenty miles? What can you do, call her?"

"Of course I can call her." She picked her purse up from the floor, and opened it, and took out a small crocodile address book. "And before you ask me why I'm going to call her, let me tell you that I've been trying to find an excuse to see her for ages and ages, and that I'm bored silly, and that I love to stick my nose into other people's business."

"Sounds reasonable to me," Jack acknowledged.

She went out to the pay phone in the corridor. Jack stood beside her as she slotted in her dime and dialed the number. From the office close by, he could hear the flat plasticky rattle of somebody typing out a story on a word processor.

At last she said, "Olive? Is that Olive? Olive, this is Helena! Helena Manfield, of course!"

They drove out to Sun Prairie under a sky that was smudged with thick charcoal clouds, past red-painted barns and dark green fields of curly kale, past silvery silos and rain-beaded greenhouses. Helena Manfield said very little, but refused to wear a seat belt and sat with her hands in her lap like two fitfully sleeping birds.

Jack drove badly, jerking the brakes at intersections and running two red lights. It was only now that he was beginning to understand how tired he was.

It was almost dark when they reached Sun Prairie. Helena directed Jack off 151 onto 19, and then down a jolting unmetaled track that finally brought them out on top of a hill, where a green-painted house stood all on its own, surrounded by grass and flowers and nothing else, as if it had been dropped out of the sky like Dorothy's farmhouse in The Wizard of Oz.

Jack parked next to an abandoned harrow and a rusty feed trough, and arm in arm he and Helena Manfield made their way against the stinging rain up to the porch.

The front door was opened almost immediately. The light from inside was reflected on the wet boards of the porch. A woman's voice said, "Come along in! Come along in!" and the next thing Jack knew he was jostling out of his coat in the smallest of hallways.

"Well, Helena!" Olive exclaimed. She was a large, big-boned woman, much taller and bigger than Helena Manfield, but attractive, too. Her gray hair was tied back from her forehead with a blue velvet band, her eyes were almost violet, and she had the broad, intelligent face of somebody who wouldn't put up with fools, but who could laugh at herself quicker than anybody else.

She wore a large dress patterned with blue-and-black flowers, striking but messy.

"Come in! Helena, you dear person! I just couldn't believe it when you called! It's been so long!"

She led them through to a parlor crowded with good but mismatched antique furniture. A French chaise longue, upholstered in green figured silk, a brown leather armchair, and occasional tables of all shapes and sizes. On the walls hung unnaturally bright watercolors of Wisconsin lakes, and framed diplomas and honorary degrees. Jack leaned over the chaise longue to examine one of the degrees more closely. From Edinburgh University, an honorary doctorate in clinical psychology, awarded to Elmer J. Estergomy, March 12, 1921.

A log fire was smoldering weakly in the grate. Olive Estergomy stabbed at it with her poker, and then said, "The wood's so damp."

"I'm Jack Reed," said Jack. "I'm the fellow who's been negotiating to buy The Oaks."

"I see," said Olive Estergomy. She looked questioningly at Helena Manfield, twisting her long amber necklace between her fingers. "How did you happen to meet Miss Manfield?" There was an odd implication in her voice that he and Helena had cooked up some kind of conspiracy between them.

"Olive, we met at the Times-Dispatch, purely by accident," Helena told her. "I was pasting clippings, and Mr. Reed was trying to find items about The Oaks."

"I was very impressed with your proposals, Mr. Reed," said Olive Estergomy. "It would be wonderful to see the place restored."

Jack said, "Has Mr. Bufo been in touch?"

"He told me your suggested price, and I accepted."

"Has he been in touch today?"

Olive Estergomy stood by the fireplace, leaning slightly to one side, like a gym teacher restraining herself from giving a practical demonstration. "Not today, no. Is anything wrong?"

"I told him that I had to speak to you face-to-face. I told him that if he didn't arrange it, the whole deal would have to be canceled."

Olive Estergomy slowly sat down. The fire began to crackle and spit. "Mr. Bufo didn't say a word about that. Not a word."

"I made a point of telling him it was urgent," said Jack.

"Perhaps he thought that it would upset me. And, as a matter of fact, it has upset me. Why should you need to speak to me in person?"

Jack laced his fingers tightly together. Here is the church, here is the steeple, open the door... "Miss Estergomy, I need to know what happened, the night The Oaks was closed down."

Olive Estergomy stared at Jack, her face rigid. It was only now that Jack noticed the faintest tic in her left eyelid, the constant fluttering of suppressed anxiety. "Nothing happened. We closed it down, that's all."

"For any special reason?"

"We didn't have sufficient patients to remain open, that's all. It was plain economics."

Jack took out his handkerchief and wiped his nose. "I was told you had one hundred thirty-seven patients the night you closed down. That was more than you'd ever had before."

"Who told you that?"

"Joseph Lovelittle, the caretaker."

"Oh, him. I hope you realize that Joseph used to be a mental patient, too."

"He seemed pretty sure about it, mental or not."

Olive Estergomy lowered her eyes and didn't reply.

"Miss Estergomy—" said Jack. "My nine-year-old son is missing. I took him to The Oaks yesterday evening and he disappeared. I'm desperate to find him."

"You took him to The Oaks?" asked Olive Estergomy flatly.

"Miss Estergomy, there's something strange about that building. I've experienced it for myself. Noises, voices, hallucinations." He didn't go further; he didn't want her to think that he was a candidate for the nuthouse, too.

Olive Estergomy remained totally silent for almost a minute. Then, as if she had suddenly arrived at a crucial personal decision, she said, "They disappeared. They all disappeared."

Jack was perplexed. "Who disappeared, Miss Estergomy?"

She looked up. "The patients, of course. Every single one of them. One minute they were all there; the next they were gone."

She fell silent again for a very long time. A minute, more than a minute.

"Can you tell me how it happened?" Jack coaxed her. It was obvious that the memory still distressed her.

"There's nothing much to tell. We were sitting together in our parlor that evening when one of the male nurses knocked on the door—shouting, frightened—and said that all the patients had escaped. Of course my father couldn't believe it. But when we went up to the first floor, we found that every single room was empty."

Helena Manfield sat down, too. "Olive," she said. "You never told me this."

"Nobody would have believed me, my dear; not even you."

"But if all those lunatics had gotten out—"

"They were gone, yes. But they hadn't gotten out. Not in the sense that they had opened their doors or climbed out of their windows. Every single room was still locked, and none of those rooms could be opened from the inside. Every single window was still intact; barred and unbroken. There were cups of coffee in the lounge, still hot, still only half-drunk. There were newspapers, dropped on the floor. Just as if they had all evaporated."

"But if there were over a hundred of them," Helena Manfield protested. "Where did they go?"

Olive Estergomy shook her head. "To this day, Helena, I simply don't know. My poor father was almost driven insane himself, looking for them. Where could they go? He called the police and of course the police found the doors locked and the windows unbroken, and at first they assumed that my father had suffered some kind of a breakdown and let all the patients free himself. They were never particularly sympathetic, the police, because my father was a great champion of rehabilitation for the criminally insane. He actually believed that they could be cured, and returned to the community, whereas all the police wanted to do was to see them exterminated."

Jack said, "What happened then?"

"The police searched the whole area. But they couldn't find a single footprint—not one—nor any sign that over a hundred people had escaped from The Oaks. They were called less than an hour after the patients disappeared, and since some of the patients were physically handicapped as well as mentally handicapped, and most of them were wearing nothing but hospital robes, and some of them were completely naked because they would have strangled themselves with hospital robes, the chances of them having gotten any further than the perimeter fence were practically nil."

"But?" said Jack.

"But they were gone," Olive Estergomy replied. "One hundred and thirty-seven patients had completely vanished."

"And you don't know where?"

Olive Estergomy said, "Perhaps God took them. Perhaps the devil took them. I don't know."

"What did the police do about it?" asked Jack.

"There was nothing they could do. There were no patients. There were no clues. None of the patients had been seen on the roads or in the woods or attempting to hitchhike. No thefts of clothes were reported. No barns broken into. Nothing."

She paused for a moment. A pretty little silver clock on the mantelpiece chimed six. "At ten-thirty that evening, a whole gang of assorted bigwigs arrived from the justice department and examined the building for themselves. They talked to my father for ten minutes, and then they officially declared that The Oaks was closed. Well, of course, it had to close, we didn't have any patients left. But the official reason they gave for its closure was that they no longer had confidence in my father's rehabilitation program."

"How did they explain the patients' disappearance? I mean, officially?"

"They waited for a week, to see if any of the patients would show up. When they didn't, the justice department announced that they had all been sent to a new high-security facility up at Lake Nokomis. After six months—when none of them had reappeared anywhere—they told the relatives of those patients who still had relatives who cared about them—and, believe me, that wasn't too many—that their not-very-loved-ones had died of food poisoning. I think they even held funerals."

"That's astonishing," said Helena Manfield.

"Of course, but what else could they do? How were they

going to tell the public that one hundred thirty-seven highly dangerous mental patients had vanished without a trace and that every effort to find them had met with complete failure?"

"Did the police have any theories about it?" asked Jack.

"No," Olive Estergomy replied. "As far as I know, they erased the case from their records, just as if it had never happened. They took away all of my father's case histories, too, and you can imagine what happened to them. It broke his heart."

"What happened to your father?" Jack inquired, as gently as he could.

"He couldn't work any longer. After The Oaks, there wasn't a state in the country that would allow him to practice. We went to England for a while, where he made some money lecturing; then we moved to France. My father drowned in 1934, while he was swimming in the sea off Arromanches. My mother died the following year."

"Your sisters?" asked Jack.

"They stayed in France. They were still living near Paris when war broke out. I never found out what happened to them."

She said, in the quietest of voices, "That evening in 1926, Mr. Reed, everything vanished out of my life. Not just one hundred and thirty-seven mental patients, but my father's career, my mother's health, my two dear sisters."

"I'm sorry," Jack told her uncomfortably. "I'm really sorry."

"But you've lost your son," said Olive Estergomy.

"He's still at The Oaks," Jack replied. "That's why I wanted to talk to you."

"I'm not sure what you mean."

"I'm not too sure what I mean, either. But I think I know where he is, and I also think I know what happened to your father's patients."

Olive Estergomy frowned at him. "You know where they went?"

Jack nodded. "I have a theory—well, half of a theory. You'll probably think that I'm just as loony as they are."

"Mr. Reed," said Olive Estergomy, trying hard to contain her ferocious curiosity, "would you like a drink?"

"Do you have whiskey? If not, a beer would go down well. And please call me Jack."

"Olive," said Olive Estergomy. "Although my friends call me Essie."

"All right, Essie." Jack nodded. "Just one question first. Can you tell me why you haven't thought of selling The Oaks before now?"

Essie was opening her stained-oak liquor cabinet. "I've had two or three offers," she said, "and once I even advertised it. But there's a clause in the deed that says that nobody must demolish the building; and until you came along with your idea of restoring it, and turning it into a resort hotel, nobody else was interested in keeping the building intact. You know yourself that it will probably take millions to bring it back up to scratch."

"Have you ever visited it?" asked Jack. "I mean, since 1926?"

"I went back to look at it about four years ago. I didn't go inside. As you can imagine, it doesn't hold very many pleasant memories for me."

"They're still there," said Jack.

She stopped in the middle of pouring out his whiskey. Her back remained turned, but he could tell from the tension in her shoulders that she knew what he meant. She was waiting for him to spell it out for her.

"The reason that nobody could find those so-called escaped lunatics was because they never escaped. They're still there. I've seen a couple of them. They're inside the walls."

Essie turned around and was staring at him wide-eyed. Helena said anxiously, "What do you mean, they're inside the walls? How can they possibly still be there? That was over sixty years ago, they would have died of old age by now. And what would they eat?"

Jack didn't take his eyes away from Essie. The emotion in her face was an inch away from total tragedy. *My father, my mother, my poor dear sisters. And they're still there! Those screaming, foaming, raging lunatics! They're still there!*

"I knew it," she said. She was trembling. "In a peculiar way, I always knew."

"But how can they be?" Helena insisted. "It's impossible! Inside the walls? In secret passages, is that it?"

Jack laid his hand on her arm. "I don't know how they got into the walls; and I don't know how they managed to survive. But they're not in secret passages. They're actually, physically, inside the bricks. I know it sounds wacky. I know it defies all the laws of physics and all the laws of nature, you know, all that stuff about two material objects not being able to occupy the same space at the same time.

"But," he said, "I've seen them. I've actually seen them. They've got my son. They almost got me."

He bent forward, lifted up the cuffs of his pants, and

tugged down his socks. "See these bruises? One of them came right up out of a solid concrete floor and grabbed me."

Essie handed him his glass of whiskey. Helena said, "You won't mind if I help myself to a gin, dear? I'm shaking all over."

"No, no, go ahead," said Essie abstractedly. Then she looked at Jack and said, "It's madness, isn't it? It's absolute lunacy."

"I know," he told her. "But it really happened. And you know it really happened because you were there when they disappeared, weren't you? And what other possible explanation could there be?"

"I've never heard anything like it," said Helena. "You've made me feel utterly unreal."

Jack said, "There's one called Lester."

"They spoke to you?" asked Essie, in astonishment.

Jack nodded. "They communicated, in a way. I'm not sure that you'd actually call it speaking."

"Lester Franks, that was his name," said Essie. "I remember Lester very well. He always appeared so sane. He used to sing songs to me and tell me stories. He couldn't have been older than eighteen or nineteen. Always helpful! Always ready to run errands! And do you know what he had done? When he was baby-sitting, at the age of fourteen, he had cut off his three-year-old sister's head. They had found him playing ball with it in the yard, throwing it up and catching it. The whole yard had been smothered in blood."

"Oh my God, Essie, you're making me sick," Helena protested.

"Oh, no—most of them had done far worse," said Essie. "Mind you, when my sisters and I were children, we used to revel in all the gory details. There was one man there, what was his name? Holman or Hofman or something like that. His wife had chattered too much, so he had tied her wrists and ankles to a dining-room chair and nailed her tongue to the table. She was there for days before anybody found her."

"Essie, I am going to be sick," Helena proclaimed.

But Essie continued regardless. "My father tried to rehabilitate this Holman or Hofman or whatever his name was by giving him odd jobs to do. One evening he didn't come in for his tea and they found him in the garden, unable to move. He had nailed his own penis to a tree."

"Essie!"

"I'm sorry, Helena," said Essie. "But that's exactly what kind of people they were. They had no feelings for human life whatever. They couldn't tell the difference between pain and pleasure. Some of them would amuse themselves by cutting off their own fingers and playing with them. They were utterly insane, Helena! You have no idea!"

"That's not the kind of people they were," Jack corrected her. "That's the kind of people they are."

"Well, Jack," said Essie, "I'm not at all sure I know how to react to that. I don't know what to say, or what to feel, or anything. I believe that you're telling me the truth, but I'm not so sure that my mind is going to allow me to believe it."

"There's one thing I need to know," said Jack. "Was there ever a priest attached to The Oaks? Or a local chaplain that the patients might have known?"

"Why, yes, of course. There was Father Bell. He was only a young priest, but he used to come out to The Oaks every Sunday for any of the patients who wanted to take Communion. Some of them were fanatically religious. One of them was quite sure that he was God, and every time Father Bell said 'praise the Lord' he used to say 'thank you very much.'"

"Do you happen to know if he's still alive?"

"I really have no idea. I haven't seen him since the night the patients disappeared. If he is alive, he must be getting on to ninety."

"He was there the night the patients disappeared?"

"Yes. He just turned up, I don't know why."

"You weren't expecting him?"

"No, it was Monday. He usually came only on Sundays. Oh, once I think he came on a Saturday afternoon, when we had a carol service. What a disaster that was! Can you imagine a hundred and fifty homicidal schizophrenics trying to sing 'We Three Kings of Orient Are'?"

Jack gave her a tight smile. It must have been essential for the Estergomy family to retain a sense of humor in the dangerous half-world in which they had been living out at The Oaks.

"Can you remember which church Father Bell came from?"

"Oh, yes. St. Ignatius, I think it was, at Portage."

Jack finished his whiskey. "Essie," he said, "I'm sorry I busted in on your privacy. But I hope you can understand that it was only out of desperation. You've been truly helpful."

Essie smiled. "I want you to keep in touch, Jack, tell me what's happening. I pray that you find your son."

She hesitated, and then she added, "If you find those people... the patients. If you find them, be very careful. They were sent to The Oaks because they were too dangerous for anybody else to take care of. They have no conscience whatsoever, and some of them are very strong.

"There was one in particular, a man called Quintus Miller. Watch out for him. He was incredibly intelligent, incredibly powerful, and totally mad. He nearly killed a woman patient once, I won't tell you how."

Jack went to the door and buttoned up his coat. "Quintus Miller," he repeated. "Lester mentioned somebody called Quintus. All right, I'll take care. And I'll call you if I find out any more."

After Jack and Helena had left, Olive Estergomy stood very still in the middle of her crowded parlor with her hands pressed together as if she were praying. The feeling of dread that she hadn't felt for sixty years had returned, cold and familiar. It was a dread that was worse than the dread of death. It was the dread of everlasting pain that couldn't be borne, and of screams and sobs and nightmarish laughter.

It was the dread of The Oaks, and of utter madness, and of Quintus Miller.

6

Jack drove back to Howard Johnson's, showered, and changed into one of three new shirts he had bought in Madison. He called his office. It had closed for the night, but he guessed that Mike Karpasian would still be there. Mike said they were up to their asses in muffler replacements, and when the hell was Jack going to sign the checks for B. F. Goodrich because B. F. Goodrich sure as hell wasn't going to supply them with any more tires unless they paid for the last consignment, but apart from that everything was going good.

Karen wasn't home. Bessy said that Karen had taken Sherrywine to the doctor because Sherrywine had regurgitated her fish fingers all over Mommy's favorite long-haired nylon scatter rug.

He called Maggie. Maggie was furious because he hadn't called her all day and she wanted to take Randy to a special Women's Consciousness-Raising Gala on Saturday. Jack said he wasn't outstandingly keen on having his impressionable nine-year-old son hanging out with a bunch of lesbians and nuclear disarmers and nonsexist knitters, but then he suddenly thought of the Turd, and of Randy rising out of the floor, and his throat tightened and he had to hang up the phone without saying good-bye.

Maggie, of course, couldn't call him back because she didn't know where he was. But he bet the phone back at home was ringing and ringing, and would probably ring all night. Maggie was that kind of a woman.

He called Daniel Bufo but Daniel Bufo had left for the day.

He ordered a New York steak and a bottle of red wine on room service. He sat with his plate on his lap watching "The Cosby Show." It was the first time he ever watched it and didn't laugh once.

He didn't know when he fell asleep, but when he woke up it was well past ten o'clock and his mouth felt dry. His half-finished steak lay on the bed beside him. He rubbed his eyes and sat up. This was no good. He had to sleep properly. He undressed, brushed his teeth, switched off the television, and climbed into bed.

He lay there awake for hour after hour, staring up at the ceiling, thinking about people who played finger puppets with their own amputated fingers and of men who tried to kill women in ways that were so horrifying they couldn't even be described.

He thought of Lester, the face on the statue. *Lester always appeared so sane.* He thought of Quintus Miller.

It was nearly three o'clock in the morning when he thought he heard a noise in his room. He lifted his head from the pillow, frowning into the darkness. The night was completely silent now. The traffic on 94 had dwindled to an occasional long-distance semi. The motel stood silent.

But there it was again. *Sssssshhhhhhhh—sssssshhhhhhhh—sssssshhhhhhhhh:* just like that noise in the walls of The Oaks.

Jack went cold. He eased up his sheets and slid sideways across the bed, trying to make as little sound as possible. But the dragging noise continued, and it was coming closer. *Sssssshhhhhh—sssssshhhhhh—sssssshhhhhh*.

He froze, trying to suppress his breathing. Maybe it would pass without realizing that he was here. He closed his eyes in the hope that it would vanish if he did, but then he immediately opened them again because he didn't want it sneaking up on him without him seeing it.

Please God may it drag itself away.

It was then that he saw a dark hump rising up beside the bed. It was brown sculptured motel carpet, but it was in the shape of a boy. *It was Randy, rising out of the floor.*

Jack lay back on the bed, staring at him in horror.

"Randy?" he mouthed. "Randy?"

The priest, Daddy. We want the priest.

"Randy—is that you? Randy!"

Bring us the priest. That's who we want. We want to chop off his fingers and guzzle his bones.

Numb with fear, Jack reached out with both hands and took hold of Randy's carpeted shoulders.

You shouldn't touch me. Daddy. You never know what might happen.

"Randy, for Christ's sake, I want you back!"

Jack tugged at him, trying to wrench him out of the carpet. But instantly Randy's head fell off, and rolled heavy and carpeted across the bed. Ice-cold blood spurted out of his neck, drenching the sheet.

Jack screamed and screamed, rigid with terror.

He screamed so loudly that he woke himself up. In fact he wasn't screaming at all, but making a hoarse *haahhhhh!*

sound. He had thrashed out with his arm and knocked over the glass of water beside his bed, splashing the sheet. There was no decapitated Randy swaying next to the bed, no carpeted head lying on the covers. It was ten after six, still raining, but already light.

He lay on his back for five minutes, breathing deeply to calm himself down. He must have slept for at least three hours, and he felt much more refreshed. He never had needed too much sleep. At last he eased himself out of bed and called room service for coffee and toast.

He drew the drapes. The raindrops freckled the windows. Beyond the motel parking lot he could see the trucks roaring through the spray, on their way to La Crosse and Eau Claire and Duluth, or southeastward toward Chicago.

Today he was going to get Randy back. He pledged himself that. No matter what it took, by nightfall tonight, his son was going to be safely back in his arms.

While he drank his coffee, he leafed through the telephone directory. There were twenty-two Bells, none of whom lived in Portage. But he did find the number for St. Ignatius. He called it, and nobody answered. It was, after all, quite unlikely that anybody would be sitting around a church at six o'clock in the morning, even in Portage. The best solution was to drive up there. It was only about thirty miles.

It took him over an hour to reach Portage because of the rain. By the time he turned onto the cracked concrete parking lot outside St. Ignatius, his eyes were strained from staring into the spray, his neck was stiff, and his back felt as if it were clamped in a vise.

He stepped on the parking brake, unfastened his seat belt, and stretched.

St. Ignatius was a small church on the southern outskirts of Portage, a gray cinderblock building with a roof of green-painted corrugated iron. On one side of it was a lumberyard, on the other side a gas station. The church boasted a spire, with a single bell, and arched wooden doors with stained-glass windows in them, but otherwise it could have been mistaken for a paint shed, or a boat shed, or any other kind of shed.

He climbed out of his station wagon and hurried across the concrete driveway with his collar pulled up against the rain. He was just about to climb the wooden steps to the front door when a voice shouted out, "Nobody there! Hey, mister! Nobody there!"

"What?" Jack came back across the concrete. A pimply teenage boy with an immense blond pompadour was leaning out of the garage pay booth.

"Nobody there," he repeated as Jack came up close.

He paused, and then obviously realized that Jack might have been going to St. Ignatius simply to pray. "Well," he said, "'cepting for God."

Jack said, "I'm looking for a priest."

The boy sniffed. "Father Dermot, he's your man. But he ain't there today."

"I was looking for Father Bell."

"Father Bell? Ain't never heard of no Father Bell. You sure you got the right church?"

Jack nodded. "Father Bell was the priest in charge here back before the war."

"My dad was in the war, Fourth Marine Regiment."

"I mean the war before the war before that."

"Huh?" the boy asked him in bewilderment, wrinkling up his nose.

At that moment a bullet-headed man in a greasy pair of overalls appeared, wiping his hands on a piece of torn rag.

"Hey, what happened to my coffee, zitface?" he demanded. He glanced at Jack and said, "How are you?"

"I forgot," said the boy.

"He forgot," appealed the bullet-headed man. "He'd forget where his frigging ass was if his body didn't bend in the middle."

The boy disappeared inside the pay booth. Jack said, "I've been looking for a priest who used to be here, at St. Ignatius. Wonder if you've heard of him, Father Bell."

"Sure," said the bullet-headed man without hesitation. "I know Father Bell."

"He's still alive?"

"Sure, he lives up at Green Bay now, in one of them senior citizens' homes. His daughter Hilda is friends with my wife, they trade recipes."

"His *daughter*?" asked Jack.

"Sure. He gave up priesting, years before I ever knew him. But everybody kept on calling him Father Bell regardless. Like kind of a nickname, you know. Or when you leave the army, people still keep on calling you colonel."

He paused to yell out, "How long does it take you to make one frigging cup of coffee? What the hell are you doing, growing the frigging beans?" He finished wiping his hands, balled up the rag, and tossed it with impressive accuracy into a trash bin on the opposite side of the forecourt. "This frigging weather, doesn't it make you want to kill yourself?"

Jack asked hesitantly, "Father Bell's daughter... can you tell me where she lives?"

The bullet-headed man gripped Jack's arm. "You drive straight down here until you reach the first turnoff to your right. You turn off. There's a yellow house directly in front of you. Well, I say yellow to be polite. More like somebody barfed their Mexican dinner all over it. That's the house."

The boy appeared with a mug of coffee.

"My son," said the bullet-headed man. "What the hell did I do to deserve a son like this?"

"I shall be eighty-eight this year," said Father Bell. "I was born on September sixth, 1901, the very same day that President McKinley was shot. Of course he didn't actually die till eight days later."

He turned away from the window and looked at Jack with sad glistening eyes. "My childhood is so clear to me now, every detail, as if I were regarding it through a crystalline window, brightly lit. Yet it was eighty years ago! So far away, and lost forever."

"Your daughter asked me to bring you these," said Jack. He held up a soft red paper package.

"Ah, bed socks," said Father Bell. "Well, that's very kind of her. She's always sending me little gifts and keeping in touch. A good girl, Hilda. A fine, gentle girl. Have you known her long?"

"I met her for the first time today," Jack told him.

"Really?" asked Father Bell in faint surprise. Then, "Really?"

Father Bell was a tall angular man, with no spare flesh on him at all. His wrinkled skin was shrink-wrapped onto his skull, so that his eye sockets and cheekbones appeared inky and cavernous. He was almost bald, but his eyebrows were dramatic and bushy, and his nose curved out like the outstretched wing of a bat, all veins and bones and translucent nostrils.

He wore a taupe-colored turtleneck sweater and a voluminous pair of brown bell-bottom pants, which he must have bought some time in the 1970s. "*Imagine me and you, I do, I think about you day and night....*"

Jack said, "I was talking to Miss Olive Estergomy yesterday."

"Essie! Were you? Now there's a surprise! I call her Essie, you know."

"I know," said Jack, and couldn't resist adding, "So do I." He paused for a moment and then he said, "Essie told me you used to administer Sunday Communion at The Oaks, back in the days when it was a mental institution."

Father Bell said nothing, but fixed Jack with unblinking eyes. Outside the window of his shadowy room, the rain coursed across Bay Beach Park. The bay itself was almost completely hidden by misty spray.

The room was modern and clean, with an orange-covered sofa bed and a pine desk and an armchair and a scrupulously neat bookshelf. But apart from a framed black-and-white photograph of the round-faced woman who lived in the house that looked as if somebody had barfed their Mexican dinner all over it, there were no personal knickknacks whatever. It was the sort of room that if you died in it at four minutes to nine in the morning, it could be ready for its next guest at eleven minutes after.

All of the books were impersonal, too: dated best-sellers like *The Holcroft Covenant* and *The Carpetbaggers*. Considering that Father Bell was a former priest, it was noticeable that his bookshelf contained no Bible.

Jack ventured, "Essie also told me that you visited The Oaks the night the patients all disappeared."

Father Bell breathed in and out, in and out, as if it were something he had to make a conscious effort to do, in order to stay alive.

Jack persisted, "Father Bell—this is kind of presumptuous of me, I know that. But the fact is that my son has disappeared, too. At The Oaks."

Father Bell turned his head in profile. For an achingly long time he said nothing at all, but occasionally moistened his lips with the tip of his tongue.

"Father Bell," said Jack, "I know my son's there. And I need your help to get him back."

At last Father Bell shifted in his chair, his hands crawling over themselves in his lap like two skeletal cats. "What you're talking about, Mr. Reed... that all happened a very long time ago."

"They're still there," said Jack.

For a moment he could see that Father Bell was considering the option of denying all knowledge of who "they" were. But Jack had said it so directly and so forcefully that there was no escaping it.

"They're *still there*?" he repeated, in disbelief.

"You know what happened to them, don't you?" asked Jack. "You know where they went."

"Yes," said Father Bell. "I know where they went."

"Are you going to tell me about it?"

The horror of what Jack had said suddenly began to sink in. "They're still there, you say? After all these years? My God... I didn't think that they would be able to survive. They should have starved, by rights. They should have died within days. Still there! My God, still there!"

"Tell me about it," Jack insisted. "You have to."

"Oho, my friend, I'm not so sure that I should. I'm not sure that I *can*. If they're still there, my God!"

"Father Bell, I have to save my son."

"I'm not a priest anymore, Mr. Reed. I have no duty to help you."

"What are you talking about, duty?" Jack demanded. "He's just a kid!"

"You don't know them, Mr. Reed. You don't know them the way I do."

"You're trying to tell me you won't help? You're eighty-eight and my son's nine. Doesn't that count for anything? He's got his whole life ahead of him!"

Without warning, Father Bell clutched the arms of his chair and twisted from one side to the other and bellowed hoarsely, "I'm terrified, Mr. Reed! I'm frightened to death! My God, do you know what you're asking me? You're crazy! You're *crazy!* You're almost as crazy as they are!"

Jack stood up, and walked across the room, and stood right over him. Father Bell rolled his eyes up toward him, then looked away. Jack said, more patiently, "It can't hurt you just to tell me about it."

"Ah, no. But if they find out—"

"They won't find out. How the hell can they?"

Father Bell shook his head. "They'll know. They'll guess! Nobody else knows what happened but me. One of them told me, during confession. That's why I couldn't tell the police. That's why I left the priesthood. I saw poor Elmer Estergomy, pilloried by the state; I saw his whole family ruined. And all the time I couldn't speak out to defend him, because of what a madman had told me in confession."

Jack said, "Damn it, Father Bell, you have to tell me now. Because, by God, if you don't tell me now, my son is going to be killed by those lunatics; and if that happens, then I'm going to kill you, and that's a promise, and damn the consequences."

Jack had never threatened anybody like that before, and he was almost as frightened by what he was saying as Father Bell was. But when the old man whispered, "You won't let them out, will you? Whatever happens, you won't let them out?" he knew that Father Bell was going to tell him what he wanted to know.

Jack dragged his chair two or three feet nearer and sat down again. "This patient who talked to you in confession— was it Quintus Miller?"

"How did you know that?" Father Bell's voice was jumpy with terror.

"Inspired guess, I guess. Essie Estergomy told me he was probably the toughest and the most intelligent of the whole lot."

"Yes, he was, by a long shot. Quintus Miller, my God. He was an extraordinary man. Short, but very broad, very muscular. He looked like a weight lifter. A neck as thick as a bull's! Black hair, greased down, parted dead center. Of course that style was fashionable then. A face like a rock. Hard eyes, eyes like nail heads, completely without expression, completely without compassion. And a tattoo on his chest like you've never seen in your life. Two tattooed hands, apparently reaching around from behind him, and tearing his abdomen wide open. His insides, tattooed in red and yellow and blue—his stomach, his liver, his intestines. It used to make me freeze just to see it."

Father Bell took a whistling breath in one nostril. "It was the way he flaunted his own mortality, that was what frightened me so much. There is nothing so terrifying as finding yourself faced with a man who does not care if he lives or dies. There were quite a few of them like that, at The Oaks, both men and women, but they were usually self-destructive. None of them frightened me the way that Quintus Miller frightened me. You felt that if *he* were faced with death, he would do everything he could to take as many people with him as he could. That man had the morals of a hammerhead shark."

Jack stayed quiet for a while, to give Father Bell the chance to calm down. Then he said, "Tell me what Quintus Miller told you in confession."

"We had many confessions. Two years of confessions, almost every week. I warned Dr. Estergomy several times that Quintus was very dangerous. But of course Dr. Estergomy knew that already, from his attempts to rehabilitate him.

"It was quite *unhinging*, listening to Quintus talk. He sounded so rational, and yet you would suddenly realize that he was telling you the most hideous, obsessive, illogical nonsense. In confession, in almost the same breath, he would admit to sins as inconsequential as stealing candies from other patients, or masturbation, or lying, or blasphemy, and then he would tell me that he had tortured his fellow patients by breaking their fingers or by crushing their testicles in his fist. He had no sense of proportion. To stub out a cigarette on somebody's eyelid was no more but no less serious to Quintus Miller than to steal a bar of chocolate.

"He tried to kill a woman patient, you know. Attacked her with his bare hands. But since he was already incarcerated for life and had already been declared by the courts to be mentally incompetent, the worst they could do to him was lock him up in solitary confinement."

Father Bell hesitated, and then he said, "After about a year at The Oaks, Quintus suddenly started talking about freedom, about getting himself out. When I asked him about it, he said he had found a way to escape. I advised Dr. Estergomy to check the building's security, but Dr. Estergomy said he was completely satisfied that not even the most determined patient could get free. In those days, of course, the whole property was surrounded by a ten-foot barbed-wire fence.

"All the same, Quintus went on and on about escaping. He said he had discovered something about the building that would help him get out. He kept rambling about mazes and what he called 'earth magic.' He became so obsessive about it that I had to ask the nurses to take him away sometimes, because his confessions were going on for half an hour at a time."

Jack said, "You still didn't believe that he could really escape?"

Father Bell shook his head. "I didn't believe in his so-called earth magic, that's why."

"And what was 'earth magic'? Did he explain it to you?"

"I knew about it already," said Father Bell. "Earth magic was the magic of prehistoric times, the magic of the Druids. The pagan priests believed that there were spiritual forces within the earth itself. They believed that all over the world, at certain precise locations, these spiritual forces manifested themselves in places of special sanctity. In Britain, there was Stonehenge and Glastonbury. Here in the United States, we have Mystery Hill, in New Hampshire, and Gunjiwaump, in Connecticut, and North Salem, New York, and—well, there are dozens of others."

"Including The Oaks, Wisconsin," Jack suggested.

Father Bell nodded. "All of these magical locations were interconnected one to the other by a pattern of unswervingly straight lines. Ley lines, they called them, which meant *lea* lines, or meadow lines. Quintus said that The Oaks had been built at the precise intersection of several of these ley lines—that, in fact, it was the principal center of earth magic in the entire North American continent—and not accidentally, but on purpose."

Jack thought for a moment and leaned back in his chair. "Then I guess it follows that what's-his-name, the beer baron, Adolf Krüger—he must have known about earth magic, too?"

"Almost certainly," Father Bell agreed. "It's hard to imagine that he built The Oaks on that precise spot by accident. I often speculated how Quintus Miller had first found out about earth magic. He wouldn't tell me, of course. But the only logical conclusion seemed to be that he had discovered a book in Adolf Krüger's library. I don't know whether you know it, but Krüger himself had left the house in very mysterious circumstances."

"But how was this earth magic going to help Quintus Miller escape?" Jack asked.

Father Bell watched the rain dribbling down the window for a while. Then he said, "At the time, when he told me, it sounded to me like the babblings of a lunatic, so I scarcely listened. But I remember him saying that the building itself was the key to the underworld. It was like a maze, he said, and if he could find his way to the center of the maze, where the ley lines converged, and where the four elements of the universe became one, he would have access to the ley lines, and be able to escape along them 'like strolling down a highway.' That's what he said. 'Like strolling down a highway.'"

Jack said, "Another thing I want to know is—how come you were up at The Oaks that night they all disappeared?"

"Chance, mostly," Father Bell replied. "I telephoned Dr. Estergomy around seven o'clock to tell him I was going to be late the following Sunday, because I had to drive some of the Sunday-school children out on their picnic. He said, 'You won't believe this, Father, but they've all gone.' Well, I remembered at once what Quintus Miller had been telling me, so I got into my car and I drove up there directly."

Quietly he said, "What I saw there filled me with complete consternation. The patients' rooms were still locked, their windows were still barred, but they were gone, every single one of them. You can imagine what I felt like. But in my consternation I recalled what Quintus had told me, that the building was a maze—and that before he could escape along any of the ley lines, he would have to reach the center of the maze. I prayed that he and his followers had not yet had the time to do so.

"I ran outside, and I circled the building, consecrating the boundary as I did so, running, sprinkling it with holy water, and reciting the prayer for keeping evil spirits at bay. I had only just finished when I heard a rushing noise, a terrible rushing noise, like a hundred barefoot people running toward me, under the ground.

"It was *them*—it was the inmates of The Oaks, and they were escaping. I was convinced of that. I was terrified. But the rushing abruptly stopped, because they had come up against the holy circle I had described around the building. I hadn't been able to prevent them from vanishing; but I *had* managed to prevent them from leaving the building.

"There was a howling beneath the ground which still gives me nightmares to this day, and a pummeling of fists against the earth, *drum-a-drum-a-drum-a-drum*, like an earthquake."

He took a deep breath, as wheezy as Joseph Lovelittle's Doberman. "I thought the patients would reappear in their rooms after a while, when they realized there was no way for them to escape. But they never did. Perhaps it was only possible for them to pass through the maze in one direction. After several weeks I could only presume that they had all perished. That was another reason why I gave up the priesthood. I believed I had the deaths of one hundred thirty-seven helpless people on my conscience."

Jack said, "What about the circle, the holy circle? Is that still there?"

"Of course it is; and it will stay there. It can only be removed by the priest who originally consecrated it, or by three cardinals acting in concert."

"And of course you wouldn't even think of removing it?"

Father Bell stared at him. "If I were to let Quintus Miller and the rest of those creatures loose on the world—as insane as they always were, and as full of vengeance and resentment as they must be now—well, that would be an act of the gravest irresponsibility. That would probably make me an accessory to *massacre*."

The door opened and a freckle-faced nurse looked around the door. "Are you ready for your supper, Billy?"

Father Bell looked up. "What is it tonight?"

"Fish cakes."

"Goddamn it, I hate fish cakes."

"Don't be long," the nurse told him brightly, and closed the door.

Jack said, "That your name—Billy?"

Father Bell's mouth sloped sideways in a cynical smile.

"My old man's idea of a laugh, calling his son Bill Bell. That's the kind of practical joke that parents used to play on their children way back then. Not that they're any better these days, calling them Wentworth and Chevy."

"How about coming out to eat with me?" Jack asked him. "I haven't eaten all day. There must be one or two reasonable restaurants here in Green Bay."

"Why should you want to take an old man of eighty-eight out to eat?" Father Bell asked him suspiciously.

"Because I'm hungry. Because I hate to eat alone. Because I want to talk to you more about The Oaks. Want any more reasons? Lobster has to be better than a fish cake."

For the first time Father Bell smiled. "You're a persistent man, Mr. Reed."

"So would you be, if your son was stuck in a wall with Quintus Miller."

Father Bell opened his eyes. "Where are we?" he said, sitting up in his seat. "I must have dozed off for a while."

Jack took the keys out of the station wagon's ignition. "I decided to take the pretty way," he said tiredly.

Father Bell wiped the fogged-up window with his hand. "Where the hell are we? This isn't Green Bay!"

"No, you're right, it isn't. We're back at The Oaks."

Father Bell stared at him in indignation. "The Oaks? You had the goddamned nerve to take me all the way back here to The Oaks?"

"You were sleeping, after all of that lobster and all of that Chablis. I guessed you wouldn't mind."

"Are you crazy? Are you stark staring crazy? This is kidnap, for God's sake! Let me out of here!"

Jack unlocked the station wagon's doors. "Go ahead. It's pouring with rain, it's three-thirty in the morning, we're ten miles away from the nearest human being, and you don't have a raincoat. Not to mention the fact that.you're eighty-eight years old, and you have bursitis."

"How do you know that?" Father Bell demanded irritably.

"You told me, over dinner. You told me a lot of things about yourself, over dinner."

"You can't do this," Father Bell protested. "You have no right."

"My son gives me the right."

Father Bell said, "Listen, my friend, I'm very sorry about your son. But I can't help you. There's nothing that I can do. I haven't been a priest for sixty-three years; and I don't have the slightest desire to be a martyr."

"You must have had some compassion for other people, to want to be a priest."

"Oh, sure, and look where it got me."

"It got you *here*, Father Bell. Right back where you left off. If you want a classic lesson in facing up to your responsibilities, this is it."

"Don't you moralize to me!" Father Bell roared back. "I did what I could; I stopped those bastards from getting away! I can't do anything else! You can't expect me to do anything else! Jesus Christ, that was back in 1926! I was twenty-five years old! I did what I could!"

"Please—you can talk to them, at least," Jack insisted. He knew that Father Bell was terrified. He knew that it had been wrong of him to drive him all the way here. Taking an elderly ex-priest against his will and driving him half the length of the state in the middle of the night was probably a criminal offense punishable by twenty years in the state penitentiary, or worse; and he probably deserved it, too. But he was too tired and too desperate to worry about the morality of what he had done. All he knew was that Lester had asked him to bring them the priest, or Randy would be crushed.

Father Bell hunched forward in his seat and peered through the darkness toward The Oaks. "Can't see it. Trees must've grown."

"I don't suppose it's changed much," Jack told him. He opened his door. "Are you coming?"

"Does that mean I have a choice?"

Jack leaned into the car. "You're here, Father Bell. You can finish what you started. You might as well give it your best shot."

Father Bell sat in the passenger seat of the car, looking yellow-skinned and fragile and very tired. "To tell you the truth, Mr. Reed, I'm not at all sure that I've got it in me."

"Will you *talk* to them? That's all I'm asking. If nobody can deconsecrate the circle around the house but you, then what have you got to worry about? The choice is entirely yours."

"I don't know," said Father Bell "I'm not too sure I want to face up to Quintus Miller again... not after all these years."

Jack walked around the station wagon and opened the door. "Come on, Bill Bell. Let's do it to them before they do it to us."

Father Bell hesitated for a moment, but then he swung his legs out and reached for Jack's hand to help him.

"God-awful night," he remarked.

The two of them walked up the gravel drive together, with Father Bell leaning heavily on Jack's arm. The wind was up, and the rain flew almost horizontally through the darkness, like a plague of ice-cold locusts. Jack had bought new batteries for his flashlight, and he flicked the beam here and there so that Father Bell could see the building he hadn't visited for more than sixty years.

"Grounds are overgrown," Father Bell observed. "Apart from that, though, can't say that it's changed hardly at all. Same look, same smell. If you knew how much I used to dislike this place."

"You and me both," said Jack.

He helped Father Bell around the back of the building to the conservatory. He opened the door, and they stepped inside. Father Bell peered this way and that in the darkness.

"Ruined," he said, touching the broken plant pots and the desiccated plants. "You should have seen it then! Every variety of hothouse flower you could think of! And a grapevine, too!"

"Come on," said Jack, and led him into the lounge.

Father Bell hesitated, stopped, and looked around him. "I can't believe it. It hasn't changed. It hasn't even been *touched*. Can you imagine coming back to a house you once lived in sixty years ago and finding it exactly the same as the day you left it? It's uncanny!"

They went through to the hallway. Jack quickly shone his flashlight on each of the marble statues, but both of them were as blind as justice. Their footsteps crunched on the gritty marble floor. Up above their heads, the huge iron lantern creaked in the early-morning draft.

Father Bell shuddered in the cold. "Do you know what night it was, they all escaped? June twenty-first, midsummer's night. Didn't strike me as relevant till years later. But that's the time when the forces of the earth are strongest. Summer solstice. One of the Druid times. One of the times when the ley lines come to life, and all the earth joins up."

"I fit mufflers," Jack told him. It was a way of saying that he had very little imagination, at least as far as magic was concerned.

"Sure you do," said Father Bell. "And I spend my time staring out of the window at Green Bay. But just because you and I are practical and pragmatic, my friend, that doesn't stop the summer solstice coming around, and that doesn't impress the elements. Earth, fire, water, and air. And the fifth element where they all meet together—the Quintessence."

They stopped in the middle of the hallway. The building was dark and silent. But Jack knew now that it was more than a building, very much more than a building. It was a mystical maze, built on one of the most potent sites in America—a site that had probably had awesome significance in the days when America had been explored by Celts and Norsemen and ancient Egyptians. Jack felt afraid, in a way that he had never felt afraid before.

"You're right, they're here," whispered Father Bell. "I can feel them."

"Wonder if they've realized we're here?" asked Jack, shining his flashlight toward the cellar door. It was slightly ajar.

Father Bell made the sign of the cross and said, "*Crux sacra sit mihi lux; non draco sit mihi lux; uade retro Satana; nunquam suade mihi uana; ipse uenena bibas.*"

Jack glanced at him. "You still remember the jargon, then?"

"It's not something that you forget."

The cellar door creaked very slightly. Jack strained his eyes to see if there was anything there, hiding in the darkness.

"Maybe I'd better call them," he suggested.

Father Bell's mouth tightened, but he said nothing. He was too concerned with looking around, and with his memories, and with his fears.

"What do you think?" Jack repeated. "Do you think I'd better call them?"

Father Bell nodded.

"Lester!" Jack shouted. "Lester, you there?"

His voice echoed around the galleried landing. He waited, but there was no reply. No sign of movement; no eyes opening; no dragging sounds.

"Lester, you asked me to bring you the priest and I brought you the priest!"

Still no reply. Father Bell touched Jack's sleeve and whispered, "They *asked* you? You didn't tell me that!"

"Would you have come up here if I had?"

"I'm here under sufferance anyway."

Jack cupped one hand to the side of his mouth and called, "Lester! Lester, where are you?"

At that instant the cellar door flew open and a large dark object came rushing across the floor toward them.

Father Bell cried out, *"Jesus!"* but Jack was too frightened even to speak.

He saw almost straightaway, however, that the dark object was Joseph Lovelittle's Doberman, Boy. Its eyes gleamed, staring and yellow in the beam of his flashlight, and its jowls were bursting with creamy froth.

It had nearly reached them when it abruptly stopped, its claws skidding on the marble floor. It let out an anguished scream. Jack had never heard a dog scream before, and he was chilled right down to the base of his spine.

A hard marble white hand had reached out of the floor and gripped the dog's back paw. Gradually, forcefully, it was pulling the dog downward.

Boy barked and yelped and scrabbled desperately at the tiles, but the hand sank smoothly back down into the marble, pulling the paw after it.

Jack pushed his flashlight into Father Bell's hands and circled the struggling dog, looking for an opportunity to seize his struggling body. He lunged forward once, and the dog's claws scratched at the back of his hand. Then he lunged forward again and caught hold of him.

"*Domine sancte, Pater omnipotens, aeterne Deus...*" mumbled Father Bell, crossing himself again and again.

Jack pulled at the Doberman as hard as he could. He could feel its muscles shuddering with pain and terror. Its spine whiplashed. But the hand that had risen from the floor was far too strong for him. All he could do was try to keep his grip as the dog's sleek-haired body was dragged into the floor.

"*Ab insidiis diaboli, libera nos Domine!*" Father Bell shouted out, in pious desperation. But his prayers were hopeless; because Boy was pulled straight into the floor without any hesitation at all.

The dog's head disappeared last of all. Its mouth gaped, its eyes bulged. It uttered one last gargling bark. Then it was gone, and the floor was as smooth as it had been before.

"*Per Dominum nostrum Iesum Christum Filium tuum, qui tecum uiuit, et regnat in unitate Spiritus sancti Deus, per omnia saecula saeculorum, amen,*" Father Bell whispered. Hopeless.

"A warning," said Jack, shivering. "I'll bet you anything you like that was a warning. Don't play any games, that's what they're telling us, or this is what's going to happen to you"

He stepped back. As he did so there was a gurgling, sticky noise from the floor in front of him. Out of the marble poured the remains of the dog, gray flesh, rainbow-colored intestines, strips of ripped-apart skin. A single severed leg, which shuddered and kicked in the last throes of nervous reaction.

And somewhere in the house, faint and clear, came the strains of a song.

Lavender blue, dilly-dilly;
Lavender green.
Here I am king, dilly-dilly;
You shall be queen.

"Quintus Miller," breathed Father Bell.

7

They climbed the stairs. Father Bell had to pause halfway up to rest for a moment or two, but Jack waited for him patiently.

"I'll show you Quintus's room," said Father Bell as they resumed climbing. "After he almost killed that woman, it was always kept locked, and he was allowed out only for exercise, and of course for therapy with Dr. Estergomy."

"Dr. Estergomy still continued treating him?" asked Jack.

Father Bell cleared his phlegm-clawed throat. "Oh, yes. He continued treating him. Elmer Estergomy believed that no disturbed mind was beyond redemption. I was a priest, you know, and a priest who had been trained as an exorcist—but I'm afraid that I disagreed with him. I saw some terrible things here, Mr. Reed. I saw men and women whom the Lord had quite plainly deserted for good and all; and for whom there was nothing left in their lives but unremitting hell. Hell on earth, and hell hereafter."

They walked along the eastbound corridor until they reached the third window. Father Bell stopped to listen. The corridor was airless and oppressive. Still very faintly, they could hear "*Lavender blue, dilly-dilly...*" quiet and mocking as a humiliating memory. Father Bell said, "He always used to sing that song, over and over. And he always used to change the words, to say *here I am king*. I suppose in a way that he was. There was nobody at The Oaks who was stronger than Quintus Miller, nor more determined."

He stopped and lifted his hand as if he were giving a benediction. In front of them, one of the doors stood ajar. Cream-painted, like the rest, but much more kicked and scratched.

"This was Quintus Miller's room," Father Bell breathed. Jack had the odd impression that Father Bell was almost relieved to see it, as if he had suspected all his life that he would have to come back here one day.

At least the waiting was over.

Jack said, "That door was locked, the last time I tried it. I tried all the doors along here."

Father Bell gave him a sideways glance that was almost mocking. Then he pushed open the door to reveal the interior of Quintus Miller's room. There was no furniture, only a mattress and a toilet without a seat. The room smelled sour and musty and indefinably evil. Jack didn't even want to go inside.

"There, on the wall," said Father Bell.

In the gloom Jack could see that a huge six-pointed star had been scrawled on the wall with some dark brown substance, a substance as dark as blackberry juice, or blood, or excrement.

"What's that?" asked Jack, peering at it in distaste. "The Star of David?"

Father Bell approached it cautiously. "Not exactly. This is the Hexagram of Solomon. It is, quite simply, the most powerful occult symbol ever known, even more powerful than the cross. It has as much meaning in pagan worship as it does in Judaism and Christianity. It looks like a star; but more accurately you should interpret it as one triangle superimposed on another. The upward-pointing triangle—you see?—which represents fire and air. And the downward-pointing triangle, here. which represents earth and water.

"Where these triangles overlap, in the six-sided figure within, there is the conjunction of all ancient power—the fifth element, the Quintessence. Presumably Quintus used this power to escape into the walls."

"Quintus? Quintessence? Do you think that could be more than just coincidence?" Jack asked him.

Father Bell shrugged. "The fifth son and the fifth element? You may be right. But I regret that my knowledge of earth magic and all its ramifications is not very extensive. I was, after all, a Roman Catholic priest, not a Druid."

Father Bell looked around. "This hellhole," he remarked. "The number of times I sat with Quintus Miller in here, trying to reason with him, trying to restore his sanity. But he was too far gone for me, and too far gone for Elmer Estergomy."

"All the same," said Jack, "maybe we ought to try calling him."

Father Bell allowed himself the weakest of smiles. "I don't think we need to call him, Mr. Reed. He knows we're here, don't you, Quintus?"

The rain prickled against the window, behind the protective steel mesh, wooly with dust, unsteady with age. The passing years had punished the building as it had punished them all. But the passing years had left Quintus Miller keener than ever for freedom and revenge, while

Father Bell had been left dried up like a chili pepper and just as frail, and craving nothing except peace, and his book-club thrillers, and his tedious pine-and-orange room. Even sixty years of disappointment and boredom were better than sixty seconds of absolute pain.

There was no response. Jack listened, but there was no *sssssshhhhhh* noise inside the walls, no telltale dragging of human bodies through solid brick and solid cement.

"Maybe we'd better try the cellar," he suggested, although the last place on the whole planet he wanted to go back to was the cellar. "That's where they tried to pull me down into the floor, and that's where I found Randy's toy."

But Father Bell lifted one hand and said, "Wait. I can feel something; I'm sure."

Jack waited and listened. "I don't know, Father. I can't hear anything."

Moments passed in soft rustling quietness, like a plaza at night when thrown-away newspapers are blown across it in the wind. Rain, the nervous banging of a downstairs door.

Father Bell approached the pentacle scrawled on the wall. "This is the entrance to the underworld," he said. "A gateway, do you understand what I mean? The pentacle gives you access to the maze; and the maze in turn brings you to the point where the ley lines intersect; and from there— well, my friend—from there you can journey anywhere you wish."

He laid his hands flat on the pentacle and examined it with a serious face. "In the fifteenth century, occultists were quite matter-of-fact about passing from one element to the next. They saw the elements simply as a kind of ladder, up which one could progress from the stonebound underworld at the bottom to the ethereal realms of heaven at the top. Given the right conditions, the human soul could exist in all of these elements, the way that fish swim around in the sea."

Jack looked around him uneasily. "What I want to know is—how did Quintus Miller and the rest of them actually get *inside* the wall. I mean you say that's a gateway. But how does it work? You can't just step into solid brick, can you?"

Father Bell continued to smooth his hands across the design on the plasterwork. "It's happened before. Some of the stories about it are ancient legends, like Theseus going into the labyrinth in Crete to kill the Minotaur. Some of them are much more recent, like the Pied Piper, who led all the children of Hamelin into solid rock."

"But how's it *done*?"

"There are rituals for entering the underworld in the same way that there are rituals for entering heaven. Substantially there is very little difference in them. In the nave of Chartres cathedral, in France, there is a maze that you can follow, and the movements you make when you follow it are a ritualistic dance that are part of the procedure for reaching a condition of divine spirituality."

Jack pounded on the wall with his fist. "But this is *brick*, for Christ's sake! There's nothing spiritual about brick. It's not a state of mind, it's hard-baked clay!"

Father Bell said, "If Quintus Miller did it, we can do it. We'll have to try Elmer Estergomy's library. We can probably find the rituals in there."

Jack stepped back. He was beginning to wonder if it had been such a good idea, bringing Father Bell back to The Oaks. Although there were rustlings and scrapings inside the walls and the whole building seemed to be agitated,

Quintus Miller and his followers were keeping themselves very well concealed, and there were no more signs of Randy, or indications from Lester or anybody else about how Jack might get him back.

"Lester!" he shouted. "Lester, I brought you the priest!"

Again, there was no response. Jack felt the cold throat-swallowing feeling of complete despair.

"Lester!" he repeated. "Lester, can you hear me, damn it! You promised to give me my son back!"

Almost immediately, in answer to his shouting, the wall inside the pentacle began fluidly to bulge out. It rose into the shape of a human face. A boy's face—Randy's face. Jack stared at it, not moving, with a mixture of horror and anticipation. Perhaps Lester was going to keep his word after all and let Randy go. The only trouble was—what was he going to expect in return?

Randy's paint white face opened its paint white eyes.

Daddy? I don't like it here. Please help me. It sounded like· an old-fashioned tape recording of Randy's voice.

Jack stepped forward but Father Bell caught at his arm.

"Don't, Mr. Reed—not yet. It could be a deception of some kind. Quintus was always very devious."

Daddy, begged Randy. *You have to help me. Please, Daddy, help me!*

"What do you want me to do, spaceman?" Jack asked him. "Spaceman" was an affectionate nickname that Jack had given Randy when he was very small, when he used to fling him, giggling, up into the air.

Daddy, they want to be free.

Father Bell clutched Jack's arm even more tightly. "No!" he breathed. "You can't let them out! That would be absolute madness! They would murder, they would rape! You have no conception of what they're like! They're scarcely human!"

Please, Daddy, pleaded Randy's masklike face.

Jack said to Father Bell, "All right, listen. You say they'd go wild if you let them out. But what can they really do? They're mentally backward. They've been shut up in this place for over sixty years. Essie Estergomy says some of them are physically handicapped, too; and half of them are bare-ass naked. What can they do? If they escape, they're going to get picked up by the police before you know it. Especially if we *tell* the police what to expect."

Father Bell still refused to release his grip on Jack's sleeve.

"Mr. Reed, you have no idea of how strong they are, and how totally *vicious* they are. Why do you think they were sent to The Oaks in the first place? Have you seen that metal mesh covering the windows by the staircases? Have you seen how dented it is? They used to throw themselves against it, from the top of the stairs. One second they would be smiling and laughing and talking as sanely as anybody you'd ever met—the next second they would be crashing themselves against the mesh, and rolling down the stairs, screaming and shuddering and foaming at the mouth."

Jack inclined his head toward Randy's face on the wall.

"That's my boy there, Father Bell," he said, his voice unsteady with tiredness and emotion. "That's my son."

"I know, Mr. Reed; and I can understand how you feel. But we have to find another way to get him out of there. We don't dare let Quintus Miller go."

"You mean *you don't dare*."

Father Bell's nostrils flared. "Very well, if that's the way you want to put it, *I don't dare.* But more than that, I won't accept the responsibility."

"Did I ask you to?" Jack retorted.

Daddy, whispered Randy. *Please, Daddy, they're going to hurt me if you don't.*

Jack abruptly twisted his arm free from Father Bell and approached the wall. "Here, Randy—take hold of my hands. Can you do that? Can you get your hands out? Come on, spaceman, I'll pull you out of there!"

"*No!*" shouted Father Bell, rushing after him.

With a jarring blow from his bony shoulder, Father Bell knocked Jack away from the wall. But as he did so two plaster white hands, far too large to be Randy's hands, came thrusting out of the wall. One of them caught hold of Father Bell's right wrist. Father Bell shouted in fear and tried to pull his wrist away, but the hands were far too powerful for him.

Jack stumbled, caught his balance, and immediately plunged forward to help Father Bell break loose. As he did so, however, Randy's face turned to him and snarled with feral teeth.

Get away, you stupid interfering bastard! A voice cement-thick with menace.

Jack recoiled. "Randy?" he called. "Randy?"

But in front of his eyes, Randy's face suddenly crumbled like dry chalk, and broke open to reveal beneath it the staring face of a man. Just as white, just as masklike, but with a narrow forehead and near-together eyes, and lips that peeled back to reveal long teeth in badly receded gums.

"Holman!" whispered Father Bell. "Gordon Holman!"

The very same, Father Bell, the face crowed at him. *What a good memory for faces!*

Jack skirted cautiously around behind Father Bell's back, looking for an opportunity to grab Holman's arm and to pull Father Bell loose. But in a high hysterical shriek, Father Bell cried out, "No! Don't! Stay well away! It's far too dangerous!"

Oh, come on, Father Bell. We're all dangerous!

"Gordon, let me go," said Father Bell. "I took care of you, Gordon, you just remember that. I brought you gum, didn't I? I brought you all of those movie magazines."

Holman smiled at the memory of it. *You were a good priest, Father Bell. We all loved you, you know; until the last. We all trusted you.*

"Come on, then, let me go," Father Bell encouraged him. "Come on, now, there's a good fellow. You're hurting my wrist."

But the narrow chalky face on the wall half closed its eyes and gave Father Bell a knowing, superior grin. *You heard what I said, Father Bell*—until the last. *That was when you betrayed us. That was when you trapped us here. Trapped, Father Bell! No way to go forward, no way to go back.*

Father Bell said fearfully, "Let me go, Gordon. No good is going to come of this."

The face laughed out loud. *You're right, Father Bell! No good at all!*

At that instant Jack lunged at Holman's arm and tried to wrench it away from Father Bell's wrist. But the arm was hard and chilled and muscular, startlingly inhuman, and Jack wasn't nearly strong enough to break its grip. There was a second's pause, and then Jack heard Randy screaming *Daddy! Daddy! Don't!* right above his head.

Horrified, confused, Jack stepped back. Randy's head and shoulders had appeared out of the ceiling, with a man's hand gripping the back of his neck and forcing his head down into the room as if he were trying to drown a puppy. Jack shouted, "Randy!" and hurled himself upward, jumping two or three times; but the ceiling was too high, and each time he missed by inches.

Daddy! Please! Save me! Daddy, they're hurting me! Daddy, they're going to—

Randy was lifted forcibly back up into the ceiling, and its molecules closed over him like the surface of a bowl of freshly mixed plaster. In fury and desperation, Jack turned back toward Father Bell, and toward the staring white face in the middle of the pentacle.

"You evil bastards! You let my boy go, you hear me? For Christ's sake, I brought you the priest, didn't I? What the hell else do you want? Let him go!"

But the voice was soft and sly and adamant. *Quintus says—only if you let us out.*

Jack shouted back, "You want out? We'll let you out! Come on, Father Bell! What the hell difference is it going to make?"

But Father Bell cried out, "Mr. Reed! Don't even *think* about letting them go! Never! Not in a thousand years! Mr. Reed—don't listen to what he says! I beg you, Mr. Reed! Never!"

Jack pointed furiously up to the ceiling. "You saw that? You saw that boy? That's my son! And what the hell *difference* does it make if we *do* let them out, that's what

I'd like to know! In any case, don't shout at me. I can't let them out, not on my own. Only you can do that. And what do you think? *You* think that it's more important to stop some—some theoretical 'revenge of the loonies'—you think that's more important than saving my son! Brother, you should have gone into politics, not the church."

"Mr. Reed," said Father Bell. He was trying to sound rational, although he was grimacing with pain. "There is nothing theoretical about these people, nor about their madness. You're misjudging them, badly. Once they get out of here, you will never be able to stop them or to control them. If they get the chance, they will slaughter everybody who gets in their way."

Oh, but we'll have our fun first, said Holman. *Like* this!"

He suddenly cracked Father Bell's right arm back and smacked it tight against the wall. Father Bell cried out, the pitiful cry of a man who was born into this world with nothing, and will leave it with nothing.

You stopped us, Father Bell, whispered Holman. *We had come through the maze, we had struggled not to panic, we had struggled to stay alive. Some of the women were as crazy as shit, do you think it was easy? But there they were. The ley lines stretched in front of us—north, south, east, west, anywhere we wanted to go. They were beautiful. The first beautiful things that most of us had ever seen. We stood there, you know? Whores and homicidal crazies and arsonists, and we all agreed that this was it, this was the future. Freedom, light! That Quintus Miller, what a magician! And we drank in that magic, and we drank in that glory.*

He closed his eyes completely. *One moment of joy! One*

moment of hope! But you know what happened then? The shutters came down! Oh, yes, you bet! The shutters came down! One by one, the ley lines were sealed off. Sealed off by darkness, just like a mine caving in; darkness—falling through the surface of the earth; rolling thunder. That was you, Father Bell! That was you, and your fancy incantations, and your holy water! And that was the last we saw of the world outside. You stopped us, Father Bell, you trapped us! But now we want out, buddy! Now we want out!

Father Bell lifted his head. His Adam's apple quivered, stringy and vulnerable.

"I can't do it, Gordon. I can't let you go."

You want to suffer?

"I've been suffering for sixty-three years. I can't let you go."

The face opened its eyes. Then—suddenly—another hand burst out of the wall and seized Father Bell's left hand. He was pulled tight up against the wall, his arms outstretched, his face pressed against the plaster. He turned his head sideways and stared back at Jack in pain and terror.

"Holman!" Jack warned the chalk white face. "Don't you touch him! Let him go!"

What he needs is suffering, the face replied. *True suffering, the way that Christ suffered. That's why Quintus chose me for this. I'm good when it comes to suffering.*

There was a deafening bang, which made Jack jump back. Father Bell screamed—a scream so high that at first Jack wasn't sure that he had really heard it. His right arm had disappeared up to the elbow into the wall. Then there was another bang, and his left arm vanished in the same way.

Father Bell screamed again and again, trying to tug his arms free from the wall. Gordon Holman's face melted away, but then it reappeared on the other side of the room, next to the door.

The crucifixion of Father Bell, Holman said, gloating.

"Let him go!" Jack shouted. "For God's sake, let him go!"

For God's *sake? We don't do anything for God's sake. And why should any of us feel sympathy for Father Bell? Think what he did to us—keeping us captive here for sixty years.*

Jack went up to Father Bell, who was whimpering and shaking in anguish. He tried to pull Father Bell's arms out of the wall, but just like Randy's woolly toy they had fused with the brickwork; flesh and brick were indivisible.

"Get him out!" he repeated, turning back to Gordon Holman.

There's only one way to get him out now, said Holman. *And that's to amputate his arms.*

"He's eighty-eight years old!" Jack retaliated. "Whatever he did when he was twenty-five, he's an old man now, completely helpless!"

That's right. The same way that we've been helpless.

"Oh God," babbled Father Bell. "Oh God, it hurts; oh God, it hurts."

"Are you crazy?" Jack screamed at Gordon Holman.

Holman tittered. *Of course I'm crazy. We're all crazy. What did you expect in a nuthouse?*

"Let him go!"

If he lets us go. we'll let him go.

"And if he won't?"

We still have your son. we still have little Randy. So if

Father Bell won't let us go. you'll just have to go off and find yourself three cardinals, won't you, to get us out, and that isn't going to be easy. Otherwise, Randy gets skrushed into something that won't even look *like a boy.*

"I beg of you, I beg of you," wept Father Bell. His sunken cheeks were wet with tears.

Jack leaned against the wall, very close to him. "Father Bell, you're going to have to let them go. You're going to have to say the words. For Christ's sake, Father Bell, that's the only way they're going to let you out of there."

"Can't," wept Father Bell. "You don't even understand what they'll do."

Is he going to help us? asked Gordon Holman. *Perhaps he needs a little more persuasion.*

"Can't you see that he isn't going to give in to you?" Jack demanded.

Oh... I don't know. Wait till we set his hands alight. We can do that, you know. Anything to do with the elements. Earth, water, air, fire. Go take a look in the room next door, and watch him light his candles to God.

The white face melted again. In blind anger, Jack stalked across the room and punched the wall where it had been. "He's an old man, you bastard! Let him go!" His fury was all the worse because he had brought Father Bell down here against his will, and in spite of Father Bell's own warnings. The responsibility for every ounce of Father Bell's agony was entirely his.

"Oh God protect me," breathed Father Bell.

Jack said, "Father, listen to me. You're not a priest anymore. You said so yourself. You don't have to feel guilty about letting these people go! It isn't your job anymore! Just let them go, and they'll let you go! You think you're going to die here, with your arms buried in a wall? Is that what you think you're going to do? You want to be a martyr, or what?"

Father Bell turned to stare at him, and as he did so his jaw dropped open in a soundless scream of absolute pain. He shuddered and shook, and hit his own forehead against the wall, but he couldn't get free.

"What is it?" Jack asked him in panic. "What are they doing to you?"

Go take a look in the room next door, and watch him light his candles to God.

Immediately Jack hurtled out of Quintus Miller's room and rushed to the door of the adjacent room. It was locked, as Quintus Miller's room should have been locked. Jack frantically rattled the handle, but it wouldn't open.

Father Bell shrieked. *"Oh God, oh God, protect me!"*

Jack lifted the brass cover over the door's spyhole. What he saw made his skin prickle and his mouth flood with bitter saliva. Father Bell's hands came right through the wall, from Quintus Miller's room, as if he were standing in a pillory. The tip of each finger was blazing and even though Father Bell was wriggling his fingers in a desperate attempt to extinguish the flames, it was clear to Jack that the fire was far too hot, far too intense.

He shook the door violently, until he heard the frame cracking. But it was far too solidly built for him to budge it. It had been designed to keep criminal lunatics locked away for life, and even the most desperate of men couldn't have forced it open.

All he could do was stare in horror as the flesh at the end of Father Bell's fingers reddened and blistered and charred, and his fingernails curled up like burned onion skins.

Already, with every agonized wriggle, the bones of Father Bell's fingers were breaking through the skin. In anoher minute, the way this fire was blazing, he would have no hands left at all.

"I'll do it!" screamed Father Bell. "Gordon! Gordon! Aaaahhhhhhh, Gordon! Gordon, I'll do it! Aaaaahhhhh! Gordon! Please, Gordon, I'll do it! *I'll do it!*"

The fire was immediately snuffed; although Father Bell's blackened fingers still smoldered like charcoal twigs and filled the room with smoke. Jack went back into Quintus Miller's room and found that Father Bell was quivering with pain and shock. Blood ran from the sides of his mouth because he had halfway bitten through his tongue, and crept along the creased of his age-weathered skin.

Jack put his arm around Father Bell's shoulders, feeling helpless and angry and nauseated. Father Bell's eyes filmed over. The pain in his hands and arms was raging so furiously that he kept lapsing in and out of consciousness.

In the corner of the room, the plaster boiled and bubbled like liquid mud. A man's form appeared, between one wall and the other, a short thin man, naked except for a shawl around his shoulders. He looked toward Father Bell with blank plaster eyes, and there was an expression of peculiarly lunatic compassion on his face.

Father Bell gasped, *"The pain—the pain I can't bear it."*

Jack turned toward the naked figure in the corner.

"Come on, for Christ's sake, let him out of this wall."

Christ suffered more, the figure in the shawl replied,

without taking his eyes away from Father Bell. *At least, that's what you Gentiles keep telling us.*

Jack took a deep breath. "For the sake of humanity, then. Let him go."

When we go, he goes. That was the agreement.

Jack held Father Bell tight. "Father Bell? Can you hear me? Just nod if you can hear me. You have to let them go now. You have to say the words."

Father Bell nodded. There was a lengthy pause, while he moistened his blood-dried mouth, and then he whispered, "In the name of the Father, and of the Son, and of the Holy Ghost... I hereby declare that this place which I have consecreated and protected..."

He hesitated, and licked his lips. He leaned his head against the wall. "I can't do it," he said. "I mustn't."

You want the fire again? the figure in the corner asked him. *You want us to burn your hands down to the wrists?*

"Father Bell," Jack insisted, holding him closer still, feeling his bony shoulders beneath his coat. "Father Bell, you have to. There's no other way out."

Father Bell took a shivering breath. Then he went on.

"This place which I have consecrated and protected from the forces of darkness and devilry... should now be deconsecrated, and returned to the natural state of its creation..."

As he spoke these words Jack felt a shifting and a stirring inside the building, as if thousands of cockroaches had been disturbed inside its walls. The figure with the shawl smiled slowly in triumph.

"...and released from the guardianship of all His holy agents..."

The shifting and stirring grew louder. It was like the sound of a huge crowd of silent people, shuffling toward a single doorway. Then it grew louder still. It was all around them. *Sssssshhhhh—sssssshhhhhh—sssssshhhhhhh*. The thick, concrete-mixer sound of human molecules being dragged through solid brick, as the long-imprisoned inmates of The Oaks made their way back through the maze of its walls, toward that ancient and terrifying place where the mystical ley lines intersected, where all four elements became one Quintessence.

"...forever, and ever..."

Father Bell finished his recitation. His face was glistening with tears and perspiration. "That's it," he said. "That's everything." But he had hardly spoken when the shuffling in the building suddenly stopped. Jack stepped back from Father Bell and listened, his head raised up.

"What is it?" he asked. He turned to the plaster white man in the corner. "Why has it gotten so quiet?"

We're still trapped. The ley lines are not yet open.

"Father Bell?" Jack demanded; but Father Bell did nothing but groan.

The deconsecration is not complete, said the figure in the wall.

"What do you mean? He said all the words, didn't he?"

The ley lines are not yet open, the figure insisted. *We are all still prisoners.*

"Father Bell?" Jack repeated. "Father Bell—you must have left something out. They're still trapped inside the building. Father Bell!"

Father Bell's head lolled. He was only half-conscious. Jack shook him and said, "Father Bell! Wake up! You must have left something out!"

Father Bell stared at Jack with misted eyes. "I have to—make—the sign of the cross."

Jack turned back to the figure in the shawl. "You *have* to let him go! He has to cross himself, otherwise you'll *never* be free!"

He has to cross himself?

"That's right, you've got it. He has to make the sign of the cross, in the air, you got it? With his hand, you stupid bastard. Otherwise spellee no workee."

The figure opened and closed its powder white eyes like a desert lizard. Then it flowed back into the corner of the room, with a billowing of plasterwork, and vanished. Probably going to talk to Quintus Miller, Jack guessed, as he heard it slide through the brickwork with a swift *sssssshhhhhing* sound.

Jack waited, supporting Father Bell's sagging body as much as he could. He was exhausted, too, both physically and emotionally. He hadn't even allowed himself to think if he could bring this nightmare to an end—or, if he did, how he was going to deal with the guilt of what he had done to Father Bell. All he wanted right now was to get Father Bell out of the wall, and to rescue Randy.

"Hilda?" asked Father Bell, deep in shock. "Is that you, my dear Hilda?"

"It's okay." Jack shushed him. "Hilda's going to be here soon."

He waited almost five minutes. Father Bell may have been emaciated, but he was big-boned, and heavy, and Jack's back began to ache from holding him up.

"For God's sake!" he shouted at the wall. "Are you going to let him go, or aren't you?"

His answer came explosively, almost at once.

With a grinding, mincing, chopping noise, Father Bell's arms were cut off just where they met the wall. His body dropped, Jack couldn't hold on to him. Blood pumped out from both of Father Bell's sheared-off elbows. Jack jumped back, sprayed with sticky scarlet. But as he did so, two white hands lunged out of the wall, fast as rattlesnakes, and seized hold of Father Bell's spurting right forearm, and flung it this way and that, *Domine sancte, pater omnipotens, aeterne Deus,* mockingly imitating the sign of the cross.

Blood filled the room in a mist of droplets and spatters. For one fraction of a fraction of a second, the bloody cross that Father Bell had described in the air with his mutilated elbows hung suspended in front of them in glistening loops of gore, just like water from a hose wiggled into a figure eight. Then everything was splashed with blood—the floor, the walls, the ceiling—and Father Bell rolled silently across the room, his severed arms held stiffly out in front of him, and the noise his body made was hollow and drumming, like rolling a Thanksgiving turkey across the floor.

He was dead by the time he reached the door.

Jack stood shocked, speechless, his own hands held out in front of him, cups of blood.

"Oh, Jesus Christ what have I done?" He could hear himself talking, but he was almost deaf with stress.

He knelt down beside Father Bell's body. Father Bell's face was pressed against the floor. His eyes were open; he was staring at nothing at all. Jack couldn't even summon up the nerve to close his eyelids. God almighty, he was still warm!

Jack looked around the room. Blood was sliding down

the walls and dripping audibly on to the floor. The air was rich with the smell of recent death, like an abattoir.

"You promised to give me my son back," he said hopelessly.

There was no reply. Only the rain. Only the slow, glutinous dripping of Father Bell's blood. Jack stood up and took two or three breaths, and admitted to himself for the first time since he had followed that scampering gray-white figure down the valley to The Oaks that he had been taken for a fool. That Quintus Miller had enticed him here; that Quintus Miller had indirectly contrived for him to go to Olive Estergomy so that Olive Estergomy could send him off to track down Father Bell.

That very first day, when the gray-white figure had run in front of his station wagon, Quintus Miller must have sensed him passing, somehow, and sensed what he wanted out of life, and drawn him here.

The rest had been done by fear, by cajolery, by blackmail, by violence. That was the kind of man that Quintus Miller was. He had all the persuasiveness of true insanity.

Jack shouted at the blank walls, "I want my son back. You hear that, you goddamned crazies! I want my son back! You promised! I want him back!"

There was a long, long silence. Then the wall flowed and rippled, and half of a woman's body appeared, a young woman, with long wavy hair, in profile. Her eyes were closed and she didn't open them once.

Quintus will keep his promise. He always does. Her voice sounded like a high-toned bell, chiming through a Sunday-morning fog.

"I want my son now," Jack told her.

Quintus will give you back your child when Quintus is free.

"Quintus is free already. You're *all* free. Come on, open your eyes. Look at this body! That's a man, an innocent man! You've tortured and killed an innocent man!"

The young woman's voice was unrepentant. *Father Bell was never innocent. You should have seen him. with some of the women patients. Especially the younger ones. Twelve, and thirteen; the ones who couldn't speak. Don't go mourning Father Bell.*

"You listen to me," Jack told her. "I don't give a shit what happened in 1926. I don't give a shit for Quintus Miller, and I don't give a shit for you. I want my son back, that's all. I want him here, and I want him now. That was the deal. You got that? That was the fucking *deal!*"

The young woman turned her face toward Jack, but still didn't open her eyes. She could have been beautiful, but there was something about her forehead that was a little too bulbous. Something about her mouth that was a little too uncontrolled and weak.

Quintus will give you your son back when he is free.

"I've told you, Goddamn it! He's already free!"

The young woman smiled without humor. *He is free of this building, yes. But of course he is not yet free of the earth.*

"I don't understand."

It requires an extra sacrifice for him to escape from the earth.

"Oh, yes? You mean he's gotten himself out of The Oaks, by walking through the walls, and through the ground outside, but he can't get himself out of the ground?"

It requires a sacrifice, the young woman told him. *A special sacrifice, to pay off the debt.*

Jack made a point of averting his eyes from Father Bell's body. He could feel Father Bell's drying blood sticking to the soles of his shoes. He said quietly, "I want you to take this message right the way back to Quintus Miller, you understand me? Either he lets my son go, and I mean *right now*, or else I'm going to bring down on top of his head more goddamned grief than he's ever known in his life. And let me tell you this—I'm not some progressive psychiatrist like Elmer Estergomy, and I'm not some softheaded sky pilot like Father Bell. I don't have any sympathy for Quintus Miller, nor for you; not one inch. I'm going to break his ass."

He stopped and took a breath. Then he said, "What do you mean, sacrifice?"

Debts have to be paid, Mr. Reed. Nothing ever comes for free.

"What are you talking about? What kind of a sacrifice?" Jack shouted at her.

A blood sacrifice. What other kind? Eight hundred lives, one for every month of our imprisonment.

"What the hell are you talking about?"

Eight hundred lives must be offered, Mr. Reed, for every life that emerges out of the earth. Eight hundred lives must be taken.

Jack stood and stared at her with his arms by his sides, quite stiff with disbelief. "Eight hundred people have to be killed? What—for *every single patient* who wants to get out of the ground?"

The white face nodded. *Eight hundred lives, for every life.*

"But that's—thousands of people! You can't kill thousands of people!"

The gods will not release us out of the earth for anything less.

Jack covered his mouth with his hand. He was beginning to understand why Father Bell had been so desperately reluctant to let Quintus Miller loose.

Eight hundred, for every one of us, the young woman told him. *It isn't much to ask.*

"So Quintus Miller won't let my son go—not until he's killed eight hundred people—and gotten himself out of the earth?"

Quintus Miller is worth eight thousand ordinary people. Quintus Miller is worth the lives of everybody else on earth.

Jack had never felt so defeated in his life. "What am I supposed to do?" he asked the young woman. "Wait for eight hundred innocent people to die? And what happens then?"

You made a deal, Mr. Reed. A deal is a deal. Your son's freedom for Quintus Miller's freedom.

"But eight hundred people, for God's sake—"

That was the deal, Mr. Reed. You made it. You have to live with it.

Jack hurried down the stairs, across the hallway, and into the night. Lightning was stilt-walking across the horizon, over toward Baraboo and Mirror Lake. He left The Oaks by the conservatory and ran along the shingled pathway toward the front of the house. Just as he reached the corner of the building, thunder compressed his eardrums, and rain lashed out of the sky so fiercely and so suddenly that he had to take shelter under the eaves of the kitchen.

He stood there panting, dripping, and praying that this was all a nightmare. *You'll wake up soon, Jack; you'll be back at home; with Maggie sleeping close beside you and the sun lighting the pink bedroom drapes; and the tinny sound of Randy's television turned low as be sits cross-legged in the living room, watching early-morning cartoon shows. If dere's one thing I can't stand... it's a flower that steals bananas from the refriger-ator-ator!*

He wiped his face with his hand. His station wagon was parked at the end of the avenue. As soon as the rain eased off a little he would make a run for it. He began to think that it had always been raining, ever since he was born. He couldn't remember any sunshine; he couldn't remember any snow. Only his father, leaning toward him and laying his hand clawlike on his knee, with the rain sprinkling across the lake outside, and saying, "When you got nothing to say—say nothing. That's my motto."

Jack had later discovered that somebody called Charles Colton had said the same thing, just about two centuries before, and at that moment the last impression of his father had disappeared, like an overexposed photograph.

He reached out to test the rain. As he did so a thin-fingered hand came out of the darkness and clutched his wrist. He shouted out, "*Nyaah!*" and jolted back up against the house, hitting his shoulder.

A flashlight dazzled him; then a face appeared. The face of an elderly woman, pale and alarmed, wearing a deerstalker hat and a brown plaid cape.

"Mr. Reed? I didn't mean to startle you."

It was Olive Estergomy—Essie. Jack lifted both of his hands in mute surrender and told her, "It's all right. It's quite all right. You surprised me, that's all."

"Mr. Reed, you have blood on you."

He looked down. His coat was spattered with Father Bell's blood; dried now, and rusty-looking, but unmistakably blood.

"It's not mine," he told her. "It's Father Bell's. He's—well, I'm sorry to tell you he's dead."

"Dead" seemed like a euphemism, after the torture that Father Bell had suffered. The fire, the agony, and the amputation.

Essie shone her flashlight toward The Oaks. "Dead?" she said.

"It was all my fault," Jack told her. "He told me how dangerous it was, but I didn't understand."

Essie shone the flashlight back at him. She seemed bemused. "Mr. Reed, I couldn't sleep. I called your motel but they said you were out. I had to come back here to see for myself; just to make sure that everything was still quiet."

Jack said, "Listen, come back to the car. Something's happened. Something bad."

"Bad? What do you mean?"

Jack said, "I found Father Bell, up in Green Bay. He wasn't a priest anymore but everybody still called him Father. He said that I was right. They were still in the walls. Quintus Miller, Lester Franks, Gordon Holman, all the rest of them. They got there by some kind of—I don't know, hard to describe it, magic almost. Earth magic, that's what he said. Something the Druids used to believe in."

Essie Estergomy stared at him from under the brim of her dripping hat.

Jack said, "They killed him." He tried to explain how. He tried to explain that Randy's face had appeared from the wall, and then Gordon Holman's and that Father Bell had been seized and burned and mutilated. But on a fresh thundery night in the middle of Wisconsin, with lightning sizzling and rain dredging the trees, his words sounded flat and unbelievable.

Essie said fearfully, "You've called the police?"

Jack looked way. "I don't know whether that's the best thing to do," he said evasively.

"Mr. Reed! A man's been murdered!"

"Yes," he said. But how could he tell her that thousands more people were supposed to be sacrificed—eight hundred unsuspecting lives for every single patient who had escaped from The Oaks? And how could he tell her that this wholesale massacre was just to restore them to the real world, the world of air and fire. God alone knew what they would do once they were free.

Jack said, "I know this sounds—well, I know this doesn't sound like the regular thing to do. But let's wait till the morning before we call the police. I need to think, you know? The police could make things worse. I need to find some way of dealing with all of this."

Essie said, "They were really inside the walls? Inside the bricks?" She shone her flashlight up the side of the building and illuminated one of the sculptured faces with closed eyes.

"I think we're better off out of here," Jack told her. "They're not only dangerous, they're angry. They want revenge for being shut up for so long."

Essie hesitated for just a moment, then she nodded. "My car's parked just beside yours."

Jack took her arm, and together they made their way back down the avenue of oak trees, their feet crunching quickly in the gravel.

"Surely the police will be able to help us," said Essie. "If the patients have gotten away, they can put out descriptions, catch them. I still have my father's list of admissions, with their original pictures."

"You don't seriously think the police are going to believe us, do you? A hundred thirty-seven lunatics have been buried in the walls of a building for sixty-three years, and now they've escaped? I can hear them laughing now."

"But surely we can show them," Essie replied. "Surely we can find some way of persuading them."

"What are we going to show them?" asked Jack. "Father Bell's body? And how do you think they're going to react to that? They're going to throw me in the slammer with no chance of bail, while Quintus Miller and all the rest of his loonies go free."

Essie stopped and clasped Jack's hand. "You didn't kill Father Bell, did you? I mean—you're telling me the truth?"

Jack looked at her and attempted a smile. "Essie," he said, "you're just going to have to trust me."

They were two-thirds of the way down the drive when they saw a small figure standing by the gates. A small figure, grayish white, like a child in a hooded rain cape. The figure had its arms outstretched, as if to bar their way, but it wasn't moving, wasn't waving. It had no face.

"That's a *child*," said Essie, in disbelief.

Jack stopped, and stopped Essie, too. "I don't think so," he said.

"But it's a little girl... what on earth is a little girl doing out here in the middle of the night?"

Jack said, "I've seen her before. I've seen *it* before. I'm not sure what it is, but it's something to do with Quintus Miller."

Essie released Jack's hand and went forward, toward the gates. The grayish white figure remained motionless, although its cape flickered in the wind, like a rain-sodden newspaper.

"Little girl!" called Essie. She quickened her pace, then slowed down again uncertainly. "Little girl?"

Essie stopped, and stood facing the figure for a very long time. Jack waited a few steps behind her. Essie shone her flashlight at the figure's head; but although its feet were pointing toward them and there were buttons down the front of its coat, all they could see was the back of its hood. Essie turned to Jack with a look of perplexity. "Her head's around the wrong way," she said. "How can her *head*—"

Jack warned, "Be careful. I'm not too sure that it's child at all."

Essie took two or three steps nearer. "Little girl?" she called. "Are you all right, little girl?"

She took one more step, and then two bare arms came crashing out of the gravel just in front of her feet and seized her ankles. She screamed, and dropped to her knees. As she did so two more arms burst out of the shingle and snatched at her arms. Her flashlight tumbled away and went out.

"Hold on!" Jack shouted, and ran up to her, kicking one of the arms away. He held her around the waist, and tried to yank her upright again, but more arms came out of the gravel and dragged him away. He kicked and struggled and thrashed, and managed to break free and to roll across the wet grass.

Essie cried out in pain as one of her legs was plunged right into the ground, then the other. "Help me! My legs! Oh God, help me!"

Jack scrambled to his feet. But as he did so he saw swiftly moving furrows in the gravel path, and arms that curved out of the ground like the arms of swimmers, just below the surface of a lake. There were five or six of them at least, and they homed in on Essie's struggling body with a slurring, crunching, gravelly rush.

Dodging the arms that snatched at him from all sides, Jack grabbed Essie under the arms and hefted her upward. She came free from the ground so easily that Jack fell backward, with Essie on top of him. She was still screaming, still frantically waving her arms. But she was no longer kicking. Her legs had been amputated, right up to the top of her thighs, and her femoral arteries spurted dark cascades of hot blood all over the gravel, and all over Jack.

Instantly, more powerful hands pulled her out of Jack's grasp and dragged her across the path. He tried to get up, but another arm burst out of the path and seized him around the neck, half throttling him and pulling him back to the ground.

He felt other hands snatching at his legs and grabbing at his clothes.

They've got me! This time they've got me! They're going to grind me up, the same way they ground up Lovelittle's dog, and spew me back out again.

He heard Essie let out one last high-pitched shriek. Out of the corner of his eye, he saw her pulled down into the gravel and disappear. He kicked out in panic at the hands that were trying to tug at his ankles; and he took hold of the arm that was gripping him around the throat and forced it downward. Then he bit it, as hard as he could.

The arm recoiled and whipped away. Jack somersaulted onto the grass, gasping for breath, staggered onto his feet, and then ran madly toward the gates. He heard the gravel *sssshhhhhhhing* right behind him as Quintus Miller's maniacs came swimming in pursuit beneath the surface of the path, their arms hooking out of the ground like shark's fins.

He squeezed through the gap beside the gate, the branches scratching at his face. Then he ran across to his car, flung open the door, and started the engine. A hand thrust itself out of the ground right beside his open door and caught hold of his foot. He slammed the door on its wrist, and felt the hand convulse. Cursing, shaking with disgust, he opened up the door again, kicked the hand away. Then he stamped on the gas pedal, and the station wagon's back wheels slithered and snaked, and he was away.

His headlights jostled and jumbled through the rain. He saw trees, hedges, rain-slicked curves. He glanced in his rearview mirror again and again to make sure that nobody was following him. About a mile up the road he hit a deep puddle, and slid sideways, and almost went off the road. He pulled in to the side, stopped, and gripped the wheel, just to stop himself from shaking.

Calm down, start thinking straight. If you start panicking, then there won't be anybody who can cope with Quintus Miller. There won't be anybody to save Randy.

He switched on the car radio. His first contact with normality all day. A woman was crowing, "*...and praise the Lord! Yesterday I was riddled with cancer, today I'm eating pork sausages!*" He switched channels, until he found a country-western station. "*He got fishing lines strung across the Louisiana River....*"

After ten minutes, still trembling but more relaxed, he pulled away from the side of the road and carried on. Right now all he wanted to do was go home, and sleep, and try to work out what he was going to do next. At the moment his mind was logjammed with sheer horror.

"*It takes him every bit of a night and a day... to even reach a place where people stay...*"

Jack had almost reached the Lodi intersection when he saw the small grayish white figure standing right in the middle of the narrow road.

Oh God, he prayed. *Please let it not be a child; not really.*

He sped toward the figure at nearly sixty miles an hour. It made no attempt to move; it made no attempt to jump out of the way. Just before he hit it, he thought, *Supposing it's deaf; supposing it hasn't seen me.* He braked instinctively. The wheels locked, the tires shrieked, and he collided with the figure head-on and heard a dreadful wet thump. His windshield was splashed all over with blood. He skidded to a stop, gasping and gagging.

Unsteadily, he climbed out. Spread across the hood of the station wagon, dripping and stringy, all tubes and blood clots and yellowish glistening sacs, were the mashed remains of a human body. They steamed in the dim reflected light from the headlights. Jack had seen more death in the past two days than he had ever seen in his life, but this was too much for him. He had deliberately slaughtered a child. He dropped on his knees by the side of the road and vomited half-digested lobster.

After a minute or two he wiped his mouth, and wiped his eyes, and stood up. He would have to clear the body off the front of his car. He had a cardboard box in the back. He guessed that he could tear off one side of it and use it as a scoop.

It had been a child, after all, and he had run it down. It had been a living child, just like Randy.

He lifted the station wagon's tailgate. As he did so he glimpsed something through the side window, on the opposite side of the road. Something blurry, something grayish white. Frowning, he stepped around the car to look at it.

The small figure was standing not far away, faceless, silent, unharmed. He stood watching it; and he knew that it was watching him back, although it had no face.

It wasn't until he had scraped a lump of raw flesh out of the gully in front of the windshield, and seen a tangle of amber beads beside the wipers, that he understood whose mangled remains had been dumped all over his car.

Essie's, Olive Estergomy's.

Which meant that all the time he had been sitting by the side of the road, listening to the radio, Quintus Miller and the rest of the patients had been following him, beneath the ground. Which probably meant that they were capable of pursuing him anywhere.

8

Adishrag dawn was smearing the sky by the time he reached Karen's house and parked. He climbed out of the station wagon and stretched his back. He felt as if he had been bruised and pummeled all over.

He leaned over the hood and inspected it carefully, just to make sure that he had left no telltale streaks of blood. He had managed to scoop most of Essie's remains into the bushes, where he hoped that they would be eaten by worms and wild animals. The rain had washed the rest of the car clean.

He was worried now that the police might be looking for him. Father Bell would have been reported missing from his senior citizens' home in Green Bay, and Olive Estergomy would certainly be missed from her house at Sun Prairie. In both cases, the last person who would have been seen with them was him.

He rang the doorbell four times before Karen came to the door. She was wearing a black baby-doll nightdress and her hair was done up in curlers. It was stale and gloomy in the living room. On the artist's-palette-shaped contemporary coffee table, next to the *capo di monte* statue of a weeping child, there was a bottle of Smirnoff vodka, nine-tenths empty, and a single lipstick-smeared glass.

Karen put her arms around his neck and kissed him. Her breath smelled of stale alcohol. "I've been worrying myself *sick*," she told him.

He peeled off his coat and sat down on the white vinyl settee. "I don't know what the hell to do next," he said. "It's been nothing but sheer bloody murder."

"I'll make some coffee," she suggested. "Come on, tell me about it. What are friends for?"

He told her what had happened, trying not to sound hysterical, trying to sound sane and collected and reasonable, trying not to leave anything out. She sat beside him with her hand on top of his. Her crimson nail polish was chipped. She said, "Uh-huh, uh-huh," and "Uh-huh?" but she didn't interrupt him or ask any questions, and he wasn't sure that she believed him.

"Well, you sure don't want to tell the police now," she said once he had finished. "That would be—you know—like suicide. Cutting your own throat."

"I don't know what else to do."

"Jack, honey, all you have to worry about is getting Randy back."

"But, Karen, they're going to kill thousands of people—literally *thousands*—that's if they haven't started already."

"Jack—it's not your fault. You've done what you can." But Jack shook his head. "It's my goddamned fault, all right. It's my fault that Joseph Lovelittle died and it's my fault that Father Bell died and it's my fault that Olive Estergomy died. Karen—it's my fault! They wouldn't have gone anywhere *near* that building if it hadn't been for me."

"But why did *you* go near it? Because Quintus Miller wanted you to. I mean whatever this little white girl is, she must be something he can *control,* you know like *thought control.*"

"That doesn't make me any the less responsible."

"Well, maybe it does and maybe it doesn't. But I'll tell you what. The way I finally got my way with Cecil was to find out how to be *stronger* than he was, and the way I could be stronger than he was, was to be *smarter*. I had the clerk at his trucking company call me up whenever Cecil was going drinking with the boys, and so I made sure that I stayed out that night, till late. In the end he grew tired of having nobody around to use as a punching bag. You can beat this Quintus Miller if you're smarter. Come on, Jack, he's a goddamned headcase, after all. It shouldn't be hard to be smarter than a headcase."

Jack sipped his coffee. "No, I guess it wouldn't."

Snuggling up beside him, Karen said, "You have to find out more about him—you know, who he was, and what they locked him up for. Find out what kind of a headcase he was; you know, maybe he was frightened of something, like spiders, or going outside."

Jack kissed her. "Hey," he told her. "You're not as dumb as you look, are you?"

"You never said I looked dumb."

"I'm sorry, I didn't mean it. It's just a saying, you know?"

"Well, you ought to find out more about this earth-magic stuff, too," Karen told him. "Maybe this Quintus Miller doesn't have to kill all those hundreds of people at all. You know, maybe it's just a what-do-you-call-it, legend."

"You're right," Jack agreed. "Father Bell said that Adolf Krüger was into earth magic, you know? And that maybe

Quintus Miller found out all about it from Adolf Krüger's library."

"There you are, then!" Karen told him. "All you have to do is to get yourself into Adolf Krüger's library, and read all about it in the same books."

"You make it sound easy." Jack smiled.

"Jack, honey, nothing is easy, you know that. Life's a joke, then you croak."

Jack closed his eyes. Karen stroked his forehead with her fingertip. "Mike was wondering what had happened to you," she said. "I told him not to worry, everything was fine. Oh—and Maggie called the works. She was going bananas about some women's weekend?"

Jack said, without opening his eyes, "I've seen people die. I've never seen that before."

"You need some sleep," said Karen.

He slept on the couch for over three hours. When he woke up, his head was thumping, and his mouth tasted like a pocketful of pennies. On the edge of the artist's-palette table, Karen had left him a note that read, *Gone 2 Work. Catch U Later.*

He opened the thin unlined drapes. It looked as if it had stopped raining at last, although the streets were still glossed with wet. He went through to the kitchenette, opened up the refrigerator, and found himself a beer. Heineken: Karen thought that it was ritzy to buy imports. He popped open the can, walked through to the bathroom, and turned on the shower. Leaning against the shower stall, he stepped out of his pants and his socks. He smelled strongly of sweat and something else: the cold vinegary mustiness that pervaded The Oaks.

After he had showered, he called Karen at the works and asked her to meet him at the Bierkeller across the street. "And don't tell anyone you're meeting me, just in case the cops come looking."

Karen said, "There's a couple of Cecil's old shirts in the closet, and some shorts, and some jeans, I think, if you look down at the bottom."

Jack dressed in a huge woolen trucker's shirt, red-and-white plaid, with the sleeves rolled up; but the shorts were like the sails of an oceangoing schooner, and the jeans were a size fifty-six waist—big enough for him and Karen together, one in each leg.

He borrowed the least frilly pair of Karen's panties that he could find—white satin with a bow in the front—and sponged as much of the blood and dirt from his own slacks as he could, and then pressed them with Karen's traveling iron on the kitchenette counter. He watched TV while he ironed. There was a news report about a fire on board the ferry steamer from Milwaukee to Ludington, and then an update report from Madison on a party of Girl Scouts who had mysteriously disappeared while camping up near Mirror Lake.

"Police discovered all the Girl Scouts' tents and camping equipment, including clothes and personal possessions... but by dawn this morning there was still no sign of the twenty-three girls and their four scout leader... no indication that they might have been attacked, or been frightened by somebody or something, and run off... in fact, the mystery

deepened later this morning when detectives revealed that the girls' footprints entered the campsite, but did not appear to exit... a fact made especially baffling because the ground all around the camping area had been softened by recent downpours."

Jack set down the iron. He felt as if somebody had hit him in the face. *They've started,* he thought. *They've taken those girls, and dragged them into the ground, the same way they dragged Essie Estergomy into the ground. They've started, and they mean what they say. Eight hundred sacrifices, for each of them. And then—*

He pulled on his slacks, switched off the iron and the television, threw his coat over his shoulders, and left the house. The day was fresh and the sky was beginning to clear. He climbed into his station wagon and U-turned it with squittering tires toward West Good Hope Road.

He sped along the puddly roads until he reached Reed Muffler & Tire. His station wagon jounced across the concrete forecourt. Mike Karpasian was standing in the tire bay, talking to a customer, but as soon as he saw Jack climbing out of his car he excused himself and came hurrying across.

"Jack? Is everything okay?"

"Not exactly. I just netted myself a couple of urgent family problems, that's all."

"You look like shit. Is there anything that I can do?"

Jack squeezed Mike Karpasian's shoulder. "Just keep the customers happy."

"Sure, no problem. But I need a couple of John Hancocks. Goodrich won't deliver any more tires until we settle their account, and we're totally cleaned out of TAs."

"Just put the checks in front of me, okay, and I'll sign them."

He crossed the noisy echoing workshop with Mike Karpasian in close pursuit. When he entered the office, Karen looked up in surprise. She was wearing the red sweater that one of Jack's customers had called "Living Jell-O" and a tight black leather skirt with laces up the side.

"What's wrong?" she asked him, her nails suspended over her word-processor keyboard.

"We have to leave right away. Can you call the agency and have them send out a temporary? And Mike wants those checks."

"Okay, sure," said Karen. She passed him a plastic folder marked "Checks for Signature," and punched out the number for Milwaukee Office SOS.

"What's happened?" she asked him under her breath as she waited for the agency to answer. "I thought you were supposed to meet me at the Bierkeller. Maggie's called three times this morning, wanting to know where you are. She says she's going to call the cops if you don't bring Randy home by lunchtime."

"They've started killing people," said Jack, glancing toward Mike Karpasian to make sure that he couldn't overhear him.

"What? What do you mean?"

"A whole troupe of Girl Scouts went missing this morning near Mirror Lake."

"You're sure?"

"It was on the news. I heard it when I was pressing my pants."

"Maybe they got lost," Karen suggested.

Jack finishing signing the checks and raised his hand to show her that he knew what he was talking about. "Believe me, it's Quintus Miller. We have to get to that library and find out how the hell to stop him."

Mike Karpasian suddenly turned around and said, "Hey, Jack. It's Maggie!"

"Oh, Jesus," said Jack. But there she was, in her square-shouldered "Dynasty" suit, the brown one from Sears, storming across the workshop, turning the heads of every fitter and mechanic she passed. *Hey, that's Jack's old lady... looks like she's ready to do some damage.*

Maggie slammed open the office door, so that the glass shook. "Where's Randy?" she demanded.

Jack made a point of ignoring her. "Did you get through to SOS yet?" he asked Karen.

"Where's Randy?" Maggie repeated.

Without looking at her, Jack said, "He's okay, he's staying with a friend at Wauwatosa."

"What's he doing at Wauwatosa? He should be at school! I called the school and they haven't seen him today or yesterday."

"Maggie, listen, he has a very slight cold. Nothing to worry about, just a sniffle. He couldn't stay home, I couldn't bring him to work, so he's staying with a friend at Wauwatosa. All right? He's well looked after, he has other kids his own age to play with. There's nothing for you to worry about."

"Where were you last night? I called you all night, last night."

"Maybe the phone was on the fritz, I don't know."

"I want to see him," Maggie insisted.

"Sure you do, but you can't. You'd probably upset Randy, and you'd certainly upset my friends. And, besides, how do I know you won't try to steal him back?"

"Because I give you my word."

Jack turned to her and said, "Listen, lady, you gave me your word that you would love, honor, and obey."

"What about Saturday?" Maggie persisted.

"What about Saturday?" Jack wanted to know.

"We're having a gala, I want to take Randy along."

"I'll think about it. What is it, lesbians?"

"God, you're a bastard, Jack. You always were. Women's consciousness raising, that's what it's all about. Learning that we don't always have to knuckle under to brainless chauvinistic bigots like you."

"I don't remember you calling me a brainless chauvinistic bigot the night that Randy was born. Or the night that he was conceived, for that matter."

Karen pressed her hand over her mouth to stop herself from laughing and Maggie gave her a glare that would have dissolved Kryptonite.

"Can I come round this evening to see him?" asked Maggie.

"I guess so," said Jack.

"Eight o'clock not too inconvenient?"

Jack nodded.

"I said, eight o'clock?" Maggie repeated.

"Sure, sure, eight o'clock," Jack told her. He turned away because he knew what Maggie was going to do next, which was to slam the door and stalk back out of the workshop in full wide-shouldered fury.

"Oh, shit," said Karen. "Oh, I'm sorry. I didn't mean to laugh."

"Did you get that temporary secretary?" Jack asked her. His heart was beating faster than normal, and his mouth felt a little dry, but Maggie hadn't upset him as much as usual. Saving Randy and stopping Quintus Miller were far more urgent than arguing with his wife. But he thought, *Why couldn't Maggie just—*

"He'll be here in an hour," Karen told him, switching off her word processor and picking up her purse.

"*He'll* be here in an hour?"

"Secretaries come in all sexes," Karen told him. "You're too old-fashioned, that's your trouble."

"What are you trying to do, make me feel old?"

Jack opened the office door and followed Karen out of the works. He could tell by the sly sideways looks they were giving him that all his mechanics thought he was taking her out for a lunchtime quickie. But right now he didn't care what anybody thought about anything he did. There were 137 escaped crazies underneath the ground, and nobody knew about it except him and Karen. Everybody else who had found out about them had found out the hard way, and was dead.

They drove back toward Madison under a misty, illusory sun. Karen said, "I wish to God you'd never gone to look at that building. That building is damned to hell."

"Me and that building both," Jack told her.

It was the first time that Jack had seen The Oaks in the sunshine, but somehow the building looked even more dilapidated and unwelcoming than ever. Its spires were shrouded in a midafternoon heat haze, and hundreds of pigeons perched on the rooftops and crowded the parapets and the gutters like lice.

He couldn't think why he had found it so exciting when he had first discovered it. Right now he would rather have turned the state penitentiary into a resort hotel than this place.

Perhaps it had been the living personalities of its inmates that had drawn him here, the lunatic seductiveness of Quintus Miller. Now *they* were gone, The Oaks was no more than a shell.

Jack was carrying the tire iron from the station wagon, in case they were attacked. He doubted if it would help him much. He had thought about bringing a gun, but he doubted if that would have helped him much, either. Still— even swinging a tire iron gave him more confidence than walking up to The Oaks empty-handed.

Karen said, "You don't think that any of them could have stayed behind?"

Jack said, "No, I don't think so. I hope not. They've been trapped in here for sixty years, remember. They all would have wanted out; and as far away as possible. Besides, if they're looking for human sacrifices, they won't find them here."

"Only us," said Karen.

The conservatory door was half-open. Jack hesitated, but then he pushed it wider and stepped inside.

"God, I hate this place," said Karen.

They walked through the lounge into the hallway. They were greeted by the blind statues at the foot of the stairs, even more luminescent than usual in the sunshine that filtered through the clerestory windows. Karen's high heels rapped on the marble flooring.

"Can you *smell* something?" asked Jack.

Karen sniffed. "I have my sinus."

"It smells like burning," said Jack. "Burning paper."

They climbed the west staircase to the landing, and then walked along the corridor to the west tower. Karen kept close to Jack, and she was obviously jumpy. "I can smell it now," she told him. "Like burning newspaper, you know?"

Jack said nothing. He was thinking about Maggie. He hadn't meant to shout at her like that. It wasn't her fault they didn't get along. And of course she was anxious about Randy, she was his mother. The only reason he had shouted at her was because he felt guilty about losing Randy, and he hated lying. But what was he going to tell her? Our son's been kidnapped by a homicidal lunatic and dragged into the ground, but don't worry, I'll try to have him out of the ground in time for your women's consciousness-raising gala on Saturday?

They reached the doors of the west tower. They were double doors, heavily padlocked, just like the east tower.

"Oh boy, the smell's really strong here," Karen said, and sneezed twice.

Bless you, thought Jack.

"How are we going to get inside?" asked Karen. "We don't have a key. Only that big fat realtor guy has a key." Jack hammered the sharp end of his tire iron into the door, behind the metal hasp. Then he levered it outward. The oak cracked, the screws cracked. He dug the tire iron further in and levered it again. After five minutes of sweating and struggling, the screws suddenly grated out of the wood, and the doors were unlocked.

When they opened them up, however, they discovered the source of the burning smell. They were in a huge library, two stories high, like Elmer Estergomy's clinic. Every wall was lined with shelves, and every shelf was crammed with books, thousands and thousands of books, wedged in tight. But at least a hundred books had been heaped into the middle of the carpet and set alight. The air was filled with acrid blue smoke. Jack knelt down beside the books and sifted his hand through their blackened remains. It had been a miracle that the whole building hadn't burned to the ground. The windows were stained nicotine brown with smoke, and a library chair stuffed with horsehair was smoldering still. The carpet had been burned right through to the floorboards.

Jack poked at the ashes with his tire iron and teased out a half-burned book.

"Look at this," he told Karen. "*Awen, the Divine Name.*"

He picked out another book and peeled back layer after layer of charred pages. "*Ye Origines and Historie of Ye Druides.* And look at this: *The Culdees in Christian Britain.* And *Druids in the Gallic Wars.*"

Karen glanced at them momentarily and then went back to fanning the smoke away with her hand and chewing gum. "Sure stinks in here. I hate it."

"Druids," said Jack, picking up more and more crumbling black pages. "This was all to do with Druids. And they've deliberately burned it all, to stop us from finding out about it."

"What's a Druid?" Karen wanted to know.

Jack stood up. "Well... they were like priests, you know? In ancient Britain. That's all they told me at school."

Karen watched him in silence for a long time, and then she said, "What are you going to do now? If they've burned all the books?"

Jack looked around the library. "I don't know. I guess I'll have to find out about the Druids some other way. But the point is—they've shown us their weakness."

"Jack, I don't understand that at all. What weakness?"

"Think about it! Why did Quintus Miller burn all these books? He burned them because he didn't want us to find out what was in them. Because if we find out what's in them, we may find out how to stop him—you know?—and send him back where he came from. Back into the walls, or wherever. By rights he should have been dead for years."

"So what do we do?"

Jack gathered together three of the less-burned books.

"The best bet is the university. They must have somebody on campus who knows about Druids. I mean they get visiting professors from all over the world."

Karen reached out and held his hand. "Jack?" she said. "What is it?"

"Well, you know this might not work out, you know? I mean—if Quintus Miller is really as bad as that priest told you he was—well, Randy might be dead already."

Jack had tried to come to terms with that possibility ever since he had found the Turd, half-buried in the cellar wall. "Yes," he said. "But we can't stop trying, can we?"

They left the library and walked back along the corridor. Karen linked arms with him. "Jack, honey—listen— whichever way it turns out, I want you to know that I love you—and if you want to move in... well, you're more than welcome."

Jack kissed her hair and squeezed her hand. "I'm not too sure that I could fill Cecil's shoes. I certainly can't fill his jeans."

Their footsteps echoed down the staircase. They left The Oaks through the conservatory door and walked down the avenue of trees where Essie Estergomy had died. Jack kept glancing from side to side for signs of what had happened, but the gravel was smooth and undisturbed, and there was no blood anywhere.

"It's time we listened to the news," said Jack. 'I want to make sure they haven't taken anybody else."

"What if they have?" asked Karen.

"Then there's nothing I can do about it."

She pecked his cheek. "In that case stop torturing your goddamn feelings of guilt and let's get down to the university."

When they reached the gate, however, they saw Daniel Bufo's Cadillac parked next to their station wagon, and Daniel Bufo sitting in it, looking dyspeptic and unhappy. As they squeezed through the gap beside the gate Daniel Bufo eased himself out of his car and came toward them, hitching up his pants.

"Mr. Reed, I have a bone to pick with you."

"Oh, yes?" said Jack.

Daniel Bufo nodded to Karen and gave her a tight grimace. "Mrs. Reed?" he acknowledged her, his eyes lingering for just a moment on the Living Jell-O.

Karen said nothing. But Jack opened the door of his station wagon so that she could climb in.

"Before you go, Mr. Reed," said Daniel Bufo, leaning his elbow on the station-wagon roof and blocking Jack's way around it, "I'm not too happy about the way this sale has been shaping up. Not too happy at all. I'm beginning to think—well, that you may not be one hundred percent motivated."

"Oh, really? What gave you that idea?"

"Well—believe me, I don't want to upset you, Mr. Reed. You showed a keen interest in The Oaks at the outset, and in spite of the fact that you made an offer that was well below the property's actual value—"

"Let's wait up a minute here," Jack interrupted. "Are we talking about market value or curiosity value?"

"Mr. Reed," said Daniel Bufo, "I don't want to cause any bad feeling here, but are you still genuinely interested in acquiring this property? Because if you're not, you could save both of us a considerable amount of time and work. Just say the word, and we'll call it a day."

"Of course I'm still interested," Jack assured him. "Everything's on track. I'm talking to my attorney later this afternoon." Daniel Bufo was standing so close to him that he could see the clear perspiration on his upper lip. In truth, after what had happened, Jack would never have considered buying The Oaks in a zillion years. But if he called the deal off now, his access to The Oaks could be severely limited, and until he had tracked down Quintus Miller, he wanted to be able to come and go from the building as often as he needed to.

"Well, I'm real glad to hear that," said Daniel Bufo, with

obvious relief. "After what you said to me yesterday—about meeting the vendor face-to-face..."

"Well, that won't be necessary," said Jack. "I guess I was just being persnickety. I've been suffering some toothache recently—tends to make me out of sorts."

"Oh, I'm sorry," Daniel Bufo told him, solicitous now that he was reassured about his sale. "I hope you manage to get it fixed soon. My sister was a martyr to toothache."

He leaned forward and leered at Karen's legs as she sat in the car. "Good to see you again, Mrs. Reed."

Jack reluctantly shook his hand, and said, "I'll be in touch, okay? Just as soon as I've talked to my attorneys."

Daniel Bufo walked back to his car, his large coat flapping in the breeze. Jack watched him go. Karen said, "You're not really going to buy it, are you, after all of this?"

Jack said, "I wouldn't buy this building if it was the only building left standing on God's good earth."

Daniel Bufo turned and gave Jack a wave before hefting himself into his car. Jack was turning away when he thought he saw a ruffling in the grass beside the road. He looked again, frowning. Must have been the wind, nothing more. But then he saw the ruffling again, and it couldn't have been the wind because it rushed along the verge like an invisible polecat running through the grass. It was headed straight toward Daniel Bufo's car.

Karen said, "What's the matter, honey?" but Jack had already started running.

"Mr. Bufo!" he shouted. "Mr. Bufo! Get the hell out of here, quick!"

Daniel Bufo frowned at him through the windshield, and then did the worst possible thing that he could have done.

He switched off his engine. Jack yelled, "*Go! Mr. Bufo! Go!*"

The furrowing movement in the grass verge reached the road itself. Suddenly an arm burst out of the solid earth, and the hard-packed roadway crackled and split. Daniel Bufo let down his car window and leaned his head out and called, "What did you say, Mr. Reed? Is there anything wrong?"

Jack had almost reached Daniel Bufo's car by now. "Go!" he shouted at him. "They're here!" He suddenly realized that he had probably made matters worse—that if he hadn't shouted and tried to warn him, Daniel Bufo would have already gone by now.

Daniel Bufo's face was large and placid. "I'm sorry, Mr. Reed, I'm not too sure what you—"

Frantically, Jack looked all around the car, to see where the furrowing had gone. The roadway had closed up behind it, as if it had never happened.

"Who's here, Mr. Reed?" asked Daniel Bufo.

Beneath his car, they heard a loud metallic clonking noise; then a sound like somebody hammering at sheet steel. The whole car shook and squeaked up and down on its suspension.

Daniel Bufo said angrily, "What the hell is *that?*"

"Mr. Bufo, if I were you, I'd—"

But at that moment there was an explosive bursting noise, metal and fabric and springs, and Daniel Bufo jumped back in his seat. A bunched-up fist with red raw knuckles came punching out of the brown hide upholstery right between his thighs.

"What the *hell!*" he exclaimed, but his voice was an

uncontrolled squeal, the same kind of squeal that a pig lets out when it suddenly realizes that it's just about to be slaughtered.

One arm thrust its way out of the seat, then another arm. They seized Daniel Bufo around the throat and jerked him violently downward. His nose hit the steering wheel, and Jack heard the bone snap.

"*Graaarrggghhh!*" choked Daniel Bufo, one arm clawing out of the car window for Jack to save him. Jack tugged at the door handle, but the car was centrally locked, and when he tried to reach inside to open it, Daniel Bufo snatched hold of his sleeve and wouldn't let him go.

The two muscular hands had pulled Daniel Bufo's head right down between his knees, so that he was bent double. He was gargling and struggling, but he couldn't find the breath to scream. Jack shouted at him, "My arm, let go of my arm!" but Daniel Bufo's panic was total, and all he could do was to clutch it tighter.

Two more hands, a black man's hands this time, wrenched their way out of the car's upholstery and caught hold of Daniel Bufo around the waist. At once they started to pull him down into the seat.

Jack held on to Daniel Bufo's hand as tightly as he could. But inch by inch, in a series of steady, irresistible tugs, Daniel Bufo was dragged doubled-up into the depths of his seat. The back of his coat mushroomed up behind him, and then he suddenly started to throw himself from side to side in wild unbearable pain. His bare back was being scraped against the torn-open metal of the Cadillac's underbody.

Jack tried to prize the hands away from Daniel Bufo's throat, but they were so strong that he couldn't even budge them. All the time he kept glancing quickly and frantically around him, just to make sure that the road wasn't furrowing up and that more of Quintus Miller's mad disciples weren't hunting him.

There was a moment when the tug-of-war between Jack and Daniel Bufo and the hands that were dragging him downward reached a shuddering impasse. Daniel Bufo was gripping Jack with one hand and the Cadillac's steering wheel with the other, desperate not to be pulled down into the ground. His knuckles were white, his whole body shook with agony and effort.

"*Arrrrgghhhh!*" Daniel Bufo gargled. Then he gasped an ounce of precious air and screamed, "*Help me!*"

They were the last words he spoke. At that moment Jack heard his rib cage crackle in a fusillade of broken bones and then his pelvis snap in half with a sound that he would never forget, like a large serving plate being snapped in half underneath a cushion.

Blood splashed out of Daniel Bufo's mouth and onto his feet. Then with one last jostling wrestle, he was pulled down into the depths of the seat, and through the floor of the car, and into the ground itself, leaving nothing behind him but ripped clothing and ribbons of bloody fat still clinging to the seat's twisted-open springs.

Jack got down on his knees, trembling and panting, to look underneath the car. For a brief second, the ground was in turmoil, the same way the ocean is momentarily churned up when a shark claims its victim.

Karen was calling, "Jack? Jack? What's going on? What are you *doing?*"

Jack climbed to his feet and leaned against the side of

Daniel Bufo's car, wiping sweat from his forehead with his sleeve.

Then, without warning, a hand clawed out of the hard-packed earth in front of him and clutched at his shoe.

He stamped at it, and jumped back. But immediately he recognized that it wasn't one of the lunatics' hands. It was pudgy, and white, with heavy gold rings. It was Daniel Bufo, making a last hopeless effort to rescue himself.

Jack reached out for the hand, but it was pulled away from him across the road—quite slowly at first, then faster and faster. It vanished into the grass with an agitated rustling, and then it was gone.

Quickly, jerkily, Jack walked back to the station wagon. Karen was waiting for him with her eyes wide and her mouth open and her chewing gum in suspense.

"What *happened* back there? Where did Mr. Bufo go?"

Jack climbed into the driver's seat and said, "Close the door. Come on, quick. We're getting out of here."

As he twisted the key in the station wagon's ignition he saw the roadway cracking over to his left. The engine whinnied, but wouldn't start. He tried again, it whinnied again.

"Come on, you bastard," he fretted.

Karen said, "I was going to tell you. Your inside lights were on."

"What?" he demanded. "You mean the map light, the door lights? I left those on?"

"I switched them off for you," said Karen helpfully.

Oh, Jesus, my battery was pretty weak already. There's a new battery under my desk at the shop. Why is it that somebody who runs an auto business is the very last person to look after their car?

He tried the ignition again. This time the engine heaved over twice, and then died. The furrow in the road was coming closer. An arm broke the surface, then another arm. Jack turned his head, and through the woods to the right of the car he saw bushes bustling and shaking, and leaves turfed up, as more furrows came rushing toward them.

"Kick your shoes off," he told Karen.

"What?"

"Kick your shoes off, we'll have to make a run for it."

"Are you kidding me?"

"Just kick your shoes off and get out of the car and run like hell and stay away from any broken ground! Now, go!"

Karen stared at him, petrified. But then the station wagon violently shook, and under the floor they heard the parking-brake wire snapping, and fists pummeled furiously at the metal beneath their seats.

"What is it?" screamed Karen. "Jack—what is it?"

"*Go!*" yelled Jack, and they flung open their doors and ran. Past Daniel Bufo's Cadillac, along the wall that surrounded The Oaks, and up the road.

"What are we—running—from?" Karen gasped.

Jack reached out and gripped her hand. "Don't—talk—run!"

He glanced behind him just once. His station wagon was shaking on its springs, and he could hear metal tearing. Then one of the tires burst, with a deafening bellow that sent the crows screaming and wheeling up from the nearby oaks.

The black gas station attendant had been watching them

approach for almost a mile: walking along the tree-lined road like the closing scene in *The Third Man*, except that Karen was hobbling in her stocking feet and a too-tight miniskirt, and Trevor Howard didn't stop to offer them a lift.

When they finally reached the Exxon station the attendant said simply, "Hi," to Jack and "hi," to Karen, and then "Breakdown?"

"Just need to use your phone, please," Jack told him.

"I can get you a tow truck," the attendant offered.

"No, thanks. All I need is a phone. And the lady here could use something to put on her feet, if you have anything."

The attendant stuck out his bottom teeth and looked down at Karen's feet. "We sell Milwaukee Brewers baseball regalia. Should have some boots your size."

Jack bought two Sprites from the Coke machine and then went to the pay phone while Karen freshened up in the ladies' room. He popped the top off one of the cans and drank almost half of it straight down. Then he called the operator and asked for the number of the University of Wisconsin at Madison.

He had just been connected to the administration office when Karen reappeared. He couldn't help smiling at her as she came flapping toward him in a pair of size-eight baseball boots.

"I don't know what the hell you're laughing at," she said as she opened the folding door and crowded into the phone booth next to him.

"Did they pick you for the team next season?" Jack asked her.

Karen nodded toward the phone. "Who are you calling? Not the cops?"

"Uh-uh. The university. You remember what I said about getting some expert help? They're trying to connect me to the religious-studies department."

"You really think that's going to do any good?"

"It can't do any harm. We have to know what we're up against here."

They waited for almost five minutes while Karen noisily drank her soda, and Jack fed the phone with quarters. At last a distracted voice said, "Department of religious studies?"

"All right," said Jack. "Do you have anybody there who knows anything about Druids? No, no, *Druids*. Yeah, that's right. It's urgent."

The minibus driver let them off on campus, beside Lake Mendota. Huge thunderclouds were building in the inky afternoon sky. "Your department of religious studies is right across there, man," the minibus driver told them. He must have been forty-six years old, with graying shoulder-length hair, impenetrable John Lennon sunglasses, and tie-dyed jeans. He had talked to them all the way from Waunakee with the sipping style of speech peculiar to those who had never quite managed to outlive The Doors and Jefferson Airplane and head shops and who spoke as if they were smoking a roach.

Jack said, "Good luck, and thank you."

"Peace," replied the minibus driver.

They hurried hand in hand across the newly mowed grass. "That's the first time I've been called 'man' in about twenty-five years," Jack remarked. He was hurrying, not because it looked as if it were going to rain, but because he felt unusually defenseless without a car.

Karen asked him, "Is this going to do any good? I mean shouldn't we be trying to find out where this Quintus Miller has actually taken off to?"

"Think about it," Jack replied. "Supposing we find him—what do we do then?"

"Well, couldn't we *shoot* him or something? You have a hunting rifle, don't you?"

"You've been watching too many *Rambo* movies. This character exists under the ground. Not just under the ground, *in* the ground. Or in solid walls, or floors. How do you shoot somebody like that?"

"I don't know," Karen admitted, bustling her bottom to keep up with him. "It's just that talking to professors and stuff... it's so kind of wimpy, you know?"

They reached the arched brick doorway marked DEPARTMENT OF RELIGIOUS STUDIES and pushed their way in through a heavy swinging door. Inside, the building was dark and stuffy, and the green-painted corridor was stacked with boxes of duplicating paper. Jack stopped a tall blond girl with a beaky nose and spectacles.

"I'm looking for Mr. Summers?"

"He's in the common room, right down at the end of this corridor," the girl told him, in an oddly dreamy voice, as if she were talking about God, or at the very least Robert Redford.

Jack and Karen walked the length of the corridor and knocked at the common-room door. There was no reply, so Jack opened the door and they went straight in. On one of a collection of motley sofas, with his feet up, they found a lanky black-bearded man in baggy green corduroy pants and a loose brown sweater, smoking a pipe and contentedly reading a copy of *Woman's Circle Home Cooking*.

"Mr. Summers?" asked Jack.

"That's me," the man replied in a British accent without looking up.

Jack held out his hand. "I'm Jack Reed. I called you earlier."

Mr. Summers looked up. His eyes were slightly bulbous and green like freshly peeled grapes. "So you did. The Druid man, yes? The *urgent* Druid man?"

"That's right. I was wondering if maybe we could talk."

"Of course. I'm not sure that I can tell you anything very useful." He swung his brown suede shoes off the sofa and stood up. "I've been trying to find out why my pot roasts are always so vile."

"You probably don't cook them slow enough," Karen told him. "That's the mistake that most people make. You have to cook them real slow, for hours and hours, otherwise they're tough and they're stringy and they taste like somebody's training shoes."

"Ah! Well, that's probably my problem," said Mr. Summers. "Too impatient! You wouldn't think that anybody who had devoted their life to the study of comparative religion would be impatient, would you? But there you are."

He frowned at Jack suddenly and said, "You were calling from a *garage*, weren't you?"

"Let me tell you something," said Geoff Summers. "These ley lines have far more power than modern scientists understand, particularly at certain times of the year. For example, the bluestones that the ancient Britons used to build Stonehenge came from the Prescelly Mountains of Pembrokeshire, one hundred thirty-five miles away from the site where they were eventually set up—even though some of the stones weigh fifty tons.

"In terms of modem science, nobody has yet been able to explain how the ancient Britons could have moved a fifty-ton stone one mile, let alone one hundred thirty-five. But the Druidic story says that the stones were simply *summoned*, and that they crept along the ley lines from Wales to Stonehenge, under the ground, by *themselves*."

"That's weird," said Karen. "That's really weird."

"Unfortunately it's impossible to substantiate," Geoff Summers replied, with his eyes fixed on the waitress. "But it's happened in America, too. At Mystery Hill, in New Hampshire, and in Arizona, too. The Pima Indians have a legend about Tcu-Wutu-Makai, the Solid-Earth-Magician, who could walk through the ground. And we've had quite a few modern sightings of earth-walkers.

"In Applebachsville, in Pennsylvania, in 1881, a woman saw the figure of a naked man moving along the wall of her farmhouse, and as recently as 1903, a farmer in Pewamo, in Michigan, swore to his local newspaper that he had seen a field full of human arms. He swore blind that they had snatched his white prize bull and dragged it right down into the ground."

"Do you believe that?" Jack asked cautiously.

"I don't know," said Geoff Summers, lighting another match and singeing the fresh tobacco in the bowl of his pipe. "But in religious studies, we're not as skeptical as anthropologists, say, or pure historians. We make allowances for the mystical side of life. And—you see—what that Michigan farmer said did actually tally with Druidic lore. Once a priest was intermingled with the earth, a blood sacrifice would be necessary to allow him to return to the air. Sometimes several blood sacrifices."

He puffed smoke, and then he said, "The Druids kept their rituals secret, so nobody can tell how many people they actually sacrificed. There are very few human remains at any of their sacred sites, two or three skulls, a couple of thighbones, so most historians have assumed that they scarcely held any blood sacrifices, perhaps none at all.

"But the stories and legends are quite explicit. The early Druids were supposed to have killed men and women by the hundreds, and not very nicely, either. They were said to have castrated the men and pulled out the women's wombs. They tore off their arms and legs, and scattered their blood on the ground. Whole villages were decimated that way. It was said that they studied the writhings of their dying victims in order to divine the future."

Karen pressed the heel of her hand against her forehead in a quick, fretful gesture. Geoff Summers said, "I'm sorry... I didn't mean to turn your stomach."

But Karen glanced at Jack and Jack knew that it wasn't squeamishness that was making her feel so upset. It was her fear of Quintus Miller and his followers, forging their way through the darkness of the ground, with an appetite for blood that was whetted in equal parts by stone-age mysticism and by sheer criminal insanity.

Jack said to Geoff Summers, "Is there any way—do you know of any way at all—in which these earth-walkers could be stopped?"

Geoff Summers observed him for a while with his grape green eyes. "Stopped, what do you mean by stopped?"

"I mean killed. Could anybody track them down and kill them?"

"Jack," said Geoff Summers slowly, "I am beginning to ask myself just what it is that you've got yourself into."

"I'm asking you a question, that's all. How do you kill them?"

Geoff Summers slowly shook his head. "I'm not saying another word until I find out what this is all about."

Jack took a deep breath. "I can't tell you anything, not yet. Somebody could get hurt. I have a young son, as a matter of fact. *He* could get hurt. Can we just make a deal? You tell me what you know about earth-walkers, and when it's safe for me to do so, I'll come back and I'll tell you everything. I'll even write it down for you."

"You bastard," Geoff Summers told him cheerfully. "Have you *found* an earth-walker?"

"Uh-uh," Jack replied. "I don't know what I've found. But, please. I need your help. I'm not asking for you to give me anything for nothing. I'll pay you. What do you want? How does twenty-five hundred sound? Cash, no taxes."

"Have you actually *found* an earth-walker?" Geoff Summers repeated.

Jack slammed the flat of his hand on the table and struggled out of his seat, bruising his thigh on the armrest. "I told you, Geoff—I need your help. I need all the help that I can get. But I can't explain what's happening because I'm not at all sure what's happening myself. If you *won't* help— well, I'll have to find somebody who will."

Geoff Summers quickly took his pipe out of his mouth

and lifted his hand. "Wait, Jack—*fanites!* Come on, now, let's not go rushing off madly in all directions. Just answer me that one question—just tell me if you've found an earth-walker. And whether your answer is yes or no, I'll tell you what I know about the Druids, I promise. It isn't very much—you could find out most of it for yourself if you knew which books to read. But after that I won't ask you any more questions till you're ready. How does that sound?"

Jack hesitated. All hell would be snapping at his heels when the police found out what had happened to Joseph Lovelittle and Father Bell and Essie Estergomy and Daniel Bufo—not to mention the Girl Scouts and all the other people that Quintus Miller and his lunatics might already have massacred. Before he confessed to any involvement in what had happened, Jack wanted to find Quintus Miller first, and make sure that he destroyed him.

And if Randy were still alive—somewhere, somehow— he wanted to save him, too.

"This is very complicated," he said. He sat down again.

"The Druids were very complicated people," Geoff Summers assured him. "They understood the world they lived in, they understood its powers, and they used them to devastating effect. Here we are, four thousand seven hundred years later, and we *still* can't come up with any rational scientific explanation for the building of Stonehenge, or Easter Island, or Carnac in France, or Mystery Hill. Either *why* they built them, or *how*."

Karen put in, "Geoff, it's true, we've found one. An earth-walker. Well, more than one, as a matter of fact."

"*Karen,*" Jack protested, but Karen said, "It wasn't your

fault. Jack! It wasn't your fault! And what else are you going to do? Somebody has to know about it. They scare me, Jack. They really scare me."

Geoff's eyes lit up, and he leaned forward on the table with his pipe puffing like an old-time locomotive. "This is great! You're going to let me in on it? I've been waiting for something like this! Listen to me, Jack, if this is true, if you've really found an earth-walker, then this is the rarest mystical event in decades. My doctorate is in the bag."

"I don't give a shit for your doctorate!" Jack retorted. "Those people have *my* son!"

Geoff sat back, abashed. "I'm sorry. Listen, I'm sorry. I didn't understand." But then he leaned forward again, with renewed enthusiasm. "If you let me in on it, believe me, Jack, I'll do everything I can to help you to get him back."

Jack repeated, with exaggerated patience, "Just tell me how to kill them."

"Well..." said Geoff, "this is only a story, you understand? There is no historical evidence for any of this. But then— ha!—so what? There's no historical evidence for earth-walking, either. To kill an earth-walker—this is what the Druids said—you have to drive him with incantations to a point where the earth comes to an end. Like the edge of a cliff, perhaps. You have to force him into an area from which he can't escape. Then you have to break apart the earth or stone in which he is hiding, and kill him in the ritual Druidic fashion."

"And pardon my ignorance, what is the ritual Druidic fashion?" asked Jack.

Geoff smiled. "You have to bend him over backward, until his spine breaks."

Jack was silent for a long time, picking up the book of matches marked "*Lindstrom's Farm*" and dropping them again. "And these—what-do-you-call-them?" he asked. "These incantations? What are you supposed to incant?"

"Nobody knows. Sorry about that. The Druids did have a written language, apparently, but—well, you know. It's like so many things. Lost in the murky mists of time."

"Lost in the murky mists of time, huh?" said Jack. "That's a fat lot of help."

"Well, I'm sorry. But that's all I know. This was over four thousand years ago. There aren't any Druids left around to ask. Well, there's a modem order of Druids, but they're nothing but a bunch of eccentric Welshmen who dress up in sheets at weekends."

But Karen had been gum chewing furiously and thinking hard. "Jack—listen—the holy water kept them there, didn't it?"

Jack said, "The holy water kept who where?" He was very tired.

She shifted her gum to the other side of her mouth. "Didn't you tell me the reason the loonies couldn't get out of the building was because it had holy water all around it? Didn't you tell me that? And because that priest had said all the right prayers. Like, you know—'stay put, you unclean spirits, or else.'"

Jack nodded. "That's right!" he said. "That's absolutely right. So if they can't escape a ring of holy water... maybe we could use holy water and prayers instead of a Druid incantation."

In their excitement they forgot about Geoff Summers, who was watching them in ever-increasing fascination and amazement.

"There must be books with all the right prayers and stuff," Jack told Karen. "Then all we need to do is to find ourselves some holy water—out of a font or something—and when we're ready we can track those bastards down."

Geoff Summers said politely, "I can help."

Jack turned back to him. "I'm sorry, believe me. But you're not supposed to be listening to any of this."

"I can *help*," Geoff insisted. "I have all of the books that you need. All of the rituals of exorcism, all of the spells for dismissing demons. Even a prayer for ridding the community of people who have an unorthodox view of the meaning of the Scriptures. Let's put it this way—I don't think 'stay put, you unclean spirits, or else' is really going to work."

Jack hesitated for a moment and then pointed a finger at him. "You want to be in?"

"Of course!" Geoff grinned. "You wanted an expert, I'm an expert. At least as far as comparative religion is concerned."

There was something about Geoff Summers's intense Englishness that made Jack feel more like Dick Van Dyke than ever. *It's Murree Poppuns!* in a fake Cockney accent.

"Okay, then," he said. "You're in. But two warnings, okay? One is, we're not yet ready to tell the police about what's been going on. If we do, we could screw up everything, even worse than it is already. Second, it's very dangerous, and I mean *very* dangerous, and there's a serious possibility of getting yourself hurt."

"Well... I think I can live with that," Geoff replied. "I

enjoy living dangerously. You know—motorcycling with no helmet, yachting with no life preserver. Having it away without a condom."

"There's one thing more," Jack told him. "This whole thing is ultimately down to me. It's my son; it's my situation. That means that you have to do what I say, and you have to do it quick, without asking."

"All right, all right," Geoff Summers reassured him. "Now... are you going to tell me what's going on?"

Jack said, "First of all, I have to find myself a car. Then we have to find a base, somewhere to sleep, somewhere to monitor the news."

"The *news*? You're expecting reports about Druids on the *news*?"

"Geoff," Jack told him, fixing him with an intent stare. "You have no idea how serious this thing is."

"No, well, obviously I don't." He grinned at Karen, and raised his eyebrows, and said, "Gosh!" and Jack suddenly realized how young he was.

9

At 5:30 that evening, a sixty-seven-year-old woman called Matilda Pancic left the Whole-Sum Discount Health Food Store on Lincoln Avenue in West Milwaukee and began to walk the three blocks west to her apartment building.

She hummed as she walked, *"This is my lovely day... this is the day I will remember until the day I'm dying..."*

Close behind her, the concrete sidewalk began to craze over, in a narrow furrow, and although she couldn't hear it because of the traffic, and because she was partially deaf, she was followed by a thick dragging noise. *Sssssssshhhhhh—sssssshhhhhh—sssssshhhhhh.*

Matilda Pancic had been a widow for four years and nine days. Her husband Milton Pancic had been a specialty baker. His photograph stood on her bureau, a bald-headed man with a drooping mustache. He had died of a perforated ulcer the night before their wedding anniversary. The cake he had made for it stood next to his photograph, under glass. For *My Sweetest Matti, Thank You for Forty-Eight Wonderful Years, Yours For Ever, Milton.*

He had brought the cake home at six o'clock. *For Ever* had lasted seventeen minutes.

These days, Matilda Pancic felt the cold, so she wore a head scarf with views of Niagara Falls printed on it, and a dull blue quilted raincoat. Her face was rounder than ever, but what else was there to do but sit in front of the television and eat tropical-fruit yogurt out of the container and think of Milton? Sometimes, in the night, she thought she heard his voice, calling her from the kitchen, as loud and clear as when he was alive.

She stopped at Carswell Drugs to buy the *Milwaukee Journal* and a new toothbrush. Mr. Druker, the horse-faced pharmacist leaned over the prescription counter and said, "You tried that ointment for your eczema, Mrs. Pancic? What did you think?"

She pulled her lips tight with distaste. "Too greasy, Herman—didn't like it. It messed up my sleeves."

"You should try it for a month, at least."

The girl in front of her was taking a long time trying to decide between Honey Dawn hair coloring or Tawny Rapture. Mrs. Pancic peered over her shoulder and said, "Take the brown. With the other, it's too light, you'll look like a floorbrush."

The girl turned round and stared at her and gave an embarrassed whinny through one nostril.

"Take my advice," Mrs. Pancic urged her. "I should know from hair coloring, look at mine. Snowy Surprise."

She cackled at her own joke. But only six inches away from her left foot, the black-and-white vinyl-tiled floor was beginning to ripple and bulge, and the dry, dragging sound seemed to be nearer and nearer to the surface.

"Just the newspaper and the toothbrush," said

Mrs. Pancic, holding them up and showing them to Mr. Druker.

At that instant, the floor beside her foot erupted, ripped-open tiles and spraying concrete, and a massive hairy-backed hand lashed out and seized her ankle.

She shrieked with shock and pitched forward onto the counter, smashing the glass partitions. She dropped heavily onto the floor in a shower of Anacin, Tylenol, Tums, and Tampax.

The girl shrieked, too, and leaped back two or three steps. Mr. Druker said, "Oh my God!"

Matilda Pancic clawed at the plinth around the counter in an effort to pull herself free. But another hand wrenched its way out of the floor and seized her right calf. All the time she said nothing, nothing at all, but lifted her hand toward the counter, trying to get a grip on something solid.

Mr. Druker shouted at his assistant pharmacist, "Call the police!"

"What?" said his balding assistant.

"Call the fucking police!" Mr. Druker screamed at him, the first time he had sworn since 1951, in Korea.

The two huge hands gripped Matilda Pancic and huried her from side to side—smashing her *crakkk*! against the counter, then *crakkk*! gainst the floor, then *crakkk*! against the Hallmark birthday-card stand. Her Niagara Falls scarf suddenly flooded crimson with blood; her arms flailed loose because they were broken. She was smashed from side to side, again and again, until she flew with the blows like a bloody rag doll.

Sirens cried like children in the street outside. A crowd had gathered outside the drugstore already, not to save

Matilda Pancic but to watch her die. Her blood and brains were sprayed against the drugstore window and all across the counter.

See that blood flying? See those whiplashing arms? Look at her face!

At last the huge hands reached up and possessively gripped her. In front of everybody's disbelieving eyes, she was manhandled down into the floor, into the concrete itself, in a tangle of blood and insides and thrown-back head, a gory human jigsaw puzzle that nobody who was watching could quite understand.

The very last thing to disappear was her swollen left foot—an old woman's foot, bandaged. It scraped into the concrete with a sound that set your teeth on edge; flesh against concrete. Flesh *into* concrete.

Then she was gone, and the floor momentarily bulged. The police rushed in, with their guns drawn. "Out of there! Freeze! Police!" But nobody could follow the deep, slurred escape of the man that somebody had once christened Lester.

Shortly after seven o'clock that same evening, a thirty-three-year-old insurance assessor named Arnold Cohn stepped out of the elevator at Parking Level 3 of the Wisconsin Mutual Assurance Building and walked the length of the parking floor, smoothing his hand through his hair.

He was meeting a girl called Naomi Breinstein that evening, for an Italian dinner, and then he hoped to take her back to his apartment in Shorewood to listen to opera. In his briefcase, apart from all the papers on that highly suspicious fire at Voight's Vegetable Warehouse, he carried a new CD recording of *Le Calife de Bagdad* by Francois Boieldieu. Arnold was a real opera buff, far beyond Verdi.

He was concerned about his hair. Even though he was only thirty-three, it was beginning to thin on the crown, to the extent that if he swung his medicine-chest mirror outward so that he could see the back of his head in the mirror in the hallway, white scalp was revealed, gleaming through soft black curls.

Arnold's father was almost completely bald, but it was okay for fathers to be bald. Arnold had never thought for a moment that it would ever happen to *him*. Particularly not *now*, when he had discovered a girl for whom he had developed the genuine hots.

Naomi was a cellist with the Milwaukee Symphony Orchestra. Her hair was dark and came halfway down her back, her eyes were as brown and shiny as all-chocolate M&Ms, her thighs were strong. Arnold had never come across a girl who exuded so much brio.

Arnold had almost reached his car when he thought he heard somebody walking behind him, dragging their feet. He stopped and looked around, but the concrete garage was empty. Arnold had been working late, and apart from his own Volkswagen, only six or seven vehicles still remained. One of those was a Corvette that belonged to his colleague John Radetzky, and which lay permanently shrouded in tarpaulin.

Arnold stayed perfectly still for almost half a minute, suppressing his breathing. But the garage was silent. He said "*hmmph*" to himself for being so nervous and continued walking. He wondered if Naomi might be persuaded to stay the night. He had watched her thighs clasped around her cello. The thought of having them clasped around his waist was enough to make him sweat.

He took out his car keys. As he did so he heard the noise again. *Sssssshhhh—sssssshhhhh—ssssshhhhh*—like somebody dragging a heavy sack. He looked up. It seemed to be coming from the *ceiling*, this noise; from Parking Level 2. Yet Parking Level 2 had been deserted, and in darkness, when he had passed it in the elevator. It was usually only used for daytime visitors.

"Anybody there?" he called out. *There?* mimicked his echo.

He unlocked his car door. *Sssssssssssshhhhhh*, whispered the noise. This time Arnold swung around really quickly.

"Listen—if there's anybody there, you'd better understand that your presence here is unauthorized, and that I'm going to inform the building super on my way out of here."

It was then that he saw the tarpaulin shroud over John Radetzky's car rippling slightly. So that was it. Somebody was hiding inside Radetzky's car. Some bum, probably. Either sleeping in it or thinking of stealing the hi-fi system.

Arnold crossed the garage floor as quietly as he could, smoothing his hand over the back of his hair. When he reached the covered-up Corvette, he hesitated for just a moment. Then he bent down and grasped the tarpaulin in both hands.

Right, you bastard. One, two, three! He whipped the tarpaulin back and shouted, "Got you!"

But the car was empty. There was nobody in it to think

what had happened to him, trying simply to get there. *Get there, then you'll be safe.*

He felt freezing cold, and his body seemed to be twice its normal weight. Every time he blinked his left eyelid, a fresh curtain of blood poured down. He tried to remember the words of *Koanga* by Frederick Delius, one of his favorite operas.

He was only six or seven feet away from his car when the concrete underneath him began to rise up, like gray swelling bread. *Earthquake*, his mind told him. But then he felt harsh and powerful arms around him, in a terrible embrace, and roughened breasts pushing themselves against his chest. He blinked his left eye and she was smiling at him, a mad triumphant frightening smile, her face freckled with oil from parked cars and spotted with Arnold's blood.

Make love to me, she demanded. *Come on, my sweetness, make love to me.*

She kissed his raw and lipless mouth, her concrete teeth scraping against his. Then with one powerful tug, she submerged like a diver into the floor and pulled him down with her.

For one split second, Arnold knew pain so intense that it transcended anything he had ever experienced. It was like falling alive into an ocean of meat grinders. As he was crushed and mangled and ripped apart he was amazed that his consciousness could have survived for so long, when his body was nothing more than fats and slimes and fragmented bones and ground-up string. He died amazed. He died in white-hot agony.

There was silence in the garage after he had vanished.

Then, almost inaudibly, the *sssssshhhhhh—sssssshhhhhh—sssssshhhhh* of human flesh moving through solid walls.

At 2:30 the following morning, Officer Gene Spanier of the Milwaukee police force was driving home northward on Lisbon Avenue when he saw what appeared to be a drunk lying on the sidewalk. He drew his car slowly into the curb, turned around in his seat, and looked back, his engine idling. Either a drunk or a stiff, although as far as he knew nobody had reported a stiff. The local residents will step over drunks, but they do prefer to have corpses taken away.

Officer Spanier was very tired. He had been working since eleven o'clock the previous day, and all he wanted was bed. But here was this figure, sprawled face down on the sidewalk, arms by its sides, and supposing this figure was a late figure, and Officer Spanier drove on?

He said a bitter prayer to the Lord God above. *O Lord, You give yachts to bank robbers and Cadillacs to pimps. How come you never give me anything but wall-to-wall buffalo chips? Amen.* He backed up his shuddering eight-year-old Oldsmobile until he was parked right next to the figure, and he examined it with some sanguinity through his tightly closed window.

Inebriated, or exited? It was hard to tell from the curbside. He couldn't detect any breathing, and the figure's face was the strangest color, almost the same color as the concrete on which it lay. Its coat was concrete-colored, too.

A man, maybe thirty-five years old, stockily built, Polish or German maybe.

GRAHAM MASTERTON

Officer Spanier backed up a foot or two farther and saw
that the figure had bare feet. Concrete-colored bare feet.

Drunk, had to be. No sign of blood. No sign of head
injury. But on the other hand, his face was that awful
concrete color—wasn't it?—and his chest didn't appear to
be rising and falling as he breathed. And even if he *wasn't*
dead—even if he was just drunk—he could be suffering
from alcohol poisoning. Officer Spanier might be able to
save his life.

*If there is any point in saving a man lying facedown-
drunk on Lisbon Avenue at two-thirty in the morning*,
thought Officer Spanier, without charity. He had never
liked the parable of the Good Samaritan. He didn't know
many policemen who did. Most of the time the people they
saved didn't even want to be saved, and the rest of the time
they weren't worth it. Bums, junkies, would-be suicides,
unemployed brewery workers, crazy Polacks.

Officer Spanier was thirty-nine years and fifty-one
weeks old, and he had just been divorced for the second
time. He opened his eyes two hours too early every single
morning and lay there wondering what his life was all
about. Next week he was going to be forty. He lived in a
two-room apartment with a soprano saxophonist upstairs
and a prostitute across the hall. The soprano saxophonist
played excruciatingly bad imitations of Roland Kirk and
the prostitute wore tight white short-shorts that cut like the
sharpest of knife cuts between her legs, and both of them
bothered him differently but equally. He drank a lot of Jack
Daniel's when he was off duty and laughed sardonically at
"Miami Vice." And why not? Neither a white Armani suit
nor a red Ferrari Daytona were necessary adjuncts to being

a happy cop. All you needed was a good wife who didn't nag you and burn your frittata and who didn't turn around when you climbed into bed looking like Frankenstein Meets the Three Stooges and then use her full-length brushed-nylon nightdress to enforce a state of monkitude on you. You could do without those fucking Milwaukee winters, too. That wind blowing right off the lake like facefuls of razors marinated in ice-cold vodka.

Grunting, and with huge reluctance, Officer Spanier heaved himself out of the driver's seat. Since his divorce, he had put on fifteen pounds, as well as growing a Teddy Roosevelt mustache. His greatest hero was Burt Reynolds. He had a signed photograph of himself and Burt Reynolds, arm in arm, at Universal Studios. *For Gene, With Best Squiggle, Burt Reynolds*. He could never make out what the squiggle meant.

He hunkered down next to the sprawled-out figure on the sidewalk. No smell of alcohol. No smell of anything. Drunks usually reeked like drunks, and stiffs usually stank of shit. Loss of anal tension. But this hombre didn't smell of anything at all. Officer Spanier regarded him with professional disinterest for a minute or two and then sniffed and said, "Hey fellow, you sleeping, or what?"

The figure on the sidewalk remained totally still. Not drunk, not dead, but completely inanimate.

Officer Spanier reached out and cautiously touched the figure's arm. It was cast out of concrete, it was a statue, for Christ's sake. Somebody had made a statue and laid it on the sidewalk.

He pushed it but it wouldn't move. He couldn't even work his fingers underneath it. It was fused into the sidewalk like it was an integral part of the concrete. Jesus. Somebody had cast a paving slab into a sculpture and just left it here. Anybody could have tripped over it, broken their leg. The whole idea of it was totally crazy, the kind of thing that happened in California, but here in Milwaukee?

Yet whoever had created it, it was brilliant. You had to scrutinize it from two inches away before you realized it was concrete. The detail was incredible. Whoever made it, they should be manufacturing rubberized women, comforters for divorced cops.

The trouble was, now that Officer Spanier had found this sculpture, Officer Spanier would have to file a report; and Officer Spanier would have to locate the sculptor, and make an arrest, if sculpting the sidewalk was an indictable offense. Maybe it came under vandalism, or public disorder.

Maybe he could solve everything by levering the sculpture off. He could use the sharp end of his tire iron and chip into the concrete. He must be able to move it. If somebody had put it here, somebody else must be able to take it away. All he had to do then was to drop the goddamned thing in the lake and pretend that it had never existed.

He went back to his Oldsmobile, opened the trunk, and stretched inside for the tire iron. While he was doing so, he thought he heard something scraping, and he stopped and looked around, but Lisbon Avenue was totally deserted. *Nothing*, thought Officer Spanier. *Late-night jitters.*

He returned to the sculpture. *I really cannot believe this. I'm supposed to be home and in bed. But here I am, chiseling a human figure off the sidewalk. I should have listened to Uncle Albie and taken up that trailer dealership.*

At least I would have made some money. At least I wouldn't be squatting on the goddamned sidewalk at three o'clock in the morning, coping with the lunatic handiwork of some fruitcake artist.

Wheezing softly, Officer Spanier knelt down beside the sprawled-out figure and positioned the chisel-shaped end of his tire iron right where its cheek met the sidewalk.

He was about to chip into the concrete when the statue flicked open its eyes and stared at him. Officer Spanier dropped his tire iron with a clang and stood up, nervously wiping his hands on the thighs of his jeans.

"You moved," he accused the sculpture. "You opened your eyes."

The statue smiled. *Nothing is ever what it seems to be. You're a policeman. You should know that.*

Officer Spanier picked up his tire iron and brandished it. "I'm warning you. Whatever the hell you are, you're under arrest. I'm going to read you your rights."

I know my rights. My rights are given by Awen, the greatest of names.

"Just stand up, mister. Stand up slow. Keep your hands in sight, no false moves."

I cannot stand. Not yet.

"I said, up!" Officer Spanier snapped at him.

That's impossible. The concrete is me and I am the concrete.

"If you don't stand up of your own accord, mister, I'm going to drag you up."

Officer Spanier seized the collar of the statue-man's coat and tried to haul him on to his feet. But—"shit!"—it was impossible. Either the statue-man was impossibly heavy, or

Officer Spanier was too exhausted after sixteen hours on duty to lift up squat, or else the statue-man really *was* part of the sidewalk. A living, breathing part of the sidewalk.

What the hell was he going to do now?

Give me your hand, the statue-man told him. His voice was thick and blurred, as if he had a mouthful of fine wet sand.

Officer Spanier shifted the tire iron to his left hand and offered his right. The statue-man reached up and clasped it. Tight. Tight like steel.

"Okay, mister, up!" Officer Spanier demanded.

No, my friend. It is you who are coming down.

Officer Spanier tugged at the statue-man's hand. But his strength was extraordinary. Officer Spanier had never felt anything like it. He tried to twist his hand free but he couldn't.

"Hey! Let go of my...!"

But the statue-man suddenly twisted in the sidewalk, with a smile on his face, and plunged into the concrete and disappeared. Officer Spanier yelled out, "*Stop!*" but then he was pulled down into concrete, too.

He had dived into Lake Michigan on a February morning to save a drowning woman. He had dived through fire to rescue two small children from a blazing apartment. He had dived through a plate-glass window to avoid being shot at by a crack-crazed Polack with a sawed-off shotgun. But nothing could have prepared him for being forced headfirst into the solid sidewalk of Lisbon Avenue. He was smashed into the concrete with such force that he felt as if his soul were coming apart. It was impossible for a human body to penetrate concrete, yet he felt the statue-man dragging him deep inside it, stripping away skin, unraveling arteries—sieving his flesh into bright red pulp.

He felt death closing in on him, like the closing shutter of a camera. *I'm dying, I can't believe it, this is the end of my life.* He thought he could hear himself screaming, but it was probably nothing more than the atoms of his brain, splitting apart like a supernova.

Officer Spanier disappeared into the sidewalk like a man sinking into a swimming pool. Lisbon Avenue remained silent and deserted. Officer Spanier's abandoned Oldsmobile stood with its door still open, the keys still hanging in the ignition.

Then, after a quarter of an hour, a dark wet stain appeared on the sidewalk, following the cracks in the concrete.

The stain grew wider and wider, and then suddenly a thick tomato soup began to gout out of the ground, quarts and quarts of it.

The soup was Officer Spanier—liquefied flesh, blood, and pulverized bone. He poured across the sidewalk and into the gutter, and then began to drip down the drains.

Early the following day, in Room 516 of the Hyatt Regency Hotel, on Milwaukee's Grand Avenue, a nineteen-year-old psychology student called Rhoda Greenberg opened her eyes and lifted her head off the pillow and frowned toward the window and wondered where the hell she was. Then she heard snorting, and so with all the fastidiousness of a mortician, she picked up the tangled blanket and inspected the gray-haired man sleeping heavily beside her, and she remembered.

You've done it again, Rhoda, you whore.

She tiredly dragged aside the blanket and climbed naked out of the bed. She went to the window, yawning and scratching her thick black curly hair, and noisily tugged open the drapes. Outside, downtown Milwaukee lay ghostly in the mist from Lake Michigan—the bell tower of city hall with its distinctive green roof rising above the haze like the tower of some Eastern European capital. The clock on the bell tower told her that it was five after six in the morning. Her mouth tasted of sour red wine, and her head pounded.

She looked toward the bed. One fat arm, skin white as liver sausage and thickly covered with gray hair, lay exposed on top of the blanket. It wore a steel Seiko wristwatch and a wedding band. Rhoda didn't know whether she felt disgusted with herself or not—or, if she did, how much. She had done this so often now that it was difficult to evaluate her sense of guilt. She knew very well that she would do it again, when the mood took her.

She stood by the window for a long time, in the pearly-colored light. She was not at all pretty. Her nose was hooked and far too large; her lips were thick and her chin was as weak as Olive Oyl's. She had photographs at home of her grandmother back in Breslau when she was young, and she could have been the same girl.

What she did have, however, was a spectacular figure. Her breasts were huge and rounded and firm, her waist was so narrow that most men could close their hands around it. Her legs were long, with slim thighs and perfect ankles.

She had learned when she was thirteen that men lusted

after her. They didn't want to be seen with her, they didn't want to take her dancing. She was too plain and toothy and frizzy-haired and she brayed when she laughed. But men used to go out of their way to touch her breasts and to slide their hands up her skirt. She had even caught her father once, staring at her in appalled fascination through the crack of the bathroom door, one hand on his heart, whiskey on his breath, his eyes the color of Spam.

Rhoda ached for friendship, companionship, love, and affection, just as much as any other girl. Just because she didn't have the face of a prom queen, that didn't mean she didn't have emotional needs. But when men looked at Rhoda, they never looked at her face; and she had never once been taken to a party. She had decided at the age of fifteen that if men weren't prepared to give her what she wanted, she would just have to take from men whatever she could get.

She had openly chased (and laid) every single boy in her senior class at High School, except for two, who were gay; and she had gone to bed with three of her teachers, too. Now that she was studying psychology at the University of Wisconsin Milwaukee, she had taken to spending her few spare evenings at the Hyatt or the Sheraton, or around the stores on Grand Avenue, picking up lonely businessmen. Cosmetic and jewelry counters and lingerie stores were always good places to find them, as they clumsily tried to find gifts to take home to their wives.

Rhoda was always so sweet and helpful. "Do you know what I would buy her, if I were you...?"

Back in their hotel rooms, however, she humiliated them; she made them crawl. She called them filthy and degrading names and made them perform the most disgusting acts she could think of. And the extraordinary part about it was, they always did what she told them. Some of them adored her so much they wanted to set her up as their regular dominatrix, in an apartment of her own.

She always refused. She didn't want to be owned by anyone. But she made thousands of dollars, and she always expected each man to give her an expensive gift. Jewelry, or perfume, or dresses.

She left the window and walked through to the bathroom without giving the sleeping man on the bed another glance. She couldn't even remember what his name was. All she remembered was that he was short and hairy, and that he had burst into tears after they had finished having sex. She never thought of what she did as "making love."

She switched on the bathroom light and looked at herself in the mirror. Dark circles under her eyes. She would have to catch up on some sleep this weekend. She brushed her teeth, spat, brushed them again.

As she was rinsing out her mouth she heard a noise behind her, like somebody brushing against the shower curtain. *Sssh.*

She looked in the mirror, but there was nobody standing in the bathroom behind her. She filled the washbasin with cold water so that she could bathe her swollen eyes. She wished that she wouldn't drink red wine; it always gave her such a paralyzing hangover.

Then she heard the noise again, longer and slower this time. *Sssshhh—sssshhhhh.*

She turned around, frowning. The bathroom was empty;

the shower curtain hadn't stirred. She went to the door and looked into the bedroom, but Short 'n' Hairy was still fast asleep, and snoring.

Oh, well, maybe it's the plumbing, she thought. *You know what these hotels are like. Every time somebody goes to the john, everybody else can hear it in graphic detail.*

She washed her face, patted it dry, and then opened up her makeup bag. She always liked to use plenty of makeup. False eyelashes, garish red lipstick. It was better to look like a hooker than a mouse.

She squeezed glue on to the first of her false eyelashes. She smiled at the memory of one of her men, who had discovered her eyelashes on the bathroom shelf and squashed them up in toilet paper and flushed them down the john, because he thought they were centipedes.

She was still smiling to herself when the water in the washbasin abruptly emptied of its own accord and gurgled away.

She jiggled the lever that operated the plug. Then she filled up the basin again; but again the water emptied itself out. She peered down at the plug. Maybe it wasn't straight.

She was still trying to work out what was wrong with the plug when she felt something catch at her hair. *Damn it,* she breathed, and tried to lift her head out of the basin; but somehow her long curly hair had become entangled in the drain, and she couldn't pull it out.

Carefully she attempted to unwind her hair from the plug. She couldn't work out how it had become so hopelessly snarled up. The more she tried to disentangle it, the more wound up it became. Her head was now being pulled quite painfully down into the basin, until her forehead was pressing against the cold ceramic.

"Oh, for God's sake," said Rhoda, not just impatient now, but panicky. She didn't want to cut her hair to get it free, but she couldn't work out how she bad gotten so hopelessly ensnared.

"Hey!" she shouted out, trying to wake up Short 'n' Hairy in the bedroom. "Hey, give me a hand here, will you? Hey!" She wished that she could remember what his name was. Something like Herman or Harry or Herbert.

"Hey, Herman!" she called. "Herman, I'm stuck! Herman, get me out of here!"

As soon as she had said that, however, her hair was forcibly wrenched downward into the drain, as if somebody had actually snatched hold of it, and pulled it. Her forehead was knocked against the basin, and she cried out in fear. *"Help me! Help me! For God's sake, Herman, help me!"*

Rhoda's face was pulled harder and harder against the washbasin. She felt the skin crackle all over her head as her scalp was being lifted away from her skull. She screamed again and again and again, but the relentless pulling continued.

"What the hell's the matter, what the hell are you screaming for?" She heard Short 'n' Hairy Herman's voice, close beside her. She opened her eyes and saw his worried face, upside down.

"I'm caught, my hair's caught, get me out!"

Herman grasped her head and tried to yank it upward. Rhoda screamed even more piercingly, and he let her go.

"Not like that, you stupid bastard!" she raged at him, her eyes filled with tears. "The plug, take out the plug!"

Herman wrestled with the plug for a while, rattling the lever up and down like a child pretending to drive a train, but then he gasped, "I can't. Your hair's all knotted up, it won't come out."

"For God's sake it's pulling me down!" Rhoda sobbed.

She glimpsed the ruffles of fat on Herman's big white bottom; his fist clenched in indecision. "Maybe I should try scissors," he suggested in a windy voice. "Do you want me to try scissors?"

"Just get me out!" she begged him. Her hair was being dragged with such force into the drain that she thought that it was going to be ripped out by the roots. Then it was tugged, and tugged, and tugged, as if in furious impatience; and the pain was so intense that it surged way beyond anything she was able to bear, and she started screaming again, blind purposeless screaming, against the cold ceramic of the washbasin.

Herman backed away. "Listen," he said, "I'd better find somebody to help. Can you hold on? Can you just hold on?"

He hurried back into the bedroom to find his clothes. "Jesus H. Christ." Rummaged wildly around for his shirt and his socks. "What the hell did I do with my necktie? Jesus, stop screaming, Jesus."

Rhoda took a deep trembling breath before screaming again; but this time she didn't scream at all. Two glistening white hands emerged smoothly from the washbasin and grasped her head on either side and pulled it downward, into the ceramic itself.

Herman reappeared at the open bathroom door, half-dressed, his cheeks stiff with fear. He saw Rhoda's naked body, bent over the washbasin, shuddering as if she were being electrocuted. The washbasin itself was brimming and slopping with blood.

Herman stared at Rhoda for a very long time. He had never seen anybody killed. It didn't even occur to him that Rhoda was dying in a way that defied all the laws of the natural world. Last night she had forced him to crawl across the carpet. Now she was bent over in front of him, her knees and elbows rigid with agony, right on the point of death.

He felt an extraordinary sexual excitement. She was naked and she was being killed and he couldn't look away.

At last, with an awkward little genuflection, he caught hold of the bathroom doorknob and closed the door. He breathed deeply. Then he took out his handkerchief and wiped the doorknob clean. He had probably left thousands of fingerprints all over the room, but somehow this one token gesture made him feel safer. It erased at least the fact that he had watched her dying. He went back to the bedroom, trembling, and sweaty, and very white, and packed his suitcase.

When he was packed, he went back to the bathroom door and listened. All he could hear was a slow, thick dripping. He wondered if he ought to take a last look, but he decided against it. If anybody asked him, he would deny that he had ever seen the girl before—she must have broken into his hotel room after he had checked out, and committed suicide. It was obviously suicide. Cut her throat, in the washbasin.

He knew that his wife Marcia would stand up for him. He could almost hear her now. "In thirty-seven years of marriage, my Herman has never been unfaithful once." That tight gray permanent wave nodding. He was sweating like a pig and he was so short of breath that he had to lean against the wall and tell himself: *Breathe, breathe, for Christ's sake, breathe.*

At last he managed to stop gasping. *You're all right, all you have to do now is to check out, and smile, and take the plane back to Indianapolis, and nobody will ever be able to prove that you had anything to do with it.*

He picked up his plaid valise and turned toward the door.

He was chilled to the spot, in a greater terror than he had ever experienced in his life.

The door itself had bulged out, into the shape of a short, muscular man. The man was staring at him and smiling, his face streaked like war paint with the brown-and-gold patterns of the wood veneer.

Herman stood and looked at the man in the door and didn't know what to do. He didn't dare to reach for the door handle.

"What do you want?" he whispered at last.

The man in the door continued to smile, continued to stare, and there was something about his smile that convinced Herman beyond any possible doubt that he would never be allowed to leave this hotel room alive.

It happened all over Milwaukee, and Wauwatosa, and Cudahy, and Whitefish Bay. On East Kilbourn Avenue, three-year-old twins were found crying in their baby buggy, apparently abandoned by their mother in the middle of shopping. On North Sixth Street, a well-known brewer vanished from his car while waiting at a traffic light, with no indication of where he had gone but the car's violently torn-apart seats.

Right beside the Domes at the Mitchell Park Horticultural Conservatory, three members of a wedding party were dragged into the pavement in front of a hundred horrified but helpless witnesses as they posed for photographs.

A thirty-two-year-old architect was coming back from the men's room at Mader's Restaurant when he disappeared without any trace at all.

Jack listened to the television news all day, trying to keep track of how many people were disappearing. By midafternoon, it was dozens, and he could tell by the news reports that a strong feeling of panic was beginning to sweep through Milwaukee. Governor Earl had already declared a state of emergency in the area, and the National Guard had been alerted.

"But the plain truth is that we have no idea of what we're trying to combat here... whether these disappearances are due to some kind of natural phenomenon, a variety of seismological disturbance... or whether they're part of some criminal conspiracy...."

Jack looked at Geoff Summers and Geoff Summers shrugged. "Should we tell them?" asked Jack.

"Do you think they'd believe us if we did?" Geoff replied.

"Not for a moment."

"Then we're better off keeping quiet and trying to work out some way of stopping them before it's too late. I'm a great believer in doing things for oneself. The minute you start bringing in officialdom, you're lost."

Geoff had arranged for them to stay in a small back-street house on the outskirts of Madison, with a veranda overgrown with gourds and a rocking chair and a scruffy overgrown vacant lot next door. The house belonged to a professor of physics who was lecturing in Scandinavia for two years, and Geoff had a key because he was supposed to water the ferns. Geoff thought it would be unlikely that anybody would find them here.

It was a dull, headachy afternoon, with the sky dark and low over the treetops and a smell of impending rain in the air. They were sitting on bean bags in the physics professor's front parlor, drinking coffee out of Garfield mugs. Jack was close to giving up. He had let loose an uncontrollable horde of violent criminals, and every life they claimed was his responsibility. He was beginning to believe that even Geoff and Karen blamed him now.

"If only we had some way of tracking them down," he said. "Some way of finding out where they are, *before* they reach out and snatch people."

Geoff was leafing through a huge musty-smelling book called *Ritual and Magic in Pre-Christian Times*. "I've been trying to find the ritual the Druids used to use for getting inside the ground. I thought that perhaps we could hunt them down that way."

"You mean, go into the ground *ourselves*?" Jack asked him.

"How else are we going to locate them?"

"God knows," Jack replied.

Karen said, "Hold on—this is the news." She lifted the television remote control and turned up the sound. On the screen were several utility workers in hard hats, talking to the police and to TV reporters.

One of the utility workers was saying, "...digging here to lay new electric cables, right? And all of a sudden my divining rods go haywire. So Louis here says what the hell's happening, excuse my French, and suddenly he falls right into the pavement, and that's it, he's gone."

"You mean he fell right into your excavation?" the TV reporter asked him.

The utility worker shook his head emphatically. "No, lady. He was nowhere near the excavation. He fell right into the road. He disappeared into solid pavement."

The TV reporter turned to face the camera. "And so here on East Wisconsin Avenue yet another unaccountable disappearance, the eighteenth in the Milwaukee area in just twenty-four hours. A utility worker vanishes into the solid roadway, leaving his coworkers mystified. The police so far are 'keeping an open mind.' But there have been calls already for a special investigation, and hundreds of Milwaukee residents are leaving the area by road or by air until the disappearances are satisfactorily explained and stopped. All roads to General Mitchell Field—"

Jack reached over and turned off the sound. He turned to Geoff with a serious face. "You know what we're going to get now? We're going to get a major hysteria. We're going to have to think of something quick."

But Geoff was looking thoughtful. "Did you hear what that utility worker said?"

"Sure. His friend disappeared into the solid pavement."

"Yes, but before then."

"I don't know. Just that they were laying electric cables."

Geoff closed his book and put it aside. "He said 'my divining rods went haywire.'"

"Oh, yes?" asked Jack, still baffled.

"Listen—" said Geoff, "the utility services use divining rods before they excavate the highway so that they can locate water and gas pipes and dig into the ground without damaging them. But the Druids used to use divining rods, too—to locate ley lines. Actually the Druids used hazel twigs... but they worked on exactly the same principle."

"So what are you trying to suggest?" said Jack.

"Well, if Quintus Miller and his chums make divining rods go haywire whenever they're around, perhaps we can recruit somebody who knows how to use divining rods to track the buggers down."

Karen said, "How about that guy on the television—the utility worker?"

"Good thinking," said Geoff. "Jack, why don't you call the electric company; see if you can find out who that chap was."

"And what are you going to do?"

Geoff picked up his book again. "I'm going to try and find out how we can deal with these maniacs once we've found them."

"I thought we had to bend them double or something," put in Karen.

"That's right... but we have to do it in strict accordance with Druidic ritual. Once they've traveled through the ground, remember, these people are not quite human anymore. They're rather *more* than human. We have to make sure that when we sacrifice them to Awen, they stay sacrificed. Otherwise they may return in an even more savage form and track *us* down."

Karen shuddered. Jack picked up the phone.

10

They met Otto Schröder in Watertower Park, underneath the 175-foot Gothic water tower that gave this part of Milwaukee's east side an incongruous similarity to Disneyland. The sky was brilliantly blue but the wind was piercing, and Otto Schröder was wearing a speckled woolly hat pulled over his ears and a leather USAF jacket with a lambswool collar, and he was jogging in place to keep himself warm.

"I feel the cold," he told them. "I should've had an inside job, you know? Bad circulation. But it's too late now."

Jack said, "Come and have a cup of coffee."

"It's okay. I just had lunch. I'm not supposed to be meeting you guys anyway. My foreman said not to talk to anybody."

"Well, we're not just anybody," Geoff told him. "We happen to know exactly what happened to your friend."

Otto Schröder sniffed and wiped his nose with the heel of his hand. "He went straight into the blacktop. He just vanished. I don't know whether the cops believed me or not."

"We believe you," said Jack. "What's more—we can probably find the people who did it."

Otto Schröder looked at Jack suspiciously, one eye closed against the cold. He was stubby and broad-shouldered, at least four inches shorter than Jack, with pugnacious wind-stung cheeks, and bright gray eyes, and the bluntest of Germanic noses. "Nobody *did* it, mister. Norman just disappeared."

"You didn't see anybody else there?"

Otto Schröder shook his head. "No, sir. Nobody. There wasn't a single person inside of ten feet of Norman when he went."

"Did you see any hands holding him?" asked Jack.

"What do you mean? I just told you. There wasn't a single person inside of ten feet of him."

Geoff said, "What Mr. Reed means is, did you see any hands coming out of the concrete?"

Otto Schröder looked from Jack to Geoff and back again. "What is this, some kind of stupid joke? Are you guys nuts or something?"

Jack said, "We're totally serious. The truth is that there are some very dangerous people who have found a way to move around under the ground. They can go through walls, they can go through doors, you name it. Brick, concrete, rock. As far as they're concerned, it's all the same."

"You *are* nuts," said Otto Schröder. He stuffed his hands in the pockets of his jacket and started to walk away.

"Mr. Schröder, will you please wait?" Geoff begged him.

"You're nuts," Otto Schröder repeated. "I took an early lunch, I wasted almost an hour, and you're nuts."

"But you saw what happened for yourself. You saw your friend disappear right in front of your eyes."

"An optical delusion," Otto Schröder told him. "That's all it was."

Jack reached into his wallet and took out two hundred-dollar bills and pushed them into Otto Schröder's top pocket. Otto Schröder stopped walking, and took the bills out, and carefully uncrumpled them.

Jack said, "There's a thousand in it if you help us. You can go on thinking we're nuts. To tell you the truth I don't give a coffee-colored shit what you think. Those people took your friend and they've taken dozens of other people, too, and they're going to take more. They also took *my* nine-year-old son."

Otto Schröder looked toward Geoff. Geoff said, "It's true, Mr. Schröder. That's why we wanted to talk to you."

"What can I do?" asked Otto Schröder.

"You know how to use divining rods, right?"

"Sure. My grandfather taught me. It's nothing special if you got the feel for it."

"Just before your friend disappeared, you felt the divining rods go out of control, right? Your exact words were, 'they went haywire.'"

Otto Schröder nodded, still suspicious.

Geoff said, "Now—whether you believe it or not—the *reason* your rods went haywire was because one or more of those people were under the ground and they were disrupting the magnetic currents close to where you were working. What exactly did the rods do?"

"They spun. They kind of spun around. Like, the left one going clockwise, and the right one going anticlockwise."

"Did you notice any change in the rods' behavior at the moment that your friend disappeared?"

"I guess I did." Otto Schröder nodded. "They stopped spinning. They stopped dead. I never saw them do that before. And they touched together at the end, just kind of kissed each other, and I got this strong feeling that there was something there. You can't explain it to somebody who doesn't dowse. But it was the same kind of feeling you get when you're close to something very big, like an underground water tank, or a tunnel."

Jack said, "Otto—it's okay if I call you Otto?"

"For sure."

"Otto, there are one hundred thirty-seven of these people. They're all maniacs, criminal psychotics. We have to find them as quick as we can, before they do to more people what they did to your friend. At the moment they can't leave the ground, or the walls—they can't walk around in the air, the same way that we can. But if they manage to kill enough people—well, they'll get out... and then we won't be able to stop them at all."

Otto wiped his nose again. "What do you plan to do with them once you've caught them?"

"The truth is, we're going to have to—" Jack began, but Geoff interrupted him.

"We have a special way of dealing with them," he said, with reassuring smoothness. "That's all you have to know. You don't have to be involved in that part of it in any way. Now—are you willing to help us, or not?"

Otto hesitated for a very long time. "This is on the level?" he asked them.

Jack nodded. "You want more money, I'll pay you twice as much. And look at it this way—if it's *not* on the level, and there's nobody there, what do you have to lose?"

"I guess you have a point there," Otto agreed.

Geoff smiled and slapped Otto on the back. "That's marvelous. And I'm especially glad that it's going to be you, because there's something else that we need."

"Oh, yeah?" asked Otto.

"A compressor and a jackhammer," said Geoff. "Your company wouldn't mind if you borrowed one for a while, would they?"

"A compressor and a jackhammer? What the hell do you need those for?"

"Digging," said Geoff succinctly. "Once we've found them, do you see? We're going to have to dig them out, like potatoes."

They met Otto again at six o'clock that evening, under the East-West Freeway, after they had taken Karen home. Geoff parked his limping Valiant opposite Otto's bashed-up GMC compressor truck and tooted his horn. Otto climbed down from his cab and came across the street.

"I don't know why the hell I'm doing this," he shouted over the noise of the freeway traffic as he climbed into the back of the car and slammed the door. "I must be out of my goddamned mind."

"Would you not slam the door, please?" Geoff asked him. "Diana is rather delicate."

"Diana?" Otto frowned.

"The car," Jack told him. Then, to elaborate, "He's British."

"Oh," said Otto, as if that explained everything.

Geoff remarked, "That truck looks pretty run-down."

"Yeah, sorry. It's the only one the foreman would let me borrow. I told him I was digging a swimming pool in my backyard. He said I was crazy. I agree with him."

"You've brought your divining rods?" Geoff asked him, unabashed.

Otto reached inside his leather jacket and produced two foot-long copper rods with bent handles. "Beauties, aren't they? Made them myself. Some people use iron or brass, but my grandfather used to swear by copper. Said it was much more sensitive than anything else.

"I'll tell you something—with these rods, I can locate a half-inch pipe within an inch of error. And that's something that nobody can do with a hazel twig."

Jack said, "Could I look at those?" and Otto handed them over. Jack swung them in his hands, but he couldn't feel anything at all. "Do you know how they work?" he asked Otto.

Geoff said, "Scientifically inexplicable. They do work—even the most skeptical of scientists have to admit to that. But nobody knows how, or why."

"How about you, Otto?" asked Jack. "Any ideas?"

But Otto shook his head and said, "Search me. It's a feeling, that's all. Kind of a buzz."

"It's something to do with the earth's natural magnetic field," Geoff added. "I was reading up about it this afternoon. The Druids used to use divining rods made out of willow or rowan branches to find out where ley lines ran. And I discovered something else interesting. Right up until medieval times, divining rods were used to track down murderers. Apparently, killers have measurably more natural magnetic charge in their bodies than the rest of us.

Nobody knows *why*—but it could help us to hunt down Quintus Miller and all the rest of his maniacs."

"How are you planning on doing it?" asked Otto, taking back his divining rods and carefully polishing the handles with his handkerchief.

"We have the location of the last reported disappearance," said Jack, opening out his street plan of Milwaukee. "We'll start there... just to see if you can pick up any vibrations."

"And what if we do?"

"Then we circle the area with holy water, and we recite the prayer of exorcism that prevents evil forces from leaving a particular location. That should stop our murderous friend from getting away."

"Then what?"

"We dig the bastard up," said Geoff, rubbing his hands together with relish.

"And then?"

"You don't need to know the rest," Geoff told him. "You can look the other way."

"Hey—I'm not having no hand in no murders," Otto protested.

"Think about your friend Norman," Geoff reminded him. "Have you talked to Norman's widow?"

"He wasn't married. I talked to his sister."

"Well, in that case think about his sister. And think about all the other people who are going to be killed the same way, unless you and I and Jack here do something about it."

Otto sat back in his seat with a deeply unhappy pout on his face. "My wife thinks I'm bowling. I never told her a lie before. Maybe I should forget all of this maniac stuff and *go* bowling."

"Otto—this is your chance to be a hero."

"I don't want to be a hero. Did I say I wanted to be a hero?"

Jack checked his watch. "It's ten after six. We'd better get moving. The first location we're going to try is North Fifth, a block north of MECCA."

Otto hesitated, but Geoff said, "Come on, Otto! Give it a try! You never know, you might enjoy it!"

"I'm dowsing for psychos," Otto muttered as he eased himself out of the car. "I don't believe it. I don't even *half* believe it."

Geoff called, "Don't slam the—" just as Otto gave the door a hefty bang behind him.

"Door," Geoff finished quietly.

For almost ten minutes they paced up and down the sidewalk on North Fifth Street while Otto held his two copper divining rods out in front of him, searching for the tiniest tremor that would tell him that one of the maniacs from The Oaks was somewhere near.

The wind was growing raw, and Jack was beginning to wish that he had brought an overcoat. He was also beginning to wish that he had picked a location that was less conspicuous. They were catty-corner to the Milwaukee Exposition and Convention Center and Arena (MECCA for short), and eleven busloads of conventioneers were arriving for the Midwestern Bakers & Confectioners Jubilee Bake-off. Several conventioneers and homegoing business people and shoppers stopped to watch Otto with guarded fascination as he crisscrossed the sidewalk with his divining rods swinging from side to side.

"Anything?" Jack asked him.

Otto sniffed. "There's a sewage duct that runs across *here*, and a telephone cable that runs across *here*. But nothing else. Nothing moving. Nothing that's what you might call *alive*."

"Keep trying," Jack urged him.

"And if I still don't find nothing?"

"Then we try someplace else."

A man in a gray suit and a snap-brim hat and horn-rim spectacles came up to Jack and said, "Pardon me, sir?" He looked as if he had just arrived from 1962 without stopping to change. "Pardon me, sir, can I ask what your friend is doing?"

"Oh, sure," said Jack. "He's field-testing a new kind of shopping cart. Well, just the handles. The rest of the cart isn't ready yet."

The man watched Otto with grave and respectful interest. "You research people sure go to some lengths," he said at last, and then walked off.

Soon, however, Otto declared, "This location is stone-cold. There's nothing here at all."

"What do you think?" Jack asked Geoff. "Give it up and try the next one?"

"All right," said Geoff reluctantly. "I was just hoping that we could find some trace—you know, even after they're long gone. I was hoping they might leave some sort of natural magnetic footprints, as it were—something to track them by."

"Nothing," said Otto emphatically.

They climbed back into their vehicles and drove east across the Milwaukee River and then south toward the large white sculptured blocks of the Performing Arts Center. A twenty-seven-year-old actress called Millicent Horowitz had vanished from the rooftop parking lot just after three o'clock that afternoon.

They parked the compressor truck and the Valiant side by side, backed up against the parapet that faced the river. Then they crossed the roof to the spot where Millicent Horowitz had disappeared. The area was still cordoned off with fluttering tapes that read POLICE LINE DO NOT CROSS, but there was nobody around to stop Jack and Geoff and Otto from ducking under the tape and approaching the actual point of her disappearance, which was marked with a cross of red adhesive tape.

"I never tried dowsing on a roof before," said Otto, taking out his divining rods again. He stood over the red tape across and moved the rods gently from side to side.

Jack said, "They said on the news that she was walking across here with her boyfriend. He turned around to look at a boat on the river, and when he turned back she was gone. Totally vanished. At first he thought that she had thrown herself off the roof."

Otto said, "I got something."

Geoff stood with his hands on his hips facing the wind. "I don't know—I'm beginning to think this dowsing wasn't such a brilliant idea after all. Especially with somebody who's only sensitive to sewer pipes. Maybe we'll have to try chasing our maniacs underground."

"Any more luck with the ritual?" asked Jack.

"I've found *part* of the ritual. I have a friend at Harvard and he found Nestor Druggett's book *Druidism and the Significance of the Megaliths* in the Harvard library. It's one of the oldest and most comprehensive texts on Druidism that exists. He read me all the relevant passages over the phone. Apparently the Druids used to draw a large pentacle in blood onto a vertical rock, then they used to recite the sacred name of Awen in all its forms, but I can't discover what they did next—what it was that actually caused the rock to open up and admit the Druids physically to the underworld. All that Druggett says is that 'they played the king and thus entered their underground kingdom.'"

"I got something," Otto repeated, his voice thick with excitement. "Here—here, I got something!"

Jack said, "What? What is it?"

The divining rods were visibly vibrating. They were pointing toward the far corner of the roof, but as Jack watched them they began to swing to the left, as if they were tracking something moving.

"What can you feel?" Geoff wanted to know, laying his hand on Otto's shoulder.

"It's like nothing I ever felt before. It's like *circling*, around the roof. Circling all around us. Like it's watching us or something. You know, like a shark circling around somebody swimming."

"Can you tell if it's human?" asked Geoff.

Otto grimaced. "I'm not too sure about that. But it's moving through the ground. It's making kind of a noise. Like a gritty kind of a noise, do you know what I mean? Like when you get sand in your mouth, down on the beach, and it crunches in between your teeth."

They watched in dry-mouthed apprehension as the divining rods swung all the way around in a complete circle. There was no sign of any rippling in the concrete floor of the parking lot, but Jack knew that one of the maniacs was there, circling and circling, watching them, and waiting.

"I feel like a goat, tied up to catch a tiger," Geoff remarked.

"It's coming in closer," said Otto. "It's got this real deep vibration. Like the bottom note on an organ, you know? I never felt anything like this before. It's deep, and it's cold, and it's making this gritty crunching noise."

"I wish to hell I could feel it for myself," said Jack.

"Believe me, you don't," Otto replied. The divining rods swung around again, their tips shuddering closer together, as if they were pointing towards something which was coming nearer with every revolution.

"You've got the prayer ready?" asked Jack.

Geoff nodded, staring at the concrete. "I've learned it by heart, it's only a couple of lines." The relentless approach of the maniac was audible now. That hair-raisingly familiar *sssssshhhhhh—sssssshhhhhh—sssssshhhhhh* that he had first heard at The Oaks.

"You've got the holy water?" asked Jack.

Geoff patted the side pockets of his coat. Then he patted his breast pocket—then his inside pocket. "Oh shit, I've left it in the car!"

"Well, get it, for Christ's sake!" Jack shouted at him. "That lunatic's going to be hitting us any second now!"

Geoff glanced at the divining rods. They were pointing to the right, to the opposite corner of the parking lot. Immediately he made a dash for the police cordon off to the left, ducked under it, and began to run across the roof toward his car.

Immediately the divining rods swung to the left, too, as if the maniac under the floor had been alerted by the vibration of Geoff's running feet.

"Geoff!" yelled Jack. "It's coming after you! Make it quick!"

Otto said, "Holy Moses, look how *fast* it's going!"

Geoff reached his car. The rubber soles of his sneakers skidded on the concrete floor. He wrenched open the driver's door and reached across for the Perrier bottle he had filled up with holy water. But at that instant, a fist burst through the passenger seat of the car with an explosion like a grenade going off and seized his wrist.

"*Jack!*" Geoff yelled out, in panic. "*Jack!*"

Jack swung under the police line and pelted across the roof toward Geoff's car.

"It's got my wrist!" Geoff shouted.

Jack dodged around to the passenger door and pulled it open. Even though Geoff was bracing himself against the door frame, his hand was already being dragged down into the seat, and his skin was being lacerated by the broken springs. Jack hesitated for a second, then bent his head forward and bit into the side of the maniac's thumb, his teeth crunching through muscle and skidding against bone.

The hand released its grip for only one split second, but it was long enough for Geoff to pull himself free. Jack retreated from the car, spitting out blood.

"The water!" he shouted to Geoff. "Pour the water around the car!"

Geoff unscrewed the Perrier bottle and shook holy

water all the way round the car, his face still white with shock. As he walked around he recited the words of the prayer of exorcism, *"Ab insidiis diaboli, libera nos Domine; ut Ecclesiam tuam secura tibi facias libertate seruire, te rogamus, audi nos; ut inimicos sanctae Ecclesiae humiliare digneris, te rogamus, audi nos."*

The concrete beneath the car shuddered with every word, as if somebody were beating against it with a sledgehammer. But when Geoff had finished his prayer, the disturbances stopped, and they could hear nothing but the wind whistling across the parking lot from Lake Michigan, and the hooting and turmoil of traffic.

Otto came over, with his divining rods still held out in front of him.

"What's happened, you got him trapped?"

Jack said, with grim satisfaction, "You bet your ass we got him trapped. Let's shift that car off there and start digging. It could be Quintus Miller himself."

Geoff climbed cautiously back into the Valiant, started the engine, and steered it across to the opposite parking area. They stood around and looked at the concrete where the car had been standing. It had been crushed into lumps where the maniac's hand had forced its way upward, but there was nothing else to suggest that the maniac was still down there.

Otto said, "That's reinforced concrete, solid. It's going to take a hell of a lot of jackhammering to break into that"

"In that case, we'd better get started," said Geoff.

"Supposing somebody asks what we're doing?" Otto asked him. "Like the cops, for instance."

Geoff said, "Urgent maintenance. This is an official utility-company truck, right? And you're an official utility-company employee."

"Jesus, this'd better be worth it," growled Otto. He went around to the back of the truck and hefted down the jackhammer. Then he started up the compressor, covered his ears with mufflers, and began to hack away at the concrete flooring.

The noise was earsplitting, and the vibration made Jack's vision blur. But Otto made faster progress than Jack had expected. The broad-bladed jackhammer chopped into the concrete and broke it into lumps, which he and Geoff cleared away with their hands and stacked against the parapet. Within a quarter of an hour, Otto had cut an oval that roughly followed the perimeter that Geoff had sprinkled with holy water. Within thirty minutes, he was clearing out the edges of the oval, and after an hour's work he was beginning to drill right into the center.

Considering the hellish noise they were making and the racketing echoes of the jackhammer from the white concrete walls of The Performing Arts Center, it was remarkable that nobody came up to ask them what they were doing. Dozens of people drove their cars up onto the roof to park—the Milwaukee Ballet was performing *Swan Lake* tonight—but nobody gave them a second glance. Anybody breaking up the ground so noisily and so blatantly must have had official approval.

But as they reached the center of their rough-and-ready excavation Otto stopped the jackhammer and took off his mufflers and said, "Damned if there's anything here. We're just digging this up for nothing."

Geoff looked across at Jack and said, "What do you think? Do you think we've missed him?"

But Jack kicked at the last remaining island of concrete and said, "This is big enough for a man to hide in, if he curled himself up. Come on, there's a chance, let's keep at it."

"You're the boss." Otto sighed and fitted his mufflers back on.

The jackhammer knocked away one chunk of concrete after another, and then suddenly Jack felt his scalp prickle in fear and excitement. Protruding from one side of the concrete island was the back of a man's bare heel. He swung himself down into the excavation, and tugged at Otto's arm, and pointed out the heel to him in jubilation.

"Got him!" he yelled over the roaring of the compressor. "Got the bastard cold!"

Otto took two or three steps back. "Holy mother of God," he mouthed.

"Come on, dig him out!" Jack urged. "Come on, Otto, before it gets dark!"

But Otto shook his head. "You want him dug out, you dig him out yourself. Jesus. I never saw anything like that, never." He laid down the jackhammer and took off his mufflers and climbed out of the pit.

Geoff said, "Come on, Otto. Be reasonable. You've come this far."

"Sure I have," Otto retorted. "And I'm the one who's been taking all the risks. Borrowing this truck, digging up city property. Who's going to fill this hole in, huh? Answer me that! And who's going to take the rap for digging it?

You? Somehow, from where I'm standing right now, I just don't see that."

"All right then, for God's sake, I'll do it," said Jack. He pressed the mufflers over his ears, and hefted up the jackhammer, and squeezed the handle. With a shattering *brrr-brrrr-brrrr-brrrrrrpp!* the jackhammer jumped sideways, almost tugging itself out of Jack's grip, and fell sideways onto the ground.

Jack was bending over to pick it up when he heard Geoff shout out, "*Jack*!"

He looked up. From the surface of the concrete island, with a thick grating sound, a concrete-colored head was emerging, followed by concrete-colored shoulders. The head swiveled around and stared at him, blind-eyed, and he recognized it almost at once. Lester—who had first demanded that he bring him Father Bell.

You bastard, spat Lester. *Quintus will kill you for this.*

Otto stared at Lester's head in total disbelief. "That's a head," he said, at last, swallowing hard. He pulled at Geoff's sleeve. "You see that? That's a *head*!"

Geoff said, "It's okay, Otto. Don't panic. This is what we came here for." All the same, this was the first time that Geoff had seen with his own eyes any of the lunatics from The Oaks, and he was stiff with apprehension, too.

Let me free, Lester demanded. *Let me free, or Quintus will kill your son.*

"You mean he's still alive?" asked Jack.

Of course he's alive. He's a prize, your son! He's our final sacrifice, the innocent one who was demanded by the ancient gods! The one whose life will set us all free!

Jack stood up, grasping the jackhammer in both hands. "You're not going free, Lester. You can threaten me all you want. But you're not going free. I'm going to jackhammer your stupid head off."

Lester said wildly, *You can break up my body, my friend, but not my soul! Quintus will restore me! You wait! As long as my dust is still on this earth, Quintus will restore me! And Quintus will crush your son, believe me! Quintus will crush your son like a fledgling crushed in its nest!*

At that moment Geoff called, "Jack?" Then he turned to Otto and said, "Turn off the compressor, would you, Otto? We won't be needing the jackhammer anymore."

The compressor chugged to a stop, and suddenly the rooftop parking lot seemed very hushed. The wind blew soft and chilly, the way it had once blown across Stonehenge, and Easter Island, and the stones of Carnac. Most of the parking bays were taken, but there was nobody around. Tonight's performance of *Swan Lake* must already have started.

Geoff said to Jack, "I want you to trust me now, Jack. Quintus Miller won't touch your son, not yet—he daren't— not if Randy's already been singled out for the final sacrifice. Those maniacs can't be finally free until they make that sacrifice, that's what it says in Druggett's book, anyway. And once they've chosen a child, that's the child they have to stick with, no changes of mind. That child's protected, until sacrifice day. Randy's safe, for the time being, anyway."

If you lay one finger on me, you filth, Quintus will have his revenge on you, Lester snarled. *You'll wish that your mother had never parted her legs to let you out.*

Geoff replied, "I'm not too sure about that, old chap.

From the way that Quintus Miller has been lording it over you, I'd guess that he's a classic schizophrenic. He's obviously quite convinced that he's Awen, the god of the Druids. Awen was a cruel god, and an extremely unforgiving god. I don't think Awen will care too much what happens to you."

I am immortal, Lester whispered. *Whatever you do to me, you can never destroy me.*

"Well—I very much hope that you're wrong there, too," said Geoff. He wiped his hands nervously on his jeans, then turned to his Valiant and unlocked the trunk. "Give me a hand here, Jack," he asked. Jack could tell that he wasn't quite as confident as he was trying to appear.

Out of the back of his dilapidated car, he wrestled a triangular wooden frame, three five-foot lengths of heavy oak, roughly sawed and nailed together. Jack helped him to lower it to the ground. It weighed nearly three hundred pounds.

"What the hell is *that?*" Otto asked suspiciously.

"The university carpentry shop made it for me." Geoff smiled. "It didn't take them long. It's an exact replica of a Druid's sacrifical rack. As near as we've been able to make it, anyway."

"It's a *what?*"

"A sacrificial rack. The Druids bent their victims backward over one side of the triangle—see here?—and lashed their wrists and their ankles together. Then they tightened the lashings with tourniquets, tighter and tighter, until the victim was bent back so far that his spine broke. Then the Druids spoke the sacrificial words, and that guaranteed that their victim's spirit was obliterated, as if it had never been."

Jack turned to stare at Lester's head, rearing out of the broken-up concrete. Lester was watching them intently.

"It was difficult finding the sacrificial words," said Geoff. "But they're all in Druggett's book on Druids. They were found on a sacrifical stone in Wales.

"Caimich mi a nochd
Eadar uir agus eare,
Eadar run do reachd,
Agus dearc mo dhoille."

As soon as Geoff had completed his recitation, without any warning at all, Lester screamed. His scream wasn't audible, but it pierced their heads like a knife blade dragged across slate.

"You see?" said Geoff triumphantly. "We've got them! We've sussed them out! We've caught the bastards!"

Lester's head submerged into the concrete. But Geoff jumped down into the excavation, and pounded on the concrete with his fists, and shouted out, "You hear me! We've got you now! *A Righ nan reula runach!*"

Almost immediately Lester's face reappeared, screaming at them even more piercingly.

"Got you!" Geoff shouted back at him. He was almost hysterical with the magic and the strangeness and the terror of what they were doing. "Got you, you murderous shit! *A Dhe mheinnich nan dula!*"

Lester, concrete-faced, gibbered, *Don't, don't! Smash me if you want to! But sixty years! Sixty years waiting! I want to get out, I want to be free!*

"Oh, there's only one way you're going to get free,

chum," Geoff told him. "And that's if you tell us all about Quintus Miller, and all about your lunatic friends. Because if you don't, it's the rack for you, and absolute extinction, courtesy of Awen, the sacred name, and Bel, the sun god, for ever and ever amen."

You can have them! You can have them! I can tell you how!

"Make it quick, then," Geoff demanded. "I'm not feeling particularly patient this evening, and I've got an appetite for extinguishing mental deficients like you."

It was all in the books... in Krüger's library... and there were diaries, too. Krüger had been studying Druids all his life. Quintus broke into the library and stole them... and he told us that we could all escape. We planned it for months. The hardest part was finding a flute, the right kind of flute. But we pretended we wanted to start our own folk-music circle... and in the end Mr. Estergomy bought one for us.

"Flute? What are you talking about?" Geoff asked him.

To play the ritual music, to open the pentacle... so that we could all escape. And we did escape.... Quintus went first, and then came through the walls and played the music and we escaped, too. One to play and the rest to follow, that was the ritual. And we did it! Right into the walls!

Geoff stood quite still, the early-evening wind blowing back his hair. "One to play and the rest to follow," he said quietly. And then he recited,

"However he turned from South to West,
And to Koppelberg Hill his steps addressed,
And after him the children pressed....

"When, lo, as they reached the mountainside,
A wondrous portal opened wide,
As if a cavern were suddenly hollowed;
And the Piper advanced and the children followed."

Even Otto knew what that poem was. "'The Pied Piper of Hamelin,'" he said in a throaty voice. "Holy Moses, the damn thing's true; and I'm seeing it here with my own eyes."

"Yes," said Geoff. "The damn thing's true; and it's happened again and again throughout history. There aren't any such things as ghosts, or poltergeists, or demons, but there are earth-walkers, and wall-walkers—people who inhabit the real underworld."

Let me free, Lester insisted. *I've told you everything I know. Let me free.*

"Jack? What do you think?" said Geoff.

Jack looked at Lester's face in the concrete and thought of Randy, and of Father Bell, and of Essie Estergomy and Daniel Bufo and Joseph Lovelittle. He felt capable of smashing Lester's face apart with the jackhammer. In fact, he would have done so, except that it wouldn't have guaranteed the extinction of Lester's unbalanced soul.

"I vote we sacrifice him," he said. "Let's show Quintus Miller we really mean business."

You gave your word! Lester protested.

"And Father Bell died in the worst goddamned agony that anybody could ever imagine," Jack snapped back.

He wouldn't give in! He wouldn't let us go! It wasn't my fault!

"How do we get him out of the concrete?" Jack asked.

Geoff held up the holy water. "Exorcised water mixed

with exorcised salt. That's the way the early Christians finally overcame the Druids. The way of the spirit versus the way of the flesh."

No! screamed Lester. *No, don't take my soul!*

Geoff unscrewed the cap of the Perrier bottle and lifted it up.

No! shrieked Lester. *I'll tell you how to find them! I'll tell you how to find them!*

Jack went right up to the concrete block and stared Lester directly in the face.

"Jack—don't go too near," Geoff warned him. But Jack was too angry to listen.

"All right, then, Lester," he said. "You tell us how to find them and we'll let you go. But I'm warning you, buddy. If you cheat us... I'm going to track you down, personally, and I'm going to break your back on that rack, and I'm going to take my time doing it."

Listen, will you, I'm telling you the truth... You have to go back to the gateway... to the place where Quintus first went into the wall.... You have to play the music... the music will draw them all back. They have to follow the music, they don't have any choice. You know it, it's the summoning music for Grian-stad...

"*Grian-stad?*" Jack asked. "What's *Grian-stad?*"

"It's Celtic for 'midsummer night,'" put in Geoff. "I don't know whether our friend here is telling us the truth, but he knows his Druidic lore. On midsummer night the Druids would play music to call everybody to the holy places."

"So we don't have to track them down individually," said Jack. "We can call them all back to The Oaks, and then we can deal with them there."

He had no idea how he and Geoff were going to be able to "deal" with one hundred thirty-six criminal maniacs, but maybe Druggett's book on Druidism would help them. Even if they couldn't destroy them—even if they couldn't do anything more than imprison them back in the walls of the building, the way they had been imprisoned before—that would be better than having them roaming the city, tearing innocent people into the ground.

Geoff said, "This music—what kind of music is it? Is it a special tune?"

Pipe music, said Lester. *Pipe music, played on a whistle. It goes like—*

"All right," said Geoff, "it's pipe music, but what does it sound like?"

But at that instant Lester screamed even louder than he had before. A harsh, grating screech of terror and total despair. Two massive hands rose out of the concrete on either side of his head and dragged him into the ground. They saw one of Lester's hands lifted desperately for a moment out of the concrete, clawing at the air. Then that was dragged down, too, and Lester was gone.

"What happened?" said Jack in bewilderment. "Where did he go?"

Geoff shouted, "Otto! The rods!"

"What is it?" asked Jack.

"Get out of the pit!" Geoff ordered him. "Ten to one it's Quintus Miller!"

They scrambled out of the concrete excavation and backed toward the compressor truck. Otto was fumbling with his divining rods, trying to hold them parallel, saying, "Nothing but goddamned trouble. Wish I'd never come."

Jack looked quickly around the parking lot, searching desperately for any furrowing of the concrete, any arms lifted like sharks' fins.

Otto said, "They're crazy! They're going crazy!"

The divining rods were swinging around and around and around, like compasses over the North Pole. Otto was trying to keep them still, but he couldn't. "It's too strong! It's everywhere! I just can't stop them from spinning around!"

Abruptly the divining rods stopped rotating and touched each other. There was a loud, sharp crackle of electrical discharge, and Otto was flung rigid against the side of his truck, knocking his head with a dull crunching sound like a run-over squirrel. He fell to the ground, quivering and trembling and muttering.

Jack knelt down beside him. His woolen hat was matted with blood, and his eyes were rolled up into his head.

"Don't touch him," Geoff warned. "He's been hit by natural magnetism... and a hell of a lot of it, too. You'd probably get a serious shock yourself if you touched him."

"You got that holy water?" Jack asked him, his eyes darting from one side of the parking lot to the other. His heart was pounding against his rib cage with the same ferocity that Lester had pounded against his concrete tomb.

"I've got it, sure—but I'm not sure how much *good* it's going to do us," Geoff replied. "Whoever pulled Lester down into the ground... he must have broken right through the circle."

"You're not a priest, remember," said Jack. "Maybe that had something to do with it. Maybe you don't have enough power."

"All right, I'm not a priest," Geoff agreed quite angrily. "But, damn it, I'm not that much of a sinner, either."

"Maybe we'd better get out of here," Jack suggested.

"I think you're probably right. Total cowardice occasionally has a great deal to recommend it."

They stood up, and cautiously backed toward Geoff's Valiant. Almost instantaneously, however, they were deafened by a shattering explosion. The concrete island in which they had trapped Lester was blasted apart, in a blizzard of grit and gravel and blinding dust. Chunks of concrete rattled and banged against the automobiles parked all around them, smashing windows and denting bodywork.

Shielding his eyes against the dust, Jack looked back toward their excavation. The central concrete island had been completely blown away, but standing in its place was a naked man, flayed of every inch of skin, glistening and scarlet and throbbing with fanlike traceries of veins.

In the dying light of the day, he looked almost beautiful, like a work of surrealist sculpture. Muscles, sinews, tendons; and arteries wriggling across his body like snakes. In spite of the rawness of his face, Jack immediately recognized him as Lester.

Lester tried to move, tried to cry out, but the pain that he was suffering was too intense. He uttered a single strangled bleat that sounded more like a slaughtered animal than a man. Then a hand reached up from out of the concrete beneath his feet and snatched his ankles and pulled him down into the ground in a grisly detonation of blood and flesh.

"God almighty," Jack whispered.

"Jack, the car!" Geoff urged him, in a voice so shocked that it was almost transparent. "Let's get out of here, quick!"

They ran the last few steps to the Valiant, tugged open the doors, and climbed inside. Geoff pulled his keys out of his pocket, but dropped them on the floor.

"Shit!" he panicked, reaching down and scrabbling around for them.

As he did so Jack heard a thumping noise and turned to his right. The car at the far end of the line in which they were parked was heaving upward three or four feet. Then it dropped down again. Then the next car was lifted up, colliding noisily with the car beside it, and the next car and the next. It looked as if something huge and powerful were making its way toward them under the ground—a tidal wave in solid concrete—lifting up each car as it approached and dropping it again.

"Geoff, get this heap of scrap iron out of here!" Jack shouted at him.

Geoff found the keys and jabbed them into the ignition. As he did so, however, they felt the Valiant shaking, and metal breaking apart underneath it. His mind blotted out with thoughts of Daniel Bufo, Jack kicked open his door and jumped right out of the car. Geoff followed him.

The car stopped shaking almost at once. They backed away two or three paces farther, then hesitated.

"This one's strong," said Geoff, wiping his forehead with the back of his hand. "This one's Quintus Miller, no doubt about it."

In front of their eyes, the windshield of Geoff's Valiant began to bend and distort. A face appeared, molded out of glass; visible only because the lights from MECCA were reflected on its cheeks and on its nose and on its lips. It was a strong, cruel face; exactly the face that Father Bell had described to Jack up at Green Bay. *A face like a rock. Hard eyes, eyes like nail heads, completely without expression, completely without compassion.*

"Quintus Miller," Jack whispered.

That's right, said a harsh, cultured, midwestern voice. *Quintus Miller in person. Pleased to make your acquaintance.*

"I want my son back," Jack told him. "You hear me? I want my son back! I want him back here and now, or else by God I'm going to give you the kind of hell that people only dream about."

Your son is very important to me, Mr. Reed. Not just important to me personally, you understand, but to my faith. Your son is going to go down in history as the most momentous sacrifice in pagan religion in two thousand years. History, Mr. Reed! Not many boys get the chance to make history. Not so young. Not so tender.

"I want to see him," Jack demanded.

You can see him, if you wish.

The windshield began to rise, as if it were being fashioned by an expert glassblower. The head and shoulders of a powerfully built man appeared, formed out of glass. Across the man's shoulders, apparently tied or handcuffed, slumped a glass boy who looked exactly like Randy. His eyes seemed to be closed, but as Jack slowly approached the Valiant he could see that the boy was still breathing. He must have been sleeping an exhausted sleep.

"Randy?" he said. "Randy?"

"Jack, keep well away!" Geoff cautioned him. "He wants to kill you—he wants to kill both of us!"

Jack stopped, hesitated, biting his lip. Quintus Miller's glass lips were curved in a shining smile.

Come closer if you want to, Mr. Reed; or can I call you Jack? It won't make any difference, now or later, I'm going to kill you, and you can be sure of that. Just the same way that Lester died, trying to tell you our holy secrets. Nobody betrays Quintus Miller, Jack. Nobody stands in his way. They named me after the Quintessence, and that's what I am. Killed my brothers, all four of them, poked out their eyes with a black-hot poker. What are you looking at me for, nobody looks at a god, not like that! *That's what I told them. And while they were sleeping... one by one. My father's leather razor strop jammed between their teeth to stop them from making a sound... then the black-hot poker right through the eyelid into the eye. Sizzle? You bet they sizzled! You ever hear optic fluid frying, Jack? That's what I heard! Eight times! Each brother blinded, dead and blind; and then my mother, too, I cauterized her, same black-hot poker, cauterized her right where she'd birthed me, sealed and purified, so no woman could ever boast that I was her whelp.*

Jack's glance slipped sideways. One of the chunks of concrete that had been blasted from Lester's tomb lay right beside his foot. He looked back at Quintus Miller, at the glass man rising from the Valiant's windshield, and he calculated that he could scoop up the concrete, swing forward and smash Quintus Miller's head, quicker than Quintus Miller could stop him.

One second. Less than a second. Scoop, swing, smash.

My father wasn't there... that was my mistake. I was planning to purify him, too. But he was away that night, without my knowing it... without my mother knowing it, either. He was sleeping with another woman, on the other side of town. Said he was walking the dog, but I knew better! Rutting, that's what he was doing! He was strong, my father... strong as a bull, like me. Big cock on him, I'll always remember his cock. It used to frighten me when I was small. I wanted to exorcise that cock, exorcise that memory altogether... But he wasn't there...

Jack scooped up the chunk of concrete. Swung. Smashed.

...opened the door and—that dog!—

Quintus Miller's head burst open like a broken light bulb. Fragments of glittering glass fell into the driver's seat.

But to Jack's horror the smashed face continued to smile, and a glass hand came lunging out of the windshield to catch hold of his hair at the back of his head. He grunted, tossed his head, and pushed against the Valiant's fender, but Quintus Miller's grip was too fierce and too tight. Gradually he was pulled nearer and nearer to the broken windshield, until he was face-to-face with a glass mouth and a smashed-open head.

Now then, Jack... you've disappointed me now. I wanted a hunt. I wanted to pit my wits against you, instead of my strength. All I have to do now is pull your throat across this glass, and that's you done for... and don't believe I'm not going to do it, because I am. I'm not so stupid that I put the hunting before the catching... I've caught you, Jack, and now I'm going to do for you.

Jack pulled his head back as far as he could. But even

though his hand was made of glass, Quintus was unbelievably powerful, and Jack found himself inched closer and closer to the broken edge just above Quintus's lips.

You ever see somebody's throat cut, ear to ear? That happened back at The Oaks once, one of the crazies broke a coffee cup, cut himself open right in front of Mr. Estergomy... nothing sharper than broken porcelain, cuts like a razor, cuts real straight... but glass is good, too, except it cuts wavy...

"Uh," Jack grunted, trying harder than ever to pull his head away. But the glass fist clutched his hair so tight that he couldn't break away, and the glass mouth smiled at him in total dispassion, glad to witness him die.

His throat was less than inch away from Quintus Miller's broken head when Jack heard a sharp shattering sound, and Quintus's grip was released. He dropped, knelt, half rolled back onto the ground, and found himself lying with his cheek against the concrete, right next to the curved pieces of Quintus's broken glass arm. Geoff was standing over him with a lump of concrete in his hand. He must have smashed Quintus's arm at the elbow.

"Let's get the hell out of here," said Geoff, helping him up. The Valiant's broken windshield suddenly collapsed into thousands of pieces, a heap of artificial diamonds piled up on to the seats. Together, Jack and Geoff ran down the exit ramp, glancing quickly behind them from time to time to make sure that the concrete wasn't furrowing up, and that Quintus Miller wasn't in hot pursuit.

They ran across East Kilbourn Avenue, gasping and puffing. At last Jack said, "Got to stop, Geoff. Sorry. Out of condition."

Geoff nodded and bent forward to touch his toes. "You and me both. All that pipe smoking. Should have kept up my squash."

"Jesus," said Jack, "I could use a drink."

They hobbled slowly together along the sidewalk, still sweating and panting. "Do you think Otto's dead?" Jack asked Geoff.

Geoff nodded. "He certainly looked as if he was."

"This whole damned thing was my fault," said Jack. "So many people have gotten killed."

Geoff gripped Jack's shoulder reassuringly. "Listen... that's the story of the human race, from beginning to end... you meant well."

"Meant well? Jesus!"

They crossed East Kilbourn Avenue, still keeping a weather eye open for cracks in the sidewalk.

"He's going to do his damnedest to kill us, you know that."

"You're not kidding. If you hadn't broken his arm back there, he would have sliced me up like a family pack of Farmer John's bacon."

"At least we're certain that Randy's still alive."

Jack said, "Yes, thank God. And I want him back."

They were still panting and talking and hobbling when a police car suddenly pulled to the curb beside them, its lights flashing. Two policemen climbed out of the car and came running across the sidewalk.

"Police! Put your hands up! Put your hands right up where we can see them!"

Jack and Geoff slowly raised their hands. One of the

officers kept them covered while the other cautiously approached them.

"You're Jack Reed, right?" he asked Jack. He was young and pimply, with a sparse black mustache.

"I'm Jack Reed, that's correct. What's this all about?"

"You're under arrest, for violating an order of the district court. I have to read you your rights."

"What are you talking about? I haven't violated any orders."

"Something to do with your son. Randolph Reed?"

Jack took a long, deep breath. "Is it all right if I put my hands down now? It wasn't reported as armed violation, was it? And—you know"—he glanced around the crowded sidewalk—"people are staring."

"Prefer it if you kept them up, sir. You have the right to remain silent, you have the right—"

Jack looked across at Geoff in desperation. If the police arrested him now, then he would have to come up with some explanation about what he had done with Randy. And what the hell could he tell them? That Randy had been abducted by a maniac who walked inside walls? That the Druids had taken him? That he knew Randy was safe, because he had seen him, fashioned out of an automobile windshield, a boy made of glass?

"—can and will be used in evidence against you."

I I

Shortly after one o'clock the following morning, Geoff was allowed to leave Milwaukee police headquarters at 749 West State Street and return to Madison. Jack was detained in a cell on the second floor, next to a drunk who kept singing over and over again, "*Oh baby, baby, it's a world wide...*"

Jack chewed gum that had surrendered the last of its flavor an hour ago, and paced up and down the floor. He was physically and mentally close to collapse, but he couldn't allow himself to slow down. He wasn't a bright or an educated man, he had no intellectual reserves on which he could draw. He couldn't theorize about the moral significance of what he had done or the religious significance of the Druids. He couldn't even quote *The Song of Hiawatha* to keep himself occupied.

But he had a native Wisconsin stamina, an unpolished energy that came from raw Lake Michigan winters and building your own business and fighting for your emotional survival.

He was going to see this through. He was going to beat this shit. He didn't believe in people who walked through walls. At least he didn't believe that anybody *should* walk through walls. It was old magic, something that ought to have been dead and buried centuries ago. This was the twentieth century, almost the twenty-first.

Most of all, he didn't believe that people should steal other people's children and put them through the god damned emotional wringer.

"*Oh baby, baby, it's a world wide...*"

"It's not a 'world wide,' it's a 'wild world'!" Jack shouted at him.

"What?" came the slurred reply.

"It's a 'wild world'!"

Long pause—and then the cheery rejoinder, "You're damn right it is!"

Jack sat on the edge of his bunk. His greatest immediate fear was that Quintus would discover that he was here, and penetrate the police headquarters, and drag him into the reinforced concrete floor of his cell. He was also afraid that after their confrontation in the parking lot, Quintus would find renewed blood lust to slaughter all the eight hundred people he needed to return to the real world, and that Randy would then be sacrificed as his final offering to Awen.

He rubbed his eyes. He had called his lawyer, Maurice Lederman, but Maurice was out of town (Miami, fishing, for God's sake) and his wife wouldn't be able to reach him till the morning. Meanwhile Jack had been formally charged with violating the court order that gave Maggie regular access to Randy, and he was being detained until Randy's whereabouts could be established.

At about three o'clock in the morning, his cell door was unlocked, and a neat-looking dark-haired man with a three-o'clock-in-the-morning shadow and a wide-shouldered gray suit came into the cell with a clipboard under his arm and two Styrofoam cups of black coffee.

"How're you doing, Mr. Reed? My name's Sergeant Charles Schiller. Thought you might care for some coffee."

Jack said, "If you're thinking of asking me any questions, you're going to have to wait until tomorrow. My lawyer's been catching marlin off Miami."

Sergeant Schiller said, "Yes, Mr. Reed, I know."

There was a sharpness in the tone of Sergeant Schiller's voice that made Jack look up. Sergeant Schiller was looking at him with an intent, cold expression that was close to being contemptuous.

"Something wrong?" Jack asked him.

"Something *wrong*?" replied Sergeant Schiller. "Well... let me put it this way. I've lived in Milwaukee all my life and I'm proud of Milwaukee. Milwaukee has warmth and friendship, do you know what I mean? *Gemütlichkeit*, that's what my father used to call it. And up until now, Milwaukee has one of the lowest crime rates in the country."

He paused for a moment, stirring his coffee with a plastic stick. Then he said, "We've had a bad time this week, people disappearing right, left, and center. People are beginning to say that Milwaukee isn't safe anymore. People are getting panicky, and aggressive, and suspicious. That isn't *Gemütlichkeit*, Mr. Reed. That's seriously antisocial behavior. And I don't much care for people who indulge in seriously antisocial behavior."

Jack said tiredly, "I'm accused of violating a court order in respect of my wife's access visits to my nine-year-old son. That doesn't exactly rank me with Al Capone, does it?"

"Can you tell me where you son is now?"

"Not until I talk to my lawyer."

"Is your son alive?"

"Of course he's alive. What the hell do you mean, is he alive?"

"How about Miss Olive Estergomy, of Sun Prairie. Is she alive?"

Jack swallowed dryly. He had been afraid of this. It looked as if the grisly events that had taken place at The Oaks had caught up with him at last.

"You do *know* Miss Olive Estergomy?"

"I have to talk to my lawyer first," Jack told him.

"But you do *know* her?"

Jack said, "Yes, I know her."

"Do you know where she is now?"

Jack shook his head.

"Is she alive, Mr. Reed?"

"I have to talk to my lawyer."

Sergeant Schiller sipped coffee and leafed through his clipboard. "All right, then," he said after a while, "how about Mr. Daniel Bufo, of Madison? Is he alive?"

"I can't answer that," Jack replied.

"Do you know where he is? We'd really appreciate knowing where he is."

"I can't help you, I'm sorry."

"All right, then... how about Mr. William Bell, of Bay Park Retirement Home, Green Bay? Is he alive?"

Jack said, "You want to explain to me what this is all about?"

Sergeant Schiller put down his clipboard. "Surely. The fact is that your son Randy and Miss Olive Estergomy and Mr. Daniel Bufo and Mr. William Bell all have two things in common. The first thing they have in common is that they are all missing. The second thing they have in common is that the last known person to see them was you."

"What does that prove?" asked Jack.

"It doesn't prove anything," said Sergeant Schiller. "But it does suggest that any line of inquiry into their mysterious disappearance ought to begin with you; and maybe end with you, too."

"Are you going to charge me?"

"Not yet. We have officers coming over from Madison tomorrow morning, and I want to talk to your lawyer, too, and to the district attorney's office. But I want to make it clear to you here and now, Mr. Reed, that if you know where these people are, the sooner you tell me, the better it's going to be for you."

Jack said, "Can I make a telephone call?"

"You want to make a telephone call *now*?"

A uniformed officer escorted Jack down the hall to one of the interview rooms. Jack dialed Geoff's number and waited and waited while it rang. The uniformed officer stood by the door and yawned. At last Geoff answered groggily, "Hello? Who the devil's this?"

"Geoff, it's Jack."

"Oh, God. How are you, Jack? They haven't started beating you with rubber truncheons yet, have they?"

"Almost. Things have gotten a whole lot worse. They've been asking me questions about Olive Estergomy and Daniel Bufo and Father Bell."

"Jack—" Geoff warned him. "Be careful what you say. They'll almost certainly have this call tapped."

"I don't give a damn if they do. You've got to help me,

Geoff. They're not going to let me out of here for days, the way things are going. It could be too late then. It's certainly going to get worse out on the streets. Geoff—come on, this is all down to me. I need to be out there, fighting it."

"What's your lawyer done to get you out?" Geoff asked him.

"My lawyer's still on his way back from Miami. Besides I don't think that he's going to be able to get me released on bail. Not until I've managed to produce Randy, and show the court that he's safe and well. And if the police charge me with abducting all these people—well, maybe not at all."

Geoff said, "I don't see what more I can do, Jack. I'm going to try tomorrow to find out everything I can about the rituals... but, you know, this all happened more than two thousand years ago. Most of it's legend, and a lot of it makes no sense whatsoever."

"All right," said Jack. He felt a sudden wave of nausea and tiredness. "I'll talk to you tomorrow, if they let me. Right now they seem to think that I'm a cross between Son of Sam and Bruno Hauptmann."

Jack was escorted back to his cell. When he got there, he found that Sergeant Schiller was still waiting for him.

"How about a bedtime chat?" asked Sergeant Schiller.

Jack shook his head. "My lawyer's going to be here in the morning. Until he arrives, nothing."

Sergeant Schiller gave him a small lipless smile, like the mark of a very sharp chisel in freshly planed pine. "I'll promise you one thing, Mr. Reed. I personally believe that you were actively involved in the disappearance of all of these people, including your son. I also believe that all of them are dead, and that you killed them. And the promise is, I'm going to nail your ass to the wall, Mr. Reed."

He went to the door of the cell and opened it. "You, Mr. Reed, are going to be locked up forever."

Jack said, "Good night, Sergeant. I expect I'll see you in the morning."

"Oh, don't worry about that," said Sergeant Schiller. "You can count on it."

Jack slept for a little over two hours, and woke up at 5:15. He lay on his bunk listening to the echoing noises of the police headquarters, the distorted shouts, the constantly slamming doors, the whistling, the abrupt bursts of laughter.

In the distance he could hear ambulance and police sirens, and he dreaded to think what emergency they were rushing to deal with. More innocent people, pulled down into the sidewalks, or smashed into solid walls. More souls sacrificed, for the grisly and glorious resurrection of Quintus Miller.

He eased himself up off his bunk and splashed his face in cold water at the tiny corner washbasin. In the plastic mirror he looked white and big-nosed and distorted, a ghost who had once been Jack Reed.

If only he could walk right out of here, right through the walls, the same way that Quintus did.

He sat down again. Supposing he *could* walk through the walls. Supposing Geoff could discover the full Druid ritual. Quintus Miller had managed to do it, after all, and Quintus Miller was a lunatic. *You have to play the music;* that's what Lester had said. *You have to play the ritual tune.*

It was a puzzle, a puzzle with pieces. Some of the pieces fitted neatly together—the way in which Quintus had found out about Druidism, for example, and the story of the Pied Piper. But there were so many unanswered questions. So many pieces that *felt* as if they ought to fit, but didn't.

Jack lay back and tried to catalog all the outstanding pieces of puzzle that he couldn't understand.

They knew most of the ritual that would take them into solid rock. But they still didn't know what the sacred tune was, the tune that the Pied Piper had presumably played to the children of Hamelin, as they walked into Koppelberg mountain.

In an odd way Lester had seemed to assume that he and Geoff should already know what the ritual tune was. *You know it*, he had said. But how could they, when they had never heard it—never seen it written down? But then Jack suddenly thought of another piece of the puzzle, another unexplained fragment.

Geoff's friend at Harvard had read him excerpts from Druggett's book on Druidism, and what had he said about the climax of the ritual when the Druids walked into walls? *They played the king.*

But Geoff had *heard* this excerpt over the telephone, rather than reading it for himself. Supposing the Druids hadn't been playing at being royalty, which is what the ritual sounded like. Supposing they had been playing "The King." A tune called "The King."

And where, recently, had Jack heard a tune about a king?

It came to him with a shiver. The distant echoing voice which he now knew to be that of Quintus Miller—in the abandoned corridors of The Oaks. That simple childhood tune that he had repeated over and over, until Jack hadn't been able to hear it without a deep feeling of dread.

Lavender blue, dilly-dilly;
Lavender green.
Here I am king, dilly-dilly;
You shall be queen.

Jack slowly sat up. The way he remembered it, Quintus hadn't sung the tune exactly right. Well—not the way it was supposed to be sung at nursery school. One or two of the notes had been different—off-key, more barbaric.

That was the tune, he was sure of it. Why else would Lester have assumed that they knew it? Why else would Quintus have sung it so often?

Because he's crazy, a small dissenting voice told Jack, inside his mind. *Crazy people never do anything for the same reasons that we do; and they never do anything predictable.*

All the same, Jack didn't have anything else to go on. He could try it, at least. All he needed were some pipes, and a razor blade to cut himself with so that he could draw on the wall the ritual pentacle of fresh blood, and a list from Geoff of all the sacred names that he was supposed to recite.

God, if it worked, Sergeant Schiller could stick his suspicions where the sun never shone.

He went to the door of his cell and called out, "Guard! Guard!"

The door at the far end of the corridor was noisily unlocked, stirring up moans and hungover groans from all the other cells nearby. A young officer with squeaky crepe-soled shoes came walking along the polished floor.

"Anything wrong?" he wanted to know.

"I need to use a telephone," said Jack.

"I have to call Sergeant Schiller, just as soon as you're awake."

"Look, all I need is to use the telephone, for two minutes."

"I have to call Sergeant Schiller, sir."

It was twenty minutes before Sergeant Schiller appeared. He had shaved, and washed, and changed his shirt, and he smelled of toothpaste and Grey Flannel after-shave, but his eyes were still swollen like overripe plums and face was gray with fatigue.

"How did you sleep?" he asked cuttingly.

"How do you think?" Jack retorted. "Is there any objection to my using the telephone? I need to talk to my friend in Madison for a couple of minutes."

Sergeant Schiller said, "Your friend Geoffrey Summers, the college professor, is that who you're talking about?"

"Geoff Summers, that's right."

Sergeant Schiller looked down at his clipboard. "Geoffrey Summers is currently not at home. Geoffrey Summers is wanted for questioning in connection with the death of one Otto Schröder on the rooftop parking lot adjacent to the Performing Arts Center, yesterday evening at approximately seven o'clock."

He raised his eyes. Calculating as spirit levels. "According to four independent witnesses, Otto Schröder was in the company of two men yesterday evening, one of whom has positively been identified from police photographs as *you*, Mr. Reed. The other man was tall and bearded. A vehicle found damaged and abandoned on the rooftop parking lot belonged to Mr. Geoffrey Summers, the friend whom you wish to telephone this morning. Mr. Geoffrey Summers, as you probably know, is tall and bearded."

Jack said nothing, but waited for what he knew was going to come next.

"Mr. Reed—you're charged with murder in the first degree of Otto Cornelius Schröder. Your rights have already been read to you, in relation to the charge of violation of a court order for access to your son, but in relation to this charge, I'd like to remind you that you have the right to remain silent—"

Jack closed his eyes while Sergeant Schiller recited his rights. He felt that he deserved this punishment, almost, for all the people who had died since he had first found his way to The Oaks. But nobody could stop Quintus Miller and his troupe of maniacs; nobody except him.

Sergeant Schiller said, "Your lawyer should arrive at General Mitchell Field at eight-oh-five. Then you and I can start talking, yes?"

Jack said nothing, but ran his hand through his hair and looked toward the wall. He was sleeping deeply, dreaming of rain, when somebody shook his shoulder and said, "Hey... your sister's here to see you."

"My sister?" He frowned, trying to focus. A ginger-haired police officer was peering into his face from less than six inches away. He could chart every freckle on the officer's nose.

"Sure. Edna-Mae? She's waiting for you in the interview room. Sergeant Schiller says five minutes only."

Jack swung himself off his bunk. His sister? He didn't have a sister. But he mutely permitted the ginger-headed officer to handcuff him and then lead him along to the interview room at the end of the corridor.

When he was ushered in, he found Karen sitting at the table, fretful and uncomfortable, in a tight turquoise sweater and a short white skirt, and a bouffant blond wig whose falseness bordered on the absurd. When Jack had sat down, she glanced all around her like a nervous chipmunk, and then she said, "They called Mike Karpasian. They told him you were under arrest for homicide. I came right away. Oh, Jack!"

"You shouldn't have come," Jack whispered at her fiercely. "They'll be looking for you, too, if they haven't started looking for you already."

"I told them my name was Edna-Mae Schultz. I went to grade school with a girl called Edna-Mae Schultz."

"I like the store-bought hair," said Jack. He couldn't help smiling. "You look more like Dolly Parton than ever."

"Geoff called me," Karen told him, still serious.

"What did he say? Him and me, we're supposed to have killed that poor guy Otto Schröder."

"I know. Geoff—" She glanced around again, and then she whispered hoarsely, "Geoff called me. He's hiding someplace. I won't tell you where, in case they're listening. But they won't find him."

"Are you okay?" Jack asked her. She didn't look pretty today, and it wasn't just the wig. She looked exactly what she was, a onetime trucker's wife with big breasts and good legs and all the tiredness and cynicism that eventually overtakes any woman who has to live in a single-story clapboard house on the outskirts of Milwaukee, rearing a spoiled abandoned daughter and watching countless hours of television and knowing that her girlhood dreams will never come true.

Come on down, the price is right!

But, Jack decided, in the bald light of this bald interview room, he would rather spend the rest of his life with a woman like Karen than all the Maggies you could gather together in the Pabst Theater. She was sexy, friendly, spirited, devoted, and completely individual; and that's what made her so feminine. More than anything else, she had taken the trouble to visit him when he was in trouble.

"Are you okay?" Jack asked her.

"Sure I'm okay."

"And Sherry?"

"Sherry's okay."

Jack leaned forward as close as he dared. He could see the ginger-headed officer watching him intently, to make sure that Karen didn't pass anything over the table. "I think I know how to get into the walls," he told Karen.

"What?" She frowned at him.

"I think I know how to get into the walls... the same way that all of those lunatics did. I think I've worked out the secret."

"What good will that do?" Karen asked ingenuously. "You're locked up in here."

"Karen, *think* about it. If I can get into the walls, then I can get *out* of here."

Realization suddenly dawned. Karen pressed her hand over her bright red mouth. "You'd really *do* that?"

"My lawyer was here earlier. He said I had about as much chance of getting out of here on bail as he did of being elected pope. Optimist of the year, huh? The trouble is, Otto Schröder was killed by a huge charge of natural energy—you know, like a massive electric shock—right out of nowhere. Quintus Miller must have done it somehow, God knows how. Otto hit his head when he fell. Geoff and I weren't even anywhere *near* him. I mean, we were about as far away as that cop standing by the door. But as far as the police are concerned, we slugged him with a lump of concrete, and he died of a fractured skull."

He paused and sat back in his chair. "Apart from that, they think that I killed all those other people—Father Bell, Olive Estergomy, Daniel Bufo. And I still won't tell them what's happened to Randy. I still *can't* tell them what's happened to Randy. So I don't have any choices. Either I stay here, or else I try to get into the wall."

Karen said, "I *know* you didn't take Randy, and I *know* you didn't kill Daniel Bufo. I was there, I can tell them."

"I know you can, but don't. It won't do any good, and they'll haul you in, too, for being an accessory. I don't think you should come here again, in any case. Find someplace you can hide for a while."

"Oh, Jack..." said Karen. "If anything happened to you... if anything went *wrong*. I mean, supposing you go into the wall and you can't get *out* again?"

"What else can I do? I can't sit here and let Quintus Miller drag a hundred thousand people into the ground, can I? And what about Randy? Karen—I *saw* Randy, he was tied around Quintus Miller's back, and he was still alive!"

Karen said, "What are you going to do?"

"I can't do anything without your help. I know this sounds weird, but I need a flute... the kind of flute the

Druids might have used. Ask Geoff about it. I need a list of names, too. The names of the Druid god Awen."

"Jack—" said Karen.

He could tell what she was thinking: that he had succumbed at last to the stress and the shock of the past few days, that he was exhausted beyond all reason, that he was almost as nuts as Quintus Miller.

"Karen," he told her. "You've been brave and you've been good. I love you, do you know that? I really do. I don't know what the hell's going to happen to me. I'm scared to death. But I have to try every possible option. Do you understand me? Every possible way out, even if it sounds screwball.

"The flute, Karen, please; and the list of names. Give them to my lawyer, Maurice Lederman, his office is in the First Wisconsin Center, ninth floor. Lederman, Pfister and Lederman. Tell him they have to be delivered to me urgently."

Karen swallowed, as if she had no moisture in her mouth at all. "Okay." She nodded. "I'll try to do it today." She leaned over the table and kissed him. "I love you, Jack."

"Hey, cut out that kissing!" snapped the ginger-haired young officer.

Karen scraped her chair back noisily and pranced toward the door with her usual walk that made her body look as if it were bouncing in five different directions at once. She lifted her nose to the officer and said, "Sir, you wouldn't know what kissing was if two elephants came up and sucked you on the ass."

She *click-clacked* off along the corridor. The ginger-haired young officer watched her go and then stared at Jack in stupefaction.

"What did she mean by that?" he demanded.

"Who knows?" said Jack. "But it sure shut *you* up, didn't it?"

He spent a long morning doing nothing but thinking. Maurice Lederman his lawyer came to see him again at three o'clock and talked to him for over an hour about preliminary hearings and finding the right kind of trial lawyer. Maurice made no secret of his annoyance at having been called back from his fishing vacation. It was the first time that he had been able to get away from his wife Sheldra for nearly nine years. He hated Sheldra. He called her the *Rebbitsin*, which meant rabbi's wife, because she spent so much time at the synagogue running around the rabbi.

Maurice was irredeemably overweight, with furrowed gray hair and a furrowed forehead and deep-set, close-together eyes that always reminded Jack of prawn's eyes. The prawn effect was enhanced by his scorched, half-completed sunburn. His skin kept flaking onto his notepad, and from time to time he had to flick it off.

"It's keeping your mouth shut that's doing you no good, Jack," he complained. "If you give the police some basic cooperation, we might be able to work out some kind of a deal. It wouldn't hurt if you gave *me* some basic cooperation."

"Maurice, I didn't touch any one of those people, and the police don't have any evidence that I did. Now that's all I'm going to say."

Maurice took a Dristan inhaler out of his shirt pocket and squeezed it sharply up each nostril. "They have a witness—Mrs. Yvonne Cropper, a supervisory nurse at the Bay Park Retirement Home, who will testify that you took Mr. William Bell out for dinner on the last evening that he was seen alive. You were also seen by serving staff at the Ship's Lantern restaurant, Green Bay, in Mr. Bell's company, talking and arguing with some animation."

"Animation? What's that? Cartoons?"

Maurice fixed him with his dull black prawn's eyes.

"Damn it, Jack, this is serious. These are charges of abduction, kidnap, and multiple homicide."

"Maurice, I'm innocent. I didn't do any of those things. I took an old guy for dinner. That doesn't prove squat."

Maurice took a deep, wheezy breath, hesitated, but then continued. "They also have a witness, Miss Helena Manfield, who says that she introduced you at your specific request to Miss Olive Estergomy. Miss Manfield says you exhibited an unusual and even morbid interest in the Estergomy family, who used to run The Oaks when it was an institution for the criminally insane. She says that on the night that Miss Estergomy was last seen alive, Miss Estergomy telephoned her and said she had been trying to contact you, and had been told that you were probably out at The Oaks. Miss Estergomy's car was found abandoned at The Oaks.

"They have a witness, Mr. Ned Pretty of Capitol Realtors, who says that the following day Mr. Daniel Bufo went to The Oaks to inspect the premises for insurance revaluation. He was also hoping to meet you there because he was concerned about the slow progress of his sale, and in fact had come to the conclusion that you were no longer seriously interested in buying the property. Mr. Daniel Bufo never returned from this meeting and later *his* car was found abandoned at The Oaks with serious damage to the interior, and shreds of Mr. Bufo's clothing and skin were found in the vehicle.

"Your own station wagon was also found at The Oaks at the same time, seriously damaged in a similar way."

Maurice paused, as if he expected Jack to say something, but all Jack could do was to shrug.

"Jack," said Maurice, "can't you get it through your head that this is real life-or-death heavyweight stuff. They could lock you up till Judgment Day."

Jack said, "Maurice—I met those people, sure. I'm not denying it. But I didn't touch them. I didn't touch Otto Schröder, either. No judge in the world is going to lock me up just because I *met* them."

"That's where you're wrong, Jack," Maurice replied. "This isn't 'The Defenders' or 'L.A. Law.' The police have witnesses who saw you and Geoffrey Summers in the company of Otto Schröder literally *minutes* before Otto Schröder was killed by a blow to the head. They have enough circumstantial evidence to tie you in conclusively with every one of these other disappearances. Jack, they don't need eyewitnesses to prove homicide. They don't need smoking guns or bloody lumps of concrete or whatever you used to kill them. They don't even need bodies."

Jack retorted, "What about all these other disappearances and murders? They've been happening all over Milwaukee! They're *still* happening! Haven't the police considered that there might be some connection?"

Maurice sniffed dryly. "I wouldn't push *that* line too hard. They might decide that the connection between all of them is *you*. Anyway, do you have any evidence that they're connected? Do you have any evidence that you didn't kill any of these people you've been charged with killing? What have you done with Randy? Come on, Jack, I've known Randy ever since he was born. If he's still alive, where is he now?"

Jack was silent. He lowered his head.

"You're going to help me, or what?" asked Maurice.

"I can't, Maurice, not just yet."

"Not just yet? They've got you trussed up like a Thanksgiving turkey, oven-ready already, and you tell me 'not just yet'?"

"I'm sorry, Maurice, that's it. I can't tell you any more. You wouldn't believe me anyway."

Maurice swept away more flakes of sunburn. "Well, then, before we do anything else, we're going to have to find you a first-class trial lawyer. I want to talk to Gerry Pfister, back at the office. I was thinking of Saul Jacob, if we can get him."

Jack looked up, startled. "Saul Jacob? Saul Jacob defended the Black What's-his-name—that guy in Minneapolis who machine-gunned all those people in that Burger King restaurant. The Black Avenger, or whatever."

"Sure, and he got him off, too."

"Got him off? Jesus, Maurice, he pleaded insanity! The guy got sent to the funny farm! I'm not insane!"

Maurice pouted his sun-sore-encrusted lips and drummed his fingers on his legal pad and wouldn't look at him straight. Jack stared at him with one elbow on the tabletop and a slowly dropping sensation in his stomach. *Saul Jacob?* Saul Jacob specialized in hopeless homicide cases; in death-row appeals and stays of execution. Saul Jacob had kept Mad Frank Maharis out of the electric chair for nearly six years, and saved the life of Don Castigliani. Maurice would only think of briefing Saul Jacob if he were quite convinced in his own mind that Jack was guilty—that he *had* killed Essie Estergomy and Father Bell and Daniel Bufo and Otto Schroder—and that he had probably killed Randy, too, for good measure.

"You think I did it," he told Maurice. "You son of a bitch. You think I did it."

Maurice still wouldn't look at him. "What I think isn't important. It's what the jury can be persuaded to think."

"Christ, Maurice, you think I did it. You've known me all these years."

"Well, everybody has their hidden side. I found out only last week that Gerry Pfister was gay."

"I suppose that made a difference?"

"I had the coffee machine changed to disposable cups. Apart from that, he's gay, who cares?"

"You know something, Maurice, you're a *schmo*. And that's the nicest thing I can think of to say to you."

Jack felt—unexpectedly—cornered. His only consolation was that if Karen could bring him the pipe, and the names of the Druid god, and if the ritual of disappearing into the wall really worked, then it wouldn't matter what Maurice believed, and it wouldn't matter what Sergeant Schiller believed, either. He would have vanished, beyond capture, and beyond the law.

"All right," he agreed. "You go talk to Gerry Pfister; whatever you think best."

"I'll be back later," said Maurice, "maybe you'll feel more forthcoming. I can't help you, Jack, if you won't tell me what really happened."

"You want me to confess to murder?"

"Anything... just so long as you tell me *something*."

Jack dry-washed his face with his hands. "Okay, Maurice, whatever. By the way... somebody should be leaving a package for me at your office, possibly sometime today. Could you make sure that you get it around here as soon as it arrives?"

"Depends what it is. They won't let you have drugs, or alcohol, or food."

"A flute, Maurice, that's all. Something to tootle on, to pass the time."

Maurice stared at him incredulously. "You want to play the *flute*?"

"I used to play the tenor sax at school."

Maurice slowly shook his head, then went to the door and knocked for the guard to let him out.

Jack said, "So long, Maurice," but Maurice hurried from the room without even turning to look at him.

At a quarter after five they let Maggie in to see him. She was red-eyed from crying, and shivering, and highly distressed, and Jack was convinced that Sergeant Schiller had sent her in to try to shame him into admitting that he had murdered Randy.

"Hello, Margaret-Ann," he greeted her.

She sat down, twisting a damp-looking handkerchief. She was wearing the wide-shouldered orange suit he particularly disliked. It always made her look pasty and unwell, even when she wasn't. What was worse, she thought it made her look like Krystle, in "Dynasty," and it made her behave that way, too. Saintly and dewy-eyed and irritatingly practical.

"Hello, Jack," she whispered, and then abruptly cleared her throat.

"How are you?" he asked her.

"Upset, what do you think?"

"How's the blessed Velma?"

"I wish you wouldn't call her that."

"All right, how's the plain and ordinary Velma?"

"She's quite well, thank you," she said, with all the politeness of true hatred.

"Herman, too?"

"He's quite well."

Jack nodded broadly. "That's excellent. Herman and Velma, a marriage made in heaven. Well, Manitowoc, anyway; and I guess that's close enough."

Maggie swallowed, and then she suddenly rushed out in a sibilant, steady monotone, "Jack, I know you don't love me anymore, I'm quite prepared to deal with that, I *can* deal with that, I have my sister and my consciousness-raising classes and plenty of supportive friends, but I have just as much right to Randy as you do and I need to know where he is."

Jack said, "I can't tell you where he is."

"But why? I have a right to know! He's my son! I love him!"

Jack repeated, "I just can't tell you where he is, that's all. I'm sorry." He was sorry. Whatever he thought of Maggie, he knew that she was suffering the same fears and the same uncertainty about Randy as he was; and it was an agony he wouldn't have wished on anybody.

"Is he safe?" asked Maggie.

Jack nodded. "I believe so."

"What do you mean, 'you believe so'? Don't you know for sure?"

"No," said Jack. "If you want the truth, I don't. But I'm doing everything I possibly can, believe me."

"Locked up in here? What can you do locked up in here?"

"I'm not too sure. But I have a couple of ideas that I'm working on."

"Jack! Listen to me! I'm *ordering* you! You have to tell me where he is!"

"Sorry, Margaret-Ann," Jack replied.

Maggie was silent for a moment or two, twisting her handkerchief and biting at her lips. Then suddenly she lunged at him, smacking his face and wrenching at his shirt.

"I hate you!" she screamed. *"I hate you! I hate you!"*

The door of the interview room was flung open immediately, and a uniformed policewoman caught hold of Maggie's arm. Maggie backed away from Jack, her face a mess of tears. "If you've done anything to harm our son," she sobbed at him, "I'm going to kill you!"

Jack turned his back on her. There was nothing else that he could do. He heard her sob once or twice more, and then leave the room, with the policewoman comforting her.

When she had gone, Sergeant Schiller came in. He stood beside Jack for a while, and then he held out something that he had been holding behind his back. A plain wooden flute, and several sheets of paper with handwriting on them. Jack glimpsed the name "Awen."

"You want to tell me about these?" he asked. "They were just delivered by your lawyer's clerk."

"Folk music," said Jack.

"*Folk music?* You've been charged with kidnap and homicide and you want to play *folk music?*"

"What's it to you?"

Jack found it quite unnerving to act so hard-boiled, but he knew that if he told Sergeant Schiller anything at all, he would forfeit any chance of stopping Quintus Miller and of rescuing Randy. Sergeant Schiller would never believe that human beings could run through walls and walk through the earth—not until it was too late, anyway; and he would never allow Jack to follow Quintus Miller.

Sergeant Schiller said, "How about telling me where you hid your boy? Then you can have the flute."

"Keep the goddamned flute," Jack told him, trying to sound as if he couldn't care less about it.

"You're going to have to tell me sometime," Sergeant Schiller warned him.

"I can't tell you something that I don't know."

"You killed him, didn't you? Come on, it's understandable. You were under stress. Your marriage was breaking up. You were tired of the responsibility of taking care of him, he reminded you so much of your wife, so you took the easy way out, and you killed him."

Jack turned around and stared Sergeant Schiller directly in the eye. "That," he said, "is bull."

Sergeant Schiller stared back at him for a moment, then handed him the flute. "I've turned over a lot of stones in the past eleven years, Mr. Reed, sir, and I've uncovered all kinds of pretty disgusting creatures. But I never uncovered anything quite like you."

With that, he snapped his fingers to the guard at the door, to order him to escort Jack back to his cell.

*

That night, the sacrificial blood lust of Quintus Miller and his maniacs raged throughout Milwaukee and Madison and along the ley lines that ran between them.

Thunder bellowed out of the sky; unnatural lightning stalked on stilts along the ley lines; and the air was thick with the tension of approaching catastrophe.

Close to Dousman, a fifteen-year-old farm girl called Sarah Lee Kodiak was dragged into the depths of a dark green kale field. She was screaming at an unearthly high pitch as she was pulled two hundred feet across the field, deeper and deeper, thigh-deep, waist-deep, neck-deep, until she was swallowed up into the rich black soil with her father and her brother still running desperately toward the spot where she had vanished.

By the light of their tractor's headlights, with rain smearing their hair against their faces, her father and brother dug with spades and picks for over two hours, sobbing with grief and exhaustion, but they couldn't find her. Black soil, stains of crimson, but no Sarah Lee.

A fifty-five-year-old banker named Lincoln Winter was pulled into the sidewalk as he stepped out of a taxi in The Avenue, Milwaukee. He opened the door, stepped onto the sidewalk, and as he did so his foot was wrenched straight into the concrete. He shouted out once, but nobody saw him, and when the mystified cabdriver climbed out of the taxi to collect his fare, Lincoln Winter had disappeared. The cabdriver didn't look down— or he would have noticed four well-manicured fingertips scraping in agony at the sidewalk, like four wriggling pink chrysalides, just managing to tip up a discarded Mcdonald's carton before they disappeared, too.

Heidi Feldman, an auburn-rinsed waitress from Karl Ratzsch's restaurant, in Milwaukee, was caught by the maniacs as she went up in the elevator to her fifth-story apartment in West Allis. She was leaning toward the mirror on the back wall of the elevator to pluck out a stray eyebrow hair, when two powerful hands shattered the glass and dragged her headfirst into the brick wall of the elevator shaft, while the elevator continued to whine on upward.

In the last instants of her life, Heidi Feldman felt as if her head were being ground like corn between two massive grindstones. Her husband opened the elevator door at the fifth floor with a smile and a large martini and found the elevator car torn open and empty.

A thirty-five-year-old television engineer named Roy Truesho was sleeping next to his wife in his duplex house in Monona, southeast of Madison, when a glistening hand emerged from his laminated wood headboard and reached quivering like a praying mantis toward his wrist. Roy was tugged, inch by inch, into the headboard, with a slow churning splintering sound. He didn't cry out. His wife opened her eyes just in time to see his left foot disappearing into solid wood, its toes stiff with pain.

Then she was alone, widowed, with two small children sleeping across the landing.

Rain swept like warm blood all the way across Green, and Dane, and Jefferson Counties.

In his cell at the Milwaukee police headquarters, Jack was sitting uncomfortably cross-legged on his bunk, waiting for midnight to pass, when the moon would rise to its zenith, even though it was hidden behind the rain clouds. *About 1 o'c*, Geoff had written, *ley-lines will be magnetized 2 their utmost—easier 4 U to penetr8, hopefly.*

The note had ended, *Meet you at the pentacle, Q's room, soonest.*

Jack closed his eyes and breathed regularly and deeply, but he knew that any attempt to sleep was futile. The trouble was, when it came down to the bottom line, he didn't believe for one moment that he was going to be able to walk into the wall at all, let alone make his way to The Oaks and emerge from Quintus Miller's pentacle with all the ease of a man stepping out of a subway. He had practiced Quintus Miller's off-key version of "Lavender Blue" over and over again (much to the fury of a vociferous and spaced-out punk in the next cell but one); he had recited the rituals and the names. It all sounded more like hocus-pocus than ever. If he hadn't seen the maniacs rising from the ground with his own eyes, if he hadn't seen Father Bell's fingers burning and Essie Estergomy dragged down into the gravel, he wouldn't even have tried.

Just before twelve, he had taken up the flute again, to play yet another reprise of "*Lavender blue, dilly-dilly; lavender green*" when Sergeant Schiller came in and stood in the doorway with his hands in his pockets and looked at him. "End of my shift," Sergeant Schiller said at last. "I'm going home now. Wondered if you felt like telling me anything that might help me sleep."

Jack looked back at him for a long time without saying anything.

"Oh well, please yourself," said Sergeant Schiller, and turned to go.

"Sergeant!" Jack spoke up.

"What is it?"

"Just to tell you, I won't be bothering you too much longer. I promise."

"What kind of a promise is that?"

"You'll see. At least I hope you will."

"You're a genuine one-hundred-percent sicko, Mr. Reed, sir. Get some sleep."

At a quarter after one, when police headquarters was comparatively quiet, only echoes and footsteps and winos and addicts moaning in their sleep, Jack lifted his head and looked around and listened. After two or three minutes, he rose quietly from his bunk and padded on stockinged feet toward the end wall of the cell. It was still raining outside. The rain sprinkled softly and suggestively against the window.

Jack thought: *This is it, at last. This is where I trust in history and ancient magic. Oh God, I hope it works. Oh God, I hope it doesn't work.*

Grimacing, he took the tiny sliver of razor blade that Geoff had secreted behind the reed of his flute and drew it across the ball of his thumb. Blood flooded out: he could hear it dropping glutinously onto the ceramic-tiled floor. *Split, splat, split, splat.* He approached the wall, holding his wrist, his thumb still dripping. He was quaking with the enormity of what he was about to do. Or perhaps with the madness of it.

It's not going to work, it's not going to work. It's far too late.

He hesitated, sniffed—then described in blood two huge triangles, one upright and one inverted, the Hexagram of Solomon. Earth and water, air and fire—and where they met, the Quintessence, the fifth element.

He stood in front of them and touched the wall, and outside the window of his cell the lightning flickered, and thunder ripped across the sky like a thousand torn bolts of broadcloth, and rain clattered onto the rooftops of Milwaukee as if God was determined to drown it, and commit it to the lake.

He lifted the scribbled papers that Geoff had sent him and began to recite the Druid rituals. *They're wrong*, he thought. *It was too long ago. How could anybody hand down these rituals for two thousand years?*

But Quintus Miller had managed it, hadn't he? Quintus Miller and all of his lunatic followers? And if Quintus Miller had managed it, then he could, too.

"Dia dha mo chaim,
Dia da mo chuairt,
Dia dha mo chainn,
Dia dha mon smuain!"

He felt like a fool. He felt like a total fool. His pronunciation was probably appalling. Even if there *were* any Celtic gods—even if there *were* any Druidic influences—they probably wouldn't be able to understand him anyway.

But he recited everything that Geoff had written for him, faithfully, down to the very last word. And then he read the list of the fifty names of Awen—Da and Yoghan, Mabo and Mabona, Lu and Lew, mab-Moi and Mabinos.

He hesitated, licked his lips, and then he played his flute, the tune that sounded so much like "Lavender Blue, Dilly-Dilly," and spoke the final ritual words that were supposed to take him into the wall.

"Caimich mi a nochd
Eadar uir agus earc,
Eadaer run do reachd,
Agus dearc mo dhoille.

"Bury me by night,
Amid the pastures and the herds.
Amid the mystery of thy laws.
My unseeing eyes."

As he recited these words, Geoff's paper trembling in his hand, he approached the pentacle on the wall of his cell, closer and closer, until his face was pressed against the gray-washed brickwork. *Bury me by night*, he whispered. *Bury me by night.*

He heard footsteps squeaking down the corridor outside his cell. The guard was coming. He heard keys jingling, and one of the winos calling out, "*Mother! Mother! Come and get me, Mother!*"

He closed his eyes. *Thou Being-of-Laws-and-of-the-Stars, help me. Bury me by night amid the mystery of thy laws.*

The cell door opened. The guard said, "You've been playing that goddamned whistle again, you're driving everybody bananas."

Jack stepped into the wall.

12

He felt as if soft dry sand were pouring over him. He couldn't open his eyes, because the brick was pouring over his face, but he found that he didn't need to open them. He could visualize where he was going inside his head, almost as clearly as if he could actually see it. The walls of police headquarters were like the dark narrow pathways of a maze, and he could walk along them, swiftly and smoothly, his own molecules passing through the molecules of brick with a deep *sssssshhhhhh*ing sound.

He walked all the way along the corridor of the cell block, through the wall. Whenever he reached one of the metal doors, the sensation of passing through it was markedly different. It felt almost like being caught by a lawn sprinkler, a sudden smack of ice-cold water. He reached the stairs, but then he realized that he probably didn't need them. The maniacs had *swum* in their earthly environment rather than walked in it. Jack tried to imagine that he was swimming; and as he did so he allowed himself to sink down through the darkness of the walls, down to street level, then *below* street level.

With the awkward grace of an inexperienced aqualung diver, he surged his way through concrete and brick and rock. Every now and then he passed through a sewer or a gas pipe or an electricity cable. He had no way of knowing it, but when he passed through telephone cables, his passing caused a sudden shadowy-sounding frizzle that could be heard by people talking on the line.

He was fascinated when he raised his head to realize that he could see or at least *visualize* everything above the surface of the sidewalks, in the same way that a swimmer can see above the surface of a pool. He could see underneath automobiles; he could see the soles of people's shoes. Their images were distorted, in the same way that the images seen above water are distorted; but when he considered that he was looking out of a very dense medium into a far less dense one—well, he couldn't remember all of his high-school physics, but he guessed it was scientifically logical.

He felt the vibration of Milwaukee's scores of public clocks striking 1:45. He was going to have to find himself a ley line: one of the main connecting lines that would enable him to make his way speedily back to The Oaks, a Druidic highway. He could sense the magnetism of the ley lines around him, in the same way that he could usually sense an electric storm approaching. It was a strange, tingling, cat's-fur feeling; and it made the hair prickle on the back of his neck, and the nerves prickle in the palms of his hands.

He went deep beneath the Milwaukee River, sliding through silt, heading eastward. It was very much blacker and colder down here, and he could feel the weight of the earth enfolding him. Curiously, however, he didn't feel imprisoned or claustrophobic, even though he usually panicked in confined spaces. He felt calm and determined and increasingly capable of surging his way through the earth.

At least he had escaped from police custody. Sergeant Schiller would go crazy! Jack wondered whether the guard had seen him disappearing into the wall. Even if he had, Jack doubted if the poor man would have believed what he had witnessed—or even if he did believe it, if he would have the nerve to tell Sergeant Schiller.

Jack was close to the foundations of the East-West Freeway. He passed through the concrete piers that supported the overhead roadway with a sharper *ssshhh! ssshhh! ssshhh!* like somebody chopping a shovel into wet cement. He could sense that he was close to a ley line now. He felt as if he were being *tugged* through the earth, his whole nervous system effervescent with natural magnetism. Southwestward, under the freeway, in the rough direction of the Wisconsin State Fair Grounds.

He was awed by the powerful forces that existed beneath the surface. He had always understood, of course, that the ocean's tides were controlled by the gravitational pull of the moon. But the vibrant patterns that ran through the soil were equally strong, if not stronger. They were capable of turning him from a man of flesh to a man of rippling soil; they were capable of dragging him along with all the force of a major river.

Jack understood now why so many legends claimed that man had been formed out of soil. When he was a kid, he had read in one of his old Buffalo Bill books that Gitche Manitou, the great god of the Indian peoples, had baked the first man out of clay—the first was burned, and became a black man; the second was underdone, and became a white man; while the third was perfect, and became a Red Indian.

Even the Bible said, *The Lord God formed man of dust from the ground*. And it was true, it had actually happened. The Druids had understood it, and so had dozens of other ancient cultures. All that Jack had done tonight was to reverse the process—not dust into man, but man into dust.

It was a transformation as ancient as the world itself: a transformation that defined man's bond with God and with the earth that God had created. God and man were one and the same substance—earth, air, fire, and water, and everything that those elements embraced and implied, melded together into the mystical and ubiquitous Quintessence.

Jack knew that even if he survived this transformation— even if he found and defeated Quintus Miller—he could never be the same man again. He had understood the meaning of Genesis; he had understood what Adam had been. He had understood the very substance of himself.

It gave him a sensation of terrible fear, yet also of limitless power. Man had lost faith with the earth on which be lived. But men like Adolf Krüger had discovered it again; and so had Quintus Miller. No wonder the early Christians had feared the Druids. No wonder they had fought so hard to destroy them.

Jack flowed his way nearer and nearer to the ley line, and at last he reached it. He could feel it all around him, a singing, reverberating river in the earth. His eyes were still closed, but he could sense the ley line running ahead of him, relentlessly straight, all the way across Wisconsin, all the way into the northlands, into the polar ice. *This* was how the Celts had traveled across the earth, bringing their

Druidic culture to North America, in countless centuries gone by. Not by boat, not by coracle, not by crossing the northern straits on foot.

All Jack had to do was to follow the ley line, and he would arrive at The Oaks. Almost certainly, it would be there that Quintus Miller would perform the final sacrificial ceremonies that would release him and his followers from the earth, and let them live again.

He traveled along the ley line, running, like a man running in a dream. The soil and the rocks poured around him, poured *through* him, as if he had no physical substance at all. Yet he could feel the power of his body, and he could feel the power of his mind. He was back in the element from which man had first gained his shape, and first gained his strength.

He couldn't tell how fast he was running, but it was impossibly fast compared with the speed that a man could normally run when he was out of his element. He lifted his closed eyes to the sky, and the night's thunderclouds roiled past him like the speeded-up thunderclouds in *Close Encounters of the Third Kind*.

All he could hear was the thick rushing noise of soil, *sssshhhhhh—ssssshhhh—ssssshhhh*, and the easy panting of his own breath.

He passed Okauchee, Waterloo, De Forest, and Morrisonville. He wasn't more than twenty miles distant from The Oaks when he became conscious of another sound. Footsteps, pounding behind him. Somebody else, rushing through the earth. Somebody fast and powerful and determined to catch up with him.

He turned his head. Less than a mile away, he could

visualize a man running after him. Two men—three. They had their heads lowered and they were running with frightening doggedness. *We're coming to get you, you bastard. We're going to tear you to pieces.*

Jack recognized the voice. Gordon Holman, the maniac who had nailed his wife's tongue to a table and his own penis to a tree, and who had set fire to Father Bell's hands. Gordon Holman was after him, and Gordon Holman was almost as mad as Quintus Miller.

Jack took a deep breath and ran harder, as hard as he possibly could. It didn't strike him as strange that he could breathe; but then fish could breathe in water, and he was using the air in the soil in almost exactly the same way. He felt the soil pouring over his face. He was running so fast now that occasional rocks and pebbles hit him and stung him nearly as viciously as if somebody had thrown them at him.

But Gordon Holman and his two companions were gaining on him. They had lived in the earth longer, their bodies were imbued with more of the earth's natural strength. Jack began to feel the vibrations of their running through the soles of his feet. They were after him, and they meant to bring him down.

This is our *day!* Gordon Holman roared at him through the thickness of the earth. *This is* our *day!*

Jack could feel that he was nearing The Oaks. The current of the ley line ran faster, like a river coming close to a precipitous waterfall. The soil rushed past, the sky rushed past, the world rushed past. Jack began to feel that he was being helplessly swept along, running down a mountain, unable to stop.

Our day, you bastard! Our day! Our day!

At The Oaks, ley lines intersected from the west, from the east, from the southwest, from the north. The spot where The Oaks had been built drew in power from all four quarters of America; but it *radiated* power, too. It was like a sun, below the ground, with a huge gravitational pull, and yet beaming out energy everywhere.

Jack sensed that The Oaks was very near. He was running through woods. The roots of the trees wriggled darkly down in the soil, like jellyfish tentacles floating in the ocean. He could *hear* The Oaks humming as low and as powerful as a dynamo. But at the same time he could feel Gordon Holman less than thirty feet behind him. He thought: *Turn—face him—hit him hard—you're as strong as he is now, you're fighting in the same element.*

But as he turned, and stopped, something jumped up on to his back, something heavy and soft, and then somebody clutched at his arms, and somebody clutched at his legs, and before he knew it he was being pulled to his knees. He twisted his head around, fighting desperately, and then he visualized them. Women, ten or eleven women, with wild expressions and wilder hair, some of them dressed in plain institutional smocks, some of them wearing cotton skirts, but bare to the waist, some of them completely naked.

They forced his head forward until his face was pressed between his knees and his arms were stretched upward and backward behind him. He tried to sink further down into the earth to escape them, grunting with the effort of it, but one of them wriggled underneath him—a big naked woman with fat shoulders and huge breasts and blisters between her legs where she had set fire to her own pubic hair.

Come down, my darling! she said, grinning at him with a toothless gummy grin. *Come down, if you want to!*

Jack twisted, heaved, but couldn't get free. It was then that Gordon Holman arrived and stood over him, naked except for a straitjacket tied around his waist like an off-white kilt. His two lieutenants stood a little way behind him, one of them constantly nodding his head, and the other motionless, with a crown of brambles around his brow, smiling at nothing at all with an empty beatific smile. St. Out-to-Lunch. But the strangest thing of all was that this confrontation was taking place twenty feet beneath the surface of the woods, in the darkness of the root-wriggled soil, between Lodi and Okee, not too far from Lake Wisconsin.

Quintus said you wanted to stop our sacrifice, said Gordon Holman. *Quintus said you wanted us earthbound for ever.*

Jack said, *Quintus is crazy. That so-called sacrifice, that's my son.*

Quintus said he wanted you dead. Dead, that's what he said, and hung out to dry! Bring me that man's skin, that's what he said! Bring me that man's liver!

The fat woman squirmed lasciviously beneath him and licked at his eyelids and his lips. He twisted his face away in disgust.

I want to make love to you while you're dying, she whispered. *I want to have you inside me while they're killing you.*

One woman laughed, and shrieked, and called out, *Pandora! Pandora! Pandora!* over and over again, until another woman wrenched at her hair.

Let him go, ordered Gordon Holman.

The women hesitated at first, but when Gordon Holman took a warning step forward, they released Jack's arms and shuffled back and left him crouching where he was. Only the fat woman beneath him remained, in case he should dive for safety deep beneath the substrata of the soil.

Do you have a prayer that you want to pray? asked Gordon Holman.

Jack remained where he was, hunched up, desperately thinking. What were those ritual words? The words of transformation and sacrifice? When Geoff had recited them to Lester, on top of the parking lot, Lester had screamed like crazy.

Caimich mi a nochd
Eadar uir something,
Eadar run do reachd,
Something something something

He was amazed that he could remember as much as that. Usually, his memory was appalling. People would call him, and he would promise to call them back within two or three minutes, and that was it—he would have forgotten about it instantly. So how could he remember Gaelic—especially Gaelic that he had heard only once and read only twice, and in the most stressful of circumstances?

Caimich mi a nochd
Eadar Uir agus eare,
Eadar run do reachd,
Agus dearc mo dhoille

There was overwhelming silence beneath the ground. Jack remained crouched with his head bent forward. At first he thought that Gordon Holman was simply waiting for the right moment to kill him. But then he felt a quivering through the loamy soil, and cautiously raised his head; and there was Gordon Holman, trembling all over, palsied with what appeared to be total terror.

He turned around. Most of the women had fallen to their knees, and they were trembling, too. St. Out-to-Lunch was frowning now, instead of smiling, and the head-nodder was nodding so violently that Jack thought he might be in danger of shaking his head off his shoulders.

The sacrifice, the transformation. The end of one life, the beginning of another. That was what frightened these pathetic lunatics so much. Those words heralded death, and change, and insecurity—the superiority of magic over human will. Those were the words that the Druids had spoken to their followers at Stonehenge and Carnac and Mystery Hill, when all the world had been ruled by magic.

Jack himself could feel the potency of what he had just said. He could feel the power of the ley line gathering itself around him in preparation for the ritual that he had already set in motion.

But now what? thought Jack. *Do I make a run for it? Will they follow me? Will the effects of the prayer wear off, as soon as I move?*

Slowly, cautiously, he stood up. Still trembling, eyes still closed, Gordon Holman watched him, but did nothing to stop him.

It's not time yet, said Gordon Holman.

What do you mean, it's not time?

I haven't taken my full eight hundred. No more than fifty! It isn't time! It can't be time!

Jack looked up and visualized lightning crackling through the trees. It was raining hard. He could feel the bone-cold water dripping from the branches and seeping through the black hairy roots of the oaks.

Besides, said Gordon Holman, more optimistically, *Quintus hasn't called us yet. Quintus hasn't called us back. Quintus will know when it's time! Quintus will know when we've all taken eight hundred each.*

Gordon Holman laughed, and the women laughed, too, although fearfully still, and with less conviction. Jack had spoken the first words of the sacrifice. What had already been set in motion wouldn't be easy to stop, not without a sacrifice, not without death. The sacrificial ritual that Geoff had begun on the rooftop parking lot had only been concluded by Quintus Miller's slaughtering of Lester. Blood was called for, human clay.

But Gordon Holman snuffled and bayed like a hound. *Don't fret! Don't fret!* he cried out to his lunatic companions. *Quintus will call us when it's time! Quintus will play his music, and then we'll know! Quintus will call us with his pipe! The calling! The calling! We haven't heard the calling yet! If we'd heard the calling, we wouldn't have had no choice! We'd've had to go! But it isn't time! Don't fret! It isn't time!*

Jack thought, *What's he talking about, the calling? Quintus has to call them with pipe music when it's time for the sacrifice?*

He held up his own pipe. Just a smooth straight cane, with holes burned into it. Maybe the music was the answer.

Maybe the music was critical. It had been a critical part of the ritual that had taken him into the wall. Maybe it was a critical part of the sacrificial ritual, too.

Quintus would play pipe music when it was time for the lunatics to assemble at the sacred place... and they would follow. Judging from what Gordon Holman had said, they would be *compelled* to follow, whether they wanted to follow or not. The same way that the children had followed the piper in Hamelin, straight into the hillside. Because from what Jack could work out, the piping was much more than music—much more than a simple signal. It was a direct summons from the Being-of-the-Law-and-of-the-Stars, God the Quintessence, a summons that called on the body just as strongly as it called on the sense of devotion.

Jack thought, *You don't turn down an invitation from God the Quintessence, even if it means that your whole life is going to be torn apart from top to bottom, and that everybody you know is going to be tortured on frames, and bent back double so that they lost their eternal souls for ever.*

You go—because you have no choice.

Jack hesitantly lifted his pipe. He didn't know if it would play beneath the ground, but he blew into the reed, and the air flowed thickly through the stem, and something that was less than a musical note but more than a musical vibration came quivering out of it, and through the soil, *Lavender blue, dilly-dilly; lavender green; here I am king, dilly-dilly—*

The effect on Gordon Holman and the rest of the lunatics was immediate and frightening. They rose up, and crowded around Jack, holding out their hands in blind supplication. They didn't speak, but their begging hands made a rustling sound like the pigeons clustering on the roof of The Oaks, and their bodies pushed through the soil with that terrible familiar *sssssshhhhhhh*.

Jack retreated, along the ley line, back toward The Oaks. He turned. The lunatics weren't following him. They were standing in the same place with their hands outstretched, their eyes closed, their faces desperate with longing.

What is it that somebody can long for so desperately? thought Jack. *What is it that means more to them than anything at all?*

He walked farther, then stopped. Still the lunatics remained where they were. He hesitated, then lifted up his pipe again and began to play the same tune, over and over and over.

This time they followed him. They seemed blind, as if they had lost the sharp sense of visualization that allowed Jack to find his way through the blackness of solid earth. They shuffled pale and anxious and mad, like medieval lepers. Even though Jack knew that they probably wouldn't hurt him, they looked so distorted and irrational and strange that he stepped back more and more quickly, still playing his flute, but anxious that they shouldn't catch up with him.

Lavender blue, dilly-dilly... the music penetrated the soil and ran along the ley lines; and where one ley line intersected with another, the music ran off again, as soft and as bright as quicksilver.

The music reached The Oaks and spread swiftly out in all directions, as high and as vibrant as the song sung by a spiderweb touched by the wind. To Janesville and Watertown and Mineral Point, to Monona and Waukesha.

All over southeast Wisconsin, deep beneath the soil, deep

beneath the concrete sidewalks, fast secreted in walls and ceilings and furniture, the remaining scores of maniacs lifted their heads, and listened, and frowned.

The calling. But the calling was far too early. Thousands more lives had still to be taken, eight hundred each. That was the law; that was the price of escape.

But no matter how many misgivings the lunatics had about how soon the calling had come, there was no question of resisting it. *The calling.* That same plaintive pipe tune, played over and over. *Lavender blue, dilly-dilly...* The oldest of sacred hymns to the Being-of-the-Law-and-of-the-Stars, Awen, the great creator.

The tune was a mystical arrangement of notes in the same way that the pentacle was a mystical arrangement of symbols. Those who heard it were physically drawn through the soil, along the ley lines, just as the bluestones of Stonehenge had been physically drawn from ancient Wales to Salisbury Plain. They came because they had no alternative. They came because they had been commanded.

They came because they were *called.*

One hundred thirty-six of them, drawn back toward The Oaks, some of them leaving furrowed paths across fields and highways, some of them passing invisibly but audibly through stores and walls and apartment buildings. Not dancing, not chattering, the way that the children of Hamelin were supposed to have danced and chattered after the Pied Piper. But running, with their eyes closed, running as if their lives depended on it.

By the time he reached the foundations of The Oaks, Jack

already realized what had happened, and that he had called them all. He could visualize them all around him, as if he were standing on a rise in the ground, and they were approaching through the night from all directions—running, their faces grim. He had gained enough confidence over the last few miles to turn his back on Gordon Holman and his horrifying friends and to march forward at his own pace, looking ahead of him for Quintus Miller.

Above the surface of the ground, thunder cracked across the sky, and rain fell on to The Oaks relentlessly, so that its broken gutters spouted water, and the swimming pool overflowed, carrying its sickening black flotsam halfway across the flooded tennis courts.

Beneath the cellar floor, Jack stood at last in the center of a silent circle of The Oaks's last residents—all there, except for Quintus Miller.

You called and we came, said a tall man with a huge encephalitic head. *Where is the sacrifice?*

I called you because we must pay homage tonight to Awen, Jack extemporized, trying frantically to sense where Quintus Miller could be.

Does this mean a sacrifice? asked a black man with a dramatically sloping forehead. *Does this mean that somebody has to die?*

Well—ah—that's right! said Jack. *Somebody has to die. One of you—to show Awen that you're not afraid to give up anything for her—including your lives, right? Including your souls.*

There were hair-raising screams of dread throughout the assembly of lunatics. They sounded like the passengers of a falling airliner. They were not afraid of sacrificing their physical lives. They were clay, after all, in their present condition, they were nothing more than soil, and just like clay their physical presence could be restored... provided their soul had survived. But if their soul were annihilated, there would be nothingness, and worse than nothingness. There would be the never-ending *consciousness of* nothingness...

Jack said, *My friend knows all about the sacred traditions of Druidism... and my friend says that by sacred tradition, your leader should be sacrificed. If you don't, you'll never know what it is to walk around in the air, ever again. You will never be given Awen's blessing to escape from out of the ground. You hear that? Your leader represents all of you... if you sacrifice him, then Awen will know for certain that you all worship him... that you are all devoted to him.*

He was breathing deeply. The air from the soil was sour and damp, and he could smell that vinegary odor that permeated The Oaks. A hundred thirty-five ill-assorted faces watched him with their eyes closed, not seeing, but sensing. Some of the faces were impossibly beautiful. Others were grotesque, like gargoyles. Others had an unhinged plainness about them, so ordinary that Jack could tell that they were dangerous.

All right... he said, raising his arms. *What we have to do is to locate Quintus Miller. You understand that? And when you've located him, you're going to have to sacrifice him. Otherwise you don't stand a chance. You'll be trapped in the ground forever.*

The man with the huge head said, *What about the eight*

hundred lives we're supposed to take? I've taken only six so far. People aboveground aren't easy to catch.

Forget about the eight hundred lives. It's Quintus Miller you have to go for first.

A woman stepped forward. Her long ash-blond hair trailed through the soil like the hair of Botticelli's Venus, except that this was a child of the earth rather than the sea. She seemed to be barely thirty: in truth she was nearer ninety. She held out her arms and whispered, *How can we trust you? We have always trusted Quintus. You want us to sacrifice Quintus, but is that because Quintus intends to sacrifice your son? What guarantee do we have that you're not deceiving us—that we will never escape?*

Jack said, *You trusted Quintus, and what happened? You spent sixty years trapped in the walls. Quintus will save himself, believe me. Quintus doesn't care about you. Quintus wants out, and as far as he's concerned that's all that matters.*

The ash-blond girl said, *He's here.*

What do you mean, he's here? Where? I don't see him.

He's here, in the building. He's here at The Oaks. Upstairs. I can sense him.

Jack's skin prickled. So Quintus was already here. But why? Jack would have thought that Quintus would have been scouring the streets for more and more people to kill so that he could walk in the real world once again. He looked up through the main supporting wall above his head, but he couldn't see anything except darkness.

Wait here, he told the assembly of lunatics. *Make yourselves ready for a great sacrifice to Awen. Pray. Think of the days when you used to walk around in the real world, okay? Those times are going to come back. But don't go away, do you understand me? I'm going to need you here to help me.*

Where are you going, piper? asked Gordon. His voice was strangely expressionless and spaced out, as if he were still under the influence of the music.

Up, said Jack. I'm going up.

He pushed his way up through the dark gray brickwork of the walls, like a diver rising toward the surface of a thickly silted pond. His cupped hands pulled him *ssssshhhhhh—ssssshhhhh—ssssshhhhh* through the cold, damp cement. An occasional splintering pine-needle prickle as he penetrated a wooden door.

He was heading for Quintus Miller's room, where the pentacle was drawn on the wall. He had a feeling that if Quintus were anywhere, he would be there, searching for a way out.

The walls of The Oaks were deceptively complicated in their construction. Every time Jack forged directly toward the second floor, he seemed to find himself confined to walls that curved over into archways and took him back down to the first floor again. Every time he turned toward Quintus Miller's room, the walls led him emphatically and quickly away.

He stopped at the end of the second-story corridor, trying to sense the whole building, trying to feel its symbolism, trying to feel its totality. *The Maze*, Adolf Krüger had called it; and it *was* a maze.

Jack thought to himself, *You're a businessman, you run a highly successful muffler and tire outfit. Use some business know-how. Use some practical thinking. These Druids lived thousands of years ago, they couldn't have thought of something that good old U.S. business acumen couldn't lick.*

He tried heading *away* from Quintus's room, the way that Alice had walked in the opposite direction when she was trying to find her way through the Looking Glass garden. But he found himself on the opposite side of The Oaks, in one of the dingiest corners, next to the broom closet.

No, he decided, the trick was more elaborate than that. He tried rushing directly back to Quintus's room, but again he found himself way beyond it. He felt as if he were taking one step forward and two steps back.

Maybe that was it. One step forward and two steps back. He tried it, and to his surprise, he managed to reach the corner of the second-story corridor. He tried it again, but this time he was farther away than ever. Maybe it was progressive. One step forward and two steps back. Then two steps forward and three steps back. Then three steps forward and *four* steps back.

After four or five more minutes, he suddenly cracked it. One step forward, two steps back. Two steps forward, one step back. He repeated the same pattern again and again, turning right and left as he went, until quite abruptly he arrived in the wall of Quintus Miller's room, opposite the hexagram.

He couldn't stop himself from letting out a suppressed grunt of shock.

Quintus Miller was already there, and so was Randy.

Quintus Miller was crouched inside the wall in the far corner of the room, not looking in Jack's direction, and too preoccupied to stop what he was doing.

Jack stayed where he was, rigid with alarm, trying not to breathe too loudly. Quintus hadn't yet sensed that he was there—or if he had, he was so contemptuous of Jack's ability to stop him that he simply didn't care.

Jack had found Quintus unnerving enough when he had appeared in the glass of Geoff's windshield. But here, in the wall, his appearance was even more daunting. He was short, big-headed, bull-necked, with slashed-back hair and a face as cold as a painted steel mask. He wore soiled gray flannel pants, and a heavy Sam Browne belt with hammers and pliers hanging around it. Quintus's back was thick with graying woolly hair, and his elbows were raw with pink-and-white eczema.

What he was doing was even more frightening. He had forced Randy to stand naked inside the wall, behind the blood-marked hexagram, with his arms and his legs spread apart to correspond exactly with the star shape of earth and water, air and fire. He had fastened Randy's wrists and ankles by forcing them through to the real world outside, small hands and small feet protruding from the plaster.

Randy had his head bent forward, resting against the inside of the wall. He looked dirty and tousled and exhausted. If Jack hadn't known just how dangerous Quintus Miller could be, he would have rushed forward then and there and taken Randy into his arms.

There was another thing: Jack didn't yet understand how Quintus and the other maniacs could reach out of the walls and the floors, while Father Bell and Randy had obviously been trapped when their hands were forced from one element into another. And Jack had seen for himself what had happened to the people whom the maniacs had dragged right into the ground.

Maybe Quintus and his followers had acquired more of the earth's natural power, from all of the years they had spent in the walls of The Oaks. Maybe they had entered the walls with a different kind of a ritual. Geoff had told him that there were scores of Druidic rituals for moving from one element to the other, most of which had been lost. Maybe Quintus had discovered one of them in Adolf Krüger's books, the books that were now burned to ashes.

Jack didn't move. He wasn't at all sure what he was going to do now. He wondered if it would be feasible to lure Quintus down to the floor below the basement, where the rest of the maniacs were assembled, ready for a sacrifice. The trouble with that idea was that he was still unsure about making his way around the maze of walls, and Quintus would inevitably catch up with him. Even if he *did* manage to lure Quintus to the basement, Jack had no guarantees that once they saw him, his followers would not remember their long-standing loyalty to their leader and help him to tear Jack apart.

His only defense was his flute, and he wasn't certain how long the influence of "Lavender Blue" could last... especially since he didn't know any more Druidic music, or any more Druidic rituals.

He was still standing stock-still in the corner of the room when Quintus bent forward so that his head was touching the floor and began to chant a long, muffled litany. Jack could only catch a few words of it, but it was definitely Gaelic.

"Failt ort fein, a gheallach ur,
Ailleagan iuil nan neul!"

Randy whimpered and moved his head listlessly from side to side, his eyes closed just as Jack's were, and just as Quintus's were.

"Failt ort fein, a gheallach ur—"
Ohhhh... moaned Randy.
"Ailleagan iuil nan neul!"

While Quintus was reciting, Jack heard a noise in the corridor outside the room. Not inside the walls, but in the corridor itself. Footsteps, voices. He glanced back toward Quintus, visualizing his crouching figure, but Quintus was too deeply involved in his chanting to have heard.

Jack suddenly recognized the voices, and the tap-tapping of high-heeled shoes. It was Geoff and Karen, at last, thank God!

Geoff was saying, "...no way of knowing if he got away. I can't exactly call Sergeant Schiller and ask him outright."

"He'll get here," Karen insisted. "If there's any way that he can do it, he'll get here. He's that kind of a guy."

"Well, anyway, let's take a look in here," suggested Geoff as they reached the door of Quintus's room. "The pentacle is the entrance and the exit to the maze. If he's going to come out anywhere, he's going to come out here."

"But how come *Jack's* going to be able to come out, when Quintus Miller can't. Leastways, not without killing all of those people?"

Geoff opened the door and stepped into the room and quickly shone a flashlight around. "Don't know for sure, to tell you the truth. But Druggett's book says that the rule was, one sacrifice for every lunar month spent in the earth. Awen demands it. Kind of compensation, I suppose, for all the power and energy that one person draws out of the soil when they're living inside it. The earth's magnetism has to be replenished, the same way that its minerals do. Awen is the earth's protector, and as far as Awen is concerned, the earth is more valuable than individual human lives."

"You're making me shiver," said Karen.

Jack raised his hand and pressed it against the inside of the wall, tried to press it *out* of the wall, to attract Geoff's attention. But the wall was too hard; he was not yet strong enough to push his way through the mystical meniscus that separated the world of earth from the world of air.

He hesitated. Quintus was still softly chanting and nodding backward and forward, as if he were slowly going into a trance. Maybe if Jack called out to Geoff, Quintus wouldn't hear him.

Randy moaned and tossed his head back, and at the moment he did so, he flapped his hands and his feet, and Geoff shone his flashlight toward the hexagram.

Because Jack had been able to visualize everything around him with his eyes closed, he had almost forgotten that it was still dark and that Geoff needed a flashlight to see what was happening. The flashlight crossed the wall in front of Jack's face and momentarily dazzled him—not the light itself, because the light couldn't penetrate the wall—but the ionized particles that streamed out of the flashlight.

"*Karen!*" called Geoff. "Look at this! Hands, and feet, at each point of the hexagram! A child's hands and feet!"

Geoff! Jack hissed. *Geoff, for Christ's sake!*

But Geoff didn't hear him. He knelt down in front of the pentacle, and took hold of one of Randy's bare feet, and said, "It's Randy! It must be! There weren't any juvenile patients at The Oaks!"

"But why are his hands and his feet sticking out of the wall?" asked Karen. Jack caught the blond nylon shine of the wig she had bought to pretend to be his sister Edna-Mae. "Is he *in* there?"

"Yes, he is," said Geoff, worried. "And the reason he's been arranged like this is because he's going to be sacrificed. This is the final child sacrifice that allows an earth-walker to emerge from the wall."

"But they haven't killed enough people," said Karen. "The news said two hundred sixteen, that's all. That isn't enough to let *one* loony out of the wall!"

Geoff! called Jack, louder this time.

Quintus Miller had stopped chanting, halfway through his ritual, and he was rising slowly to his feet. His face was expressionless, his eyes unblinking, but Jack could tell how angry he was at being interrupted. The muscles across his shoulders and back were bunched up and wriggling with swollen arteries, and the sinews in his huge neck were as taut as braided steel cables.

"Can you get Randy *out*?" Karen was asking Geoff.

Geoff! screamed Jack. *Quintus Miller is here! Get away from that wa—*

Without any hesitation, Quintus thrust his arm out of the wall and seized Geoff's beard, pulling Geoff facefirst into the wall.

Geoff roared out in pain. Karen screamed. Immediately Jack ran around the walls of the room and snatched hold of Quintus Miller by the shoulders, shaking him as hard as he could.

Quintus released Geoff, who fell back bloody-faced into the room. He turned on Jack and this time his eyes were open, they were gleaming like steel studs. His chest rose and fell with fury, and now that he was facing him, Jack could see the full horror of the tattoo on his abdomen.

Two tattooed hands appeared to be reaching around Quintus's waist and dragging open his skin and his flesh, so that all his internal organs were exposed. Whoever had created this grisly trompe l'oeil, he must have been an obsessive but consummate tattooist, because Jack had to look twice to make sure that Quintus hadn't really been disemboweled.

The dark mauve liver, the glistening beige pancreas, the pale loops of large intestine—everything had been depicted in meticulous detail.

Quintus said, in a tensile voice, *I warned you. You meddling malicious bastard. I warned you.*

I want my son, Jack demanded.

Quintus came closer, and Jack backed away. *Your son belongs to me now. Your son is my passport.*

I won't let you take him, Quintus. You'll have to kill me first.

With pleasure. Quintus grinned and swiftly advanced.

Jack thought, *Shit, this is it*, and braced himself. But

Quintus was even stronger than he had expected. Quintus came at him with the unstoppable force of a speeding truck, seizing both of his wrists, and head-butting him so hard that he was momentarily dazed. Then Quintus punched him twice in the stomach and once in the chest. He heard a rib snap, but his lungs were empty of air, and he couldn't even cry out.

Quintus lifted him up bodily and flung him the entire length of the wall, so that he landed on his shoulder right next to Randy.

Now I'm going to tear your arms off, Quintus promised. *I'm going to tear your arms off and stuff them down your throat.* He came toward Jack with both hands raised and a look of calculating madness on his face that turned Jack's spinal column to ice water.

Quintus grabbed hold of Jack's right arm, but as he did so he flinched and turned around in fury. Then he flinched again, and smacked at his shoulder as if he had been stung, and let Jack go.

Stunned, winded, Jack looked into the room and saw that Geoff was standing in the middle of it with his Perrier bottle of exorcised water, spraying the walls.

"*Ab insidiis diaboli, libera nos Domine!*" he was calling out, through swollen and bloodied lips. "*Audi nos!*"

Quintus bellowed in anger, a harsh throat-tearing sound that made Jack involuntarily jump.

The Christian priests had used the powerful rituals of the Holy Church to supersede the Druids, and now Geoff was using the same rituals to hold back Quintus Miller.

Each splash of exorcised water sizzled on Quintus Miller's flesh like acid. The hair on his back shriveled and burned. But he advanced on Jack yet again, keeping up that steady and terrifying roaring. *Pieces! Damn you! Pieces! That's all that anybody's ever going to find of you! Pieces!*

Quintus's outline must have bulged from the surface of the wall, because now Geoff was sprinkling the exorcised water directly onto him, a shower of holy brine. Quintus's face blistered, his earlobe sizzled, skin twisted and scorched on the side of his arm.

"Ut inimicos sanctae Ecclesiae humiliare digneris, te rogamus, audi nos!"

Quintus gripped Jack's arms with fingers that quivered with power and pain. He stared Jack straight in the face and Jack believed in that instant that he was going to be killed. But then the exorcised water lashed down again, a cat-o'-nine-tails across Quintus's back, and Quintus threw Jack away from him with a hideous screeching shout.

Jack tumbled backward, overbalanced, but just managed to catch hold of Randy's arm as he somersaulted.

The two of them exploded out of the hexagram on the wall, and rolled arms and legs across the floor.

Behind them, the plaster gray bas-relief figure of Quintus Miller, still imprisoned, roared and raged at them in frustration. Geoff stepped up to him, spraying him again and again with the sign of the cross, until he suddenly vanished.

Karen, down on her knees, held Jack tightly in her arms and shuddered with shock and relief. Jack kept his arm around Randy, covering him up with his dusty shirt. His face and his hair were thick with dry plaster, and there was black soil under his fingernails.

"You made it, I can't believe it!" Karen sobbed. "You went through the walls and you made it!"

Jack looked up at Geoff. Geoff was holding a blood-spattered handkerchief to the side of his face, but he was smiling.

"Thanks to you, good buddy," Jack told him.

"You had the guts to do it, old chap," Geoff replied. "And you saved your son, too."

"That hurt?" asked Jack as Geoff dabbed at his cheek.

Geoff shook his head. "It's not much more than a scratch."

Jack said, "Randy? How are you feeling? Do you feel okay?"

Randy coughed, and rubbed his eyes, and stared up at his father numbly. He couldn't understand yet that he was free. "Do you have a root beer?" he asked.

Karen squeezed him. "Honey, I wish we had. But we'll get you some water."

Jack eased himself painfully up. "I think that son of a bitch broke one of my ribs. I was lucky he didn't kill me."

Geoff said, "I think we ought to get out of here as quickly as we can. Quintus needs a last sacrifice to get out of the walls, preferably Randy, but Karen would make a reasonable second-best, and he'd use one of us at a pinch—so don't believe that he's going to let us go easily."

"I thought he had to kill eight hundred people before he could get out of the walls," said Jack.

"Well, me too," Geoff agreed. "Lester said so and Druggett's book said so. But it seems as if he's ready now. And, believe me, he won't stop at anything. I've seen some of his medical records. I've been hiding here at The Oaks ever since the police started looking for me. I went through Elmer Estergomy's files and found quite a few references to Quintus Miller. His personal file's gone... the police must have destroyed it when the patients first disappeared. But Estergomy made lots of peripheral notes, and he kept a daily diary, too, which is pretty revealing."

Geoff helped Randy on to his feet. Then he struggled out of his hairy brown pullover and tugged it over Randy's head. "There? How about that? That should keep you warm till we get to the car."

They left Quintus Miller's room and started to walk back along the darkened corridor, following Geoff's darting flashlight. Jack kept one arm around Karen and the other arm around Randy. He was determined not to lose either of them—especially not to Quintus Miller.

As they went he told Geoff as much as he could about his surrealistic journey along the ley lines, and the way that he had summoned the maniacs back to The Oaks.

"They're down there now, as far as I know, still waiting."

"In that case," said Geoff, "we'll do what Father Bell did, and circle the building with holy water, and hope that they don't get out a second time."

"It's Quintus Miller we have to deal with," said Jack.

"Yes," Geoff replied. They were nearing the landing now. "Elmer Estergomy's notes on him were fascinating. Quintus is a classic paranoiac who came to believe from reading Adolf Krüger's books on Druidism that he was the only true son of Awen, the Druid god. He had delusions of grandeur, but he also had delusions that everybody was persecuting him. That's why he took revenge on his family, by blinding them and stabbing them.

"He was very charismatic, too, according to Elmer Estergomy—although of course he didn't use that actual word. He always commanded attention from the staff and his fellow patients, and his charisma occasionally went beyond that. Some of the staff were supposed to have seen him roll pencils across the table by the power of his mind alone, and once he was supposed to have torn up sheets of newspaper just by staring at them. Strange, huh? Elmer Estergomy wrote again and again in his daily diary that Quintus was probably the single most dangerous patient he ever had to deal with."

Jack grimaced and pressed his hand against his ribs. "I'd agree with that. But what about weaknesses? Doesn't he have any weaknesses? Karen suggested we should find out what he's afraid of, if he's afraid of anything at all, and play on that."

They had almost reached the landing, and Geoff cautiously played the flashlight from one side of the corridor to the other.

"From what I could read from Elmer Estergomy's diaries, Quintus Miller is morbidly afraid of dogs. He tore all pictures of dogs out of magazines and shredded them up, and if anybody talked about dogs he went into a fit. Elmer Estergomy guessed that it was something to do with the night he killed his brothers and his mother. His father came home and found him and set the family watchdog on him... apparently he was almost killed. He had himself tattooed to cover the scars, and also to taunt his father that he had nearly been ripped open. But that's the only specific phobia Estergomy mentioned."

Jack said to Karen, "That's probably what kept Joseph Lovelittle alive for so long. Quintus Miller didn't want to come anywhere near him, not with that Doberman of his."

They reached the landing. Jack recognized the pale blind

statues and the skeletal hanging lamp and the dull gleam from the marble floor. God, he hated this place, and feared it, too. He had never hated any building the way that he hated The Oaks. Somewhere, he could hear rain clattering through the ceiling on to the floor, and the distant grumbling of thunder.

They were just about to start down the staircase when a flashlight dazzled them from down below in the hallway, and a woman's voice said sharply, "Who's there?"

Jack frowned into the darkness. "Geoff," he said, "give me the flashlight."

The woman's voice repeated, "Who's there? Jack? Is that you?"

"Jesus Christ," said Jack. "It's Maggie."

13

Maggie walked smartly across the marble, floor until she reached the foot of the staircase, her Burberry raincoat rustling. She prodded the beam of the flashlight up the stairs, first into Jack's face, then into Karen's face, then down at Randy.

"Randy!" she cried out. "Thank God you're safe!"

She ran up the stairs, her court shoes tapping, and knelt down and hugged him tight. Randy burst into tears.

"What have you *done* to him?" Maggie snapped. "What have you done with his clothes?" She stared fiercely at Karen and said, "I might have known that *you* would be here!"

Jack retorted, "What I'd like to know is what the hell *you're* doing here. What time is it? It isn't even light yet!"

"Sergeant Schiller called me, as a matter of fact, to warn me that you'd escaped, and that you could be dangerous."

"Well, thanks. I've just saved Randy from being sacrificed alive and now I'm supposed to be dangerous."

"I never believed that you'd killed him," Maggie replied. "I may not love you, Jack. In fact I think I probably hate you. But I know you better than that. It just occurred to me that you might have *hidden* Randy someplace, and that if you'd escaped you'd be going to get him so that you could take him away. The only place I could think of where you might have been able to hide him was here. I knew that I would have to be quick, so I drove here at once."

Geoff said, "Mrs. Reed... this building is extremely dangerous. We have to leave here right away."

"Who's this?" Maggie demanded. "I warn you—I'm going to call the police!"

"At this moment, Mrs. Reed, the police are the least of my worries. Now, shall we go?"

"If you think I'm going to let you get away, you've got another thing coming," Maggie told Jack. "You've put me through absolute hell!"

She took hold of Randy's hand and began to march down the stairs with him, swinging her flashlight. Geoff looked at Jack and raised his eyebrows, and Karen said, "If she calls the cops..."

But Maggie was only a third of the way down the staircase when she screamed, and Randy screamed, too. Geoff flicked his flashlight toward her, and to Jack's horror, he saw that two gray, blistered hands had thrust themselves up from the stairs and were pulling Maggie and Randy into the marble treads.

"Maggie, hold on!" Jack shouted. Both he and Geoff ran down the stairs, and while Jack kicked viciously at Quintus Miller's fingers, Geoff shakily opened up his bottle of exorcised water and sprinkled it all around. Maggie screamed and screamed and clutched Jack's leg, but then the water sizzled into Quintus's flesh and his grip relaxed, and Jack was able to drag Maggie back up the stairs. Randy came running up, too, weeping and shaking.

Geoff was still spraying water around when another

hand reached out of the stairs behind him and grabbed at his ankle.

He turned, slipped, and almost lost his balance. The Perrier bottle fell out of his grasp, bounced once, and rolled away.

"We'll have to make a run for it!" Jack shouted. "Down the stairs, across the hall, and out through the lounge, as fast as we can!"

Geoff said, "Come on, then! The quicker the better!"

He launched himself down the staircase, but just as he reached the bottom stair a forest of marble hands rose from the hallway floor, clawing blindly at him. The lunatics had left the basement and had risen through the building in search of their promised sacrifice. The hallway looked like some hideous asparagus bed of pallid arms.

"*Up!*" Geoff yelled, and came running back up the stairs again. As he passed the place where Quintus Miller's hands had emerged the marble steps suddenly cracked and exploded, and a thunderously splintering furrow came chasing up the stairs after him.

Geoff snatched hold of Karen and Maggie and dragged them forcibly along the corridor at full tilt. Jack came hop-hobbling behind them, his broken rib jabbing into him with every step, tugging Randy along as fast as he could run.

Only feet behind them, the linoleum floor of the corridor was ripped furiously open as Quintus Miller relentlessly pursued them, mad for revenge, mad for sacrifice, mad to tear them apart.

"We'll have to go up!" Geoff gasped as they reached the landing outside Elmer Estergomy's office. "Then along the top corridor—down the other staircase!"

Maggie screamed, "What is it? Jack, what is it?"

But Jack shouted back at her, "No time! Get up those stairs!"

"But what *is* it?"

"*Maggie!*" Jack bellowed as the floor burst apart all around them. "*Get up those fucking stairs!*"

They scrambled up, hands and feet, like scampering children, and right behind them the stairs split and the banisters burst open, and the steel mesh over the windows rattled and vibrated.

"I can't—I can't run any further—" Karen panted. But Jack said to Maggie, "Take Randy's hand!" and hefted Karen up in his arms. The pain in his rib was excruciating, but he staggered up the next flight of stairs, with Chinese whiskers of blood running from the sides of his mouth, until they reached the very top landing.

Behind them, the stairs were furrowed up in a relentless *crickle-rackkle-crikk-crackkle* and plaster showered off the walls in a blinding gray fog.

Jack dropped Karen back onto her feet. Then he gasped, "Okay—we'll run along here—to the other end—then down again—see if we can't—"

But Karen cried out, "*Look!*" and pointed along the corridor ahead of them.

Surging toward them at a steady walking pace came the head of Gordon Holman, the tongue nailer, his face breaking the surface of the floor like a buoy being dragged behind a boat. Geoff shone his flashlight toward him, and for a second Gordon Holman's eyes gleamed over the crest of the rippling floor, as red as the eyes of somebody caught in a surprise-party photograph.

Jack twisted around. Quintus had almost reached the head of the stairs. There was no way back down, in either direction.

"There!" Jack said, pointing toward the ceiling. "Geoff, there must be a loft up there!"

Set in the ceiling, right above the head of the staircase, was a small square trapdoor. A frayed cord hung down from the catch, but when Geoff reached up for it, he found that it was four or five inches out of reach. He jumped, and flicked it, but he still couldn't get a grip on it.

The top stair cracked apart, and broken banisters tumbled down the staircase with a hollow ringing noise. Gordon Holman's head was only a dozen feet away from them, along the corridor, and surging closer. One of his hands suddenly emerged from the floor, ready to snatch at their ankles.

Jack swung Randy up in his arms and said, "Grab it, Randy! Grab the cord!"

Randy tugged the cord but nothing happened.

"Again, Randy!" Jack shouted.

This time the trapdoor abruptly came free, and a wooden ladder came banging down with it; but at the same time they were drenched by a heavy slippery torrent of black putrescence, smelling so strongly of vinegar that Karen retched out loud.

"Jesus, what is it?" screamed Maggie.

"I don't know! Up!" Jack ordered her.

"Up *there*? I can't! Oh God I can't!"

But Geoff suddenly shouted out in pain, and they looked around to see that Quintus Miller's hands had risen out of the linoleum and seized his right ankle.

"Up!" Jack shouted at Maggie. "You, too, Karen! And take Randy!"

Maggie closed her eyes for one split second, then pushed Randy ahead of her up the wooden ladder. The rungs of the ladder dripped with black loops of decomposing mush, and as they climbed up, more strings and bladders of unidentifiable slop came dropping on to the floor.

Jack kicked viciously at Quintus Miller's hands, but this time Quintus was determined not to let go.

Geoff held on to Jack tightly, his eyes wild. "Jack—for God's sake—save yourself! Just make sure—make sure he doesn't sacrifice me—don't let him—not the ritual—otherwise—he'll be *free*, Jack! Don't let him get free!"

Quintus dragged Geoff's right foot deep into the solid floor. Geoff screamed, and his ankle welled with blood. But he stiffly took his hands away from Jack and said desperately, "Save—yourself—Jack—"

Jack turned. Gordon Holman had almost reached him, his eyes gleaming with blood lust. Karen was disappearing up the slithery ladder into the loft.

Geoff gave him a rictus smile, and a rigid shake of his head, and then threw himself backward and sideways with all his strength. He tumbled over the banisters, blood spraying from his ground-up foot, and fell all the way down to the landing two floors below. Jack heard a terrible smashing noise as he landed.

He almost gave up there and then, and threw himself after Geoff. But he turned, with tears of frustration and fury filling his eyes, and kicked Gordon Holman straight in the forehead. Then he grabbed hold of the slippery stinking ladder and climbed quickly up into the loft.

The scene in the loft was appalling beyond anything that Jack could ever have imagined. It ran the entire length of The Oaks, apart from the spires at either end, and it was illuminated only by Maggie's flashlight and by occasional shivers of lightning through the tiny eye-curved windows. The noise of the rain falling on the wooden shingles directly above their heads was deafening, and it was accompanied by the spouting of broken gutters and the persistent *trickle-click-trickle* of water running through corroded flashings.

Maggie and Karen and Randy stood in the middle of the loft in complete horror. The floor was a foot deep in decomposed human remains, some of them mummified, so that they crunched underfoot, others much more recent, but decomposed to the point of liquefaction. The air was almost unbreathable. Vinegar had been emptied in gallons all over the bodies—presumably to mask their smell. Jack guessed that vinegar was all that Quintus had been able to find in a long-abandoned asylum—but the combined stench of vinegar and human decay was numbing in its intensity.

Jack waded across the slithery floor. He saw a bag or a sack of some kind lying in the ooze and picked it up, allowing it to spin around slowly in the light from Maggie's flashlight. He read the name on the stained label. "Gale McReady, University of Wisconsin La Crosse." Then he let it drop. "You see what Quintus has done here?" he said, his voice hoarse with awe. "He's already taken his eight hundred lives, or most of them, anyway. In sixty years, he's been killing anybody who's visited The Oaks—bums, hitchhikers, who knows—anybody who crashed out here or squatted here, or came to take a look around. He's killed them all. And he's probably enticed some here, too, with that little gray child of his, that little gray child who's nothing but newspaper."

He tried to swallow, tried to breathe, but he couldn't. "He could do that, you know. Tear up paper without touching it, make things move. That was the way he brought me here to The Oaks. The only way he could reach me."

He looked around, and he was crying so much from grief and disgust that he could hardly see. "He must have been so damn close to taking his eight hundred lives... maybe the other crazies knew, maybe they didn't. But Quintus himself—Jesus, look what he's done!—Quintus was almost ready to break himself out of here—into the real world. That's the only reason he didn't kill me, too. That's the only reason that *I'm* not lying here. Somebody to be sent off to find Father Bell. Some poor gullible bastard."

Maggie staggered toward Jack with her arms outstretched, choking with fear. "Jack—you have to get us out of here. *Jack! You have to get us out of here! I can't stand it! I can't stand it! I can't stand it!*"

He took hold of her wrists, steadied her. "Don't drop the flashlight, whatever you do. Look—there's a larger window over there. We can climb out on to the roof—then maybe we can climb down the drainpipes."

"*I can't stand it, I can't do it! Jack, you have to get me out of here!*"

Jack dragged her over to the semicircular window. Its glass was thick with grease and dust, but when he wiped it with the edge of his hand, he could see the parapet of the mansard roof outside, brimming with water. The rain was cascading down on all sides, and lightning flickered over the distant treetops like serpents' tongues. Jack made a point of not looking down to see what he was treading in, but it felt like a greasy heap of rubber gloves.

He tried the window catch. It was an old-fashioned brass lever, dulled to green. It was stiff, and he had to force it down with both hands, but to his surprise it actually opened, and the window groaned open sideways, and he was spattered in the face with cold refreshing rain.

He leaned out, his eyes squinched up against the wind and the rain. The parapet had flooded because the drains were blocked with sixty years of leaves and pigeon droppings, but if they balanced ten or twelve feet to the corner of the east tower, there was a vertical pipe in the angle between the tower and the main wall that looked as if it would be comparatively easy to climb down. Brackets every four feet, and plenty of handholds. He turned back to Maggie. "You see that? You see that drainpipe?"

"What?" she asked him, her hands over her ears, her eyes tight shut.

"Maggie, look at me! Listen! Do you see that drainpipe? There—in the corner?"

She glanced quickly and then nodded.

He took hold of her shoulder and said, "What you have to do is—climb along the parapet—okay?—keep your hand on the roof for support—then climb down the pipe to the ground. Then run. Do you understand me?"

Maggie nodded, her eyes still shut tight.

"Maggie, for God's sake, do you understand me? You have to climb down the pipe!"

"Yes! Yes! *Yes!*" she shouted at him. "Yes, I understand!"

"All right, then, go! Randy will come right after you, then Karen."

Maggie opened her eyes and stared at Jack wildly. The pupils of her eyes were tiny with shock. "*I can't do it!*" she screamed. "*How can you expect me to do it?*"

Just then, however, Karen said, "Jack—there's something moving in here. Jack, hurry, please! There's something moving."

Jack grasped Maggie's wrist and half helped, half heaved her out of the window. She stood on the parapet ankle-deep in rainwater, her Burberry flapping in the wind, her eyes closed, her hands pressed against the tiles of the roof.

"Edge your way along!" Jack shouted at her. "Edge your way along to the corner—then climb down the pipe!"

Maggie nodded, dumbly, and began to make her way along the parapet, shuffling one step sideways at a time, groping with her hands. Jack watched her with crushing impatience as she made her way gradually to the corner of the tower. There she paused, reaching behind her with one foot, her eyes still closed.

"Kick your shoes off!" Jack shouted at her. "And for God's sake open your eyes!"

He turned to Randy, who was white and shivering in Geoff's huge brown sweater. "What do you say, spaceman? Think you can do it? Along the ledge till you get to the corner, then climb down the pipe. All you have to do is watch what you're doing and hold on tight."

"Yes, sir," Randy said, quivering. Jack lifted him out of the window, and he followed his mother into the rain, his feet splashing in the flooded parapet.

God, that's my boy, Jack thought. *Sure of himself, knows what to do.*

He shone the flashlight back into the loft. He tried not to focus on any of the grisly heaps of shining flesh. Karen was balancing her way toward him, her nose wrinkled in disgust, her legs streaked with putrefying ooze.

He reached out his hand for her. "Come on, honey, we're going to make it now. Quick as you can!"

But ten feet behind her, the piles of human detritus suddenly shuddered. Something was forcing its way up from underneath them. Coils of shining intestines snaked swiftly and sulkily off to one side; jellified flesh slithered apart; skulls rose and fell as if they were floating on the tide. The floor of Quintus Miller's slaughterhouse almost seemed to *boil* as a powerful wave of energy forged its way toward them—a wave that could only have been caused by the vengeful and unerring form of Quintus Miller, swimming his way through the floor.

"*Faster!*" shouted Jack. Karen turned around, and uttered a short single "*Ah!*"

"*Faster!*"

Karen reached out for him—"*Jack, please*"—her hands quivering in panic and desperation. Her blond wig had skewed to one side; her face was distorted with fear. She had almost reached him when she slipped, stumbled, and fell to her knees.

Instantly, voraciously, Quintus Miller's hands surged out of the bloody mass of decomposed bodies, and seized her ankles, and yanked her away.

"Karen! Hold on!" Jack shouted, and waded through the flesh toward her.

Karen screamed and thrashed. But Quintus kept dragging her farther and farther away. Jack yelled, "Hold on! Keep kicking!"

At that moment, however, Randy appeared at the window,

white-faced, his hair dripping with rain, his sweater black and soggy. He let out a piercing shriek, *"Daddy! Daddy! Mommy's falling! Daddy, come quick!"*

Jack looked in horror at Karen, then back at Randy.

"Please, Daddy—Mommy's falling! She can't hold on!"

"Ja-a-a-cckkk!" screamed Karen.

Jack took two or three heavy, sloshing steps toward Karen. She was being pulled face down across the floor now, toward the trapdoor. She raised her head from the glutinous mire and her face was a rigid mask of absolute terror.

"Daddy!" Randy wailed. *"Daddy, please!"*

Jack turned to the window, then turned back toward Karen, then turned to the window again. He covered his face with his hands and roared out loud in anguish.

He didn't know why he decided to keep his back turned on Karen. It wasn't a conscious decision. But the next thing he knew, he was wading his way back to the window.

He grasped the window frame and was just about to lift himself out when he heard Karen utter a hopeless gurgle, and then a last compressed cry of *"Jack! Save me!"*

Trembling, he climbed out onto the flooded parapet and balanced his way toward the drainpipe at the corner of the tower. The rain lashed at his face like cold steel wire, but he almost welcomed it. It concealed the tears that coursed down his cheeks, and it gave him an excuse to shiver.

Randy followed just behind him, saying, "Quick—quick, Daddy, quick!"

Jack knelt down and looked over the edge of the roof. Maggie was only six or seven feet below the parapet, clinging to the drainpipe and moaning in fright.

"It's okay!" Jack shouted. "Maggie, it's okay! I'm coming down! Just hold on tight and stay where you are!"

He heaved himself over the parapet, his broken rib digging into his lung, and carefully climbed down to the place where Maggie was huddled.

"I'm going to climb over you—you got me? I'm going to climb over you so that I can get underneath you—then I can help you down!"

Maggie didn't reply, but continued to shudder and to moan.

"Margaret-Ann!" Jack screamed at her. "Hold on tight, I'm climbing down over you!"

Carefully, keeping one hand pressed against the side of the tower, Jack climbed over Maggie, until he was right behind her. The drainpipe creaked threateningly, and one of the brackets began to ease itself out of the brickwork.

"Oh God, I'm terrified," said Maggie, with her eyes closed. Her wet Burberry kept wrapping itself around Jack in the wind, and he found it almost impossible to get himself free.

"Listen," he told her, "I'm going to climb down just below you. I'll guide your feet with my hands. Just hold on tight and keep on coming and you won't fall."

"Oh, God," she prayed.

"Margaret-Ann, do what the hell I tell you and climb down!" Jack shouted *"Otherwise, God help me, I'm going to leave you here!"*

"I'll climb down, I'll climb down," Maggie promised him. "Don't shout at me anymore, Jack, I'll climb down."

Inch by painful inch, they descended the drainpipe. As soon as Maggie was well clear of the parapet Jack called up to Randy to climb down, too. Randy had climbed trees that were almost as high as The Oaks, and he came down without any difficulty. Maggie prayed and moaned all the way to the ground, and when Jack guided her last step on to the gravel, she turned, and she flung her arms around him, and smothered his unwilling face with wet kisses, and cried hysterically.

Jack pushed her aside and held her arm so that she stayed well away from him. He watched and waited until Randy had jumped down, and then he said, "Where's your car?"

"Back by the gates," Maggie told him. But then she looked up toward the rooftops, and said, "Where's Karen?"

"Never mind about Karen, run to the car, take Randy with you, and get the hell out of here. Go home, don't stop."

"But I thought Karen was right behind us!"

"Maggie, go home! Now!"

Dazed, Maggie took Randy's hand, and the two of them walked quickly down the avenue of oaks toward the gates.

"Run!" Jack shouted, and they started to run.

Jack stood watching them go with emotions so strong that he could scarcely breathe. Then he turned back toward the dark spires of The Oaks. He had the most vengeful of all scores to settle with Quintus Miller.

He skirted around the kitchens and around the back of the house to the conservatory. The heavy rains had brought down more of the glass roof, and water was splattering noisily all over the tiles. He hesitated for a moment, then stepped inside, leaving the door wide open behind him.

He made his way through the darkened lounge until he reached the hallway. The two blind statues watched him without opening their eyes. There was no sign of the clutching hands that had risen from the marble floor. No sign of Quintus Miller or Gordon Holman or any more maniacs.

The hallway stood silent.

Jack darted the beam of his flashlight all the way around the perimeter of the hallway. At last he caught the flash of green glass. Geoff's Perrier bottle of exorcised water. He waited, and listened, straining for that telltale *sssshhhh— sssshhh—sssshhhhh*, but all he could hear was the rain. Maybe Quintus was resting, after his orgy of violence.

Karen, he thought, with a sudden pang of grief.

He tiptoed across the hallway and picked up the Perrier bottle. Then he retreated, whipping the flashlight this way and that, nervously searching for hands or faces coming out of the walls.

The exorcised water made a soft slopping sound in the bottle. He prayed that it would work, the same way that it had worked for Father Bell. He didn't know any of the prayers of exorcism, but he hoped that the sincerity of his determination to rid the world of Quintus Miller and all of his homicidal maniacs would prove to be exorcism enough.

To his relief, he reached the conservatory doors unmolested. He stepped out into the rain, and unscrewed the top of the Perrier bottle, and began to circle The Oaks, sparingly sprinkling what remained of the holy water and reciting his own version of a prayer to keep unclean spirits imprisoned for ever.

"Oh God, if You love the world... if Thou lovest the world... if Thou lovest life, and happiness... keep these people locked up inside this circle for time everlasting... the power and the glory, amen."

He had almost finished his circle when he began to hear a pummeling deep within the ground, almost like the engines of the Morlocks thumping in *The Time Machine*.

Then he heard a high keening sound, and he stood alone in the rain and realized that it was the lunatics, crying inside the walls. He had trapped them all back in The Oaks. He had caught them; and this time they would never escape, because *he* had imprisoned them, and the only person who could let them out was him. Either him, or a trio of cardinals.

"*Bastards!*" he screamed, up at the sky. "*Bastards!*"

He stepped back across the gravel and looked up at the sinister neo-Gothic skyline of The Oaks, and wished he could raze the whole building to the ground.

He was still blinking against the rain when he heard a deep *ssssshhhhh* sound in the gravel off to his right, close to the bathhouse. He pointed the flashlight in the general direction of the noise, but at first he couldn't see anything.

Then he heard it again. *Sssssssssssssshhhhhhhhhhhhh*— quicker and quicker, building up toward a crescendo. *SssssssSSSHHHHHHHHH...*

He flicked the flashlight from one side of the gravel path to the other. Suddenly he saw the huge tidal wave in the shingle, bearing toward him faster than a man could run.

He didn't have to see who it was. He *knew*. Quintus Miller must have left The Oaks before he had sprinkled his circle of holy water. And now Quintus Miller was blasting through the ground toward him with limitless rage and unstoppable power.

The gravel seethed and sprayed apart. The turf sprayed apart. Two stone urns detonated like bombs. Then Jack was running down the slope toward the tennis courts, pursued by a huge furrow of bursting grass and earth.

Quintus Miller was so close behind him that Jack didn't dare even to stop, and turn, and confront him with the holy water.

He ran and ran until he was running so fast that he couldn't have stopped even if he had wanted to. He crossed the flooded tennis courts, his shoes splashing in the puddles. The asphalt was ripped up only three feet behind his heels. He reached the edge of the overflowing swimming pool, tried to avoid it, slipped, arms whirling, *Hold on to that holy water, whatever you do*, then fell sideways into the murky, cold, repulsive depths of the deep end.

He gasped with the cold, struggled—lost his flashlight—saw it falling dimly to the bottom.

Then the tiled sides of the pool were smashed open, and Quintus Miller came surging into the water in a massive explosion of bubbles and dirt and churned-up filth. Jack screamed underwater, thrashed to the surface, sucked in air. But Quintus immediately seized at his ankles and dragged him back under again.

Jack kicked and twisted, but this time Quintus was determined not to let him go. He grabbed Jack around the waist, and then around the chest, and bent him backward.

Desperate for breath, Jack felt Quintus's powerful fingers digging into his face, searching for his eye sockets.

He hit back at Quintus with the Perrier bottle, missed, and lost his grip on it. In retaliation, Quintus seized hold of his throat, forcing his thumbs underneath his jawbone, gradually pushing it apart. Jack's eyes bulged and bubbles of air began to leak out between his tightly clenched teeth. He felt as if Quintus were going to break his whole face in half.

Jack thrashed his arm out—and touched something repulsively familiar. The sack containing the decomposing remains of Joseph Lovelittle's two-headed German shepherd. Instinctively he pulled it toward him.

He's frightened of dogs—his father set the family dog on him after he had killed his brothers and his mother—almost killed him—frightened of dogs—

Sniffing in nostrilfuls of water, Jack brought up his knee and hit Quintus sharply in the chest—once, twice, three times. Quintus released his grip on Jack's face, but came circling around to grab him around the waist and bend him backward.

Jack pulled open the neck of the sack, fumbled disgustedly inside, and then dragged out the two-headed dog by the sodden scruff of its neck. He couldn't see it, in the filthy darkness of the swimming pool, but Quintus would be able to visualize it as clearly as if it were floodlight.

There was a split second when Jack believed that it wasn't going to work. But then Quintus convulsed, and convulsed again. He churned away from Jack, but Jack could still feel his epileptic spasms through the water, and a bubbling screech of abject terror.

He kicked himself to the surface of the pool, still clutching the monstrous dog. He could see which way Quintus had gone by the shuddering ripples that led to the edge. The sky was beginning to grow lighter now, even though it was still raining.

The tiles at the far side of the pool cracked and splintered as Quintus convulsively left the water and crept back into the earth. Jack struck out after him and reached the ladder. As he did so he heard something clinking close beside him. It was the Perrier bottle, floating on the surface. He lifted it out, and he could have kissed it.

Heaving himself up the ladder, with water draining from his clothes, Jack followed Quintus's progress across the grass. He held the corpse of the two-headed dog up in front of him, like a shield, like a grisly talisman.

Quintus reached the low brick retaining wall that separated the lawns from the woods. From the shifting and the shuffling of the brickwork, Jack could see that he was creeping into one twelve-foot section of it, between two sets of stone steps, in the same way that a man suffering from chronic influenza creeps into the warmth of his bed.

Jack dropped the dog's body close by, and then purposefully unscrewed the bottle of exorcised water, and walked all the way around the section of wall, reciting his prayer and sprinkling his water.

"Quintus!" he shouted. "Can you hear me, Quintus? You're trapped now, you can't get out!"

There was no reply, but the bricks dryly rubbed against each other, like somebody with a mouthful of sand grinding their teeth together.

"Quintus, where's Karen? What have you done with her, Quintus? I'm not going to let you sacrifice her, Quintus! Do you hear me?"

You pathetic idiot, Quintus's harsh, midwestern accents suddenly replied. *I couldn't sacrifice her because she's dead. You didn't even give me time, you and your holy water and your half-assed prayers! I killed her because of you!*

"You're lying!" Jack shouted at the wall. "You've got her hidden!"

I wish I had. But she's dead, Mr. Reed. Tomato puree.

Jack took two quick, quivering breaths. "O Lord keep this sinner trapped in this wall, because he deserves everything that's coming to him, amen."

He turned stiffly and trudged back toward The Oaks. He was too exhausted to run. Close to the back of the conservatory, he had seen a gardening shed, and where there was a gardening shed, there were usually tools.

The shed was padlocked, but so dilapidated that he kicked the door off its rusted hinges. Inside, he found stacks of flowerpots, a petrified lawn mower, gasoline cans, bunches of garden canes, and just what he was looking for—a pick.

He walked wearily back down the lawns to the wall in which Quintus was imprisoned. A weak sun showed its face behind the clouds and glistened on the rain-soaked grass.

He lifted the pick and hacked away two of the top layer of bricks. Then more, and more, until the wall began to collapse onto the grass.

Quintus began to rage at him. *Stay away, you bastard! Stay away! I'll kill you for this, I'll tear you to pieces!*

But Jack didn't reply. He was too tired to reply. He kept

on swinging the pick and chopping down more of the wall, until Quintus was crowded into the very end of it.

No! screamed Quintus. *You touch me now, and I'll kill you!*

Jack swung the pick again. *Clokk.* And the bricks barked against each other as they rolled across the lawn. "You don't have anyplace left to go, Quintus. This is it."

Quintus shrieked. A sound so piercing that Jack could hardly hear it.

He swung the pick, and the bricks dropped away, and there was Quintus's face, his eyes wide open, his mouth stretched in a scream of paranoiac agony.

Jack swung again, revealing Quintus's shoulders, then his chest. Then there was nothing but a half-naked trembling man crouched amidst the scattered bricks.

Quintus raised his eyes. Metallic, unforgiving, expressionless.

You shall be damned forever and ever for this.

Jack said, "God forgive me," and swung the pick, and the point hit Quintus straight in the forehead.

Quintus broke apart, like two halves of a statue, and then collapsed into lumps. Jack bent forward and picked up one of the lumps, and that was brick, too—brick that crumbled between his fingers, into dust.

He stayed where he was by the broken wall for a very long time, while the sky cleared, and the rain began to dry, and The Oaks behind him was shrouded in mist. Then he dropped the pick and began to walk back up the hill.

Two of the gasoline cans were still three-quarters filled with gasoline. Jack hefted them out from the back of the shed and carried them over to the conservatory door, his back hunched because of the weight.

He knocked off the lids and threw them into the reading lounge. They banged and echoed and tumbled over; then all he could hear was gasoline glugging onto the floor.

He had no more prayers, no more cries of furious revenge. He took out a book of matches with shaking hands and tossed three flaring matches into the lounge, one after the other.

The first two fizzled, but when he threw in the third, the lounge suddenly *whoomphed* into flame.

The burning of The Oaks was spectacular. Floor by floor, window by window, fire raged up toward the roof.

The lunatics trapped inside the building's fabric must have risen higher and higher through the maze of the building's walls, because it was only when the fire reached the third story that Jack heard screaming.

He stood on the lawn, his hand shielding his face against the heat, while the Gothic outlines of the massive building pulsed with sparks, and fire waved in the early-morning wind like a huge orange flag.

They screamed in panic and anguish and pain, and in the total despair of having survived for sixty years only to die like this. *Rats in a trap*, thought the man who had piped them here.

The spires collapsed; the staircases fell. The blind faces dropped from the parapets. The screaming went on and on, a hundred and thirty human spirits roasted into extinction. Jack watched and waited with hollow-eyed patience until the very last scream had died away.

He could hear sirens in the distance. He wiped his heat-reddened face with the back of his sleeve. He took one last look at The Oaks, and then he walked away through the woods.

Sergeant Charles Schiller crunched through the smoldering ashes of The Oaks, his hands in his raincoat pockets. Not far away, a demolition crew was bringing down two pale soot-streaked statues, which had miraculously been left standing when the hallway collapsed.

The fire chief came trudging over, sniffing and rubbing his hands together. "Some blaze, huh?"

"How long before our forensic people can get in here?" Sergeant Schiller asked.

"Four or five hours. Give it a chance to cool off."

Sergeant Schiller circled the demolition site, feeling the heat of the recent fire through the soles of his borrowed fire-department boots. He picked up fragments of broken marble, pieces of cracked china, a twisted fork. There were bones here, too, but he didn't touch them.

It was only when he was ready to leave that he saw something gleaming in the ashes. He squatted down and teased it out of the ground with his pen. It was still too hot to touch. He lifted it up and let it dangle on the end of his pen.

A cheap gold necklace, fashioned into the letters K-A-R-E-N.

Jack never went home. He took the last of his money out of the First Milwaukee Savings Bank and bought himself a faded beige Plymouth from a retired apple farmer in Standard, Wisconsin, and drove north undetected over the Canadian border.

His name is Jack Pontneuf these days, and he works as a foreman for St. Basile Muffler close to Quebec and speaks passable French. His drinking friends call him Jack the Dry, because three drinks is all he will drink, and he hates the rain, and he never talks much, except about mufflers, and there isn't much to say about mufflers.

He rents a room in a small blue-painted house in a nondescript suburb of Quebec and spends most of his time looking out of the window at the telegraph poles and the weather and the children playing in the street.

His landlady is a woman called Cécile de Champlain. A widow of forty-five, plain, sweet, and sad. She places a jelly jar of fresh flowers in his room every two or three days, but rarely talks to him.

He has asked her to tell him immediately if she ever hears a rustling noise in the walls, or if she ever sees the ground breaking up for no reason, or if a small child in a gray-white raincoat ever crosses her path.

She has promised faithfully that she will.

He has also asked her (awkwardly, his eyes focused on something quite different, far away) never to sing the children's song "Lavender Blue."

She has promised faithfully that she won't.

Cécile de Champlain thinks privately that Jack probably needs some psychiatric help. They have homes for people like him.

About Graham Masterton

GRAHAM MASTERTON is best known as a writer of horror and thrillers, but his career as an author spans many genres, including historical epics and sex advice books. His first horror novel, *The Manitou*, became a bestseller and was made into a film starring Tony Curtis. In 2019, Graham was given a Lifetime Achievement Award by the Horror Writers Association. He is also the author of the Katie Maguire series of crime thrillers, which have sold more than 1.5 million copies worldwide.